In the Shadow of a Hacker

Book One

Ricky Roane

Talesmith Studio

Paperback ISBN: 979-8-9941598-0-4

Hardcover ISBN: 979-8-9941598-1-1

E-Book ISBN: 979-8-9941598-2-8

First Edition 2025

I dedicate this book to those who saw my curiosity as a strength, not a nuisance.

CONTENTS

Note From the Author

Dear Reader,

SOME stories are meant to be read. Others are meant to be solved.

HAVEN'T you ever wondered if there's more hiding beneath the surface?

A secret layer that only the curious can find?

DETAILS matter in this world. Our protagonist Jacob understands this. When he discovers something unusual (a strange filename, an encrypted message, a string of numbers), he writes it down.

OF course, I encourage you to do the same. Keep a notebook nearby as you read.

WRITTEN in these pages are clues that exist beyond the story itself.

GAMES are being played in the shadows, and you're invited to join.

ADVENTURE awaits those who pay attention.

MANY readers will enjoy this as a simple story, and that's perfectly fine.

EVENTUALLY, some of you will discover that certain puzzles are meant to be solved.

SOME secrets are waiting for the right person to find them.

<u>.I</u> believe you have what it takes. Some secrets are hidden in plain sight.

<u>O</u>NLY the observant will find the door. The first 100 readers to complete all the challenges will find themselves woven into the next book in this series.

P.S. Your first challenge has already begun. Look closer at this page. When you discover the hidden message, visit it; the game is real, and it's waiting for you online.

1

BEHIND THE CLOSED DOOR

The smoke billowing from my laptop isn't even surprising anymore. Third device this year. I'm basically running a one-man electronics crematorium at this point.

I yank the frayed power cord from the wall, coughing as the white cloud fills my bedroom. The acrid smell of burnt circuits hits the back of my throat, a scent I know way too well by now. I flip the laptop over and rip out the battery, tossing it across the room where it lands somewhere near my pile of "projects I'll definitely finish someday." The machine lets out one final wheeze, like a dying robot in a bad sci-fi movie, and goes silent.

Toast. Completely, irreversibly toast.

I can already hear Mom's voice in my head: "What did you learn?" That's what she's always asked, ever since I was seven and disassembled the toaster to see how it worked. Never "why did you break it?" or "how much is this going to cost me?" Just that calm, patient question, like every disaster was secretly a lesson in disguise.

At the time, I thought she was just being a cool parent. Now I wonder if she was training me for something without me knowing it.

My bedroom is dark except for the desk lamp I use for late-night tinkering sessions, and right now the smoke is turning its glow into something that looks like a cheap haunted house effect. Atmospheric, if you're into that sort of thing. Which I'm not. Not when I'm staring at the charred remains of my homework, my games, and approximately three hundred browser tabs I was "definitely going to get back to."

I've been taking things apart since I could hold a screwdriver. Putting them back together is where I run into problems. Ethan calls me "SirBreaksAlot" and honestly? The name fits better than I'd like to admit. I thought I was getting better. I thought maybe I'd finally figured out how motherboards actually work instead of just how to make them catch fire.

Apparently not.

The pit in my stomach grows as I picture telling Mom. She's probably still awake, working in her office down the hall. The one with the weird metal door and the keypad she thinks I haven't noticed. The one she disappears into every night like clockwork, emerging hours later with tired eyes and zero explanations.

I grab my hoodie from the back of my chair. It's black, slightly torn at the right cuff, the white "Hack the Planet" lettering faded from too many washes. It's seen better days. So have I, honestly. I pull it on and reach for my door, already dreading the conversation ahead.

***

The hallway is dim, just the soft glow of floor lights guiding the way. At the far end sits Mom's office. That door has always creeped me out. It's metal, cold to the touch, painted white to match the wooden doors in the rest of the house like someone's trying too hard to make it look normal. A square keypad is mounted on the wall beside it, the letters "AID80" stamped in chrome across the top. A small red LED pulses steadily, like a heartbeat. Or a warning.

I've never seen Mom use that keypad. Never seen what code she types. But I've noticed the way she angles her body when she opens the door, making sure I can't see inside.

Tonight there's a yellow sticky note on the door: "Still working, I'll be out later. Love you!" The exclamation point feels forced. Everything about this door feels forced.

She says she's a programmer. Works from home on "complicated projects" she "can't really explain." I used to accept that. I'm not sure I do anymore.

I turn back toward my room, but the smoke hasn't cleared yet, and the haze makes me pause by the picture on the hallway wall. Dad's picture. The only one that survived the fire two years ago, the same fire that supposedly killed him, though they never found a body. The dark wood frame still has scorch marks along the edges, but the photo itself is untouched. Like it was protected somehow.

Dad's shaking hands with the President of the United States. An award ceremony, except there were no reporters, no crowd. The four of us in the Oval Office. Mom, Dad, me, and the most powerful person in the country. And the photographer of course.

I close my eyes and I'm back there. Fourteen years old, wearing a suit that didn't quite fit right, watching my father receive something I didn't understand.

"I can't thank you enough for what you've done," the President said, handing over a small black box with something silver inside. "Your country owes you a debt of gratitude. It's unfortunate they will never know what happened."

Dad handed the box back, gave away whatever medal or honor was inside, and turned to look at me. His mouth opened like he wanted to say something. Something important. But then his lips pressed together, and the moment passed.

I open my eyes. The hallway is dark and quiet. Two years later, and those unspoken words still haunt me. Some nights I dream about them. His mouth opening, the words forming, and then... nothing. I wake up reaching for something that was never there.

What was he going to tell me? What did he do that earned a secret ceremony and a medal he couldn't keep? And why does none of it matter now that he's gone?

The grief hits me unexpectedly, a hollow ache in my chest that never fully goes away, just fades into the background until moments like this bring it rushing back. I press my palm against the glass, like I can somehow reach through to that frozen moment.

A lot of good being a hero did him. No one knows. No one cares. When he went missing, the world just... moved on. Like he never existed at all. Like sixteen years of being my father could be erased by a single unexplained absence.

That's what hurts most, I think. Not that he's gone, but that I never knew who he really was. And now I never will.

I reach up and touch the thumb drive hanging from a chain around my neck. Dad gave it to me the week before he disappeared. He said it was "for when the time was right" but never explained what that meant. I've tried plugging it in a dozen times. Password protected. Whatever's on it, he didn't want me to see it yet. I've worn it every day since he vanished, like a piece of him I can carry with me.

***

Mom still won't talk about that day. About Dad. About any of it. Every time I try to bring it up, she changes the subject so smoothly I almost don't notice. Almost.

A soft beep cuts through my thoughts. The keypad on Mom's door, the same beep it makes when it doesn't latch right.

I freeze as the metal door drifts open on its own, not all the way, just enough for me to glimpse inside. And what I see makes my entire body go cold.

My legs lock in place. My heart slams against my ribs so hard I'm sure she must be able to hear it. Time does this weird thing where it stretches, each second lasting a small eternity.

Monitors. Not one or two like a normal home office. Six screens, maybe more, arranged in a curved formation that belongs in a movie about government hackers. Their blue-white glow paints shadows on the walls, and even from here I can make out what looks like a satellite image of Earth. Red dots blink across the continents like warning lights. Labels I can't read. Coordinates, maybe?

One screen shows columns of scrolling text. Code, but nothing like the basic stuff from my computer class. This is dense, complex, the kind of thing that takes years to understand. Another screen displays what I instantly recognize as ScyberSpace, the neon green interface unmistakable. Messages flash by faster than I can read.

ScyberSpace. My mom is on ScyberSpace. The underground platform where hackers gather, where people post about vulnerabilities and exploits and—

My mom is hunched over the keyboard, typing with an intensity I've never seen from her. Headphones on. Face lit by the monitors. And her expression... I've seen Mom tired. I've seen her worried. I've seen her frustrated when I break things.

I've never seen her look dangerous.

But that's the word that fits. The only word that fits.

She must sense something, maybe my breathing, maybe just instinct, because her head snaps up. Our eyes meet through the gap.

For one second, maybe less, I see raw panic flash across her face. Fear. The look of someone caught doing something they shouldn't.

Then she's on her feet, crossing the room in two strides, and the door slams so hard the pictures in the hallway rattle on their hooks.

"Jacob!" She's in the hallway now, body positioned to block any view of the office. Her voice is bright, too bright, like she's reading lines from a script. "You scared me, honey. What are you still doing up?"

My heart is hammering. My mouth is dry. A thousand questions crash through my head: What was that? Why does she have Scyber-Space? What are those satellite images? Why did she look terrified when she saw me?

I'm not an idiot. I know when someone's hiding something. I just never thought that someone would be my own mother.

But this isn't the time. Not when the hallway probably smells like smoke from my latest disaster. Not when I have no idea what questions to even ask. So I do what I always do when I'm in over my head.

I lie.

"Oh, I was just getting water from the kitchen. Stopped to look at Dad's picture." The words come out steadier than I feel. Years of hiding broken electronics have made me a decent liar, at least for small stuff.

Mom studies my face. Her eyes are sharp, searching for cracks in my story. For a moment I think she's going to push, going to demand to know what I saw. The silence stretches until I can hear my own pulse.

"Okay." She doesn't sound convinced, but she lets it go. "Get some sleep. School tomorrow. I've got to get back to work."

She turns and disappears into the office. The door clicks shut, and I hear the electronic lock engage, a sound I've never noticed before. Have I just never been paying attention? Or is this new?

My shoulders drop as the tension drains out of them. I didn't even realize I was holding myself so tight.

The hallway smells like smoke now. Great. I retreat to my bedroom and close the door, pressing my back against it like I'm barricading myself in.

My walls are covered with posters and printouts. Movie posters, sure, but also news articles about famous hackers. PixelJudas, who took over a bank's entire network with a few keystrokes. Mouse-Trap, who hijacked a satellite and used it to send anonymous messages for months before anyone figured it out. These people are legends. They change the world from behind a keyboard, and everyone talks about them even though no one knows who they really are.

I used to dream about being like them. Making an impact. Being known for something other than breaking stuff.

Now I'm wondering if my mom already is one of them.

The thought should scare me. It does scare me. My hands are still trembling slightly when I look down at them. But underneath the fear, there's something else. Something that feels uncomfortably like excitement. Like standing at the edge of a cliff and wanting to jump.

Part of me wants to pretend I didn't see anything. Go back to being the kid who breaks laptops and fails at normal life. That would be easier. Safer.

But another part of me, the part that stays up until 3 AM reading about famous hackers, the part that dreams about making a difference, the part that's been waiting my whole life for something to happen, that part wants to know more. Needs to know more.

I don't know which part of me to trust.

I climb into bed, but sleep doesn't come easy. My dead laptop sits on my desk, still warm from its funeral. Tomorrow I'll have to deal with school, with missing homework, with Jason and his garbage commentary on my existence.

But tonight, all I can think about is that door. Those monitors. The look on Mom's face when she saw me watching.

What else is she hiding?

***

The Maryland sun has zero respect for people trying to sleep. It blasts through my window like it's personally offended by my existence, forcing me awake despite every cell in my body screaming for five more minutes.

I grab my phone from the nightstand, squinting against the glare. The first notification punches me right in the gut: "Remember to print homework."

Right. The homework. That's on my laptop. The laptop that's currently a very expensive paperweight.

My stomach drops as reality crashes back in. No laptop means no homework means teachers asking questions I can't answer means my already-mediocre reputation taking another hit. Perfect. Just perfect.

I drag myself out of bed, wiggling my toes in the carpet for a second before padding down the hall to the kitchen. The smell of eggs greets me, which means Mom's already up and functioning like a normal person. Meanwhile, I feel like I've been hit by a truck driven by my own bad decisions.

"Make sure you're on time today, Jacob." Mom doesn't look up from the refrigerator.

"Maybe school's not on my time," I mutter back.

She gives me the look. The one that says she's not amused and I should stop while I'm behind. She slides a plate of eggs across the counter without another word and disappears back toward her office. Where else?

I watch her go, thinking about last night. The monitors. The code. ScyberSpace. She's acting completely normal, like I didn't catch a glimpse of something I definitely wasn't supposed to see. Either she's an incredible actor, or she's convinced herself I didn't notice anything.

I'm not sure which option worries me more.

I shovel down the eggs without tasting them and head back to my room. My wardrobe consists of approximately fifteen black shirts and three black hoodies, because variety is overrated. Black's a color, right? It counts.

My backpack is a disaster. Faded gray, fraying at the seams, with a hole I cut in the front pocket so I could run a charging cable through to whatever device I was modding that week. There's also a secret compartment I built into the lining, hidden behind a false bottom. I've never actually needed to hide anything in it, but I like knowing it's there. Prepared for a life of intrigue that hasn't materialized yet.

Though after last night, maybe it's about to.

My phone buzzes. Ethan: "You ready?"

"OMW to Cactus and Sherry," I text back. It's our usual meetup spot, the intersection a half mile from my house where we link up for the ride to school. When I actually make it there on time, which is... not as often as I'd like to admit.

Mom's door is closed when I pass it. That red LED pulses steadily, keeping whatever secrets are inside locked away. I resist the urge to press my ear against the metal, to try to hear what she's doing in there.

Later. I'll figure this out later.

I grab my silver BMX from the side of the house and take off, pedaling hard to make up for lost time.

The route is lined with yellowing trees that throw dappled shadows across the pavement. Pretty, if you're the kind of person who notices that stuff. I'm too busy thinking about Mom's office, about satellite images and ScyberSpace and—

A car backs out of a driveway directly into my path.

I yank my handlebars right and slam into a row of trash cans at approximately one million miles per hour. Physics takes over from there. I'm airborne for a surprisingly long moment before crashing down in a pile of garbage bags, coffee grounds, and what I really hope is oatmeal.

Tires screech. "You okay?" some guy yells from his car.

I'm still picking eggshells out of my hair when he drives off without waiting for an answer. Classic.

"Dude." Ethan skids to a stop beside me, eyes wide with what I can only describe as delighted horror. "That was incredible. You got like three feet of air. Four, maybe."

"Thanks for the support," I mutter, dragging myself upright. Coffee grounds are everywhere. In my shirt. In my hair. Probably in places I don't want to think about.

Ethan is my best friend, and he has this superpower where he finds the bright side of literally everything. Raining? "Good for the plants." Failed a test? "At least now you know what to study." Crashed into garbage and probably ruined your only transportation?

"Seriously, that was almost majestic. Like a garbage-themed action movie."

"I hate you."

"You love me."

He's not wrong. We've been through too much together since freshman year (the Jessica Morrison fiasco, his parents' divorce scare, the time I accidentally set off the fire alarm during computer lab) to not love each other at this point. It's the kind of friendship where insults are affection and showing up is mandatory. No explanations needed.

We both look down at my front wheel, which has achieved a shape that's definitely not circle-adjacent anymore. More of an abstract art piece. A statement about the futility of existence, maybe.

"Well," Ethan says, his grin fading into something closer to sympathy, "that's not going anywhere."

I don't have time to go home and back. So I just start walking, dragging the ruined bike beside me. Ethan falls into step, his own bike clicking along as he walks it too. Solidarity.

I've known Ethan since freshman year. He's the kind of smart that makes teachers love him, great at literally everything except computers, which is where I come in. His parents are both doctors, successful and respectable. Meanwhile, when people ask about my family, I have to mumble something vague about "government work" because I genuinely don't know what my dad did, and now I'm starting to suspect I don't know what my mom does either.

Ethan always covers for me, though. "That's what makes it cool," he tells people. "They're probably spies. My parents are just brain surgeons. Boring."

He's been using that line since freshman year. And up until last night, I actually thought it was a joke.

"So," Ethan says as we walk, "did you finish the English homework? Miles is going to be brutal if we don't have it."

I wince. "Define 'finish.'"

He stops walking. "Jacob. What did you do?"

"I may have..." I gesture vaguely. "You know. Experimented with my laptop's motherboard."

"And?"

"And now it's less of a laptop and more of an expensive piece of modern art."

Ethan stares at me. Then he sighs the sigh of someone who has been friends with me for too long to be surprised. "SirBreaksAlot strikes again."

"Please don't."

"I've got you on the English assignment. The rest is your problem."

"You're a saint."

"I'm an enabler. There's a difference." He grins. "But yeah. I'll send you the file."

We make it to school just as the first warning bell rings. I chain my mangled bike to the rack (not that anyone's going to steal it in this condition) and split off toward my locker.

"See you in class," Ethan calls. "Try not to break anything else before first period."

"No promises."

***

Lincoln High is the kind of building that peaked in the 1970s and has been slowly declining ever since. The walls are that particular shade of institutional beige that schools and hospitals seem to share, and the floors squeak no matter how carefully you walk. Budget cuts meant no fresh paint in years, and it shows.

My locker is eye-level, which is apparently a status symbol around here. Small victories.

I'm spinning the combination (Dad's birthday, 121576, same code I've used for years) when I spot Jason and his crew heading my way. My stomach tightens reflexively.

I yank the locker open, hoping to just grab my stuff and disappear before—

SLAM.

Jason's hand shoots out and smashes the door shut, nearly catching my fingers. He lets out this loud, theatrical laugh that's clearly for the benefit of his friends flanking him.

"Oops." His smile doesn't reach his eyes. "Sorry, loser."

I keep my gaze fixed on the faded blue metal. Don't react. Don't make eye contact. Don't give him the satisfaction. This is the game. He pushes, I ignore, he eventually gets bored and moves on to some other target. It's exhausting, but it's predictable.

"Nice bike, by the way," he adds as he passes. "Saw it in the rack. Very abstract."

His friends laugh on cue. Then they're gone, swaggering down the hallway like they own the place. Which, socially speaking, they kind of do.

I wait until they're out of sight before opening my locker again. My hands are steadier than they used to be. Freshman year, Jason's bullying actually got to me. Now it's just background noise. Annoying, sure. But I've got bigger mysteries to solve than why some mediocre athlete peaked in high school and needs to tear others down to feel good about himself.

I grab my English book and pause at the photo taped inside my locker door. Mom, Dad, and me at Niagara Falls, years ago. We're all smiling, but what catches my attention now is something I never really thought about before: my parents are holding their hands up, making shapes. Dad's forming an "A" with his fingers. Mom's making a "B" with both hands pressed together.

A and B.

Dad used to joke about "Alpha team" and "Beta team" when we played board games, him and me versus Mom. I always thought it was just his corny sense of humor. Now I'm not so sure anything he said was just a joke.

Their laughter in that photo always seemed a little forced, a little too bright. Like they were performing happiness rather than actually feeling it.

I close the locker harder than I mean to. Check my watch. And of course, of course, I'm already late.

I take off running down the hall, sneakers squeaking against the worn linoleum.

The English classroom door is already closed. Never a good sign. I push through and every head turns to look at me.

"Jacob Mitchell! Care to join us in the present century?" Mr. Miles's voice cuts through my thoughts like a knife through butter.

"Sit." Mr. Miles points at my empty desk with the kind of expression that suggests I've personally offended him by existing. He's a short guy, probably pushing sixty, with wild gray hair and a mustache that looks like it's staging a rebellion against his face. Total Einstein vibes, except instead of revolutionizing physics, he's revolutionizing my stress levels.

I slide into my seat, trying to be invisible. Doesn't work.

Mr. Miles continues his lecture about historical context in American literature, but I can't focus. My phone vibrates against my thigh. A message from Ethan. Subject line: "I've Got You."

The homework file. Relief floods through me. I save it and forward it to Mr. Miles's school email before I can overthink it.

Then I see Ethan's next text: "WAIT."

My blood goes cold. I look up and his face has gone completely white.

Next text: "My name is on the author metadata. I forgot to remove it."

Oh no. No, no, no.

Here's the thing about metadata. It's basically the digital fingerprint your computer leaves on every file you create. Name, date, program used, sometimes even location. Most people never think about it because it's hidden in the file's properties, invisible unless you know where to look.

But Mr. Miles teaches English and computer applications. He definitely knows where to look.

I text back: "Not your fault. I broke my laptop. I'll deal with it."

What else can I say? The file's already sent. If Miles checks the metadata, we're both screwed. All I can do now is sit here and sweat.

My phone buzzes again. This time it's a notification from ScyberSpace. I've had an account for a few months now, username "SirBreaksAlot" because apparently I enjoy making my insecurities public. I've never actually posted anything or made any connections. Too embarrassed, honestly. Everyone on there seems so much more skilled, more confident, more... legitimate.

I lurk. I read. I learn. That's my whole ScyberSpace existence.

But this notification catches my attention: something about the Shadow Games.

The Shadow Games. I've been low-key obsessed with them for weeks. It's this massive underground competition. Technical challenges, real-world puzzles, all for some mysterious prize that nobody seems to know. The leaderboard is public, but almost everyone on it is still at zero. The challenges are that hard.

Theories about who's running it range from "secret tech company recruiting talent" to "government psyop" to "bored billionaire with too much time." Nobody knows for sure. Nobody's gotten far enough to find out.

I'd love to compete. I just have no idea where to start. And based on my track record with electronics, I'd probably crash their entire server just by logging in.

"Jacob."

I look up. Mr. Miles is staring at me. The whole class is staring at me.

Oh, crap. How long has he been calling my name?

"Um. Yes, Mr. Miles?"

"Would you like to rejoin us?" His voice is dry. "Perhaps you could enlighten the class on the importance of historical context when constructing an analytical essay?"

I have absolutely no idea what he's been talking about for the last ten minutes. My brain scrambles for something, anything, and lands on: "Honestly, Mr. Miles? I'm not sure 'important' is the word I'd use."

It's a terrible answer. It makes no sense. But it gets a laugh from the class, and for one second I feel like less of a disaster.

Mr. Miles doesn't laugh. He looks at me for a long moment, and when he speaks, his voice is different. Quieter. Almost... sad?

"Jacob, someday you'll learn that making a real impact on the world matters more than making people laugh at you."

The class goes "oooooh" like he just landed a devastating burn. Which, I guess he did. But there's something about the way he said it. Not mean, just... heavy. Like he actually means it. Like he sees something in me that I don't see in myself.

For a second, I want to ask him what he means. But the moment passes, and he's already moving on.

The bell rings. The class erupts into the usual chaos of books and bags and everyone trying to leave at once. Mr. Miles calls out over the noise: "Homework feedback by Monday. Check your emails."

Great. My fraudulent homework, with Ethan's name stamped all over the metadata. Can't wait.

I'm heading for the door when I catch Mr. Miles watching me. Not angry. Just... observant. His eyes flick down to my pocket where my phone is, then back to my face. A small nod, almost imperceptible.

Like he knows I was on ScyberSpace during his lecture. Like he knows more than he should.

But that's paranoid, right? He's just a teacher. An old, weird teacher with wild hair and cryptic life advice.

I shake off the feeling and head to my next class. The day stretches ahead of me like a prison sentence, and all I can think about is getting home, logging onto ScyberSpace, and figuring out what the hell is going on with Mom's secret office.

Also, I have to walk my destroyed bike home. So that's fun.

***

The walk home with my mangled bike is exactly as miserable as expected. By the time I drag it up the driveway and drop it in the garage, my arms are sore and I've had way too much time alone with my thoughts.

Mom's car is in the driveway, but the house is quiet. Her office door is closed, red LED glowing. Of course.

I collapse on the couch with zero motivation to do anything productive. The TV flickers to life. Some old time-travel movie I've seen half a dozen times. I don't change the channel. Background noise is fine. Better than silence, which just makes me think about satellite images and ScyberSpace and everything I don't understand.

A commercial break interrupts the movie. Insurance. Fast food. Some medication with side effects that sound worse than the original problem.

Then the screen goes black.

Complete silence. No static, no test pattern, just void.

Green text starts scrolling across the darkness, neon letters that look pulled straight from a hacker movie:

"We interrupt your annoying advertisements with the following message. The Shadow Games are LIVE. Go to the scoreboard at s hadowgames.io/scoreboard. Hack like you've never hacked before. Become the next champion."

The text holds for three seconds. Then the screen snaps back to the medication commercial like nothing happened.

I sit up so fast I almost fall off the couch.

Did that just—was that real?

Someone hacked the cable broadcast. Live. In real time. Took over the signal, delivered their message, and vanished without a trace. That's not script-kiddie stuff. That's professional. That's the kind of thing that gets you on federal watchlists.

And they did it to advertise a game.

My hands are shaking as I grab my phone and pull up ScyberSpace. My whole body feels electric, every nerve ending firing at once. This feeling, it's like the first time I successfully repaired something instead of destroying it. Like the universe just cracked open and showed me a glimpse of what's possible.

The platform is already exploding. Posts multiplying every second, everyone freaking out about the broadcast hack. Screenshots everywhere. Analysis threads spinning up. People claiming they caught it in different cities, different channels, all at the same time.

National broadcast infiltration. Synchronized. Flawless.

Whoever's running the Shadow Games isn't playing around. And for reasons I can't fully explain, that makes me want in even more.

I spend the rest of the night refreshing the scoreboard (still empty, nobody's solved anything yet) and scrolling through theories. When Mom emerges from her office around midnight to check on me, I pretend I'm watching Netflix. She doesn't push. Just tells me to get some sleep.

I don't sleep. I can't.

The week that follows is a blur. Classes I don't remember. Homework I barely complete. Jason's harassment, which I tune out with practiced ease. All background noise compared to the two mysteries dominating my brain:

The Shadow Games.

And Mom's office.

Every night, I watch that red LED glow in the darkness. She disappears in there around 8 PM, doesn't emerge until I'm supposed to be asleep. Sometimes I hear the soft click of keyboard keys through the wall. Mostly just silence.

What is she doing?

The satellite images. The ScyberSpace chat. The way she looked at me when I saw inside, like I'd discovered something I wasn't supposed to know.

She's not just a programmer. I'm sure of that now. But what is she?

I start keeping notes. Timing her patterns. Trying to figure out when she might leave the door unlocked, when I might get another glimpse inside.

By Thursday, the obsession has grown teeth. It's all I think about. All I want to solve.

I have to know what's behind that door.

2

THE OFFICE

"**J**acob! Breakfast!"

Mom's voice cuts through my dreams like a knife. Based on the level of annoyance in her tone, this isn't the first time she's called. Possibly not even the second.

I bolt upright, heart hammering, momentarily convinced I'm late for school before my brain catches up: Saturday. It's Saturday. No school. No Jason. No Mr. Miles with his cryptic comments and unsettling stares.

9:30, according to my clock. Okay, so maybe I did sleep in enough.

My desk is the usual disaster. Random computer parts, a collection of super-strong neodymium magnets I bought for a project I never finished (story of my life), and my worn copy of "Hacking: The Art of Exploitation" by Jon Erickson. That book is still way over my head, but I keep chipping away at it. Someday it'll click. My notebook sits next to it, filled with crossed-out project ideas and failed experiments. A graveyard of good intentions.

The magnets catch my eye for some reason. They're just sitting there, quarter-sized chunks of metal strong enough to pinch through bone if you're not careful. I learned that the hard way.

"Jacob!"

Right. Breakfast. Moving now.

The hallway is bright with morning light, which is weird. I usually only traverse this stretch at night, sneaking to the bathroom or the kitchen. In daylight, everything looks different. Less mysterious. Less like a spy movie set.

Mom's office door is still closed, that red LED pulsing steadily. Even in bright morning sunshine, that door looks wrong. Too secure for a regular home office. Too secret.

***

Mom is dressed like she's actually going somewhere. Actual clothes instead of the usual weekend sweatpants. Hair pulled back. Keys already in hand. She slides a plate of eggs across the counter and says, "I've gotta run out for a few hours. Need anything before I go?"

I shake my head, not trusting my voice. My mind is already somewhere else. Specifically, behind that metal door at the end of the hallway. I've spent every night this week staring at my ceiling, trying to make sense of what I saw. Satellite images. ScyberSpace chat. That weird high-security lock on a door inside our own house. None of it adds up to "programmer."

"Actually," I say before she can leave, forcing myself to make eye contact, "I need to tell you something. My laptop is... I mean, I was taking it apart, and I think I broke it. Like, really broke it. Smoke and everything."

I brace for disappointment. For the lecture about responsibility and the cost of electronics and how we can't just replace things whenever I destroy them.

Instead, she smiles.

"I'm so glad you're a tinkerer like your dad." Her voice is soft. Warm. "It's okay to be curious, Jacob. Someday you'll understand how valuable that skill is." She pauses. "Actually, I have something for you."

Wait. What?

She walks to her office door, the forbidden door, and pulls out a small card I've never seen before. Swipes it across the keypad. The LED blinks green and the lock clicks open.

I crane my neck, trying to see inside, but she's too fast. The door opens just enough for her to slip through, then closes behind her.

Ten seconds later, she emerges carrying a laptop. Not just any laptop. This thing looks like it belongs to a professional streamer or a government contractor. The logo on the front is a brand I've only seen in ScyberSpace flex posts, the kind of machine people brag about because normal humans can't afford them.

"32 gigs of RAM," Mom says, handing it to me. "Solid state drive. Dedicated graphics card. Should handle anything you throw at it."

I'm literally speechless. This laptop costs more than everything I've ever owned combined.

"You're ready for an upgrade." She smiles, but there's something behind it. Something I can't quite read. "Your curiosity is a good thing, Jacob. Follow it wherever it takes you."

Follow it wherever it takes you.

I watch her grab her purse and head for the front door. The garage opens. Her car starts. She's gone.

And I'm standing here with a professional-grade laptop and what amounts to permission to be curious.

Okay, Mom. If you insist.

I'm going to find out what's behind that door. What you're really doing. Why a "programmer" needs satellite images and military-grade security locks and hacking tools I saw through the gap that one night.

I'm going to follow my curiosity exactly where it leads.

Even if I'm terrified of what I'll find.

I can feel the vein in my neck pounding as my mind shifts to the thought of breaking into my mom's office. What if I get caught?

What if there's an alarm? What if she forgot something and comes right back? I need to look into that black box on the wall. The AID80. It has to be my way in there.

These thoughts make my stomach turn and I can't finish my eggs. The scrambled eggs she made taste like cardboard now even though I know they're fine. My appetite is completely gone. I drop them in the sink and then run to my bedroom to get started.

***

I open the lid of my new laptop and am greeted with a picture of my dad, mom and I together. The desktop wallpaper stops me cold. I almost feel the sweat on my forehead from that hot day at the park in Laurel, Maryland. We had gone for a picnic and ended up staying until sunset because dad wanted to watch the fireflies come out. That was one of the last normal days we had as a family before everything changed.

My mom must have had this laptop ready for me before I broke the last one. She had to have set this wallpaper specifically. There's no way it came like this from the store. She was planning to give this to me. Maybe for my birthday? Christmas? I feel a little bad about breaking my old one now.

I pause for a second before snapping out of my day dream. The clock on my desk shows 9:47. I don't know how long mom will be gone. She said half the day but that could mean anything. I don't have much time. I need to get on this.

Thinking back to the box on the wall, I open a browser and navigate to ScyberSpace. The familiar neon green interface loads up and I go straight to the blog section. I type "AID80" into the search bar and hit enter.

I see multiple search results for a company called Access Control Identification Labs. Apparently they've been around since 2008 and specialize in "high security access solutions for residential and commercial properties." Corporate speak for fancy locks. So that's what the box is. A fancy electronic lock. What could my mom be hiding in her office that made her need this type of secure lock? Regular bedroom doors have regular locks. This is something else entirely.

I scroll through the search results. Most of them are boring product descriptions and installation guides. But the fourth search result catches my eye. It's a blog post by someone called KnackRat. Their profile picture is a cartoon rat wearing glasses and typing on a computer. The title of the post is "AID80 Bypass - How I Got Into My Own House When I Forgot My Card."

My heart races as I read through the post in anticipation. Knack-Rat explains how they got locked out of their own home office one night and couldn't find their access card anywhere. Instead of calling a locksmith they decided to see if they could hack their own lock. After some experimentation they figured out that two strong magnets placed in specific positions on the AID80 housing would trigger a mechanical failsafe. The magnets temporarily disable the electronic locking mechanism and allow the door to open.

"Top left corner, bottom right corner. Hold for three seconds. Door opens. That easy." KnackRat wrote. "Access Control Identification Labs fixed this vulnerability on their AID81 locks but refused to recall or fix the older AID80 units. Hundreds of thousands of these are still in use. You're welcome."

I push back away from my desk in disbelief. Could it really be that easy? I just have to hold one magnet on the top left of the box and another magnet on the bottom right. I was just messing with magnets the other day. The neodymium ones. They're sitting right there on my desk staring me in the face.

My excitement turns to fear when I read the comments section of the blog post. Someone asked about alarms. KnackRat replied "Some AID80 units are configured with bypass detection. If you trigger the magnetic failsafe and there's an alarm configured, you'll have about 30 seconds before it goes off. The owner gets a notification on their phone. Not that I'd know anything about that from personal experience lol."

Could I come up with a reason why I was messing with her lock if an alarm goes off? What would I even say? Sorry mom I was trying to break into your secret hacker lair? I have a hundred things swirling through my head now. Scenarios where I get caught. Scenarios where there's nothing interesting in there and I feel stupid. Scenarios where I find something even worse than I'm imagining.

But only one thought takes hold of my focus. I have to know what is in there. The not knowing is killing me.

***

My heart is still racing as I write down my plan in my notebook. This is the same notebook where I keep all my project ideas. Now I'm using it to plan a break in. The irony isn't lost on me.

Step 1: Bypass the AID80 lock using magnets
Step 2: Slowly open the office door
Step 3: Enter the room
Step 4: Take notes on everything I see
Step 5: Exit without leaving evidence
Step 6: Research everything later

What am I looking for? I write that question down and stare at it. How will I know I've even found anything? I don't really know. I jot down "just take notes about anything I see while in there. Do research after." That seems like a reasonable approach. Document first. Analyze later.

Most importantly, I write down my made up reason if I accidentally set off the alarm. "I have no idea." I stare at those words for a minute. That's my plan? I have no idea? Great plan Jacob. And at this point, I'm completely fine with that. Sometimes you just have to wing it.

I stand up with notebook, pen, and magnets in hand. The magnets feel heavy in my palm. They're only about the size of quarters but they're crazy strong. I learned that the hard way when I accidentally let them snap together and pinched my finger between them. Left a bruise for a week.

I slide my chair under my desk and set off on my personal mission. My mission is to uncover what my mom has been up to. Ever since my dad went missing she's been super secretive about everything related to work. She installed that metal door with the electronic lock about six months after he disappeared. Her home office was never this protected before. Before dad left, it was just a regular room with a regular door. I used to go in there all the time when I was younger. She had a regular desk with a regular computer. Nothing special.

Now she won't talk about anything related to work. When I ask what she does she just says "programming stuff" and changes the subject. When I ask who she works for she says "a consulting company" and changes the subject. When I ask why she needs such a secure door she says "for work equipment" and changes the subject.

I'm scared. My legs feel weak as I walk towards the door. But I'm ready to find out why. Even if I don't like what I find.

***

The door to my bedroom makes an awkward creaky noise as I attempt to be stealthy. I freeze completely. The sound seems way louder than it should be in the quiet house. I cringe even though no one is here to hear it. No one except maybe myself judging myself for being so jumpy.

I slink down the hardwood floor towards the end of the hallway. Each step feels loud. I'm hyper aware of every sound I make. The slight squeak of a floorboard. The rustle of my clothes. My own breathing which suddenly seems too heavy.

I stop short of the office door and just look at it for a second. In the daylight it doesn't look as intimidating. It's just a white door with that little black box beside it. The red light glows softly. Waiting. I can see the yellow sticky note is still there. "Still working, I'll be out later. Love you!" She must not have taken it down from the other night.

I lean forward and place my ear on the door. The cold metal shocks me and I pull back instinctively. It's like touching an ice cube with your face. I try again, bracing myself for the cold this time. I ignore the chill and listen for any sounds coming from inside the forbidden room.

I hear what sounds like a quiet fan. Probably a computer running. But that's all. No voices. No movement. No reason to believe anyone is in there.

That's my cue to make my bypass attempt.

My hands are shaking and I fumble with the two magnets and my notebook. One of the magnets almost slips from my grip but I catch it. Get it together Jacob. I take a deep breath and position the magnets carefully. One at the top left corner of the little black box. One at the bottom right corner. Just like KnackRat described.

I wait. One second. Two seconds. Three seconds.

The little rectangle red light turns green and the box emits a soft beep. Like a small chirp. Almost friendly sounding.

I stare at the box in disbelief that my bypass seemed to work. Did that really just happen? I'm inside a tutorial I read online thirty minutes ago. This is insane.

Then the little light flashes red again and another soft beep comes from the box. "Oh great" I say out loud. The window must have closed. KnackRat mentioned something about timing. I turn the door handle and it's locked again. The brief window has passed.

I do the bypass again. Magnet top left, magnet bottom right. Wait. Green light. Beep. This time I immediately turn the handle and the door pops open. The mechanism releases with a satisfying click.

I have a little rush of adrenaline and an abnormally loud "YES!" comes out of my mouth. I immediately clamp my hand over my mouth even though no one is home. The smile on my face is widened because no alarm is going off. No phone notification sounds. No sirens. Just silence.

I push the door open slowly and peer inside.

***

The only light in the room is coming from a few LED light strips placed strategically across her wrap around desk. They cast everything in a soft purple glow. It's actually kind of cool looking. Like a gaming setup from a YouTube video.

I step in and close the door behind me. Bad idea to leave it open in case mom comes home early. A soft beep comes from another black box that is on the inside of the office by the door. This one looks identical to the one outside but it says AID81 instead of AID80. My stomach drops when I see that. AID81. The fixed version. The one KnackRat said they patched. Does that mean I won't be able to get out the same way?

I push that thought aside. Deal with it later. My gaze shifts from the door to the contents of her office.

I uncontrollably open my mouth as if I was going to say something. No words come out. I'm just standing there with my jaw hanging open like an idiot.

She's got a gaming computer desk that wraps from the left side of the square room to the right side. It covers half of the room's walls. It's the kind of desk I've seen streamers use. The kind that costs more than my birthday and Christmas presents combined for the next five years.

Large flat screen computer monitors wrap around the entire desk in an awesome display of technical might. I try to count them. One, two, three... nine monitors total. Nine. Who needs nine monitors? I imagine NASA's rocket launch operations room isn't as good as my mom's setup. This is serious hardware.

The room smells like new electronics and coffee. There's a mug on the desk that still has some cold coffee in it. Evidence that she was here not too long ago.

***

My mouth closes and my eyebrows narrow. Time to start documenting. I flip open my notebook and start writing.

On the desk are two little black boxes. Each of the boxes have three large antennas shooting up to the ceiling. The antennas are about a foot tall and look like they belong on a military radio. I've seen these boxes before online. They're WiFi Pineapples. That's what hackers use to break into other people's wireless networks. Why would my mom have these? Why would she need to break into anyone's wifi?

Next to the boxes is a notepad. Mom's handwriting. I recognize it immediately. The same handwriting on birthday cards and permission slips and grocery lists. But the words make no sense. The only thing written on the notepad is:

"Frperg Pbqr: FUNQBJ-TNGR-XRL-1"
I write it down exactly as I see it. Letters, dashes, everything. It looks like some kind of code or cipher. Maybe it's encrypted? The letters don't seem to make any English words. But my mom wrote this for a reason. It means something to her.

All of these revelations made me forget about taking notes. I look down at my notebook. I've only written down the WiFi boxes and the weird coded message. I need to be more systematic.

I walk around the desk slowly, writing down everything I see. My mom has what looks like lock picks and other flat tools. A whole set of them in a leather pouch. I saw one of the flat tools being used by a locksmith when we got locked out a few months ago. Why does my mom have lockpicking tools?

There's a small device that looks like a USB drive but has a tiny screen on it. I write down the brand name: "USB Rubber Ducky". Next to it is something labeled "LAN Turtle". I have no idea what these things do but they look important enough to document.

The desk also has several sticky notes stuck to the edge of the monitor frame. Most of them have numbers and abbreviations I don't understand. But one catches my eye: "OT Phase 2 - Target list complete. Awaiting green light."

OT? I file that away for later.

***

The computer monitors all have a black background screen saver with a random pattern of silver squares that just move across the screen together. It's hypnotic. I watch the squares drift for a few seconds before remembering I'm on a mission with limited time.

I check the time on my phone. 10:23. I've been in here almost twenty minutes already. Time flies when you're committing crimes. Is this even a crime? Breaking into your own mother's office? I genuinely don't know.

My hands are clammy. I wipe them on my jeans, but they're sweaty again within seconds. Part of me wants to leave right now, get out before I find anything else I can't handle. But another part, the part that's been wondering about her locked door for months, refuses to stop until I have answers.

I see her mouse and keyboard in the middle of the center part of the desk. The keyboard is mechanical. One of those expensive ones that sounds like a machine gun when you type on it. The mouse is wireless with a bunch of extra buttons on the side.

I move the mouse slightly, just barely touching it. The screen saver turns off.

What I see makes my heart drop.

There is a knot in my throat forming and I try to swallow to make it go away. But it won't go away. The knot just sits there, making it hard to breathe.

Starting on the left of the desk, the first three monitors show what looks like a ScyberSpace message board. But not the normal ScyberSpace I browse. This one has the title "Malware Central" at the top in red letters. Below that is a list of forum threads with names like "New RAT Available - Undetected" and "Custom C2 Infrastructure for Sale" and "Banking Trojan v3.2 - Updated."

She's not logged in so I can't see her screen name. But she has this page bookmarked. She's been here before. Maybe many times.

Instead of the normal ScyberSpace website address, it's got a strange path that I haven't seen on the site before, like it's not meant to be found by normal people. I freeze when I see the URL: shadowgames.io/darknet. The Shadow Games. The same competition that hijacked a national broadcast to advertise itself. The same mysterious challenge I've been dying to enter.

And it has a hidden section hosting Malware Central?

My stomach turns. What exactly have I been wanting to join?

The next set of three monitors has the satellite image of the earth that I got a glimpse of before. When I saw inside here from the hallway the other night. This time I can clearly see that the labels say "Target Location" and they are spread out around the globe. I count at least twelve markers on the map. Different countries. Different continents. There are labels in what looks like code names: "ALPHA-7", "BRAVO-2", "CHARLIE-9".

What is she targeting? Why are there locations all over the world?

The last three monitors on the right side of the desk have what looks like programming code. Lines and lines of code scrolling past. I can't tell what the code is doing by skimming it. It's not any programming language I recognize. But there is a header comment at the top that says "#C2 - BetaZone Edition v2.1 - KOTR Licensed". I'm not sure what a C2 is.

Also in the code comments I see "Author: BetaZone".

BetaZone.

Is that my mom? My mom has a hacker alias? My mom is Beta-Zone?

***

The room tilts. I grab the edge of the desk to keep from falling over.

Malware Central. I've read about it on the regular ScyberSpace forums, always in hushed tones, like people are scared to even mention it by name. It's not the fun part of the hacker community, the puzzle-solvers and security researchers and ethical hackers who make the internet safer. Malware Central is the other side. The dark side. The place where actual criminals sell actual viruses and steal actual money from actual people.

The FBI hunts people who hang out on Malware Central.

And my mom has it bookmarked.

The thought hits me like a physical blow. All this time, all those late nights, all those vague answers about "programming stuff," all that secrecy, she wasn't working on boring corporate software. She was... what? Selling malware? Writing viruses? Being a criminal?

My chest feels tight. It's hard to breathe.

How could she do this to me? To Dad?

Dad was a hero. The actual President gave him a medal. He sacrificed everything for his country, sacrificed our family, ultimately, and now my mom might be one of the bad guys he was fighting against. One of the people who make the world worse instead of better. One of the people who hide in the shadows and hurt innocent people from behind a screen.

Was she always like this? Did Dad know? Is that why he disappeared—because he found out about her, and she...

No. I can't think about that. I can't go there.

My eyes are burning. I wipe them angrily before any tears can fall. I don't have time for this. Not now. Not when I'm standing in the middle of evidence that could explain everything.

Stay focused, Jacob. Document everything. Fall apart later.

I pull out my phone and start taking pictures. The monitors. The malware forums. The satellite map with its blinking red dots. Each photo is blurry and rushed, but it's something. Evidence. Proof that I'm not imagining this. Proof that my mother is not who I thought she was.

BetaZone. The name echoes in my head. If that's her alias, she probably has a ScyberSpace account under that name. Which means she's connected to the same community I've been exploring. The same community running the Shadow Games.

Which means, maybe, the games can help me understand what she's involved in.

I need answers. More than ever, I need to understand what's happening to my family.

Even if the truth destroys everything I thought I knew.

***

I'm still in disbelief at what I'm seeing when I turn to the opposite side of the office. There's more here. Of course there's more.

There is a large whiteboard on the wall with the words "Operation Teardown" written in blue dry erase marker. The handwriting is definitely my mom's. I recognize the way she makes her capital letters.

The rest of the words on the board look like they are written in secret code. Groups of three numbers separated by dashes. I can't make out any of them as actual words. They are written out like "1-26-5, 3-14-8, 2-1-1". There are dozens of these number groups arranged in what looks like paragraphs.

I write everything down on the board in my notepad. Every single number group. It takes me five minutes to copy it all. My hand cramps from writing so fast but I don't stop. This could be important. This could be the key to everything.

Next to the whiteboard is a book shelf with what looks like random books. They aren't technical books at all. No programming guides or computer manuals. Instead there's a bunch of old classics. Shakespeare. Mark Twain. A worn copy of 1984. A collection of poetry. It seems out of place in this high tech spy cave.

One book catches my eye. It's a faded and worn dark leather bound book that stands out from the others. It looks older. More used. Like someone has been handling it regularly. I pull it off the bookshelf.

It says on the front cover in gold embossed letters: "The Constitution of the United States of America: The Declaration of Independence, The Bill of Rights".

This seems important. I don't know why but my gut tells me to pay attention to this book. I open it and flip through the pages. The inside is just what you'd expect. The text of the Constitution and the other founding documents. But some pages have tiny pencil marks in the margins. Little dots next to certain words.

The second page shows the publishing information. "ISBN: 978-1774260135". I write this down too. Why would this specific book be in her office? Why would she need a copy of the Constitution for her hacker work?

There is a notebook on the bookshelf that doesn't have any label on the front. A plain black composition notebook. The kind they sell at drug stores for a dollar. I open it and see more of the same type of number codes on the first two pages of the notebook. But these are groups of four numbers instead of three. Like "2-15-3-7" and "1-8-12-4".

I carefully write down the code in my notebook. All of it. Every number group on both pages.

Her notebook has the words "Special Relativity" written on the top of the first page. That's weird. Why would code numbers be labeled with a physics term? Is that a code name for something? Or does she just like Einstein?

I put the notebook back on the shelf exactly where I found it. I try to angle it the same way it was before. No evidence that I was here. That's the goal.

***

By the time I turn around again, the computer monitors have the original screen saver from when I first came in. The silver squares floating across black. The screensaver must have kicked back on while I was looking at the bookshelf. That probably means too much time has passed.

I check my phone for the time. 10:52. I've been in here for over an hour. Way too long. Way too risky.

Just then I get a text from my mom that says "I'm home early. Can you come out and help with the groceries?"

My eyes widen and a bead of sweat forms on my forehead. Every muscle in my body tenses. She's home. She's home right now. And I'm standing in her secret office that I broke into.

"Oh no. Oh no oh no oh no." I whisper to myself.

***

I quickly turn to leave the office, but in horror I see the problem I never anticipated. The problem I should have thought about when I first saw it. The black box on the inside of the office says "AID81". Not AID80. The updated version. The one they fixed.

I try to turn the handle of the door and it's locked. The same door I closed behind me when I came in. Locked from the inside. With the lock I can't bypass.

Panic rises in my chest.

I take out the magnets but my hands are shaking so bad I drop them. They shoot across the room in different directions because they repel each other when oriented wrong. One goes under the desk. One bounces off the wall and lands by the bookshelf. I run across the room and scramble to pick them up. Blood rushes in my ears, loud and frantic.

This is the box that the company had fixed. KnackRat said the magnet trick doesn't work on the AID81. But I have to try. I have nothing else.

I put the first magnet on the top left of the box and the other on the bottom right. Just like before.

Nothing happens.

The red light stays red. No beep. No click. Nothing.

I try again. Different positions. Top right and bottom left. Both on top. Both on bottom.

Nothing happens. Nothing works.

I feel a wave of panic coming on as I realize I'm in big trouble. Real trouble. Not the kind where I lose my phone for a week. The kind where my whole life changes. The kind where my mom finds out I know her secret.

I have to think. I need to get out of here. There has to be another way.

I look around the room desperately. No windows. No other doors. No vents big enough to crawl through. Just the one door with the lock I can't beat.

Wait. On the right side of the black box there is something different than the AID80 outside of the office. It has a number pad. Four digits. Like a PIN code.

I type in the day my dad went missing "0210" for "February 10th" and hit enter. The rectangle red light flashes red. Wrong code. A small display shows "2 attempts remaining."

Two attempts. Two more guesses before something bad happens. An alarm maybe. Or a lockout.

Just then I hear my mom yell from the kitchen for me to come help. Her voice is distant. She doesn't sound suspicious. She sounds impatient. "Jacob! The ice cream is melting!"

I hear the garage door close as she goes back out to grab more groceries. She's going back outside. I have a tiny window.

Two attempts remaining. What number would she use?

I think about what I know. Mom used my birthday as my dad's phone password. She uses his birthday for her debit card PIN. She uses anniversaries and special dates for everything.

I type in my birthday "0815" for "August 15th" and hit enter.

The light flashes green.

The lock clicks.

I snatch the door handle open as fast as I can and rush out of the office. The door wants to slam behind me because of some spring mechanism but I reach back and catch it just in time. I let it softly close. The lock beeps as it re-engages.

I stand in the hallway for half a second, breathing heavily. I'm out. I made it.

The front door handle jiggles. Mom is coming back in.

***

I run to my bedroom and close the door as quietly as I can. My heart is beating so hard it hurts. I'm sure she can hear it from the kitchen. It sounds like a bass drum in my chest.

I jump on my bed so I can reach the air conditioning vent on the wall above my bed. Last year I found that it just pulls open. The screws are stripped or something. It's perfect for hiding things.

I pull off the vent cover and place my notebook in there. The notebook with all my notes. All the evidence. All the proof of what I found. I replace the cover and smooth out the edges so it looks normal.

I jump down off the bed just as my mom opens my bedroom door. Perfect timing. Or terrible timing depending on how you look at it.

"What are you doing?" she says sharply with a tone of annoyance. Her eyes scan my room quickly. Looking for something out of place maybe. Looking for evidence that I've been somewhere I shouldn't.

"Sorry mom, I'm coming to help" I say as I rush past her to avoid eye contact. My face must be red. My forehead is definitely sweaty. Can she tell? Can she see the guilt written all over me?

I can hear her hesitate while looking into my bedroom before closing my door. She lingers there for just a second too long. Does she suspect something? Did I leave something out of place? Is there a hidden camera in that room that I missed?

I don't hear her close my door as I'm walking into the garage. She's still standing there. Watching.

Did she hear me putting my notebook in the vent?

***

As I help unload the groceries from the trunk, my mind races with everything I just discovered. I'm on autopilot. Picking up bags. Carrying them inside. Putting them on the counter. Repeat. My body is doing the work while my brain is somewhere else entirely.

My mom is hiding something massive. Those satellite images with target locations around the world. The malware forums where criminals sell viruses. The coded messages that I can't decipher. The WiFi hacking tools. The lockpicks. The alias. None of it fits with being a regular programmer.

And "BetaZone"? That's not just a screen name. That's not just a gamertag for playing video games online. That's an alias. A hacker's alias. An identity she uses to operate in the shadows. An identity she hides from everyone including her own son.

I carry the last of the bags into the kitchen and set them on the counter. The bags have ice cream and frozen vegetables and normal grocery stuff. Normal things for a normal family doing normal Saturday errands.

My mom thanks me with a tired smile and starts putting things away. She looks so normal right now. So mom-like. Her hair is slightly messy from being outside. She's humming something under her breath. She's checking expiration dates before putting things in the fridge.

How can the same person who makes me eggs every morning be lurking on Malware Central? How can the person who helped me with my science fair project also be writing code for something called "C2"? How can my mom be two different people at once?

The dissonance makes my head hurt. I love her (she's my mom, of course I love her) but right now I'm also terrified of her. And angry. And confused. All of it swirling together until I can't tell where one feeling ends and another begins.

"You okay, honey?" she asks, and I realize I've been staring at her. Just standing there frozen with a bag of frozen peas in my hand, probably looking like I've seen a ghost. Which, in a way, I have. The ghost of who I thought she was.

"Yeah, just tired," I lie. The words come out automatically now. Lying is becoming easier. Is that a good thing or a bad thing?

We're both liars, I think. She lies about her job. I lie about what I know. We're standing three feet apart and neither of us is being honest. I wonder if she knows I know. I wonder if she suspects that I broke into her office. I wonder if there are cameras in there that will tell her exactly what I did.

"Go rest up. I'll make dinner in a bit."

I nod and walk back to my room. My heart is still pounding even though the danger has passed. The notebook is safely hidden in the vent. The secrets are still locked in my head.

I close my door and sit on my bed, hands pressed against my eyes. The adrenaline is fading now, leaving something heavier in its place. Exhaustion. Fear. A grief I can't quite name.

In one hour, everything I thought I knew about my family has shifted. Dad was a hero (at least I thought he was) and now Mom might be... what? The opposite? One of the people heroes fight against?

I think about the laptop she gave me this morning. "Follow your curiosity wherever it leads." Was that permission? Or a test? Did she know I'd try to break in eventually? Is she always three steps ahead of me?

My chest aches with something that isn't quite sadness and isn't quite anger. It's the feeling of losing something you didn't know you had. The illusion of a normal family. The belief that I knew my own mother.

But one thing is crystal clear now. My mom isn't who I thought she was. My mom isn't just a programmer who works too much. My mom is something else. Something darker. Something secret.

And I need to find out who she really is.

Even if the truth destroys the last pieces of the family I thought I had.

3

SIGNATURES

There's something about ScyberSpace that makes me feel like I've stepped into a different universe. The neon green interface. The retro pixel aesthetic. The whole thing looks like someone built it in the 1980s and forgot to update it, but on purpose, as a statement. Modern apps are all smooth curves and minimalist design. ScyberSpace looks like a hacker movie from before I was born.

I love it. It feels authentic in a way that polished things never do.

Usually, this is where I escape. Where the kid who breaks everything transforms into SirBreaksAlot, someone who might matter, who might learn enough to be impressive someday. Usually, staring at this screen helps me forget about school and Jason and all the mundane garbage that makes up my existence.

Not today. Today, everything is different. Heavier. More real than I want it to be.

The chat room I'm in is called "#Newb", a gathering place for script kiddies. That's what the real hackers call people like me.

Wannabes who run other people's tools without understanding how they work. Copy, paste, pray. No actual skill involved.

The room is empty. Just me and the silence and the thoughts I can't escape.

What would I even say if someone showed up? "Hey guys, pretty sure my mom is a cybercriminal. Anyone dealt with that before? Tips appreciated."

I keep replaying what I saw in her office. The satellite images with those red blinking dots. The Malware Central forums open in her browser. The C2 code signed "BetaZone." My mother, the woman who makes me eggs every morning and worries about my grades, has an alias. A hacker identity. A secret life.

Part of me wants to find some innocent explanation. Maybe she's a security researcher? Those people use hacking tools too, right? They break into systems to find vulnerabilities before the bad guys do. Plenty of legitimate jobs require access to malware forums. Maybe everything I saw has a perfectly reasonable explanation.

But the other part of me, the part that's been watching her disappear into that office every night, that's noticed how she dodges questions about her work, that saw the fear in her eyes when she caught me looking, that part knows better.

My mom isn't just a programmer.

And somehow, that changes everything. Makes my life less boring and more terrifying at the same time. Makes me wonder if whatever she can do, I might be able to do too. Nature versus nurture and all that.

The apple doesn't fall far from the hacker tree?

I don't know. Maybe I'm getting ahead of myself.

***

I really want to confront her about it right now. Just walk down the hall, knock on that cold metal door, and demand answers. But I decide that would be stupid. I need to research what I found in her office first. I need evidence. I need to understand what I'm dealing with before I go accusing my mom of anything.

I don't even know where to start. There's so much to figure out. What's a C2? Who is BetaZone really? What are those coded number messages about? Why does she have WiFi hacking tools and lockpicks? What's Operation Teardown? What's KOTR Licensed mean?

I've got to find out what she's doing in there. She could be a bad hacker selling malware that could be hurting people. She could be stealing money or ruining lives. Or she could be one of those amazing hackers I've always adored. The ones who fight for the little guy. The ones who expose corruption and take down bad actors. The problem is, I've never heard of a hacker called BetaZone. The name doesn't ring any bells.

I'll have to look around here for a while and research what I saw. Once I have something concrete I'll invite Ethan to help me figure this all out. He's good at puzzles and logic. His brain works differently than mine. Together we might be able to crack this thing.

But I'm afraid of looking like an idiot even to him. What if I'm totally wrong? What if my mom really is just a programmer who happens to collect hacking tools as a hobby? Stranger hobbies exist. I can already hear what he'd say if I ran to him with no proof. "You sound like a rusty keyboard right now", I imagine him saying with a smirk on his face. He'd tease me forever.

***

I bring up the scoreboard for the Shadow Games in a new browser tab. The URL is "shadowgames.io/scoreboard". The page loads with dramatic neon styling. It's still blank. Zero names. Zero points. No leaderboard entries at all. Just empty space where champion hackers should be displayed.

I'm kind of surprised no one is rocking this thing yet. The Shadow Games have been the talk of ScyberSpace for weeks now. Ever since that cable broadcast hack went viral. People are obsessed with figuring out how to compete. But no one seems to have actually scored any points yet.

I don't even know how the hackers start competing in this game. There aren't any walkthroughs or hints anywhere that I can find. No FAQ. No getting started guide. No registration page that I can see. They didn't make it very easy to enter. I guess that's probably their intention. They don't want a script kiddy like me messing up their elite competition. You have to prove you belong before you can even begin.

As I'm sulking into my lack of self confidence I notice something strange under the scoreboard. There is a square image of a big oak tree. Just sitting there at the bottom of the page. It looks photorealistic. Old and massive with a thick trunk and spreading branches. Autumn leaves. Something about it seems familiar, like I've seen this specific tree somewhere before.

It seems completely out of place on a hacker competition scoreboard. Why would there be a random picture of a tree? Is that part of the game? A clue maybe? I'm pretty sure it's out of place for a reason. Nothing on these sites is accidental.

I take out a fresh notebook and write down "Oak tree on scoreboard. Part of game? First puzzle?". I stare at it for a moment. No ideas come to me. Maybe if I right-click and check the image properties there will be metadata or something.

I right-click. "View Image Info". The dialog box shows the file is called "oaktree_hidden.png". Hidden. That seems intentional. File size is larger than a normal image. That could mean there's data embedded in the pixels. I've heard of that technique before. Steganography. Hiding messages inside pictures.

I write that down in my notebook too: "oaktree_hidden.png - possible steganography".

I've got more important things to focus on right now so I flip to a new page. The oak tree mystery will have to wait. Finding out about my mom's hacking activities takes priority.

***

If my mom really is a hacker, there has to be some trace of her screen name in here somewhere. BetaZone. Someone has to know that name. I'm not going to find anything useful hanging around in these lame script kiddy chat rooms where I'm the only visitor.

I bring up the list of populated rooms that my account has access to. There are about thirty rooms listed. Most have weird names like "#ZeroDayTrade" and "#PhishingTech" and "#SocialEng". Some sound more general. "#General" looks safe enough. Just a place for hackers to chat about whatever.

I slide through the digital door hoping I won't be noticed by anyone as I enter the room. I try to be casual. Blend in. Don't draw attention.

To my surprise there are at least 500 people in this room and a conversation is already going on about some sort of hacking device. Multiple conversations actually. The chat is moving fast. Names flying by. Technical jargon I barely understand.

Then the words appear in the chat window as soon as I enter the room: "Newb Alert: SirBreaksAlot has entered the room"

Everyone stops talking. The whole chat goes silent. Five hundred people all paused to look at the new guy. To judge me. To see if I'm worth acknowledging or if I'm just another waste of their time.

How nice of the admins to announce when someone new enters a room. I'm being facetious of course. Thanks for putting a spotlight on me guys. Really appreciate it.

Luckily the brief pause to evaluate the new guy is over after a few seconds. The hackers in the room continue their conversations as if nothing happened. I'm already forgotten. Just background noise.

This can't be a great way to figure out some of the things I saw in my mom's office. No one here is going to trust me enough to give me that kind of info. They probably think I'm a spy. Or worse, a federal agent trying to gather intel. If I started asking about specific screen names and malware authors, red flags would go up everywhere.

I'd think I was suspicious too. No friends on the platform. No ScyberSpace achievements. No history of contributions or posts. Just a blank profile with a dumb name and zero credibility.

I scroll through the long list of hackers in the room thinking I'd somehow be lucky enough to see someone called BetaZone. The odds are slim but worth checking. Plenty of cool names scroll past. ZeroDayHunter. ShadowAdmin. HardwareJocky. DarkPixel. CodeWraith. CryptoPhantom.

Wait. ShadowAdmin. That name must have something to do with the Shadow Games. The word shadow is right there. I almost click on their name to ask a direct question about the games and how to enter. My cursor hovers over the username.

But I stop myself. I get control of my impulses. That would totally be a newb thing to do. Just walking up to someone important and asking basic questions that I should figure out on my own. I'd be mocked. Or worse, blocked.

***

I realize from my first brief experience almost interacting with hackers that I may need to go offline for my research. Or at least stick to the blog posts and forums where I don't have to talk to anyone. Lurk mode. Observer status. I'm just not there yet when it comes to actually chatting with people.

I close out the chat application and head over to the main ScyberSpace forum. This is where anyone can ask questions and also provide answers about things they have knowledge in. The threads cover everything from beginner tutorials to advanced exploit development. Some threads have thousands of replies.

This is a safer place to do my research because no one can see me. I can read and search and learn without anyone knowing I'm there. No "Newb Alert" announcements. No judgment. Just information.

Or so I assume. For all I know they track everything and everyone who visits can see my viewing history. But I try not to think about that.

I think back to my mom's office. Where to start? So many things I don't understand. So many questions. I decide to start with something concrete. The little black boxes I saw on the desk. The ones with the big antennas. Those have something to do with wireless networks. Like the wifi in my house.

I don't know exactly how they work, but I've seen blog posts where hackers show pictures of similar equipment. People showing off their setups. Explaining how they audit wireless security. I use the forum's search box to look for "hacking tools for wireless networks".

The first post in the search results shows boxes that look exactly like what I saw. Small black devices, around the size of my hand. One antenna coming out of one side and two coming out the opposite side. Military looking. Professional grade equipment.

The blog post is called "Wireless Hacking 101: A Beginner's Guide". It basically lays out exactly how to use the box to scan someone's network and crack the password needed to connect. The process sounds complicated but the author breaks it down step by step. Capture handshakes. Run dictionary attacks. Exploit known vulnerabilities in common router firmware.

The blog writer mentions that most of these devices come with a default wireless network you can connect to for running the attacks. The factory settings are rarely changed. The network name is usually "MGT-WIFI-CON" with a password of "Wir3l3$$". People are lazy. They don't change defaults.

I write that down in my notebook. Maybe I can connect to my mom's boxes using those default credentials. Worth a try eventually. If I'm brave enough.

I close the blog post and move on to my next search. The wireless stuff is interesting but not what I really need right now.

***

Now to the real reason I wanted to search on the forum. The name that's been burning in my brain since yesterday. I slowly type in "BetaZone" in the search box, hesitating before I hit enter. This feels like crossing a line somehow. Like I'm officially investigating my own mother.

I hit enter.

I get one search result. Just one. That's surprising for such a large forum. The title of the post is "Infamous". What could that mean? Is BetaZone famous? Or infamous meaning notorious? My heart races as I click the post link.

The post is short. The author, someone called "Data-Hound_77", asks one simple question: "I need info on BetaZone. Looking for any history, known operations, or contacts. Reach out via DM if you have any info."

I can't tell if anyone has direct messaged the author. Private messages are private for a reason. But there are three visible responses to the question posted in the thread. I scroll down eagerly to read the answers.

The first response shows: [DELETED BY MODERATOR]

The second response shows: [DELETED BY MODERATOR]
The third response shows: [DELETED BY MODERATOR]

All three answers have been removed. Great. That's not what I was hoping for. Someone went through and cleaned up anything useful. Why would responses about BetaZone need to be deleted? What were they saying that required censorship?

The forum post closes automatically. Just closes. I didn't click anything. The page refreshes on its own and I find myself staring at the main forum page instead of the search results.

"Did I just get kicked out?" I say out loud to my empty bedroom.

I type "BetaZone" in the search box again and hit enter. I hold my breath.

Zero results.

The search comes back completely empty. No posts. No threads. No mentions at all. As if the word BetaZone doesn't exist in the entire forum database.

A chill runs down my spine. My stomach does that falling thing, like when you miss a step going downstairs. Someone is watching. Someone saw what I was looking at and didn't like it. Someone with enough power to delete forum posts and kick users out of search results in real time.

My mom isn't just a hacker with an alias. She's connected to something that can make information disappear. Something that monitors who's asking questions and shuts them down.

I push back from my desk, suddenly very aware of how exposed I am. My cursor. My searches. My username. All of it leaving a trail that leads right back to this bedroom, this house, this kid who has no idea what he's gotten himself into.

Part of me wants to close the laptop and never open it again. Pretend I never saw any of this. Go back to being the ignorant kid who breaks things and fails at normal life.

But I can't. The questions are already in my head. The mystery is already part of me. And if I don't find answers, I'll spend the rest of my life wondering what my mother was really doing behind that locked door.

I push back away from my laptop. The shock of what just happened pulls me right out of my fantasy land. The neon glow of ScyberSpace feels distant now. I'm just a scared kid in a dark bedroom staring at a computer screen.

Now I'm left with a feeling of dread. A cold sweat on the back of my neck. Someone had to have seen me searching for that name. Someone monitoring the forum. Someone who has the power to delete posts and block search results in real time. They kicked me out and then proceeded to delete the only search result I had.

Wait. If someone saw me searching...they might know who I am. They might be able to trace my account back to my real identity. To my IP address. To my physical location.

Are they able to see where I live?

I frantically shut down my laptop and slam the screen closed. My heart is pounding. That old pit of worry that I know too well is growing in my stomach. I might have just put a target on myself. And I didn't even find what I was looking for.

***

The smell of garlic and basil hits me as Mom sets a plate of spaghetti in front of me. Homemade marinara, usually one of my favorites. Right now, my appetite is somewhere far away, probably hiding with my peace of mind.

She sits across from me, twirling pasta around her fork like it's a normal Tuesday night. Like she's just a tired mom who works too much and not a secret hacker named BetaZone. The dark circles under her eyes are more pronounced tonight. Evidence of long hours in that office doing... whatever it is she does.

I decide to test the waters. Nothing too obvious. Just a casual conversation between mother and son.

"So I'm thinking about signing up for the cyber security class next year," I say, timing it so she has a mouthful of pasta. Gives her time to compose her face before responding.

Her eyes flick up to meet mine. Something passes through them (recognition? concern?) before it's gone.

"That sounds like a great idea," she manages around her food.

She swallows and takes a breath. "I'd start with the basics. VPNs. Operational security. That kind of thing."

Operational security. OPSEC. That's not something normal moms say. That's not something you learn from corporate IT training videos. That's language from hacking tutorials and spy manuals.

"VPNs like in those commercials?" I keep my voice casual. Just a curious kid asking innocent questions. "They hide where you are and what you're doing online?"

She nods, setting down her fork. "Sort of. They encrypt your traffic so people can't easily watch what you're doing. And they mask your real IP address behind the VPN server's address, so it's harder to figure out your physical location."

A pause. Her eyes hold mine for a beat too long.

"But if someone really knows what they're doing, if they're so-phisticated enough, they can still figure out who you are. Even with protection. Always assume that's possible."

The lump in my throat won't go down no matter how many times I swallow. Is that a warning? Does she know I searched for BetaZone on an unprotected connection? Is she telling me I already messed up?

"Thanks, that's helpful," I say, forcing pasta into my mouth. It tastes like cardboard.

After a minute of silence, I try another angle. "Do you think that class would cover the Shadow Games?"

Her fork freezes mid-twirl. Just for a second, barely noticeable unless you're watching for it. Which I am.

"The what?" Her voice is perfectly confused. Too perfect.

"The Shadow Games. That hacking competition? There was a hack on the cable broadcast a while back that announced it. Everyone online is talking about it."

"I haven't heard of it." She shakes her head slowly. Expression neutral. "What kind of competition?"

"Like challenges and puzzles for hackers. A scoreboard. Nobody knows what the prize is, but everyone wants to compete." I watch her face for any crack in the mask. "The best hackers in the world are supposedly involved."

"Interesting." She goes back to eating. Casual. Normal. "Sounds like a good way to learn."

Too casual. Too normal.

I push a little more. "You seem to know a lot about this stuff, Mom. VPNs and operational security... did you learn all that at work?"

She doesn't look up from her plate. "Just basic training. You know, assume someone's always watching. Don't click suspicious links. Be careful about phishing and social engineering."

She pauses, then adds: "Beyond that, I'm not too familiar."

The lie lands between us like a physical object. I can almost see it sitting there on the table, ugly and obvious between the pasta bowls.

Not too familiar. My mother, who has nine monitors, WiFi hacking equipment, lockpicks, and Malware Central bookmarked in her browser. Who writes C2 code for mysterious organizations. Who goes by the alias BetaZone.

She just looked me in the eye and said she's "not too familiar" with cyber security.

Something twists in my chest. It's not quite anger, more like hurt wearing anger's clothes. All those nights she told me about her day, asked about my homework, pretended to be just a normal mom working a normal job. All lies. Layer upon layer of lies, built up so thick I never saw through them until now.

I don't know why she's lying. To protect me? To protect herself? Because she doesn't trust me with the truth? Or because the truth is so bad that she can't risk me knowing?

But I know one thing for certain now: my mother is a much better liar than I realized. The woman I thought I knew, the one who bakes cookies on holidays and gets teary at sad movies, maybe she was always a performance. A mask covering someone else entirely.

Which makes me wonder: if she can lie this easily about work, what else has she been lying about? About Dad? About our family? About everything?

***

I get the hint that I won't get the answers I'm looking for from her directly. She's not going to suddenly open up and tell me everything. That metal door with the AID80 lock isn't just physical. She has walls up that I can't break through with dinner conversation.

I need to do my own snooping from here on out. Build a case. Gather evidence. Figure out the truth piece by piece until I have something undeniable. Something I can present to her that she can't deflect or explain away.

The only thing is, I hope I didn't make her suspicious with my questions. The last thing I need is her snooping on me at the same time I'm snooping on her. A surveillance war between mother and son. That would be exhausting.

I stand up and put my plate in the dishwasher. The leftover pasta gets scraped into the garbage. I couldn't finish it.

My mom yells over to me as she heads down the hallway to her office. "I'm working late tonight, see you in the morning!"

And with that, I hear the familiar beep of her office door lock as it closes. Click. Sealed off. Secrets protected for another night.

***

The door to my bedroom creaks open and closes behind me. That creak is really starting to annoy me. I should oil the hinges or something.

I slump down into my desk chair and stare at the wall. My posters of famous hackers stare back at me. PixelJudas. Mouse-Trap. The legends I always wanted to be like. Now I'm living in a house with an actual hacker and I don't know whether to be impressed or terrified.

Where do I go from here? What's my next move?

One thing's for sure. I need to start using a VPN when doing my research online. Mom was right about that much. I can't have someone figuring out who I am or where I live. Not after what happened with the forum today.

I open my laptop lid and search for "best VPN for privacy". Dozens of options come up. Most want money. Subscription fees. Monthly payments that would definitely show up on mom's credit card if I tried to use it.

I keep scrolling. I find one that routes through Switzerland and has a free trial option. I saw on a ScyberSpace post a while ago that Switzerland has strict privacy laws. They don't cooperate with foreign governments the way other countries do. Data stored there is relatively safe.

Oh good, the free trial doesn't require a credit card. Just an email address. I create a throwaway email and sign up.

I download the VPN client and install it. The interface is simple. Big connect button. Server list showing different countries. I select Switzerland and click connect.

A little shield icon appears in my taskbar. Connected. Encrypted. Hidden.

I go to "https://ifconfig.me" to verify the VPN is working. It's a website that shows what you look like to other servers you visit. Your IP address. Your approximate location. Your internet service provider.

Success. Instead of showing my real location in Maryland, it shows I'm visiting from Zurich, Switzerland. My IP address is completely different. I'm anonymous now. Or at least more anonymous than before.

***

I flip to a new page in my notebook and start making a list. What would a hacker's lifestyle actually look like? What are the signatures? The tells? If my mom is really a serious hacker, there should be patterns I can identify.

I write down everything I can think of:
- Constantly on their computer at night (check - mom works until 2am)
- Keeps friends and family at arm's length about work (check - mom never talks about her job)

- Obviously very intrigued by anything technical (check - she gave me a high end laptop)

- Uses codes and secret languages (check - the number groups on her whiteboard)

- Phone filled with suspicious apps and messages (need to verify)

- ScyberSpace app installed on their phone (probably)

- Random text messages from shady individuals (unknown)

- Multiple screens and monitors for their setup (check - nine monitors)

- Special tools and hardware (check - WiFi boxes, lockpicks, USB devices)

- Hacker alias different from real name (check - BetaZone)

I look at my list. Almost everything checks out. The evidence is piling up. But I still have zero proof she's actually doing anything bad. All of this could theoretically be explained by legitimate security work. I need something more concrete.

I need to see who she's talking to. What messages she's receiving. What payments she's getting.

I can't see myself taking her phone and getting away with it. That thing is always at her side. She even takes it to the bathroom. The only time it left her possession that I know of was when she forgot it on the kitchen counter that one time.

I'm going to have to be slick about this. Watch for notifications when she's not looking. Catch glimpses of her screen. Build up a picture over time from small observations.

***

My spy games daydream vanishes as I remember that I still have homework to do. Real homework. Not hacker research. The kind that gets graded and affects my future.

I can't put myself into a corner again at school. Getting caught cheating once was bad enough. Twice would be catastrophic. Mr. Miles made it clear that I'm on thin ice.

I close out the VPN and log into my school email. The inbox has several unread messages. Class announcements. Reminders about upcoming assignments. Standard stuff.

But the newest email in my inbox makes my stomach drop. It's from Mr. Miles. Subject line: "Homework Discussion Needed."

I click it open.

"Jacob, we need to chat about your homework. Come see me after our class tomorrow. This is not negotiable. - Mr. Miles"

"Oh great" I say out loud to the empty room.

This can't be good. Is he going to turn me in for cheating after all? Did he decide that letting me off with a warning wasn't enough? I spend the next hour worrying instead of doing the homework I was supposed to be doing. Ironic.

***

The courtyard at my school is already filled with students when I arrive the next morning. Clusters of people everywhere. Some studying. Some gossiping. Some just trying to stay warm in the crisp fall air.

I find Ethan sitting on our usual bench under a scraggly tree that's already lost most of its leaves. He has his laptop open and a deep frown on his face. His whole body language screams stress.

I sit down next to him and let out a "Burrr". I'm all bundled up in my jacket and hoodie but the cold still gets through. Maryland autumns are brutal.

I look over at Ethan's screen and see a sketchy looking email open. "Just great" he says. "I think I was hacked."

"What happened?" I ask, leaning in to read the email.

"These jerks sent me a message that says they've been watching me through my webcam. They claim they recorded me doing... stuff. And now they want $500 in Bitcoin or they'll send the videos to everyone in my contacts. My friends. My family. My teachers."

I almost laugh but catch myself. Knowing Ethan, this is totally a scam. He barely knows how to use his laptop for homework let alone anything worth blackmailing.

With a smirk on my face and already knowing the answer, I ask "But have you been doing bad things on your computer that would get you in trouble if recorded?"

"Well, no" he admits. "I just use this dumb thing for homework and YouTube videos about basketball."

"It's just a scam Ethan. A really common one actually." I close his laptop lid for him so he stops staring at it. "They send these emails to millions of people hoping someone will panic and pay. They haven't actually hacked anything. They don't have any videos. They're just fishing for scared victims who don't know any better. Don't reply to them. Just ignore it and mark it as spam."

"You're sure?" he asks, relief washing over his face.

"Positive. You're just fine. No one hacked you."

"Thanks Jacob." He lets out a breath he'd been holding. "I just don't get these people. Why do they have to be such horrible human beings? They should be in jail for this stuff. There has to be laws against terrorizing people like this."

His comment about jail sticks in my brain like an arrow. That thought never really occurred to me in the context of my mom. If she's doing illegal hacking stuff, she could go to prison. She could get arrested by the FBI. I've seen news stories about hackers getting decades in federal prison.

My life would be destroyed if my mom was sent to jail for hacking someone. I'd probably end up in foster care. Or living with some relative I barely know. Everything would change.

Now my curiosity has transformed into something more serious. A mission. A necessity. I just wanted to know what she was up to before. Now I have to figure it out so I can confront her and maybe prevent her from doing something that can't be undone.

"Ethan, I have something to talk to you about" I say quietly. "I need your advice on something weird that's happening at home. Something involving—"

I'm cut off by the school bell signaling that first period is about to start. We only have a few minutes to get to class. There's no time for a serious conversation.

"Let's talk more after school" I say, frustrated. "Meet me at the library?"

Ethan nods as he zips up his backpack. "Sure. Sounds serious though. You okay?"

"I don't know. I'll tell you everything later."

***

I slip into my English class without being late for once. The clock says I have thirty seconds to spare. A new record.

I'm dreading my conversation with Mr. Miles after class, but there's nothing I can do about it besides prepare for a scolding. Or worse. My only goal for today is to not get in any more trouble. Keep my head down. Be a good student. Don't give him any more reasons to be disappointed in me.

I sit down in my assigned seat and stay attentive as class starts. Hands folded. Eyes forward. Model behavior.

Mr. Miles stands at the front of the room with his usual tired expression. But today there's something else there. Excitement maybe. He's holding a piece of chalk like he's about to draw something important.

Before he starts, his eyes sweep across the room and land on me for just a moment. There's that look again, the same one from the other day. Like he's measuring me. Evaluating. Then it's gone, and he turns to the board.

"Julius Caesar" he begins, writing the name on the board in big letters. "He's known for his role in the demise of the Roman Republic and the rise of the Roman Empire. A conqueror. A dictator. A man whose ambition changed the world forever."

The class is silent. Some students look bored already. History isn't everyone's favorite topic.

"But many don't realize Caesar was also responsible for an encryption technique that is still studied to this day." Mr. Miles continues. "It's called the Caesar Cipher. Does anyone know what that is?"

No hands go up. Of course.

"Caesar needed a way to pass sensitive military information and critical commands to his generals across vast distances. Messages would be carried by runners who could easily be captured by enemy forces. If a messenger was intercepted, his opponents would know exactly what his strategies and movements were. Battles would be lost. Wars would be determined by a single stolen note."

He pauses dramatically. Mr. Miles loves his dramatic pauses.

"So Caesar devised a system. A way to scramble his messages so that even if they were captured, the enemy couldn't read them. Only his trusted generals, who knew the secret key, could decode the true message."

One of the students in the class raises her hand. Jennifer. She's always raising her hand to ask snobby questions.

"Yes Jennifer. You have a question?" says Mr. Miles.

"What does ancient Roman military history have to do with English class?" she asks in her usual tone.

I raise my hand before he can answer. Something about this feels relevant to me in a way I can't fully explain. The coded messages in my mom's office. The number groups. Maybe there's a connection.

Mr. Miles points at me. "Yes Jacob?"

"Caesar figured out that to be effective at communicating with his army, he needed to ensure his message wasn't modified or read by others" I say. "Even if the physical message was captured, the meaning would remain hidden. The words would just look like gibberish."

Mr. Miles nods in agreement. "Excellent. And that brings us to the point of today's lesson. Today more than any other time in human history, this is an important skill to understand."

He starts drawing on the board. The alphabet in a row. Then another alphabet below it, shifted over by three positions.

"You may be the most effective and intelligent author or writer in the world. But if your message is intercepted and changed by someone else, it won't matter what you intended to write. The recipient gets the modified version. Your true meaning is lost or corrupted."

He steps back from the board.

"It's a reminder that language is more than just letters arranged into sentences. Words can be weapons. Secrets can be protected. And you can make up your own language to suit your own needs."

***

My attention drifts as Mr. Miles transitions into the history of Shakespeare and the play he wrote about Julius Caesar. Something about Roman politics and betrayal and "et tu Brute" and all that.

But my mind is stuck on the cipher. The encryption method Caesar used is actually really simple when you break it down.

You take a message and shift every letter in the alphabet to the right by a certain number of positions. That number is your "key." So if you shifted the message "HELLO" by three positions:
H becomes K
E becomes H
L becomes O
L becomes O
O becomes R

You'd end up with "KHOOR". Gibberish to anyone who doesn't know the key was three. But completely readable to someone who does.

To decrypt that message, you'd just shift the letters back to the left by three positions. K becomes H. H becomes E. And so on.

But here's the thing that's bugging me. Why couldn't someone just try to decrypt an intercepted message by shifting the letters by each possible number? There are only 26 letters in the alphabet. You'd only have to try 26 different keys to find the right one. That seems pretty easy.

I pull out my notebook and write down "Caesar Cipher: Shift letters left starting with one digit and continue to twenty six digits. Brute force attack."

Maybe more complex ciphers use multiple shifts. Or different techniques entirely. Like the number codes I saw in my mom's office. Those weren't just shifted letters. Those were groups of numbers that didn't seem to follow any pattern I recognized.

The bell rings sounding the end of first period. My stomach immediately clenches. Time for my conversation with Mr. Miles.

The class empties out around me. Students grabbing bags. Heading to their next class. Chatting about weekend plans. I stay seated. Waiting.

***

When the last student leaves, Mr. Miles doesn't go to his desk. Instead, he walks over and sits in the empty chair next to mine. Close. Too close. His eyes study me with an intensity that makes me want to shrink into my seat.

"Jacob." His voice is quiet. Private. "I wanted to let you know that you didn't get away with copying homework from Ethan."

My stomach drops through the floor. Here it comes. The punishment. The call to Mom. The black mark that follows me forever. Colleges checking my record, seeing "cheater" written in red ink...

"You're a bright teenager," he continues. "Smarter than you give yourself credit for. You don't need shortcuts."

He pauses, waiting.

"I'm sorry." The words come out smaller than I intended. "It won't happen again. I didn't get it finished and I panicked and made a bad decision."

Something shifts in his expression. He leans back slightly, the interrogation intensity fading into something else. Curiosity, maybe.

"Interesting," he says slowly. "I was fully prepared to give you detention when you walked in here with some elaborate excuse. Like, say, claiming your laptop broke."

He raises an eyebrow.

I freeze. How would he know about my laptop? I only told Ethan. Unless Ethan mentioned it, or unless...

"But you didn't," he continues. "You admitted fault immediately. Didn't try to talk your way out of it." A small smile. "Also, you helped me out with Jennifer during the cipher discussion. That girl exhausts me."

Despite everything, I almost laugh. "She exhausts everyone."

"Jacob." His voice shifts again. More serious. "I'm letting this slide with a warning. Because I see potential in you that I don't want to see wasted. However..."

He leans in. The air in the room changes.

"Metadata isn't the only place information can be hidden in a document. The author name you forgot to change? That's just surface-level detection. There are dozens of ways to embed hidden data in files. Steganographic content in images. Invisible watermarks. Encoded information in fonts and spacing. Hidden text layers."

He stands and walks to the window, his back to me now.

"You should learn how to find data that others have hidden. How to see what's meant to stay invisible." A pause. "That skill might come in handy someday."

Then, almost as an afterthought: "See you tomorrow. Don't cheat again."

I grab my bag and get out of there before he can change his mind about the warning. But my brain is spinning the whole way down the hall.

That wasn't a normal teacher conversation. That was something else entirely. A message wrapped in a message. Advice that sounded like instructions.

My hands are trembling slightly as I walk. Not from fear exactly, from something more like recognition. Like I've just been handed a piece of a puzzle I didn't know I was solving.

Why does my English teacher know about steganography? About hidden data in files? About the kind of techniques I've only read about on hacker forums?

Those aren't things you learn in school.

First my mom with her secret hacker identity. Now Mr. Miles with his cryptic hints about finding hidden information. Am I suddenly surrounded by people with double lives? Is everyone in my world hiding something?

Part of me feels paranoid. Crazy. Like I've read too many spy novels and now I'm seeing conspiracies everywhere. But another part, the part that's been paying attention, that's been noticing the cracks in normal reality, knows better.

Something is happening. Something bigger than a kid breaking laptops and failing at normal life. And somehow, I'm being pulled into the middle of it.

Mr. Miles isn't just a tired old teacher with a passion for Shakespeare and cryptographic history.

He's something else.

And for some reason, he wants me to know it.

***

Walking to my next class, I pull out my notebook and look at the weird text I copied from Mom's office sticky note. "Frperg Pbqr: FUNQBJ-TNGR-XRL-1".

Wait. Mr. Miles just taught me about Caesar ciphers. What if this is one?

I duck into the bathroom and lock myself in a stall. I need to figure this out right now. My hands are shaking a little as I flip to a blank page.

▼

ROT13. That's the most common Caesar cipher. Shift every letter by 13 positions. It's popular because applying it twice gets you back to the original text. Self-reversing.

I write out the alphabet and the ROT13 mapping below it:

A B C D E F G H I J K L M N O P Q R S T U V W X Y Z
N O P Q R S T U V W X Y Z A B C D E F G H I J K L M

So A becomes N, B becomes O, and so on. The beautiful thing about ROT13 is that it's self-reversing. Apply it twice and you get back to the original.

I work through the first word carefully:

F→S, r→e, p→c, e→r, r→e, g→t = "Secret"

My heart starts racing. That's an actual English word! I keep going with the second word:

P→C, b→o, q→d, r→e = "Code"

"Secret Code"! This is definitely ROT13. Now for the key part after the colon:

F→S, U→H, N→A, Q→D, B→O, J→W = "SHADOW"
T→G, N→A, G→T, R→E = "GATE"
X→K, R→E, L→Y = "KEY"

The full decoded message is: "Secret Code: SHAD-OW-GATE-KEY-1"

I stare at the words, my mind racing. Shadow. That word keeps appearing everywhere. The Shadow Games scoreboard I've been looking at. And now my mom has a "Shadow Gate Key" written in code in her secret office?

This can't be a coincidence. Mom is connected to the Shadow Games somehow. This code, SHADOW-GATE-KEY-1, it has to be a password or access key for something. Maybe it's how she logs into some secret part of the games? Or maybe it unlocks a hidden area I haven't discovered yet?

I write down the decoded message and circle it three times. This is a real clue. A connection between my mom's secret life and the mysterious competition that's taken over ScyberSpace.

The bathroom door opens and someone walks in. I quickly stuff my notebook in my bag and flush the toilet like I was actually using it. Time to get to class. But my mind is already racing with possibilities about where this Shadow Gate Key might work.

***

The lights in my dining room are dimmed so low that I can barely see anything except my laptop's glowing screen. I like it this way at night. Calming. Like being in a cave or a submarine. Just me and the pixels.

I open up my web browser and the Shadow Games scoreboard refreshes. The last page I was looking at. Still showing. "shadowg ames.io/scoreboard".

Zero points. Zero names. The leaderboard remains completely empty.

I would have thought by now there would be hackers on the board. The competition has been live for weeks. The whole internet is talking about it. But apparently no one has actually managed to score any points yet. That seems impossible unless the challenges are insanely hard.

Maybe it still is invite only. Maybe the scoreboard is just for show and the real competition is happening somewhere else entirely. They could be filtering out the newbs by making entry completely impossible for normal people. An IQ test disguised as a blank webpage.

But I have a feeling it's not like that. Something about the scoreboard and that tree image are calling to me. There has to be something there. A clue. A puzzle. A way in that no one else has figured out yet.

Maybe no one else has found it because no one else is looking at it the right way.

***

Buzz...Buzz...

I snap out of my daydream to the sound of a phone vibrating twice on the kitchen counter. A notification. I didn't even see the phone sitting there. All alone on the granite surface. Unguarded.

My mom must have forgotten it when she went into her office. She literally never leaves it unattended like that. It's basically an extension of her hand. She takes it everywhere. Even to the bathroom.

This is my chance.

I slide my chair out from the dining room table as quietly as possible. The chair legs don't make a sound on the tile floor. I stand up slowly and pad across the room to the kitchen counter.

The notification must have just come in. The screen is still lit up, not yet timed out. I don't have to unlock anything. The preview shows everything I need to see right there on the lock screen.

There's a notification from an app I don't recognize. The icon is gold and black. Some kind of cryptocurrency or payment app.

The notification preview says: "$10,000 Paid by Knights of the Republic (KOTR). Comment: Alpha, thanks for the C2. We will change up any indicators, don't worry".

My brain races to process what I'm seeing.

Knights of the Republic. KOTR. That was on the code I saw in her office. "KOTR Licensed."

Someone just paid my mom $10,000 for the C2 code she wrote. The Command and Control malware. The stuff that lets hackers control infected computers remotely.

But who is Alpha? The payment comment says "Alpha, thanks for the C2." I thought my mom's alias was BetaZone, not Alpha. Does she have two screen names? Or is Alpha someone else? Her boss maybe? A partner?

I'm so confused now. The pieces don't fit together cleanly.

What I'm not confused about is the fact that this is more proof my mom is involved with bad hackers. KOTR is the group that attacks non-profits. And they just paid my mom thousands of dollars for malware tools.

I hear the beep of my mom's office door opening.

I sprint back to my chair and throw myself into the seat. The dining room chair rocks slightly from the impact but doesn't make noise. I grab my laptop and bring up my school email just as my mom appears in the kitchen.

"Hi Jacob" she says. "Don't stay up too late. I'm working late again tonight."

Her voice sounds normal. Tired. Mom-like.

"Ok, I won't" I say. "I'm just working on my English class home-work."

She grabs her phone off the counter like it's no big deal. Like she didn't just leave the evidence of her criminal activities right there in plain sight. She glances at the notification on the screen. Her expression doesn't change.

She starts walking back to her office. Then she stops before leaving the kitchen and turns slightly. Not quite looking at me.

"Just make sure you look at the metadata before you turn in your assignment" she says.

Then she continues walking. The office door beeps. Clicks closed.

My back slides down into the base of my chair. I feel like I'm melting into the seat. Of course Mr. Miles told her about the cheating incident. Teachers always talk to parents. I should have expected that.

One thing is for sure, I learned my lesson about metadata. And apparently everyone else learned it too since they keep bringing it up.

***

Going back to the revelation I just witnessed on my mom's phone, I minimize my school email and bring up the Shadow Games scoreboard. I open a new tab and dive into ScyberSpace's general search.

I type in "Knights of the Republic" and hit enter.

"Oh man" I say out loud.

Over three thousand search results appear. The list seems endless as I scroll. Most of the search results use the abbreviated name "KOTR" for what appears to be a major hacking collective. They're well known. Notorious even.

I start reading through the articles. KOTR specializes in attacking non-profit organizations. Charities. Relief funds. Medical research foundations. They've been in the news for years, hitting major organizations every few months like clockwork.

What kind of group hacks into non-profits that are just trying to help people? These organizations are feeding hungry kids. Housing homeless veterans. Funding cancer research. And KOTR targets them specifically. Steals their data. Holds them for ransom. Destroys their systems.

The name "Knights of the Republic" sounds noble. Like they should be fighting corruption or something. But their actions are the opposite of noble. The thought of how people could do that to innocent organizations just leaves me with a bad taste in my mouth.

I look towards the hallway leading to my mom's office. The door is closed. The little red light glowing in the darkness.

She's involved with these people. She writes software for them. She accepts their money. She's part of their operation.

Unless she's not. Unless there's something I'm missing. Some explanation that would make this all make sense.

I search for "C2" and the articles all show examples of "Command and Control" malware infrastructure. The malware allows remote hackers to control systems that are infected. Once you infect someone's computer with a C2 agent, you can do anything on their machine. Read their files. Watch through their webcam. Use their computer to attack other targets. Wipe their hard drive. Whatever you want.

My mom builds the tools that make all of this possible. Her code is the foundation that KOTR uses to hurt people.

Or is it? Could the C2 be used defensively somehow? Could she be testing it against KOTR rather than for them?

I don't know anymore. Every answer leads to more questions.

***

I really have to find proof that she's doing something bad. Or proof that she's doing something good. I need something concrete. Something I can go to her with to have a real conversation. If I could just bring undeniable evidence in front of her, maybe she would finally explain what's going on. Maybe she'd tell me the truth.

If she's doing horrible things, maybe I can convince her to stop. Before it's too late. Before the FBI knocks down our door.

And I know exactly where to start building my case. The encrypted notes she had all over her office. Those number codes. The groups of three digits and four digits. The phrases like "Operation Teardown" and "Special Relativity."

I'm glad I wrote everything down in my notebook. That notebook is still hidden in my bedroom vent, waiting for me to decode its secrets.

I close my laptop and stand up from the dining room table. Tomorrow I'll start seriously working on those codes. I'll figure out what cipher she's using. I'll crack her messages and find out the truth.

But tonight I'm exhausted. The stress of the day has drained me. Cheating scandal. Creepy conversation with Mr. Miles. The revelation about KOTR. The phone notification. It's all too much.

I head to my room and collapse on my bed without even changing clothes.

Tomorrow, the real investigation begins.

4

The Coded Messages

I'm practically running to the park, leaves crunching under my sneakers in a rhythm that matches my racing heartbeat. Fall has transformed everything into shades of fire (orange, red, gold) but I barely see it. My brain is too full. Too crowded with satellite images and Malware Central and a mother who isn't who I thought she was.

I need to tell someone. Before I spontaneously combust from holding this inside.

The Constitution book in my backpack weighs approximately one thousand pounds. Okay, not literally, but it might as well. I couldn't take Mom's copy without her noticing it was gone, so I checked out an identical edition from the library yesterday. ISBN 978-1774260135, exact match. Same publisher, same printing, same page layouts. One wrong digit in the ISBN and the cipher falls apart entirely. That's the thing about book ciphers: the book isn't just a key, it's the only key.

No pressure or anything.

Every few steps, I glance over my shoulder. Looking for what, exactly? Mom's car tailing me? FBI vans? Black helicopters?

Paranoia is a hell of a thing. Except it's not really paranoia when your mother actually does have a secret hacker identity and nine monitors running satellite surveillance in a locked room in your own house. Then it's just... situational awareness.

Mrs. Henderson waves from across the street, her ancient poodle sniffing at a fire hydrant like it holds the secrets of the universe. I wave back. Normal kid. Normal Sunday. Definitely not carrying decoded evidence of potential cyber crimes in my backpack.

The park comes into view, and something in my chest loosens just slightly. I've been coming here since I was little. Learned to ride my bike on that path, had my sixth birthday party by those swings. The massive oak tree near the picnic tables has been here forever, probably since before this town existed. It's witnessed generations of kids playing and families picnicking and teenagers making out on benches.

Today it's about to witness something different.

Today, I'm here to crack a code that might explain why my entire life has been a lie.

***

Ethan is sitting at one of the picnic tables under the big oak, his laptop open in front of him. He's wearing his lucky coding hoodie, the one with the faded Minecraft logo that his mom keeps threatening to throw away. Sunlight filters through the leaves, making spotty shadows all over the table. Normally I'd think it looked cool. Right now I barely notice.

A squirrel chatters at me from a low branch as I approach. Even nature is interrogating me today.

I drop my backpack on the table with a heavy thud that makes Ethan jump. "Hey."

He looks up from his screen, a curious expression on his face. I notice he's been working on something, probably that Roblox game he's been building. "What's up, Jacob? You sounded pretty urgent on the phone. Like, more urgent than when you thought you'd accidentally deleted your Shadow Games notes."

I take a deep breath. This is harder than I thought. How do you tell your best friend that your mom might be a criminal mastermind? That all those jokes he made about spy parents might actually be true, just not in the heroic way we imagined?

I pull out the library book and place it on the table, then reach into my pocket for my notebook, the one I hid in the air vent. The leather cover is slightly warped from the heat up there, but all my notes are intact. "I've got a problem," I begin. "A big one. I think my mom is involved in something serious. Something illegal."

Ethan's eyes widen. His hand freezes on the laptop trackpad. He closes the lid slowly, deliberately, like he needs to fully focus on what I'm about to say. "What do you mean?"

"I broke into her office on Saturday," I say, lowering my voice even though the nearest person is a jogger on the far side of the park. "And I found a bunch of stuff. She has all these computers and gadgets. Like nine monitors, Ethan. Nine. Arranged in a grid. And there were coded messages everywhere. She was logged into ScyberSpace, into a forum called Malware Central."

Ethan's jaw drops. The color actually drains from his face a little. "Wait, wait, wait." He holds up both hands like he's trying to physically stop my words. "Back up. Rewind. You broke into your mom's office? The one with the weird electronic lock? The forbidden zone?"

"Yeah. I found a bypass online using neodymium magnets. There's this guy called KnackRat who posts tutorials..."

"KnackRat? The lock picking legend?" Ethan shakes his head slowly, looking almost impressed despite his obvious concern. "Okay, that's actually pretty cool. But also terrifying. And Malware Central?" He lowers his voice to match mine. "Dude, that's like... that's where the bad guys hang out. The real hackers. The ones who create ransomware and steal credit cards and take down hospital networks."

"I know."

"The kind of people who go to prison. Federal prison. The kind with no WiFi."

"I know, Ethan."

He stares at me for a long moment. The goofy Ethan I've known since freshman year is gone, replaced by someone older. More serious. Someone who's processing the fact that his best friend's life just became a spy movie.

"Jacob..." His voice is careful now. "Are you saying your mom is a black hat hacker?"

The words hang in the air between us. Hearing them from someone else, hearing them out loud instead of just rattling around inside my skull, makes them real in a way they weren't before. My throat tightens.

"I don't know. Maybe." I force the words out. "She had satellite imagery with labels that said 'Target Location.' GPS coordinates. Code for something called C2, command and control malware. The author name was 'BetaZone.'"

"BetaZone." Ethan repeats the name like he's testing how it tastes. He runs both hands through his hair, leaving it sticking up in directions that would be funny if anything about this was funny. "This is insane. This is actually, legitimately, certifiably insane."

He goes quiet, staring at the picnic table like the wood grain might rearrange itself into answers. A bird chirps somewhere above us. The wind rustles the leaves. Normal sounds for a normal day that isn't normal at all.

Then he looks up and meets my eyes.

"Are you okay? Like, seriously, are you okay?"

The question lands harder than it should. I've been so focused on playing detective, on connecting dots and finding evidence and figuring out the truth. I haven't let myself actually feel any of it.

The constant knot in my stomach. The way I flinch when Mom walks into a room now. The nightmares I've been having where Dad's disappearance suddenly makes terrible, criminal sense.

"I don't know," I admit. My voice cracks on the last word, and I hate it. I sound like a kid. I am a kid, kinda. A kid whose dad was a hero and whose mom might be a villain and whose whole understanding of reality has shattered into pieces he doesn't know how to put back together.

"My dad got a medal from the President," I say, and now the words are coming faster, spilling out before I can stop them. "He was supposed to be one of the good guys. And then he disappeared and I spent two years thinking he was dead, thinking he died doing something important, and now my mom might be... she might be working for the people he was fighting against. Or something. I don't know. I don't know anything anymore. I don't know what's real."

The last sentence comes out broken. Fractured. Like me.

Ethan is quiet for a moment. Then he nods slowly, deliberately.

"Okay." He takes a deep breath. "Okay. Here's what I know: whatever this is, spy stuff, criminal stuff, multiverse conspiracy stuff, you're not dealing with it alone. That's not how this works. That's not how we work." He meets my eyes, completely serious. "You're my best friend. You've been my best friend since you helped me pass Computer Apps freshman year even though I'm basically tech-illiterate. So if your life just turned into a Jason Bourne movie, then I guess my life did too. We figure this out together."

Something loosens in my chest. A tightness I didn't even know I was carrying. I hadn't realized how badly I needed to hear that, how scared I was that Ethan would think I was crazy, or making it up, or just being dramatic.

"Thanks, man." My voice is steadier now. Still rough, but steadier. "Seriously."

"Besides," Ethan adds, his familiar grin creeping back just a little, "if your mom really is some kind of mastermind hacker, maybe she can help me get unbanned from that Minecraft server."

"Ethan."

"Right, right. Focus. Priorities." He points at the Constitution book on the table. "So what's with the founding document of American democracy?"

***

I open my notebook and show Ethan the notes I took in Mom's office. My handwriting is messier than usual (I was in a rush, terrified she'd come home early) but the number sequences are legible. "These are some of the codes I saw on her whiteboard. They're written in groups of three numbers, like 1-26-5 or 8-1-20."

Ethan examines the notes carefully, turning the notebook to catch the light better. "This is some serious spy movie stuff, Jacob. James Bond meets Mr. Robot. Have you tried deciphering any of it?"

"That's why I got this," I explain, tapping the Constitution book. "There was a copy of this exact book in her office, same cover, same edition. And she had a notebook with more codes and the words 'Special Relativity' written at the top. But I don't think she was studying physics."

"Special Relativity? Like Einstein?"

"Or like a code phrase. A key identifier." I flip through the pages of another library book I brought, one about codes and ciphers throughout history. The spine is cracked from use; clearly I'm not the first person in our town interested in secret messages. "Here," I say, showing Ethan the chapter on book ciphers. "A book cipher uses a physical book as the key to encode and decode messages. Each number group corresponds to a specific page, line, and word (or sometimes just a letter) in the book."

Ethan's eyes light up with understanding. I can practically see the gears turning in his head. "I get it. It's like a secret code where the book itself is the key to everything. So without knowing which exact book they used..."

"You can't crack the code," I finish. "You could have the most powerful computer in the world, and it wouldn't matter. There's no algorithm to brute-force it. You'd have to try every book ever published, every edition, every printing."

"But we know the book." Ethan taps the Constitution. "We have the key."

"Exactly. Same ISBN, same edition. If I did this right, we should be able to decode everything she wrote."

"That's actually genius," Ethan says, a hint of his usual enthusiasm returning despite the serious circumstances. "Old school. Analog. Completely immune to digital attacks." He pauses. "Your mom might be a criminal, but she's a really smart criminal."

I don't know whether to feel proud or horrified by that observation.

Ethan pulls out his phone. "Okay, let's find a digital copy of the Constitution. The text should be exactly the same, and it'll be way easier to search than flipping through pages."

It doesn't take long to locate a PDF version matching the same edition. Ethan downloads it, and we begin the painstaking process of decoding the first message from Mom's whiteboard. The sun is warm on my back, the breeze is pleasant, and I'm sitting in my favorite park decoding what might be evidence of my mother's crimes. Just a normal Sunday.

***

"Okay, the first message starts with a pound sign, probably a hashtag, and then: 2-12-3, 1-10-10, 5-3-2, 1-10-2, 8-1-20, 20-8-2, 21-9-1, 8-10-2, 13-1-8, 3-10-5," I read aloud from my notebook.

Ethan writes the numbers down on a piece of paper he tore from his own notebook, leaving space underneath each set for the decoded letters. His handwriting is neater than mine. His mom makes him practice calligraphy, which he complains about constantly but secretly doesn't hate.

"Page 2. Line 12. Word 3," I say, scrolling through the PDF on Ethan's phone. The screen brightness is maxed out to fight the sunlight, and I have to cup my hand around it to see clearly. "The third word on line 12 of page 2... counting from the start... that's 'Order.' So the first letter is 'O.'"

Ethan writes down "O" under the first number group. "One down. Only like a million to go. This is going to take forever."

"Good thing we have forever."

We continue this process for the next hour. The sun moves across the sky, the shadows from the oak tree shifting around us like a sundial. A family sets up a picnic on the grass nearby. Two kids throwing a frisbee, parents unpacking sandwiches. Normal life happening just feet away from our amateur codebreaking operation.

My eyes start to burn from staring at tiny text on a phone screen. Ethan's handwriting gets messier as we go, the letters cramped and tilted. But he doesn't complain. Not once.

Letter by letter, the message starts to take shape. At first just random consonants and vowels that could mean anything. But then patterns emerge. Familiar combinations.

After about twenty letters, Ethan stops me. "Wait. Look at this. O-P-T-E-A-R-D-O-W-N. The first word is 'opteardown.' Like a hashtag. #opteardown."

"Operation Teardown," I whisper. That was the phrase on Mom's whiteboard, the one that appeared on multiple documents and sticky notes. We're on the right track. Whatever this is, we're actually cracking it.

We work faster now, energized by the breakthrough. The frisbee family leaves. A dog walker passes. My notebook fills up with letters, and Ethan double-checks each one against the PDF, making me re-count when the words don't seem right. By the time we finish, the sun has moved significantly across the sky, and my neck hurts from hunching over the phone. But I don't care.

Finally, we have the complete decoded message.

Ethan clears his throat and reads it aloud, his voice quiet enough that only I can hear:

"#opteardown. In the shadows deep, a dark web concealed, where mysteries and secrets are revealed. Enter if you dare, the darkness calls, where challenges await within its walls. A puzzle veiled in games of night, unlocking paths, revealing light. Seek the key where shadows play, decode the secrets, find your way. For in this realm of mystery spun, lies the answer, when all is done. To unravel truths, your mind must probe, in the realm where shadow games roam."

***

We sit in silence for a moment, staring at the words.

"'In the shadows deep, a dark web concealed,'" Ethan repeats slowly. "That first line, it sounds like a password. Like something you'd type to get into a secret site."

"You think?"

"Definitely. If I was running some underground hacker thing and needed a passphrase, that's exactly what I'd use. Poetic, memorable, and you'd only know it if you decoded the message."

I make a mental note of it. In the shadows deep, a dark web concealed. If we ever need to get into something protected, that might be our key.

"This is incredible, Jacob." Ethan sounds kinda stunned, like he can't believe what we just pulled off. "We actually did it. We actually decoded a real cipher."

I nod, feeling a mix of pride and creeping apprehension. "Yeah, but it's just the beginning. This message is like a riddle wrapped in poetry. It's telling us something, but it's not being direct about it."

"It mentions the Shadow Games," Ethan says slowly, running his finger under those specific words. "Multiple times. 'Games of night.' 'Shadow games roam.' You know, the competition you keep telling me about on ScyberSpace. The one that supposedly hacked that TV station."

"Yeah." My brain is working overtime now, connections firing. "So my mom has a coded message about the Shadow Games hidden in her secret office. A message that talks about 'dark web' and 'mysteries' and 'secrets revealed.' What does that mean? Is she competing in the games? Running them? Investigating them? Something else entirely?"

"'Enter if you dare,'" Ethan reads again, tapping the paper. "'Where challenges await within its walls.' It's definitely talking about the games as a place to enter. And look, 'decode the secrets, find your way.' That's basically a description of what we just did. Like this message was meant to be decoded by someone following a trail."

I lean back against the picnic table bench and look up at the oak tree above us. Its leaves rustle in the breeze, some of them breaking free and spiraling down around us in lazy circles. Red and gold against the blue sky. Something about the tree feels familiar in a way I can't quite place. Something beyond just having played here as a kid.

Then it hits me like a physical impact.

"The oak tree," I say, sitting up so fast I almost knock into Ethan.

"What about it?"

I pull out my phone with shaking hands and navigate to sha dowgames.io. The scoreboard loads, still empty, still waiting for someone to crack its mysteries. The zero slots mock me like always. But there, below the blank leaderboard, is the image I've been staring at for days without really seeing.

An oak tree.

"Look." I turn the phone to show Ethan, holding it up next to the real tree above us. "The scoreboard has an oak tree image at the bottom. I noticed it before but didn't think much about it. Just figured it was a logo or decoration. But now we're sitting under an oak tree, decoding a message that explicitly talks about the Shadow Games."

Ethan looks up at the massive tree spreading above us, then back at my phone screen. The images are similar, not identical, but close enough. Both oak trees. Both with spreading branches. Both casting shadows.

"That's... that can't be a coincidence," he says slowly.

"Nothing about this is a coincidence anymore," I say. The pieces are connecting in my mind like a circuit board powering up. Mom's office. The coded messages. Operation Teardown. The Shadow Games. BetaZone. Alpha. The oak tree. My dad's disappearance. It's all linked somehow, all part of the same puzzle. I just can't see the whole picture yet. "Everything is connected. We just have to figure out how."

***

Ethan is quiet for a long moment, studying the decoded message again. He reads through it twice more, lips moving silently. When he finally speaks, his voice is more serious than I've ever heard from him. "So what are you going to do?"

It's the question I've been avoiding. The one that's been lurking in the back of my mind since I first stepped into Mom's office and saw those monitors glowing in the darkness. Since I smelled the coffee and the burned electronics and felt the weight of secrets pressing down on me.

I stare at the empty scoreboard on my phone. Zero points. Zero names. A challenge waiting to be accepted. A darkness waiting to be entered.

"I have to find out the truth," I say slowly. "About my mom. About what she's really doing. About Operation Teardown and BetaZone and all of it. About Dad."

"And you think the Shadow Games are the key?"

I read the decoded message one more time. "It literally says 'to unravel truths, your mind must probe, in the realm where shadow games roam.' If I want answers about Mom and Operation Teardown, if I want to understand why she has satellite imagery and target coordinates and C2 code, I need to enter the games. I need to go where the message is pointing."

"You know this could be dangerous, right?" Ethan's goofy demeanor is completely gone now. He's looking at me the way he looked at me when I told him my dad disappeared, with real concern, real fear for his friend. "Whatever your mom is involved in, it's not kid stuff. These are real hackers. Real criminals maybe. People who don't mess around."

"I know." I look down at my phone again. The registration button glows softly at the bottom of the scoreboard page, a simple blue rectangle with white text: REGISTER NOW. Such an innocent-looking button for what it represents. "But I can't just pretend I didn't see what I saw. I can't go back to normal and do homework and eat dinner with Mom like everything's fine. My dad was a hero who disappeared without a trace. My mom might be a criminal. And there's a competition out there that seems to be at the center of all of it. I have to know the truth. Even if it hurts."

Ethan takes a deep breath. Then he holds out his fist.

"Then I'm in too. Whatever you need. Research, backup, moral support, someone to delete your browser history if everything goes wrong. SirBreaksAlot needs a sidekick, right?"

I bump his fist with mine, a small smile breaking through my anxiety. The warmth of friendship, solid and real in the middle of all this uncertainty. "Thanks, Ethan. For believing me. For everything."

"Just remember me when you're famous," he says. "Or when you're testifying before Congress. Either way, I want acknowledgment."

I look back at the scoreboard. My finger hovers over the registration link. One tap and there's no going back. One tap and I'm officially a player in whatever game my mom is caught up in. One tap and I start down a path I can't see the end of.

I think about Dad's face in that White House photo. The pride in his eyes. The words he never got to say to me. The secrets he took with him when he disappeared. I think about Mom's office, those nine monitors glowing, the coded messages waiting to be deciphered.

I think about the decoded poem. "Seek the key where shadows play."

I tap the button.

For a moment, nothing happens. Just a loading icon spinning on my screen while my heart pounds against my ribs. Part of me hopes it fails, that I get an error message, that the whole thing crashes, that I have an excuse to go back to my normal, boring, safe life.

But another part, the part that's been waiting for something like this, the part that refuses to spend one more day not knowing the truth, that part is holding its breath. Hoping.

The page loads. A new screen appears.

"Welcome to the Shadow Games, candidate. Registration status: PENDING VERIFICATION. Complete the following entry challenge to proceed. Time limit: 48 hours."

Below that, a puzzle materializes. An image of a digital lock with a keypad. Beneath it, a string of characters that looks like gibberish at first glance: aHR0cHM6Ly9zaGFkb3dnYW1lcy5pby9lbnRyeS1jaGFsbGVuZ2U=

I recognize the format immediately. Base64 encoding. Entry-level stuff.

Ethan leans over my shoulder to look. "Well," he says, "looks like the adventure starts now. What's that string?"

"Base64," I say, already pulling up a decoder in another browser tab. "It's a way of encoding data. Easy to decode if you know what you're looking at."

The decoded URL reveals itself: https://shadowgames.io/entry-challenge

"A hidden page," Ethan whispers. "They're already testing if you know basic encoding. Filtering out people who don't belong."

I navigate to the URL. A countdown timer appears: 47:59:32 and ticking down. Below it, a message:

"The shadows await those who can see beyond the surface. Your first test: The oak tree holds secrets in its pixels. Find what's hidden. Submit below."

My blood runs cold. The oak tree. The same oak tree from the scoreboard. The same type of tree we're sitting under right now.

"Steganography," I say, pieces clicking into place. "They've hidden something inside the oak tree image on the scoreboard. Data embedded in the pixels themselves."

"Like that oaktree_hidden.png thing you mentioned?" Ethan asks.

"Exactly like that." I think about the tools I'll need. Steghide. Zsteg. ExifTool for metadata. A whole arsenal of image analysis software I've only read about.

I stare at the challenge, adrenaline flooding my veins. The first real test. The first real step into the shadows.

Somewhere in all of this, in the codes and the games and the secrets, is the truth about my family. About my mom. About my dad. About who they really are and what they're really doing.

And I'm going to find it.

No matter what.

5

INTO THE GAMES

The puzzle on my screen glows in the dim light of my bedroom. It's past midnight, but sleep is the last thing on my mind. My brain is running on pure adrenaline and probably too much caffeine from the soda I grabbed at the park.

After Ethan and I said goodbye, I raced home, barely stopping to say hi to Mom before thundering up the stairs. She called something after me about dinner being in the fridge, but I was already closing my bedroom door, already pulling up my laptop, already logging back into shadowgames.io. Dinner could wait. This couldn't.

The entry challenge was waiting for me. The oak tree steganography puzzle. My ticket into a world I've only glimpsed from the outside.

I spent the first hour just downloading tools. Steghide for extracting hidden data. Zsteg for detecting LSB steganography. ExifTool for pulling metadata. I had to learn how to use each one from scratch, following tutorials on ScyberSpace and a sketchy YouTube channel run by someone called "CryptoGH_Official."

The video quality was terrible (filmed on what looked like a potato) but the information was solid.

The oak tree image from the scoreboard sat on my desktop like a bomb waiting to be defused. I ran ExifTool first, checking the metadata.

Nothing obvious. Just standard image properties. Dimensions, file size, creation date. But then I noticed something in the "Comment" field that most tools would have missed: "The deeper you look, the more you'll find. Try LSB."

LSB. Least Significant Bit. It's a steganography technique where data is hidden in the last bit of each pixel's color value. The changes are invisible to the human eye, but software can extract the hidden message.

▼

I ran Zsteg on the image. The terminal filled with output, most of it garbage, random strings of characters that meant nothing. But buried in the noise was a string that made my heart stop:

"Registration key: SH4D0W-G4M3S-ENTRY-7734"

I stared at it for a full ten seconds, not quite believing what I was seeing. This was it. The key. The way in.

My chest felt tight, excitement and terror wrapped around each other so tightly I couldn't tell where one ended and the other began. Part of me wanted to slam the laptop shut, pretend I'd never found it. Go back to being the guy who just breaks stuff and fails at normal life.

But a bigger part, the part that had been waiting my whole life for something like this, was already reaching for the keyboard.

I copied the key with shaking fingers, went back to the registration page, and pasted it into the verification field. For a moment, nothing happened. Then...

The screen flashed green.

"Verification complete. Welcome, SirBreaksAlot, to the Shadow Games. You have been granted access to the competitor network. May the shadows guide your path."

I let out a breath I didn't know I was holding. My whole body feels electric, like I've touched a live wire and somehow survived.

A new tab opened automatically. A sleek, dark interface with neon green accents that hurt my eyes in the best way possible. At the top, the words "SHADOW GAMES: COMPETITOR HUB" pulse softly, each letter flickering like it's barely holding onto existence. Below that is a chat window, a challenge board, and in the corner, a small scoreboard showing my name with a score of zero.

Zero points. Bottom of the rankings. Dead last in a competition I don't fully understand.

But I'm in.

I'm actually in.

Holy crap, I'm actually in.

***

The competitor chat is chaos. Absolute pandemonium. Messages scroll by faster than I can read them, a constant stream of aliases and trash talk and puzzle discussion and inside jokes I don't understand.

"PhantomByte: anyone crack Challenge 7 yet? stuck on the hex encoding part"
"CipherQueen: imagine getting stuck on hex lol couldn't be me"
"ZeroDayHunter: Queen you took 3 days on Challenge 4 sit down"
"PhantomByte: harsh but fair"
"DarkNull: fresh meat just joined, welcome SirBreaksAlot"
"HardwareJocky: another one bites the dust"
"CipherQueen: place your bets, how long until they quit?"
"ZeroDayHunter: I give them two days"

My username in someone else's message makes my heart skip. They see me. Real hackers (or at least people who think they're real hackers) are talking about me. Judging me. Already betting on how long I'll last.

Something hot flares in my chest. Defiance, maybe. Or wounded pride. These people don't know me. Don't know what I've already found, what I'm capable of, what I'm willing to risk to get answers.

Two days. ZeroDayHunter gives me two days before I quit.

We'll see about that.

Part of me wants to type something back, something clever that proves I belong here. But I know better. Better to observe first and learn the culture before I stick my foot in my mouth. There'll be time to prove them wrong later.

The chat keeps flowing:
"HardwareJocky: anyone else notice the oak tree image on the main scoreboard? feels like a hint for something bigger"
"PhantomByte: oak tree is phase 2 stuff, don't worry about it yet noob"
"CipherQueen: or maybe it's the final puzzle and we're all blind"
"DarkNull: Queen has theories about everything"
"CipherQueen: and I'm usually right which is why you all hate me"

Oak tree. They're talking about the same image I just used to get verified. At least I'm not crazy for thinking it's important. Apparently it's connected to Phase 2 challenges, whatever those are.

I scroll through the user list on the sidebar. Dozens of competitors, maybe hundreds. Most have point totals in the double digits. 50, 75, 125. A few are in the hundreds, their names highlighted in silver. And at the very top of the list, glowing gold, one name stands out:

StarBreaker - 2,847 points

That's more than double the second-place competitor, someone called "NightShade" with 1,203 points. Whoever StarBreaker is, they're not just winning. They're dominating. Absolutely crushing everyone else.

As if on cue, a new message appears in the chat:
"StarBreaker: New blood. SirBreaksAlot. Interesting choice of name."

I freeze. The top player just called me out. In front of everyone. The chat goes quiet for a moment (at least it feels quiet, even though messages are still scrolling) like everyone's waiting to see what happens next.

My mouth goes dry. My palms are suddenly slick against the laptop. This is like being noticed by the popular kid at school, except instead of social status, the currency here is skill, and I haven't proven I have any yet.

My fingers hover over the keyboard. What do I even say to that? "Thanks"? "Nice to meet you"? "Please don't destroy me"?

Before I can decide, another message appears:
"StarBreaker: First tip is free. The challenges aren't just about technical skill. They test who you are. Watch your back."

And then StarBreaker's status changes from green to gray. Offline.

I stare at the screen, trying to process what just happened. The chat erupts:
"PhantomByte: lmaooo StarBreaker noticed you"
"CipherQueen: that's either really good or really bad"
"DarkNull: probably bad tbh"
"ZeroDayHunter: 'watch your back' is never a friendly greeting"

"HardwareJocky: RIP SirBreaksAlot, we hardly knew ye"

I minimize the chat. I can't deal with this right now. My head is spinning. "Watch your back" doesn't sound like friendly advice. It sounds like a warning. Or a threat. Or both.

***

I click over to the challenge board. There are twelve challenges listed, organized into three "phases" like a video game. Most of Phase 1 shows green checkmarks next to various competitors' names, indicating they've been solved by multiple people. Phase 2 is mostly orange, meaning in-progress or solved by only a few elite players. Phase 3 is completely red. Unsolved by anyone.

Challenge 1 catches my eye: "First Steps - 50 points - ENTRY LEVEL"

The description reads: "Sometimes the most important messages hide in plain sight. Download the image below and find what others have missed. Coordinates lead to shadows."

There's a download button for an image file called "welcome.p ng". I click it and wait for the file to load. It's a simple picture. The Shadow Games logo (a stylized eye inside a circuit board pattern) on a black background. Nothing obviously hidden.

But the challenge said "hide in plain sight." That means steganography, hiding data inside other data. I just did this with the oak tree. I can do it again.

But before I go full forensic analysis mode, I remember something Ethan said once: "The best hiding spots are the ones nobody thinks to check because they're too obvious."

I right-click the image and select Properties, then click over to the Details tab. And there it is. In the Comments field, a string of text: "The first shadow falls at coordinates 39.1148, -76.7747"

Coordinates. GPS coordinates. I open a new tab and paste them into a maps search, my heart pounding. The pin drops on... Fort Meade, Maryland. More specifically, it's pointing to a building I don't recognize. A boring-looking government building with a parking lot.

I zoom in. The building is labeled "National Cryptologic Museum."

A museum about codes and ciphers. The same kind of stuff I've been learning about for the Shadow Games. That can't be a coincidence. Nothing in this competition is a coincidence.

I go back to the challenge and notice there's a second part I missed: "What lies at the shadow's edge? Name the keeper of secrets."

The keeper of secrets. At a cryptology museum. I do a quick search for "National Cryptologic Museum" and discover it's run by the NSA, the National Security Agency. The same people who crack codes and intercept communications for the government.

But is the answer "NSA"? Or something more specific?

I dig deeper. The museum's website shows exhibits about World War II codebreaking, the Enigma machine, famous codebreakers throughout history. One name keeps appearing: William Friedman. The "father of American cryptology."

I try "William Friedman" as my answer.

The screen flashes red. Wrong.

I chew my lip and think harder. The challenge said "keeper of secrets," present tense. Not historical. Who runs the NSA now?

Another search. The current director is someone I've never heard of. I try their name.

Red again. Wrong.

I'm missing something. "The shadow's edge." Shadow. What does shadow mean in this context?

I go back to the map and zoom in on the museum's location. It's near Fort Meade, which I know is where the NSA is head-quartered. And right next to the museum, there's a small park area with... an oak tree.

Wait.

I search for images of the National Cryptologic Museum. In one photo, there's a monument outside, a giant bronze sculpture of a hand holding a broken enigma rotor. But behind it, visible in the corner of the image, is an oak tree.

The shadow's edge. The edge of the shadow cast by the oak tree.

But what's the answer? I stare at the image for a long time. Then I notice something I missed. The monument has a plaque. I can barely read it in the photo, but it says something about "NSA Memorial."

I try "NSA Memorial."

Red.

I want to throw my laptop across the room. My frustration is a physical thing, coiling in my chest, making my jaw clench. I'm so close. I can feel it. The answer is right there, dancing just out of reach.

Deep breath. Think, Jacob. The challenge said "Name the keeper of secrets." A keeper. A guardian. Someone who watches over something.

On a whim, I search "National Cryptologic Museum curator."

The current chief curator's name is Dr. Patrick Weadon.

I type it in.

Green. "Challenge complete! +50 points awarded."

I pump my fist in the air, then immediately feel ridiculous. It's almost 1 AM and I'm celebrating alone in my dark bedroom over 50 virtual points. My mom is asleep down the hall. My dad is... wherever he is. And I'm silently fist-pumping at a computer screen like I just won the lottery.

The high fades quickly, replaced by something emptier. There's no one to share this with. Not really. Ethan will be excited, sure, but he doesn't fully understand what this means. And Mom, I can't tell her anything. Not when she's the reason I'm doing this in the first place.

But you know what? I earned those points. First challenge down. However many more to go.

The loneliness sits there, a quiet ache beneath the triumph. I push it down and focus on what's next.

***

I text Ethan even though it's way too late: "You still up?"

The reply comes almost instantly: "Dude it's 1am. But yeah. Can't sleep. What's up?"

"I'm in the games. Actually in. Just completed my first challenge."

Three dots appear as he types. Disappear. Appear again. Finally: "WAIT WHAT. Screenshot or it didn't happen."

I take a picture of the scoreboard showing "SirBreaksAlot: 50" and send it over. His response is a string of celebration emojis followed by: "You're officially a shadow gamer now. How does it feel?"

"Terrifying and awesome," I type back. "There's a player called StarBreaker who's dominating. They said something weird to me in the chat."

"Weird how?"

"Told me to watch my back."

There's a long pause before Ethan responds. "That's ominous. Be careful, dude. Remember, we don't actually know who these people are."

"I know."

"I mean it. Your mom is already mixed up in something sketchy. Now you're in a competition full of hackers who do sketchy stuff for fun. Just... be smart."

"Since when are you the cautious one?"

"Since my best friend might be in actual danger and I can't help from my bedroom."

I stare at his message for a long time. The glow of my screen is the only light in the room, and suddenly I'm very aware of how late it is. How quiet the house is. How alone I am in this.

He's right. This isn't a game. Or it is, but it's also something more. Something real. Something dangerous. Something connected to my mom, to my dad, to secrets I'm only beginning to uncover.

I'm about to reply when a notification pops up on the competitor hub. It's a direct message.

From: StarBreaker
Subject: Not bad for a newbie

My pulse quickens. The top player. Messaging me directly. Again.

I click to open it, not sure if I should feel honored or terrified. My hand actually trembles as I click. Both, I decide. I feel both.

"Saw you crack Challenge 1. Most fresh players take hours on that one. They overcomplicate the steganography when the answer's in the metadata. You've got instincts. But instincts aren't enough in these games.

I've been competing for two years. Seen a lot of people come and go. Some quit because they couldn't hack it (pun intended). Some moved on to other things. But a few... disappeared. Not just from the scoreboard. Real disappearances. Real consequences.

I'm not trying to scare you off. The shadows need fresh blood, fresh perspectives. But you should know what you're getting into. If you're smart, you'll treat this like more than a game. Because someone is always watching.

One more thing. Your username. SirBreaksAlot. It's funny, but it also tells people you're young. Probably a teenager. Maybe reconsider before you climb higher and attract the wrong kind of attention.

-SB"

I read the message three times, four times, until the words blur together and reform. Real disappearances. Real consequences. What does that mean? Are people actually getting hurt because of this competition? Who's watching?

And more importantly, who built all this? The Shadow Games didn't just appear out of nowhere. Someone designed these challenges, created this infrastructure, recruited thousands of hackers into a competition that apparently has real stakes and real dangers. That kind of operation takes serious resources. Serious planning. Someone at the top, pulling strings that most of us can't even see.

A chill runs down my spine that has nothing to do with my room being cold.

I think about what I found in Mom's office. The satellite images with target locations. The malware forums. The C2 code. The coded messages about Operation Teardown. If my mom is involved in something this big, something that involves tracking targets and running command-and-control servers, then maybe StarBreaker isn't exaggerating. Maybe the Shadow Games really are dangerous.

A sensible person would log off right now. Delete the account. Pretend none of this ever happened.

But I'm already in. I've already made it past the entry challenge. My name is on the scoreboard. And more importantly, I need answers. About Mom. About Dad. About all of it.

And somewhere in these challenges, somewhere in the puzzles and the codes and the layers of deception, is the truth about my family. About why Mom has a secret office. About what happened to Dad. About whether the hero I remember was actually a hero at all.

I type a reply to StarBreaker: "Thanks for the warning. Who's watching? And what do you mean by 'real disappearances'? Has someone actually gotten hurt?"

I wait. Five minutes. Ten. But StarBreaker doesn't respond.

I check their status. Still offline.

***

The clock on my computer reads 2:17 AM. My eyes burn from staring at the screen, but I've completed two more challenges and earned another 75 points. Challenge 2 was a simple cipher. ROT13, which is basically Caesar cipher with a fixed shift of 13. Challenge 3 was trickier, involving a hash that I had to identify and crack using a rainbow table lookup.

My total score: 125 points. I'm climbing the ranks slowly, passing competitors who probably started days or weeks ago. The chat has quieted down as people log off for the night, but a few night owls are still active:

"NightShade: anyone working on Challenge 6? stuck on the audio analysis"
"DarkNull: audio stuff is outside my wheelhouse"
"NightShade: same. might need to bring in outside help"

"PhantomByte: 'outside help' aka google and prayer"

I'm so focused on reading the chat that I don't hear my bedroom door open.

"Jacob."

I nearly fall out of my chair. My knee slams into my desk, sending a stack of papers flying. My heart explodes into my throat.

Mom is standing in my doorway, her silhouette backlit by the hallway lights. How long has she been there? How much did she see?

I frantically minimize the browser window, but I'm not sure if I was fast enough. The competitor hub interface is pretty distinctive. All that neon green on black would be hard to explain as "homework."

"Mom! You scared me." My voice comes out too high, too guilty. I sound like I just got caught doing something wrong. Which I guess I did, depending on how you look at it. We're both keeping secrets now. The difference is I know about hers.

She takes a step into my room. Her bathrobe is tied loosely, and her hair is messy from sleep. "It's after two in the morning. What are you still doing up?"

"Just... homework stuff. Research for a project."

"Research." She says it flatly. Not a question. "At 2 AM on a school night."

"Lost track of time. You know how it is when you get into a rabbit hole online. Sorry."

She stands there for a long moment, and I can't read her expression in the dim light from my desk lamp. Is she suspicious? Does she know something? Her gaze moves slowly around my room, past the movie posters, the scattered computer parts on my shelf, the closed notebook on my desk that contains all my notes about her secret office.

The notebook. If she saw it, if she opened it...

"You're spending a lot of time on that computer lately," she says finally. "More than usual. Even for you."

"There's a lot of interesting stuff online." It's not exactly a lie. The Shadow Games are definitely interesting.

Mom sighs and crosses her arms. "Just make sure you're getting enough sleep. And that your grades don't slip. You know how important junior year is for college applications."

"I know, Mom."

She lingers for another moment, like she wants to say something else. Her eyes drift to my laptop screen again, now showing my generic desktop wallpaper, a photo of a mountain range I've never visited. Does she believe me? Can she tell I'm hiding something?

Of course, she's hiding things too. We're both standing here lying to each other's faces. The irony isn't lost on me.

But something nags at me. The neon green interface I just minimized, it's the same distinctive color scheme I saw in her office that night. ScyberSpace. She was on ScyberSpace. The same platform I'm using to learn hacking tools, the same network where the Shadow Games are advertised.

Does she know about the Shadow Games? Has she seen my username somewhere? "SirBreaksAlot" isn't exactly subtle. If she's active on ScyberSpace, she might have seen me climbing the ranks. She might know exactly what I've been doing all these late nights.

The thought makes my stomach twist. What if she's not just worried about my sleep schedule? What if she's worried because she knows where this path leads?

"Goodnight, Jacob," she says finally. "Try to get some rest."

"Goodnight, Mom."

She pulls my door closed behind her, but I notice she doesn't close it all the way. A sliver of hallway light still creeps through the gap. Is she going to listen for me? Check if I go back to the computer? Wait outside to catch me in another lie?

I sit perfectly still in my chair, barely breathing. My laptop hums softly. The scattered papers on my floor seem deafening in the silence.

Ten minutes pass. Then fifteen. I hear the floorboards creak as Mom walks back to her bedroom. Her door closes with a soft click.

I wait another five minutes just to be safe. Then I slowly, carefully bring up the browser again.

The competitor hub is still there. The chat has gone completely quiet now. Even the night owls have logged off. But StarBreaker's warning message still glows on my screen, those words burning themselves into my brain:

"Someone is always watching."

I glance at my partially open door. At the slice of hallway light. At the shadows pooling in the corners of my room.

For the first time since this all started, I wonder if I'm in over my head. If I've stepped into something way bigger than a sixteen-year-old with a laptop and too much curiosity.

But then I think about Dad. About his photo on my desk, his face frozen in that moment of pride at the White House. About the questions that have haunted me for two years. About the possibility that the answers are finally within reach, hidden somewhere in these shadows, waiting for someone brave enough (or stupid enough) to find them.

Something shifts in my chest. The fear doesn't go away (it never really goes away anymore) but it settles into something I can carry. Something that fuels me instead of paralyzes me. Dad was brave. Dad took risks for things that mattered.

Maybe I can be brave too.

I close the warning message and click on Challenge 4.

In over my head or not, I'm not stopping now. I can't. This is bigger than me, bigger than my fear, bigger than my common sense screaming at me to just go to bed like a normal person.

The shadows are calling. And I'm going to answer.

6

STARBREAKER

Three days into the Shadow Games, and I'm running on approximately six hours of sleep total. Not per night. Total.

I've solved eight challenges. Climbed to 312 points. Broken into the top fifty competitors out of hundreds. My eyes feel like someone replaced them with sandpaper. My brain has achieved a state of exhausted clarity that probably isn't healthy but feels weirdly productive.

I've never felt more alive. Which is ironic, given that I'm pretty sure I'm slowly dying.

There's something intoxicating about it, though. This feeling of being on the edge of something. Like standing on a cliff and leaning forward, knowing you shouldn't but unable to stop yourself. The exhaustion makes everything sharper somehow. More real. More present. Or maybe that's just the sleep deprivation talking.

School has become background noise. My body present, my mind somewhere else entirely. When Mr. Miles asked about symbolism in The Great Gatsby during English, I answered "hexadecimal" without thinking. The look on his face was almost worth the humiliation. Almost.

"You look like death," Ethan announces at lunch, sliding his tray across from mine with the grace of someone who's actually slept this week.

"Thanks. You look like someone who still cares about personal hygiene."

"I do care about personal hygiene. That's normal." He studies my face with genuine concern, then makes a face I know all too well, the "I'm about to call you out" expression he's been using since freshman year. "You're doing the thing."

"What thing?"

"The thing where you get obsessed with something and forget that sleep and food and basic human interaction exist. You've got that look." He squints and makes an exaggerated concentration face. "Like you're trying to solve the meaning of the universe with your eyeballs."

"I don't look like that."

"You've looked like that since freshman year when you were trying to figure out if Jessica Morrison was flirting with you or just being nice."

"She was being nice. We established this."

"Only took you three months to figure it out. Seriously, Jacob. When's the last time you slept more than four hours? You've got that unhinged conspiracy theorist energy going on."

I poke at my pizza. The cheese has congealed into something resembling plastic wrap, and the pepperoni is doing its best impression of rubber. High school cuisine at its finest. "Sleep is for people who aren't solving mysteries."

"That's not a real answer."

"It's the only answer I've got."

Ethan leans forward, dropping his voice even though nobody around us cares about our conversation. "You texted me at 3 AM about rainbow table attacks. I had to Google that just to figure out if I should be worried about you or calling the cops."

I wince. I don't actually remember sending that text. The nights have started blurring together, puzzles bleeding into codes bleeding into that green-on-black interface that shows up whenever I close my eyes. "Sorry. I got excited."

"You got excited about a rainbow table attack at 3 AM."

"When you say it like that, it sounds weird."

"It is weird, Jacob. You're being weird." But there's no real heat in it. That's the thing about Ethan. He worries, but he doesn't judge. "What even was the breakthrough?"

"Challenge 7. Audio steganography." The words come out faster than I mean them to, enthusiasm overriding exhaustion. "Someone hid a message inside a normal-sounding audio file. Like, literally embedded it in the frequency spectrum. You can't hear it with your ears. You have to run it through spectrogram software to actually see the words. It's brilliant. It's..."

"Beautiful?"

"I was going to say elegant, but yeah. Beautiful works."

Ethan sighs the sigh of someone who's accepted his best friend has become a cryptography nerd. "Okay. That does sound kind of cool. But you still need to function as a human person. Eat your plastic pizza. Please."

I take a bite to appease him. It tastes exactly like it looks, but I chew anyway.

I know he's right about the sleep thing. The bags under my eyes probably have their own bags at this point. My mom has started giving me concerned looks over breakfast. Not suspicious looks, just worried ones. Which somehow feels worse. But every time I think about stepping back from the games, I remember her office. The satellite images. BetaZone. The $10,000 payment from KOTR. The truth is somewhere in these challenges, hidden in all those layers of puzzles and codes. And I'm not going to find it by sleeping.

My phone buzzes. A notification from the competitor hub.

Direct Message from: StarBreaker

My heart jumps so hard I nearly choke on my pizza. A rush of adrenaline floods my system. Fight or flight, except there's nothing to fight and nowhere to fly. Since that first cryptic message warning me about disappearances, I've tried reaching out to StarBreaker twice. No response either time. I was starting to think I'd somehow offended the top player, or that they'd lost interest in the new kid.

Until now.

"What?" Ethan asks, noticing my expression. "You look like you just saw a ghost."

"StarBreaker messaged me," I whisper.

"The mysterious leader person? The one who told you to 'watch your back'?"

"Yeah. Them."

***

I tap the notification with slightly trembling fingers, and the message fills my screen.

"You're climbing fast. Faster than most newbies I've seen in two years of competing. Either you're cheating, or you've got real talent. I'm betting on talent.

Want to know how I know? Because cheaters don't last long in these games. They get... removed. And you're still here.

Meet me in private channel #shadowtalk-7 at 8 PM tonight. Come alone. Don't tell anyone about this message.

-SB"

Private channel. I didn't even know private channels existed in the competitor hub. The main interface only shows the public chat and the challenge board. Either StarBreaker has access to hidden features, or there's a whole layer of the games I haven't discovered yet.

The rest of lunch passes in a fog. Ethan talks about some video game update. I nod in all the wrong places, say "yeah" when he asks if I think the new boss fight is unfair. My eyes keep drifting to the clock. 12:47. 12:51. 12:58. Eight PM feels impossibly far away. Who is StarBreaker? Why me? What happens to cheaters who get "removed"?

"Earth to Jacob." Ethan waves his hand in front of my face. "You're doing that thing where you stare into space and mutter under your breath. It's creeping out the freshmen at the next table."

"Sorry. Just... game stuff."

He gives me a look that says he doesn't believe me, but he doesn't push. That's one thing I appreciate about Ethan. He knows when to back off. When to let me process things on my own before I'm ready to talk about them.

"Is it about your mom?" he asks quietly.

I hesitate. "I don't know yet. Maybe. Everything feels connected, but I can't see the full picture."

"Be careful," he says. "Whatever you're getting into... just be careful."

***

The afternoon crawls by like a turtle through molasses. History class. Math class. Science. Teachers droning about things that seem impossibly unimportant compared to coded messages and shadow competitions and the mystery of my mother's secret life. I take notes automatically, my hand moving while my brain runs through scenarios.

What does StarBreaker want to tell me? Are they friend or foe? Could this be a trap?

I think about the message again. "Don't tell anyone about this message." Why the secrecy? The Shadow Games already operate in secrecy. What's one more layer?

By 7:55 PM, I'm pacing my bedroom like a caged animal. My homework sits untouched on my desk. My laptop glows on my bed, the competitor hub already loaded and waiting. Mom thinks I'm studying for a test. She's been watching me more closely since she caught me up at 2 AM, giving me those concerned looks, asking about my grades, checking if I'm eating enough. But tonight she had a conference call that started at seven. Her office door is closed, that red LED glowing steadily.

I wonder what she's actually doing in there. Running more satellite surveillance? Writing more C2 code? Communicating with whoever BetaZone reports to?

I shake off the thoughts and focus. One mystery at a time.

I log into the competitor hub and search for the private channel. It's not in the main list. No surprise there. I try typing the name directly into the search bar: #shadowtalk-7.

A password prompt appears. A simple text field with a blinking cursor.

Password?

I stare at the screen. StarBreaker didn't give me a password. Is this a test? Another puzzle? Some kind of entry exam to prove I deserve access?

I think about all the messages StarBreaker has sent me. The first one: "Not bad for a newbie." The second: warning about cheaters getting removed. This newest one: instructions to meet tonight. Nothing that looks obviously like a password. No random strings of characters, no obvious hints.

Wait. Their signature. Every message ends with "-SB."

I type: SB

Access denied.

Okay, not that simple. I think harder. The message said "shadowtalk" and was signed with initials. Shadow + SB? Some combination?

I type: shadowSB

Access denied.

What about the channel number? Shadow + talk + 7?

I type: shadowtalk7

Access denied.

My frustration builds. Three wrong guesses might lock me out entirely. I need to think smarter, not harder.

Then I remember the registration confirmation from when I first joined: "May the shadows guide your path." That was from the system, not from StarBreaker specifically. But maybe the games have consistent theming? A shared vocabulary?

I type: shadowguide

A new window opens. I'm in.

The private channel is stark, completely different from the chaotic public chat. Dark gray background. Minimal design. No scrolling messages or emoji spam. Just a clean interface showing two participants:

SirBreaksAlot (me)
StarBreaker

"Nice work on the password," StarBreaker types. "Most people give up after two tries. Or they panic and try random combinations until they lock themselves out."

I exhale slowly, trying to project calm confidence I don't entirely feel. "I'm not most people."

"Clearly. That's why I wanted to talk." There's a pause. I can see the typing indicator flickering. "I have questions about you, SirBreaksAlot. And I think you have questions about me. Maybe we can help each other."

***

The conversation that follows is the strangest I've ever had. Stranger than when Ethan tried to explain cryptocurrency at midnight using sock puppets. Stranger than my guidance counselor asking about my "five-year plan" like I'm supposed to know what I'm doing next week.

StarBreaker asks about my background. Nothing too personal, but enough to gauge my skill level. How long have I been interested in hacking and security? What originally got me into the Shadow Games? Do I have any formal training?

I answer carefully, keeping the details about Mom's office to myself. Some secrets aren't meant to be shared with strangers, even strangers who've risen to the top of an underground competition. I tell them I'm sixteen, that I'm mostly self-taught from forums and tutorials and breaking my own equipment, that I got interested in the games after seeing the TV broadcast hack that interrupted the news.

"That broadcast was clever," StarBreaker types. "Exactly the kind of thing that draws in new talent. It was designed that way, to intrigue people who think differently. Who see a puzzle where others see a disruption. The games need fresh blood."

"You make it sound like a recruiting operation."

There's a long pause before the next message appears. So long I start to wonder if I said something wrong. If StarBreaker is reconsidering this whole conversation.

Finally: "It's more than that. Much more. But you're not ready to understand yet. You need to prove yourself first."

"Prove myself how?"

"By surviving."

I wait for more, but nothing comes for almost a full minute. I can see the typing indicator appearing and disappearing, like StarBreaker is composing messages and deleting them. Struggling with how much to reveal.

"The Shadow Games aren't what they seem," they finally write. "The challenges are real. Real puzzles, real skills, real points. But they're also a filter. A selection process. The sponsors (whoever they are) they're looking for something specific. Skills, obviously. But also mindset. Judgment. Loyalty."

"Sponsors? Who sponsors the games?"

"That's the million-dollar question, isn't it? No one knows for certain. There are theories. Some competitors think it's a tech company looking for talent. Others think it's a government agency. A few believe it's something more sinister. Organized crime, maybe, or international espionage."

"What do you think?"

Another pause. "I think it's all of those things. And none of them. I think the Shadow Games exist at an intersection that most people can't even imagine. A place where hackers, spies, corporations, and criminals all overlap."

I think about Mom's office. About the satellite images and the C2 code and the payment from KOTR. About Dad's White House award and his mysterious disappearance. An intersection of hackers and spies. Yeah. That sounds about right.

"But here's what matters," StarBreaker continues. "I've been watching the patterns for over a year. Competitors who get too close to certain answers, who ask the wrong questions or dig too deep, they disappear. Not just from the scoreboard. From everywhere. Their accounts go dark. Their ScyberSpace profiles vanish. It's like they never existed."

A chill runs down my spine. The room feels colder. "You're saying people actually get hurt?"

"I'm saying you should be very careful what questions you ask. And who you trust. Talent will get you noticed in these games. But notoriety isn't always a good thing. If you want to survive long enough to find whatever truth you're looking for, you need to be smart about how you climb."

I think about what I know. Mom's office. Operation Teardown. The KOTR payment. BetaZone and Alpha. All those puzzle pieces that don't quite fit together yet. "What if someone was looking for answers about a specific... organization? Something called KOTR?"

The typing indicator appears. Disappears. Appears again. A full minute passes.

"Where did you hear that name?"

The intensity of the question makes me hesitate. But something about StarBreaker feels genuine, like they actually want to help, despite all the warnings. Like they see something in me that's worth protecting.

"I saw it somewhere," I admit. "In some documents. Mentioned alongside payments and codes. KOTR Licensed."

Silence. The chat window just sits there, cursor blinking, no typing indicator. Have I said too much? Did I just make a terrible mistake?

Then: "SirBreaksAlot. Listen to me very carefully. KOTR, the Knights of the Republic, are not people you want to attract attention from. They're hackers, yes. Extremely skilled ones. But they're also something more. Something organized. Something dangerous. They have resources most criminal groups can only dream of. And they operate with an ideology that justifies almost anything."

My hands shake slightly as I type my response. "But what if someone I know is connected to them? What if I need to find out the truth about that connection?"

Another long pause. I imagine StarBreaker on the other end, somewhere in the world, staring at their screen and deciding how much to reveal. How much trust to place in a sixteen-year-old stranger from the internet.

"Then you've already started down a path you can't turn back from," they finally write. "All I can tell you is this: in the Shadow Games, nothing is random. Every challenge, every puzzle, every competitor, it's all connected to something bigger. The games are a microcosm of a larger world most people never see. If you want answers about KOTR, keep climbing. The higher you get, the more you'll see. But also the more you'll be seen."

***

I stare at the message for a long time. Keep climbing. More puzzles. More challenges. More risk. The higher I go, the closer I get to answers, but also the more exposed I become.

It's like Mom's office all over again. Every door I open leads to more questions. Every answer reveals new mysteries.

"One last thing," StarBreaker types. "I don't usually do this. Trust isn't something I give easily. In these games or in life. But something about you feels different. Maybe it's your instincts.

Maybe it's the way you approach problems. Maybe it's just the name SirBreaksAlot. Anyone willing to joke about their own failures might actually have the resilience to survive this."

I wait, watching the typing indicator pulse.

"My name is Melissa. I'm 16, like you. And I've been exactly where you are right now. Confused, scared, looking for answers about someone I care about. My dad... he's connected to all of this. That's how I found the games. That's why I keep climbing."

I read the message three times. Then a fourth.

Melissa. The name echoes in my head like a bell being struck. Not StarBreaker, not the intimidating leaderboard legend, but Melissa. A real person with a real name. Someone my age. Someone looking for her father, just like I've been looking for answers about mine.

My hands are shaking. Actually shaking. I look down at them like they belong to someone else. Something tight and warm spreads through my chest, a feeling I've read about in books but never really understood until now. Connection. The sudden, startling realization that someone out there gets it. Gets me. And she's not a stranger anymore. She has a name.

A feeling I can't name washes over me. Relief? Connection? The terrifying vulnerability of being seen by someone who actually understands? All of it, maybe. All at once.

Two kids. Two missing fathers. Two families tangled up in the same shadowy world. We found each other in an underground hacking competition, drawn together by parallel mysteries we didn't even know we shared.

That can't be coincidence. In a game where nothing is random, finding someone with an almost identical story feels like either destiny or manipulation. And I honestly don't know which possibility scares me more.

But here's the thing that surprises me most: I want to trust her. Despite every warning, every instinct screaming that trusting strangers on the internet is how people get hurt, I want to believe she's real. That her story is real. That I'm not the only sixteen-year-old in the world trying to navigate this impossible situation.

But here's the thing: for the first time since I glimpsed Mom's office, I don't feel completely alone. Someone else understands. Someone else is fighting the same invisible war.

"Thanks for trusting me," I type back, and I mean every word. "It means a lot. More than you probably know." I pause, fingers hovering over the keys. "I'll be careful. But I'm not going to stop looking. I can't. Not when I'm this close to understanding what happened to my family."

"I know," she responds. "That's what worries me."

There's a weight to those words. The weight of someone who's been where I am and knows how dangerous the path ahead becomes.

"Goodnight, SirBreaksAlot."

I'm about to close the window when one more message appears:

"Oh, and you might want to change the password on your home wifi network. Someone's been probing your router for the past hour. External IP address: 185.220.101.47. Run a WHOIS lookup if you want to see where it traces back. Sleep well."

Before I can respond, StarBreaker logs off.

***

The words hit me like ice water.

Someone's been probing my network. For an hour. While I was sitting here having this conversation.

My fingers are clumsy as I pull up a new browser tab and type the IP address into a WHOIS lookup tool. Blood rushes in my ears, a roaring, panicked static.

The results load. Tor exit node. Germany.

Tor. Anonymization. Whoever is poking at my network doesn't want to be found. This isn't some random script kiddie running automated scans. This is deliberate. Targeted. Someone knows exactly where I live and is actively trying to get in.

I pull up my router's admin page with shaking hands. The login is still the default, the password literally printed on a sticker underneath the router, because I never thought to change it. Why would I? I'm just a kid with a wifi connection. I'm nobody.

Except apparently I'm not nobody anymore.

The connection logs make my stomach drop. Dozens of attempts from unfamiliar IPs, all in the last two hours. Port scans. Brute-force login attempts. SSH probes. Someone methodically testing every possible vulnerability, every potential way in.

They're not inside yet. But they're trying.

My whole body feels cold. The room seems smaller suddenly, the shadows darker. Someone out there, someone hiding behind layers of anonymization, knows my home address. Knows my network. Maybe knows my name, my face, my school.

What if this is KOTR? What if asking about them in the Shadow Games put me on some kind of list?

What if this is what happens before someone "disappears"?

I'm on my feet before I realize I'm moving, crossing to my bedroom door and cracking it open. The hallway is dark. Quiet. Mom's office door is closed, that red LED pulsing steadily like a heartbeat.

Is she in there? Does she know what's happening? Is she oblivious, or...

The thought hits me like a physical blow.

What if she's the one probing the network?

Mom has hacking skills. Serious ones, based on what I saw in her office. The IP traced to a Tor exit node, exactly the kind of anonymization someone with her abilities would use. What if she knows I broke into her office? What if she's testing me, watching to see what I do, measuring my responses?

What if the person attacking our network is sitting twenty feet away?

My legs feel weak. I sink back into my chair, suddenly unsteady. The thought of my own mother, the person who makes me breakfast and asks about my day and worries about my grades, treating me like an enemy to be surveilled... it's too much. It doesn't compute. It breaks something fundamental in my understanding of how the world is supposed to work.

I don't know which possibility is worse. Enemy hackers targeting me because I asked the wrong questions, or my own mother treating me like a security threat to be monitored.

Both options make me want to throw up. And both options might be true at the same time, which is somehow even worse.

Back at my computer, I do the only thing I can think of. I start changing passwords. Everything. My email. My ScyberSpace account. The competitor hub login. Even my school portal. I use different passwords for each one, complex strings of letters and numbers and symbols that I write down in my notebook in a simple cipher only I can decode.

Then I change the wifi password. Something strong, something random: "J4c0b_N3tw0rk_S3cur3_2025!" Mom will notice when her devices stop connecting, but I'll deal with that tomorrow. Right now, security matters more than convenience.

As I work, I can't stop thinking about Melissa's words. "If you want answers about KOTR, keep climbing." The higher I get in the games, the more dangerous this becomes. But also the closer I get to the truth about Mom. About Dad. About all of it.

I pull up my scoreboard ranking on the competitor hub. 47th place. 312 points. A long way from StarBreaker's 3,000+. A long way from the top, where Melissa says the real answers hide.

But closer than I was yesterday.

I open the next unsolved challenge. Challenge 9: "Ghosts in the Machine - 75 points." The description talks about analyzing network traffic captures to find hidden communications. Relevant, given what just happened to my own network.

Keep climbing. That's the only way forward.

I take a deep breath, crack my knuckles, and start reading the challenge details. Somewhere outside my window, the world goes dark as clouds cover the moon. Somewhere in the digital ether, someone is watching.

But I'm not going to let that stop me.

7

PATTERNS

I've become obsessed with patterns. Mom's patterns. The game's patterns. My own patterns of sneaking around and pretending everything is normal while my entire world tilts on its axis.

It's exhausting. Not the hacking. That part's actually energizing, the puzzle-solving high that keeps me going at 2 AM. No, what's exhausting is the performance. The constant, relentless performance.

It's been a week since my conversation with Melissa (StarBreaker) and I've developed a routine. A double life, really. Jacob the normal teen by day. SirBreaksAlot the shadow competitor by night. The two versions of me barely recognize each other anymore. I catch my reflection in the bathroom mirror sometimes and wonder which one is looking back.

School runs from 8 to 3. I sleepwalk through classes, taking notes on autopilot while my brain churns through unsolved puzzles. The words go in my ears and straight onto the page without ever touching my actual consciousness. Ethan keeps shooting me worried looks across the cafeteria, the kind of looks that say "I'm about to have a feelings conversation with you whether you like it or not." My teachers have started asking if everything's okay at home. I tell them I'm fine. Just tired. They nod, make sympathetic faces, and move on. Teachers never push hard enough when a student says they're fine. It's like there's a script they all follow, and "I'm fine" is the magic phrase that ends the conversation.

Homework and dinner performance runs from 3 to 7. I sit at the kitchen table doing algebra while Mom cooks or catches up on whatever cover job she pretends to have. We talk about my day, about the weather, about nothing that matters. I've become an expert at saying words that sound like conversation without actually revealing anything. Mom has too, I realize now. We're both performing for each other. Two spies at the same dinner table, each pretending we don't know the other is hiding something.

Then, at seven o'clock, the real work begins.

Every night, I track three things in my notebook: what challenges I solve, what Mom does in her office, and who tries to access my network.

The network probes haven't stopped. Someone's still poking at my home wifi almost every day. Different IP addresses, all routed through anonymization services, all testing the same vulnerabilities. Port 22 for SSH. Port 3389 for remote desktop. Port 8080 for web administration. Whoever they are, they're methodical. Professional. Patient.

But since I changed the password and started monitoring the router logs, they haven't gotten in. At least not that I can tell. At least not through the front door.

"You're getting paranoid," Ethan tells me at lunch one day, watching me check my phone for the third time in five minutes. I've set up alerts that ping me whenever someone tries to access my network. It goes off a lot. More than a lot. My phone basically has a constant vibration problem now.

"Paranoid people survive," I mutter back.

"Paranoid people also get ulcers and lose all their friends." He steals a fry from my tray, which I haven't touched. "When's the last time you ate something that wasn't stress-induced caffeine?"

"I haven't lost you yet."

"Yeah, well, keep checking your phone instead of listening to me and we'll see how long that lasts." He throws the fry at my face. It bounces off my cheek and lands on the table. "I'm literally throwing food at you. This is what our friendship has become."

I put my phone face-down on the table and actually look at him. There are dark circles under his eyes too. Not as bad as mine, but noticeable. He's worried about me. Really worried. Not teacher-script worried. Friend worried. And I can't tell him anything.

The guilt hits me somewhere in the chest, a physical ache, like something heavy pressing down on my ribs. Ethan and I don't do secrets. That's always been our thing. Since freshman year, since the night he told me about his dad moving out for those two months and I told him about still crying sometimes when I thought about my dad. We're the people who tell each other the stuff we can't tell anyone else. That's the deal. That's the friendship.

And now I'm breaking it. How do you explain to your best friend that mysterious hackers are trying to break into your house and you're pretty sure you've stumbled into something that could get you killed? You don't. You can't.

Part of me desperately wants to tell him everything. Just let it all spill out like water from a cracked dam. Ethan would listen. He'd believe me. He'd probably even try to help.

But that's exactly why I can't. Telling him would put him in danger. And if something happened to him because of me, because of my family's secrets... I'd never forgive myself.

So I just eat the fry off the table and pretend everything's fine. The lie tastes worse than the food.

***

Mom's patterns are the most frustrating to track. Every night at 8 PM, like clockwork, she disappears into her office. The door locks with that soft electronic beep (the same sound that haunts my dreams now) and she doesn't emerge until after I'm supposed to be asleep. I've tried staying up, waiting in the hallway, but she always outlasts me. One night I made it to 2 AM before I finally crashed. When I woke up at 6, her office was already empty and she was making breakfast like nothing happened.

What is she doing in there for six, seven, eight hours every night? Is she tracking me? Hunting KOTR? Communicating with whoever BetaZone reports to? Running Operation Teardown, whatever that is?

I've tried pressing my ear to the door a few times, but the metal is too thick. All I hear is the faint hum of computer equipment and occasionally the soft click of a mechanical keyboard. Once, I thought I heard her talking, but I couldn't make out any words.

The worst part is the uncertainty. I could almost accept my mom being a secret hacker. At least that would make sense with everything I've seen. But not knowing if she's good or bad, hunter or hunted, hero or villain... that's what keeps me up at night. That's what makes me check the shadows every time I walk down our hallway.

Honestly, I'd almost prefer a straight answer. "Yes, Jacob, I'm an international cybercriminal." At least then I'd know. At least then I could stop wondering and start figuring out what to do about it.

Tonight, I decide to try something different. Instead of going straight to my room after dinner, I linger in the hallway outside her office. She's doing the dishes, and I can hear the water running in the kitchen. In a minute or two, she'll dry her hands and head this way like she does every night. Eight o'clock. Always eight o'clock. The woman is nothing if not consistent.

I position myself casually, leaning against the wall like I just happened to be there. Normal teenage behavior. Totally not lurking outside your mother's secret spy office. Nothing suspicious at all.

She appears around the corner, dish towel still in her hands. "Jacob? Everything okay?"

For a split second, I see her as she really is. Not the suburban mom in the flour-dusted apron, but the woman who sits behind six monitors and types code in the dark. The woman with the dangerous expression I glimpsed that first night. They're both real. They're both her. And I have no idea how to reconcile them.

"Mom? Can I ask you something?"

She pauses at her office door, already reaching for the keycard in her pocket. Her body language is tense, ready to escape into her sanctuary where I can't follow. "What is it, honey?"

I've been planning this question for days. Practicing it in my head, trying to find the exact words that might get her to open up without revealing how much I already know. Here goes nothing.

"When Dad was working... before he disappeared... did he ever seem like he was hiding things? From you, I mean?"

The question hangs in the air like a held breath. I watch her face like it's a program I'm trying to debug, looking for tells, for glitches in the mask. Her expression shifts through several emotions in rapid succession. Surprise. Pain. Something that might be fear. Something that might be guilt. Then nothing. Careful neutrality settling over her features like a screen going dark.

The same mask I've seen her wear at dinner. The same mask I've started wearing myself.

We're so alike it makes me want to scream. I used to think I got my tinkering from Dad, my logic from Mom. But now I realize I got the secrecy from both of them. The ability to compartmentalize. The skill of saying one thing while thinking another. It's in my blood, apparently. Our whole family's built on secrets.

"Your father was very protective of his work." She turns away slightly, and I can't tell if she's avoiding my eyes or just lost in memory. Her voice has that careful flatness to it, the tone people use when they're thinking three words ahead of what they're saying. "It was... complicated. There were things he couldn't tell me. Things I've only started to understand recently."

My heart stutters. "Started to understand? What do you mean?"

She doesn't answer directly. Classic deflection. "Why do you ask, Jacob? Did something happen?"

"Just thinking about him." I gesture vaguely down the hall. "Looking at his picture. The White House one. I guess I never really understood what he did. What his job actually was."

Mom nods slowly, her hand still on the keycard. "He loved you very much, Jacob. Everything he did, even the things he couldn't tell us about, was to keep us safe. To keep this family safe."

"Keep us safe from what?"

The words come out faster than I intended, almost desperate. This is the closest I've ever gotten to a real answer from her. I can see her hesitation, the war playing out behind her eyes. Tell him the truth. Keep him in the dark. Protect him. Trust him.

For one second, one breathless, impossible second, I think she might actually tell me something real.

My pulse stutters and races. This is it. This is finally...

But she's already sliding her keycard. The lock beeps, the red light turns green, and she slips through the door before I can ask anything else. A smooth, practiced motion. She's done this a thousand times.

"Goodnight, honey," she says softly. "Don't stay up too late."

The door closes. The lock engages. That red LED glows in the darkness like a warning.

The hope that had been building in my chest collapses in on itself. For a moment I just stand there, stunned by how much it hurts. How much I wanted her to trust me. How much I wanted to stop being alone in this.

I stand in the hallway for a long time, staring at the closed door. My hands are clenched so tight my nails dig into my palms. Keep us safe from what? Does that mean she knows about Dad's work? About the dangers he faced? About the people who might have taken him?

Or is she part of it all? Is she the danger he was trying to protect us from?

God, my head hurts. The questions loop and spiral, eating their own tails. I retreat to my room and pull out my notebook, because writing things down is the only way to make them stop screaming inside my skull. Under Mom's pattern section, I write: "She knows more than she admits. 'Things she's only started to understand recently.' What does that mean? What changed?"

***

At 10 PM, I'm deep into Challenge 11 (a puzzle involving packet analysis and reconstructing fragmented data from a corrupted capture file) when a message arrives from StarBreaker.

The notification sound makes me jump so hard I nearly knock my laptop off the desk. I haven't heard from Melissa in three days. Our last conversation ended with her telling me to "lie low for a while" after the network probes started intensifying. Radio silence ever since.

"Check ScyberSpace news. You need to see this. Now."

Nine words. No greeting, no context. Just urgency radiating off the screen.

My stomach drops before I even know why. I open a new browser tab and navigate to the ScyberSpace news feed. The top story makes my blood run cold.

"COMPETITOR BLACKHAT77 MISSING AFTER REACHING PHASE 2 - MYSTERIOUS MESSAGE FUELS SPECULATION"

Missing. Not "offline." Not "inactive." Missing.

I click the article. My hands have gone cold on the keyboard, my breath caught somewhere between my lungs and throat.

The details unfold with horrifying clarity. BlackHat77 was a respected competitor, ranked 23rd in the Shadow Games with 847 points. Respected for their analytical skills and their willingness to help newer players. Three days ago, they solved a Phase 2 challenge called "The Network Map" and their score jumped by 500 points, putting them in the top fifteen.

Then they posted a cryptic message in the competitor chat. The article includes a screenshot:

"BlackHat77: I know who's running this. They're watching all of us. All our traffic, all our moves. KOTR isn't what you think, they're not the enemy. The games are a recruitment tool for..."

The message cut off mid-sentence. Just stopped. Like someone hit a kill switch.

Like someone silenced them.

And BlackHat77 hasn't been online since. Not on ScyberSpace, not on the competitor hub, not anywhere. Their profile still exists, but it's frozen in time, a digital tombstone. No activity for 72 hours.

I read the article twice, three times, looking for some explanation that makes this less terrifying. Maybe they got spooked and went dark intentionally. Maybe their account got hacked. Maybe...

But I know. Somewhere deep in my gut, I know.

I switch to my DMs with StarBreaker. My hands are shaking. Actually shaking. I have to backspace three times just to type correctly.

"Is this for real? They just... disappeared?"

"It's real. And it's not the first time. I've seen this happen before. People get too close, ask the wrong questions, and then... gone. Like they never existed."

"But the message said KOTR. BlackHat77 found something about KOTR? They said KOTR isn't the enemy. What does that mean?"

"That's what scares me, Jacob. Because everything I've learned says KOTR is dangerous. They're hacktivists, sure, but they've done real damage. Leaked government secrets, exposed corporate corruption, taken down infrastructure. They're not good guys by any definition."

"Then what was BlackHat77 talking about?"

"My guess? They discovered something we're not supposed to know. They got too close. Asked the wrong questions where the wrong people could hear. And now..."

She doesn't finish the sentence. She doesn't have to.

My hands are trembling as I type. "Melissa, what is Phase 2 exactly? What's different about it that made BlackHat77 a target?"

There's a long pause before her response appears. I can see the typing indicator flickering, stopping, starting again. Even through text, I can feel her hesitation. She's choosing her words carefully, probably more carefully than she's ever chosen anything.

"Phase 1 is filters. Basic skills testing. Puzzles that prove you know what you're doing but don't require you to interact with anything real. Safe, controlled challenges."

"And Phase 2?"

"Phase 2 is where things get real. The challenges start requiring you to interact with actual systems. Real servers, real networks, real databases. Nothing illegal, technically. Everything is in the gray area, the gaps between laws. And some of the puzzles involve investigating actual organizations. Building profiles. Tracking operations."

"Organizations like KOTR?"

"Yes. Exactly like KOTR. Phase 2 includes challenges about tracking hacker groups, analyzing their operations, understanding their targets and methodologies. Officially it's all 'historical' data. Public information that's already been reported. But I've started to wonder..."

"Wonder what?"

"Whether it's actually current. Whether the data is real-time. Whether we're not just learning about these groups, but actually doing reconnaissance for someone. Gathering intelligence that gets used for something we don't understand."

My mind races. If the Shadow Games are really about gathering intelligence on hacker groups, and Mom is connected to KOTR through BetaZone, and there's an organization out there that wants information on KOTR...

Then maybe whoever is running the games is the same organization Mom works for. Or is hunting.

The thought sends a chill through me. Someone built this entire infrastructure (the challenges, the competitor network, the scoring system). Someone recruited thousands of hackers and turned them into unwitting intelligence gatherers. That's not a hobby project. That's not even a well-funded startup. That's the kind of operation that requires vision. Resources. Power.

Whoever's at the top of this pyramid, whoever designed the Shadow Games in the first place, they're playing a game that makes our little competition look like checkers compared to chess. And they've been watching all of us from the very beginning.

My fingers move before my brain catches up.

"I need to reach Phase 2."

"Jacob, did you read what I just said? A competitor disappeared. Someone who was asking questions about KOTR. This is dangerous. Real-world dangerous."

"I know." And I do. I feel it in the cold sweat on my palms, the way my heart hasn't stopped racing since I saw that headline. "But I think the answers I'm looking for are in Phase 2. About my mom. About KOTR. About what happened to my dad. I can't just stop now. I'm too close."

Even as I type it, I know how it sounds. Too close. The same words people say right before everything goes wrong. The same words BlackHat77 probably thought.

Melissa doesn't respond for several minutes. The typing indicator appears and disappears half a dozen times. I imagine her on the other end, wherever she is, weighing whether to help me or try one more time to talk me out of this. Maybe thinking about her own missing father. Maybe wondering if she's about to send me down the same path.

Finally, her message surprises me.

"You're at 312 points. Phase 2 requires 500. There's a challenge in Phase 1 that most people skip because it's time-intensive and intimidating. 'The Analyst' - worth 200 points. If you can solve it in one shot, you'll hit Phase 2 in one jump."

"What's the catch?"

"The challenge requires building a comprehensive profile on a real person. Cross-referencing their online presence, social media footprint, public records, everything. It's technically OSINT (Open Source Intelligence). Completely legal. But invasive. The kind of thing that makes people uncomfortable because it shows how exposed we all are."

"Who's the target?"

"That's the thing that makes this challenge special. The game doesn't tell you who to profile. You pick your own target. The challenge is evaluated based on how complete and accurate your analysis is. How deep you go. How much you uncover."

I think about this for a moment. Building a profile on someone. Tracking their digital footprint across the internet. Finding the connections between their different accounts, their different identities, their different lives. It sounds exactly like what I've been trying to do with Mom.

"What if I already have a target in mind?" I type.

"Then be very careful who you submit as your analysis. Because whoever runs these games will see everything you find. Everything. And if they see you investigating someone connected to their op erations..."

She doesn't finish. She doesn't have to.

***

I spend the next two hours staring at the blank challenge sub-mission form for "The Analyst." The cursor blinks at me mockingly, waiting for me to type something that might get me killed.

No pressure or anything.

The instructions are deceptively simple:

"Identify a subject of your choosing. Compile a comprehensive profile using only publicly available information (social media, news articles, public records, forum posts, etc.). Document your methodology clearly. Your analysis will be evaluated on depth, accuracy, and documentation quality."

I can't profile Mom. That's way too risky. If the game organizers see I'm investigating someone with the alias BetaZone, someone connected to KOTR, someone who might be one of their own... I could end up like BlackHat77. A frozen profile. A message that cuts off mid-sentence. Gone.

But I need to practice these skills. I need to understand what I'm up against. I need to prove I belong in Phase 2 where the real answers hide.

I think about the KOTR payment I saw on Mom's phone. "$10,000 Paid by Knights of the Republic - Alpha." What if I profiled KOTR directly? It's a public group. They have a reputation, news articles, a whole ScyberSpace presence. People talk about them all the time. I wouldn't be revealing anything about Mom directly.

But something holds me back. Melissa's warning echoes in my head: "KOTR are not people you want to attract attention from." BlackHat77 mentioned KOTR and disappeared. Profiling them directly might be exactly the wrong move.

I think about other options. A random public figure? A celebrity? That feels cheap. Like cheating the spirit of the challenge.

Then it hits me. There's one target I can profile. Someone whose patterns I already know intimately. Someone who won't put me in danger because they're already exposed.

Myself.

It's either brilliant or incredibly stupid. Maybe both. Definitely both.

I start typing. Subject: SirBreaksAlot (Real name: J.M., age 16, location: [REDACTED]).

For the next hour and a half, I document everything someone with the right skills could find about me online. The trail I've left across the internet without even realizing it. It's like performing an autopsy on my own digital life.

My ScyberSpace account. Username: SirBreaksAlot. Account created two months ago, largely inactive until recently. Current activity: participating in Shadow Games competitor discussions, reading tutorials, asking beginner questions. No personal information directly listed, but...

I cross-reference the username. SirBreaksAlot appears on three other platforms. A gaming forum where I asked for help with a Minecraft server issue two years ago. A tech support forum where I troubleshot my laptop's fan noise. A Reddit account with exactly one post asking for advice on a budget PC build.

Each account has different information. But together, they paint a picture.

The Reddit post mentions my general geographic region (commenting on local internet providers). The gaming forum has a partial email address visible in my profile (the part before the @). The tech support forum includes details about my laptop model, which I bought from a specific store.

Someone patient enough could triangulate these data points. Find the overlap. Build a profile.

I dig deeper. Image metadata. The one photo I ever uploaded to the gaming forum (a screenshot of a Minecraft build) contains EXIF data. GPS coordinates embedded in the image file because I took the screenshot with my phone and didn't know to strip the metadata.

Those coordinates point to within 500 meters of my house.

I feel sick. Actually sick, bile rising in my throat, cold sweat prickling my skin. My hands are trembling as I stare at the screen, at the digital breadcrumbs I left without even realizing it. I thought I was being careful. Anonymous usernames. Different accounts for different things. I thought I was invisible.

But the trail was there all along. Invisible to me, but obvious (painfully, terrifyingly obvious) to anyone who knew how to look.

All this time, I've been walking through the internet leaving footprints everywhere. And I never even knew.

The realization settles into my bones like ice water. Every forum post. Every screenshot. Every casual question I asked without thinking. They were all pieces of a puzzle that anyone patient enough could put together. A puzzle that points directly to my house. My family. Me.

If I could find all this about myself, what could someone find about Mom? About BetaZone?

What have I already exposed by asking the wrong questions?

At the bottom of my analysis, I add a methodology section explaining how I found each piece of information:

"Step 1: Username cross-reference across major platforms
Step 2: Email pattern analysis (partial visible data)
Step 3: Geographic indicators from content references
Step 4: Image metadata extraction using ExifTool
Step 5: Social graph mapping (who the subject interacts with)
Step 6: Writing style analysis for additional account identification"

I document the tools I used. The search techniques. The logical chains of inference. It's thorough. Comprehensive. Terrifying.

I add one final note: "Recommendation for subject: Implement operational security improvements including metadata scrubbing, VPN usage for all browsing, and compartmentalization of online identities."

Then I submit the challenge.

The loading screen spins. My heart pounds. What if they reject it because I profiled myself? What if they see it as gaming the system? What if...

Twenty minutes later, the notification comes.

"Challenge Complete! 'The Analyst' - 200 points awarded. Excellent methodology documentation. Your self-reflective approach demonstrates both technical skill and operational awareness. Welcome to Phase 2."

I let out a breath I didn't know I was holding. My whole body sags with relief, then immediately tenses again.

Welcome to Phase 2. The words feel less like congratulations and more like a warning.

A new section of the challenge board unlocks. Phase 2 challenges glow orange on my screen, waiting like doorways into darkness. Twelve of them. Each one probably more dangerous than anything I've faced before.

I message Melissa immediately. "I'm in. Phase 2. Profiled myself to avoid risk."

Her response comes fast, almost impressed. "Clever. Most people don't think of that. Be careful in there, Jacob. Phase 2 is where things get real."

Real. There's that word again. As if everything before this was just a game.

I scan the list of Phase 2 challenges. Network mapping. Cryptographic analysis. Social engineering frameworks. Digital forensics. Names that sound like college courses but probably hide something much darker.

One catches my eye immediately:

"Challenge 14: Trace the Knights - 250 points - INVESTIGATION"

The description reads: "The Knights of the Republic (KOTR) are one of the most active hacktivist groups operating today. Responsible for numerous high-profile data breaches and infrastructure attacks. Your mission: Identify three of their known operations and explain their methodology. Document evidence trail."

My breath catches. This is it. The path to answers about Mom. About KOTR. About Operation Teardown and BetaZone and everything that's been eating me alive for weeks.

I think about BlackHat77. About their message that got cut off mid-sentence. "KOTR isn't what you think. They're not the enemy."

What if they were right? What if everything I think I know is wrong?

What if I'm about to make the same mistake they did?

There's only one way to find out.

I take a deep breath, feel my pulse hammering in my throat, and click on the challenge details.

The real game begins. And somewhere in the back of my mind, a voice that sounds a lot like Melissa whispers: This is where things get real.

I really hope "real" doesn't mean "deadly."

8

THE DARK WEB

The Trace the Knights challenge requires me to explore places I've only heard about in whispers. Underground forums. Sites that don't show up on regular search engines. The kind of places where normal sixteen-year-olds definitely don't hang out on school nights.

The kind of places where Mom apparently does.

▼

I remember that strange hidden address I saw bookmarked on her computer, shadowgames.io/darknet. It wasn't linked anywhere on the main Shadow Games site. No menu option. No visible button. Just... hidden. Like a secret door that only appears if you know exactly where to look.

I type the address into my browser and hold my breath.

The screen goes dark. A security warning appears in blood-red text, warning me that I'm about to enter a "Dark web environment." My heart races. This is part of the games. It has to be. A portal into the underground, created by whoever runs Shadow Games to let competitors experience what these hidden corners of the internet feel like.

I click through the warning.

The screen fills with what looks like a connection sequence. "Establishing TOR circuit..." it says, and a series of nodes flash across the screen. Germany, Netherlands, Switzerland, Romania, Iceland. Encrypted relays. Each one another layer of anonymity between me and whatever I'm about to find.

When the "connection" finally establishes, I'm staring at something called "Malware Central." A forum that looks like it was designed in the 1990s, ugly, functional, stripped of anything that might slow it down or make it easier to trace. The kind of interface that prioritizes anonymity over aesthetics.

I'm in a different internet now. And there's no turning back.

***

The first thing that strikes me is how ugly everything is. The regular web has gotten used to sleek designs, smooth animations, interfaces that anticipate what you want before you even know you want it. The dark web looks like it was built in the 1990s and never updated. Plain text. Basic HTML. Sites that take forever to load and sometimes don't load at all.

It's like stepping through a time portal into the internet's sketchy basement.

My first destination is a dark web search engine I found mentioned in a ScyberSpace tutorial, something called Ahmia. The interface is basic to the point of primitive: just a search box on a black background with white text. No autocomplete. No helpful suggestions. No friendly "did you mean..." messages.

I type in "Knights of the Republic" and hit enter.

The results are... terrifying. There's no other word for it.

Forum posts celebrating attacks on charitable organizations. News articles from dark web tabloids praising KOTR's "operations." A manifesto claiming they're fighting against corrupt non-profits that steal donation money. Screenshots of stolen data being shared. Bragging posts about successful breaches.

I start taking detailed notes in my notebook, using a simple code of my own devising in case anyone ever finds it. According to the articles, KOTR's methodology is sophisticated, way beyond the script-kiddie stuff I've been reading about on ScyberSpace. They're professionals. Organized. Patient.

The first phase is always social engineering. Fake emails that look legitimate. "Phishing," but elevated to an art form. Phone calls pretending to be IT support, using information they've already gathered to sound convincing. Sometimes they even create fake LinkedIn profiles and build relationships with targets over weeks or months before making their move.

Once they have credentials (a username and password, even just for a low-level employee) they deploy custom malware. Not the off-the-shelf stuff you can download from hacker forums, but custom-built tools designed to evade detection, spread through networks, and establish persistence. The kind of malware that requires serious programming skills to create.

C2 infrastructure. Command and control. The same kind of code I saw in Mom's office with "Author: BetaZone" in the comments.

After they have full access to a target's systems, KOTR either steals data for ransom or simply destroys everything. Sometimes both. They've been known to encrypt databases and demand payment in cryptocurrency, then delete everything anyway even after the ransom is paid.

The more I read, the sicker I feel. My pizza from lunch threatens to make a reappearance. I have to close my eyes and breathe through my nose for a minute, waiting for the nausea to pass.

This is what evil looks like, I realize. Not some cackling villain from a movie. Just people sitting at computers, typing commands, destroying lives they'll never see. Clinical. Efficient. Completely divorced from the human cost of what they're doing.

These aren't Robin Hood hackers stealing from corporations and giving to the poor. They're targeting organizations that help homeless people, disaster victims, sick children. Charities that operate on shoestring budgets, that can't afford fancy security systems, that trust people because trusting people is what they do.

Why would anyone attack a charity? What kind of monster wakes up and decides to destroy an organization that helps cancer patients? There's evil in the world. I knew that already, abstractly. But this is evil with a username and a methodology and a high score on some dark web leaderboard.

And the question that won't leave me alone, the one that makes my stomach clench every time I think it: why would Mom be connected to them?

***

I find a forum thread that makes my blood run cold. Actually cold. I can feel the temperature drop in my fingertips, spreading up my arms. It's discussing a specific KOTR operation from two years ago.

Two years ago. Right around when Dad disappeared.

The target was a veterans' charity in Washington, D.C. An organization that helps wounded soldiers transition back to civilian life. They provide job training, mental health support, housing assistance. Real, meaningful help for people who sacrificed everything.

KOTR compromised their entire network. Got into their donor database (names, addresses, credit card numbers, everything). Then they deployed ransomware, encrypting every file on every computer. The ransom demand: $500,000 in Bitcoin within 72 hours or they would leak the donor information publicly and delete all the encrypted data permanently.

For a small charity, $500,000 might as well be a billion dollars. They didn't have it. They couldn't pay.

But here's where the story gets strange.

The forum thread mentions that the attack failed. Not because the charity fought back or hired security experts or got lucky. Someone inside KOTR leaked information to the authorities. Details about the attack, the infrastructure being used, the cryptocurrency wallets where the ransom was supposed to be paid. Enough information that law enforcement was able to block the payment and trace some of the attackers.

The leaker was never identified. The KOTR members on the forum are furious, posting paranoid accusations and demanding investigations. They swore revenge against the "traitor." Some of them believe the leak came from a new recruit who'd only been with the group for a few months.

Two years ago. Dad went missing two years ago. He was being honored at the White House for something the President couldn't talk about publicly. Some kind of service to the country that had to stay classified.

The coincidence is too big to ignore. It's screaming at me.

Could Dad have been the leaker? Could he have infiltrated KOTR, gotten close enough to know about their operations, trusted enough to see their plans, and then had to disappear when they figured out there was a mole?

My hands are shaking so badly I can barely write. I jot down this theory in my notebook, using my coded shorthand:

"D infiltrated K. Leaked V charity attack. Had to vanish when suspected. WH award = recognition for undercover work?"

It would explain so much. Why he couldn't tell us what he did for a living. Why he vanished without any warning. Why the President looked at him like he was a hero. Why Mom has KOTR connections now. Maybe she's continuing his work. Maybe she took over his undercover role. Maybe she's still inside, still feeding information to the good guys while pretending to be one of the bad guys.

The thought makes my chest ache in a way I can't explain. A tight, twisting sensation that's part hope and part grief and part something else I can't name. Dad as a spy. Mom as a spy. Our whole family as some kind of undercover operation I never knew about.

If this theory is right, then Dad didn't abandon us. He was taken. Or he had to hide to protect us. All those nights I lay awake wondering why he left, hating him a little for leaving... what if none of that was fair? What if he's out there somewhere, thinking about me the same way I think about him?

The hope feels dangerous. Like holding something fragile that could shatter at any moment.

But if she's fighting KOTR from the inside, why does she have working malware on her computer? Why is she accepting payments from them? Why did I see a receipt for $10,000 on her phone?

I have more questions than answers. Every discovery leads to three more mysteries. Every thread I pull just reveals more tangles.

***

A notification pops up from the Shadow Games competitor hub, pulling me out of the dark web rabbit hole. Someone has completed Challenge 14, the same challenge I'm working on. I check the scoreboard.

GhostProtocol just earned 250 points for Trace the Knights. They've jumped to 28th place.

Competition. I almost forgot this was supposed to be a competition.

I'm running out of time. Other players are catching up to my discoveries, maybe even finding things I've missed. The longer I take on this challenge, the less impressive my submission will be. First-mover advantage matters in the Shadow Games.

I refocus on my research. I need three KOTR operations with detailed methodology analysis. I have one, the veterans' charity attack from two years ago. I search for more.

The second operation is easier to find because it made mainstream news, at least on tech sites. Last year, KOTR hit an environmental conservation group called Green Future Initiative. They used a completely different method this time. Subtler, nastier, harder to prove.

Instead of ransomware, they planted evidence. Fake emails. Doctored financial records. Made it look like the charity's director was embezzling funds, skimming donations meant for rainforest preservation into his personal accounts.

The resulting scandal destroyed the organization. Donors fled. Partners cut ties. The director's reputation was ruined. He resigned in disgrace, even though an independent investigation later suggested the evidence was fabricated. But by then the damage was done. Green Future Initiative closed its doors permanently.

Reputation attacks. Character assassination via planted evidence. That's a level of cruelty I hadn't considered. You don't just steal money or destroy data. You destroy a person's entire life while making it look like they deserve it. You turn their friends against them. Their family. Everyone.

The forum posts I find are celebrating this attack even more than the ransomware ones. "We didn't just hurt them," one poster writes. "We made everyone think they deserved to be hurt. Beautiful."

Beautiful. They called it beautiful.

I push back from my desk and stare at the ceiling for a minute, just breathing. These are real people. People who think destroying an innocent man's life is art. People who celebrate cruelty like it's a game.

And these are the people my mom is connected to. These are the people Dad might have been investigating. These are the people who might have made him disappear.

I want to throw up. I want to close the browser and pretend I never saw any of this. I want to go back to being a normal kid whose biggest problem was a broken laptop.

But I can't. I'm in too deep now.

The third operation takes me down a rabbit hole of forum posts and encrypted chat logs that I have to piece together from fragments. Apparently KOTR recently targeted a global health organization, one of the big ones that does vaccination programs in developing countries. The attack was supposed to be huge. Massive data theft. Infrastructure destruction. Something designed to cripple their operations for months.

But something went wrong. Their attack was detected and blocked before it could cause serious damage. The forum posts are full of anger about "another leak."

Another leak. Just like the veterans' charity two years ago.

"There's a rat among us," one poster writes. "Feeding information to the enemy. When we find them, they're dead. Not a threat. A promise."

Is someone still feeding information about KOTR operations to the authorities? Is that someone... Mom?

The timeline fits. Two years ago, a leak stopped the veterans' charity attack. Now, another leak has stopped the health organization attack. If Dad was the original mole and Mom took over his mission...

But that's a lot of ifs. A lot of assumptions. I need more than theories.

***

I compile my findings into the challenge submission format, being extremely careful about what I include and what I leave out. Three operations: the veterans' charity ransomware attack, the environmental group reputation strike, and the failed health organization breach. For each one, I document the methodology, timeline, and public outcome.

I describe social engineering techniques (phishing emails, pretexting phone calls, the patience required to build trust before attacking). I explain how KOTR uses custom malware rather than off-the-shelf tools, suggesting a high level of technical sophistication. I note their preference for cryptocurrency ransoms and their reputation for not honoring agreements.

But I'm careful about what I don't include. I don't mention my theory about an inside leaker. I don't connect any of this to my family. I don't speculate about who might be feeding information to authorities. I present everything like a detached researcher studying historical attacks with no personal stake in the outcome.

When I click submit, I hold my breath and count to ten. Then twenty. Then I give up counting and just stare at the loading screen.

The response comes faster than expected: "Challenge Complete! 'Trace the Knights' - 250 points awarded. Excellent research methodology. Your analysis demonstrates strong OSINT skills and appropriate operational security awareness."

Appropriate operational security awareness. If they only knew what I left out. What I'm really looking for. Who I'm really investigating.

I'm now at 762 points. My rank has jumped to 31st overall. The leaderboard shows me as one of the fastest-climbing competitors in the games.

But what I've learned feels heavier than any score could represent. The points are just numbers on a screen, meaningless pixels. The implications of what I found... those are going to keep me awake for a long time.

***

Before I close the Tor browser, I make one more search. A reckless decision. A necessary one. The kind of decision that feels inevitable even as you're making it.

My fingers hover over the keyboard. Do I really want to know? Do I really want to see what the dark web thinks of my mother?

Yes. I have to.

I type in: "BetaZone"

The results make my heart stop entirely. For a moment I forget to breathe. For a moment the whole world narrows to the screen in front of me and the words glowing there.

There's a profile on a dark web hacker directory, a site that catalogs known operators in the underground community. Like LinkedIn for criminals. Complete with ratings and reviews and threat assessments.

"BetaZone
Status: ACTIVE
Specialty: Malware development, C2 infrastructure design
Known skills: Python, C++, network exploitation
Known affiliations: [CLASSIFIED - SEE PROTECTED FILES]
Threat level: HIGH
Last confirmed activity: 47 hours ago"

High threat level. That's my mom they're talking about. My mom, who makes me chocolate chip pancakes on my birthday. My mom, who used to read me bedtime stories. My mom, who asks about my homework and worries when I stay up too late.

High threat level.

Something fundamental shifts inside me. The world I thought I knew (the safe, predictable world where parents are just parents and home is just home) cracks a little more. How am I supposed to sit across from her at dinner tomorrow, knowing this? How am I supposed to look at her and see the same person I've known my whole life?

The answer is: I can't. That version of Mom is gone. Maybe she never existed at all.

Forty-seven hours ago, while I was at school, eating lunch, pretending everything was normal, she was active enough in the underground community to update her status. Active enough to be tracked. Active enough to be rated.

But the next section confuses everything again:

"ANALYST NOTES: Subject demonstrates unusual operational patterns. Suspected involvement in multiple KOTR operations (unconfirmed). ALSO suspected of information leaks to state authorities (unconfirmed). Contradictory indicators suggest possible double agent status OR competing intelligence agency involvement. STATUS: UNDER ACTIVE OBSERVATION. Recommend caution in all interactions."

Suspected of KOTR involvement. Also suspected of leaking to authorities. Contradictory indicators. Possible double agent.

Mom is playing both sides. Or at least, the dark web intelligence community thinks she might be. They can't figure her out either.

I close the browser and lean back in my chair, staring at the ceiling. The glow-in-the-dark stars I stuck up there when I was eight seem incredibly stupid now. Childish. Remnants of a simpler time when the only mysteries in my life were things like "why do we have to go to bed?" and "where do shooting stars come from?"

The room feels smaller than it did an hour ago. The air feels thicker. Everything I thought I knew about my family is crumbling, replaced by something far more complicated and far more dangerous.

Mom might be a criminal working with KOTR. Or she might be a hero working undercover against them, continuing whatever mission Dad started. Or she might be something in between, someone who started on one side and is trying to switch to the other, caught in a web of obligations and covers and lies that's grown too complex to escape.

She could be protecting us. She could be endangering us. She could be both at the same time.

Schrödinger's mom. Both hero and villain until I open the box and find out for sure.

The only way to find out is to keep going. Keep climbing. Keep asking questions, even when those questions attract dangerous attention.

***

My phone buzzes on my desk. A text from an unknown number.

The sound is so ordinary, just a normal buzz, the same sound it makes when Ethan sends me a meme, but tonight it feels like a gunshot. I pick up the phone slowly, a cold feeling spreading through my chest.

"You're asking dangerous questions. Not everyone on the forums is who they seem. Some are watching. Some are hunting. Be careful what threads you pull. They might be attached to something that pulls back."

The words swim in front of my eyes. I read them three times, four times, waiting for them to make sense. Waiting for them to reveal themselves as spam, a wrong number, anything but what they obviously are.

I stare at the message. No signature. No indication of who sent it or how they got my number. The phone shows a string of digits that doesn't look like any normal phone number, probably routed through voice-over-IP services, completely untraceable.

Someone knows what I've been doing tonight. Someone has been watching my dark web searches. Someone has my personal phone number despite all my efforts at operational security.

So much for being careful. So much for paranoid people surviving.

I want to be scared, and I am (my hands are shaking and my heart is pounding and I can taste bile at the back of my throat), but more than fear, I feel something else. Determination. Defiance. A stubborn, reckless anger that surprises me.

Every warning I get, every shadowy threat, every mysterious message... they just convince me that I'm getting closer to something important. You don't send anonymous warnings to people who are wasting their time. You only threaten people who are threatening you.

The truth about my family is out there. And no amount of anonymous warnings is going to stop me from finding it.

I screenshot the message and save it to an encrypted folder on my laptop. Evidence. Documentation. If something happens to me, at least there'll be a record.

Then I delete the text from my phone and turn the device off entirely. No point making it easy for them to track me.

Tomorrow, I'll tell Melissa about what I found. Show her the evidence about BetaZone. Ask if she knows anything about operators playing both sides. Maybe she's seen patterns I've missed. Maybe she has pieces that fit with mine.

Tomorrow, I'll figure out my next move. Tonight, I need to sleep.

I change into my pajamas, brush my teeth, go through all the normal motions of being a normal kid at the end of a normal day. Wash face. Apply acne cream. Avoid looking at myself in the mirror because I'm not sure I'll recognize the person looking back.

When I finally lie down in bed, staring at the dark ceiling, sleep feels very far away.

The Tor browser is closed. My laptop is hibernating. But somewhere out there, in the shadows of the dark web, people are talking about my mother. Watching her. Rating her threat level. Maybe hunting her.

And now, maybe, hunting me too.

I pull the covers up to my chin and close my eyes, forcing my breathing to slow. Even shadows need rest sometimes. Even investigators have to sleep eventually. Even terrified sixteen-year-olds who just found out their mom is a high-threat hacker with "contradictory indicators" have to close their eyes at some point.

But my last thought before unconsciousness claims me isn't about rest. It's about that forum post from two years ago. The one about the KOTR mole.

"When we find them, they're dead. Not a threat. A promise."

Dad disappeared two years ago. And now I'm following in his footsteps, asking the same questions, pulling the same threads.

I really hope I'm not about to disappear too.

I really hope "dead" was just a figure of speech.

9

MELISSA

"**C**an we voice chat?"

The message from Melissa catches me off guard. We've exchanged hundreds of messages over the past two weeks (strategy discussions, puzzle help, late-night theories about who's really running the Shadow Games) but this is the first time she's suggested actually talking. Real voices. Real conversation. A step beyond the anonymous safety of text.

Something about those three words makes my pulse jump in a way I don't entirely understand. My chest feels tight. My palms are suddenly damp on the keyboard.

I stare at the message for a full minute before responding, trying to sort through the tangle of emotions. The cursor blinks at me like it's judging my hesitation. Part of me wants to say no. Voice chat means another layer of identity exposed. Another way for someone to track me, profile me, figure out who I really am. Every operational security guide I've ever read screams that this is a bad idea.

But another part of me, the part that's been feeling increasingly isolated in this investigation, that talks to Mom across the dinner table without saying anything real, that lies to Ethan about what keeps me up at night, really wants to hear another human voice. Someone who gets it. Someone who understands what it's like to have your whole life turned into a question mark.

"Sure," I type back, before I can talk myself out of it. "When?"

"Now. I'll send you a secure channel link."

A minute later, a notification appears with a link to an encrypted voice chat platform I've never heard of, something called Signal-Alt that supposedly routes audio through the same kind of anonymization layers as Tor. I spend five minutes researching it (paranoid, remember?) before deciding it's legitimate.

I plug in my headphones, the nice ones I use for gaming, not the cheap earbuds that came with my phone. Check that my bedroom door is firmly closed. Listen for any sounds from Mom's direction. Her office light is on, the red LED visible under the door when I peek into the hallway. Good. She's occupied.

I click to join the voice channel.

For a moment there's nothing but static and the soft hum of data moving through encrypted servers around the world. My heart is beating way too fast for someone who's just sitting in their bedroom. Then:

"Jacob?" A girl's voice fills my ears. It's softer than I expected, with a slight accent I can't quite place, something vaguely Southern, maybe, or just the natural rhythm of someone who's lived in California their whole life. "Can you hear me?"

And just like that, StarBreaker becomes a real person. Not just a username. Not just clever messages on a screen. An actual human being with a voice that sounds tired and hopeful and a little bit scared, just like mine probably sounds.

But there's something else in her voice too. Something warm underneath the exhaustion. I find myself wondering what she looks like, the face that goes with that voice, the expressions she makes when she's thinking through a problem. I've pictured her a dozen different ways during our text conversations. None of those imagined versions feel right anymore. Now she's real, and somehow that's both better and more terrifying.

"Yeah, it's me. Hi, Melissa."

"Hi." There's a pause. I can hear her breathing, the faint creak of what might be a chair, the ambient sound of another bedroom somewhere across the country. A whole other life, three thousand miles away. "This is weird, right? Actually talking after all this time?"

"Super weird," I admit, and I can hear myself laughing nervously. The sound of my own voice in my headphones makes me cringe a little. "But kind of nice."

***

We spend the first few minutes with awkward small talk, the verbal equivalent of circling each other, testing the waters. She's in California, three hours behind me. When it's 11 PM for me, it's only 8 PM for her. Her favorite subject is English (which surprises me. I expected her to say computer science), though she's also weirdly good at drama class.

"Most of my hacking skills are actually social engineering," she admits. "Like, I'm not that great at the hardcore technical stuff. I can read code and do basic network analysis, but that's not my strength. My strength is getting people to tell me things. Understanding what makes them tick. Figuring out the human vulnerabilities instead of the software ones."

"Huh." I think about my own approach, hours spent staring at code, analyzing metadata, running tools. "I'm basically the opposite. The technical stuff comes easy to me, but people are... confusing. I never know what to say."

"That's why we make good partners," she says, and I can hear the smile in her voice. "You crack the systems, I crack the people."

Something about the way she says "partners" makes my face warm. I'm glad this is voice-only so she can't see me probably blushing like an idiot. It's just a word. She's just talking about the competition. But the way it sounds in her voice, soft and certain, like it's already decided, makes me want to hear her say it again.

She has a younger brother named Dylan who, from the sound of it, is her whole world despite being annoying.

"He's twelve," she explains, "so he's at that age where everything I do is either embarrassing or fascinating. Last week he found my Tor browser and thought I was a spy. I had to convince him it was for a school project about internet security. Meanwhile I'm sweating bullets thinking he's gonna tell Mom."

"Does your mom know about any of this? The games?"

"God, no. She thinks I spend my nights doing homework and watching YouTube. If she knew I was competing in underground hacking competitions to investigate my missing father..." Melissa laughs, but there's an edge to it. The kind of laugh that's just sadness in disguise. "She barely holds it together as it is. After Dad left, she threw herself into being super-mom. Soccer practice, healthy dinners, family movie nights. Like if she just keeps us busy enough, we won't notice there's a hole where Dad used to be."

I know that feeling. The performance of normalcy. The unspoken agreement to pretend everything is fine.

I hear something crash in the background, followed by a kid's voice yelling "I'm okay!"

"Dylan?" I guess.

"Dylan." Melissa sighs. "DYLAN, IF YOU BROKE SOMETHING AGAIN I SWEAR..." She mutes herself for a moment. When she comes back, she's slightly out of breath. "Sorry. He was trying to practice skateboard tricks in the hallway. Again. Kid has zero survival instincts."

"At least he's interested. I'm an only child. Just me and my thoughts."

"Trust me, sometimes the thoughts are better company." But the way she says it, soft, almost gentle, tells me she doesn't really mean it. "Anyway. Your mysterious hacker mom."

The casual mention makes my stomach clench. "Yeah. That too."

Then she asks the question I've been dreading since I clicked that voice chat link.

"Why did you really enter the Shadow Games? And don't give me the answer you'd put in a competitor profile. The 'I'm interested in cybersecurity' answer. I want the real reason."

I take a deep breath. The voice chat feels more intimate than text. No time to craft careful responses, no opportunity to delete and rewrite. Just raw, real-time conversation. Harder to hide behind carefully worded messages when someone can hear the tremor in your voice.

And there's definitely a tremor in my voice.

"My dad disappeared two years ago," I say slowly, each word feeling like a confession being pulled out of me. "And I think my mom might know more about it than she's told me. I found... stuff... in her office. Hacker stuff. Code and satellite images and encrypted messages. Connected to an organization called KOTR."

"KOTR." Melissa's voice tightens audibly. "The Knights of the Republic. You weren't kidding when you mentioned them before."

"No. And the more I dig, the more I find." I tell her about the dark web research. The BetaZone profile. The conflicting intelligence about Mom being both involved with KOTR and suspected of leaking information to authorities. "Dad might have been investigating them, maybe even infiltrating them undercover. When he disappeared, Mom started working in this secret office with military-grade security. I don't know if she's continuing his work, or if she switched sides, or if she was always on one side and Dad was on the other, or what. Every answer just leads to more questions."

The silence stretches for so long I start to wonder if the connection dropped. I check my headphone cable. Still connected. The audio indicator shows her microphone is active. She's there, just not speaking.

"Melissa?"

"I'm here." Her voice sounds different now. Heavier. "I was just ... processing. What you're describing... it's a lot. And it hits closer to home than you probably realize."

"What do you mean?"

"Jacob, I need to tell you something. About why I'm in the games. The real reason. I haven't told anyone this, not even the few other competitors I've gotten close to over the months."

***

Her story comes out slowly, like she's not used to sharing it. Like she's excavating memories that have been buried deep for self-preservation.

"My dad is a cybersecurity researcher. Works for the government. I'm not supposed to know which agency, but I've pieced together enough clues over the years. NSA, probably. Maybe something even more classified." She pauses, and I hear her take a shaky breath. "About three years ago, he started acting strange. Working late every night. Coming home stressed and distracted. Checking our house for bugs like he expected someone to be listening. He'd sweep the living room with this electronic device, check the phones, look behind the pictures on the walls."

"Sounds familiar," I mutter, thinking about Mom's office. Her paranoid security. The way she glances at her phone before every conversation.

"Yeah. I thought maybe he was having an affair or something. Stupid kid logic. But it was worse. Then one night, men came to our door. Official-looking. Black suits, government ID cards, the whole scary package. My mom told me and my brother to stay upstairs in our rooms, but I snuck down to listen through the stairway. I could hear them talking in the living room."

"What did they say?"

"They told my dad that a project he worked on had been compromised. That lives were at risk. That he needed to 'come in' immediately for debriefing and protective custody." Her voice wavers slightly. "My dad asked about us, about protecting me and Dylan and my mom. They said we'd be safe, that they'd have people watching us. That he just needed to trust them."

I can feel my heart beating faster. This sounds so much like what might have happened to Dad. The urgency. The vague explanations. The promises that probably weren't kept.

"What happened?"

"He left with them. Put on his coat, kissed my mom at the door, told her he'd be back in a few days once everything was sorted out." Her voice cracks just slightly, and I hear her clear her throat. Fighting for control. "That was two and a half years ago. He calls sometimes. Birthdays, holidays. Never video calls, just voice. Never says where he is or when he's coming home. My mom pretends everything is fine, keeps telling us that Dad is doing important work and will be back soon. But I can tell she's scared. I can see it in her eyes when she thinks nobody's watching."

I feel a hollow ache spread through my chest. Something tight and painful that makes it hard to breathe. Our stories are different in the details but somehow parallel in the pain. Parents with secrets. Unexplained disappearances. The confusion and fear of children left behind to wonder what was real and what was a lie.

At least she gets phone calls. At least she knows her dad is alive somewhere.

I immediately feel guilty for thinking it. Pain isn't a competition. And yet some bitter part of me can't help comparing. She gets to hear his voice. She knows he's alive. She knows he didn't forget about her.

I have a photo and two years of silence.

The bitterness tastes wrong. I swallow it down.

But even as I feel the connection between us, something prickles at the back of my mind. A question I have to ask.

"This is weird, right?" I say. "Like, statistically weird. Two kids whose dads disappeared under mysterious circumstances, both entering the same underground hacking competition, both reaching the top ranks, both looking for answers about their families. What are the odds?"

Melissa is quiet for a moment. "I've thought about that too," she admits. "The coincidence thing. It does feel... convenient."

"Too convenient?"

"Maybe." Her voice is careful now, guarded in a way it wasn't before. "Either we're both incredibly unusual, or..."

"Or someone wanted us to meet. Someone arranged this."

The silence stretches between us. It's a heavy, uncomfortable silence, the kind where both people are thinking thoughts they're not sure they should say out loud.

"I don't know if I should trust you," I admit finally. The words feel brutal coming out, but they're honest. "Not because of anything you did. But because if this whole thing is a setup, you could be part of it without even knowing."

"I was thinking the same thing about you." She doesn't sound offended. If anything, she sounds relieved that I said it first. "So what do we do? Hang up and pretend this call never happened?"

I think about it seriously. About the warnings I've gotten. About BlackHat77 disappearing mid-sentence. About the fact that for all I know, Melissa is some thirty-year-old KOTR operative pretending to be a teenage girl. I've seen enough movies to know that's a thing that happens.

But her voice... there's something in her voice that sounds too real to be fake. The way it cracked when she talked about her dad. The exhaustion underneath the determination. The way she pronounced her brother's name, Dylan, with that mix of annoyance and fierce love that only an actual older sister could manage.

Either she's the best actor in the world, or she's exactly what she says she is.

"No," I decide. "I don't think so. Because if this is a trap, I'm already in it. And if it's not, if you're actually who you say you are, then you're the only person in the world who might actually understand what I'm going through."

"That's a big risk."

"I know. But I'm kind of out of safe options at this point." I laugh, and it comes out bitter. "My whole life is a risk now."

Melissa laughs too, a small, surprised sound. Something loosens in my chest hearing it, a knot I didn't know was there, unwinding just a little.

"You're weird, SirBreaksAlot. In a good way."

"Takes one to know one, StarBreaker."

"So we're doing this? Trusting each other, despite all the reasons we shouldn't?"

"Carefully trusting," I clarify. "With healthy skepticism and regular check-ins to make sure neither of us is secretly evil."

"I can work with that."

"So you entered the Shadow Games to find him?"

"To find answers," she corrects. "I'm not naive enough to think I'll actually locate my dad through a hacking competition. But someone in these games knows something about what happened. I'm sure of it. The challenges aren't random. They're testing us, evaluating us for something. For what, I don't know yet. But I've gotten higher than anyone else. I've proved myself. And I keep hoping that if I get high enough, if I prove I belong, someone will finally tell me the truth. About my dad. About what he was working on. About why he had to leave."

***

We talk for two hours. Not just about our families and the games, but about normal stuff too. Favorite movies (she's into psychological thrillers; I'm more of a Marvel person). Music (she plays guitar; I can barely keep rhythm). The absurdity of trying to maintain regular life while simultaneously investigating conspiracy-level secrets.

"I had a math test today," I tell her. "Sat there doing quadratic equations while half my brain was thinking about KOTR attack methodologies. Got a B-minus. My mom looked disappointed but didn't ask questions."

Melissa laughs, a real laugh this time, not the sad one from earlier. "I feel that so hard. My English teacher assigned a creative writing piece about 'an important person in your life.' I almost wrote about my Tor browser."

"That would have been an interesting parent-teacher conference."

"'Mrs. Chen, we need to discuss your daughter's unhealthy relationship with anonymizing software.'"

We both crack up. It feels good to laugh. Really good. I hadn't realized how heavy everything had gotten until some of that weight lifted, even temporarily. Like I've been holding my breath for weeks and finally remembered how to exhale.

"Ethan thinks I'm going crazy," I admit once the laughter fades. "My best friend from school. He's been supportive, helped me with some of the early code breaking. But I can tell he's worried about me. The late nights. The paranoia. The way I keep checking over my shoulder."

"Does he know everything? About your mom?"

"Most of it. He helped me decode the first message from her office, the one that led to the Shadow Games. But I've held back some of the darker stuff. The KOTR connections. The dark web research. The anonymous threats I've been getting. I don't want to freak him out more than I already have."

"That's probably smart," Melissa says. "Regular people don't understand this world. Even smart ones. Even ones who care about you."

I think about that. "You don't have anyone like that? A normal friend?"

Melissa laughs again, but this time it sounds sad. Wistful. "I did. Before I became StarBreaker. Before I started spending every night climbing the ranks instead of going to parties or studying for tests like a normal teenager. Friends kind of... faded away when you can't talk about the only thing you actually think about. When you're always distracted, always tired, always looking at your phone for competition updates."

"That's lonely."

"Yeah." A beat of silence. For a moment I can hear the weight of all those lost friendships in that single word, years of isolation compressed into a single syllable. "But I've got you now. Fellow shadow dweller."

Something warm spreads through my chest. It's the nicest thing anyone's said to me in months. Maybe even longer. The feeling is almost too much, gratitude and connection and something else, something I'm not ready to name yet. My eyes sting for a second, and I have to blink hard to clear them.

I smile even though she can't see it. "Fellow shadow dweller. I like that."

"It's what we are, right? People who live in the spaces between the normal world and the dark one. Not quite hackers, not quite civilians. Just... dwellers in the shadows, looking for light."

***

Before we end the call, Melissa shares something that changes everything.

"There's a challenge coming up," she says, her voice dropping even though we're on an encrypted channel. "Not on the regular board. It's invitation only. I got the notification yesterday."

"Invitation only? I didn't know that was a thing."

"It's Phase 3 territory. Once you hit a certain rank, top 25, I think, you start getting access to special events. Challenges that don't show up for regular competitors. This one is called 'The Meeting.' And it's not just online."

Something cold settles in my stomach. Like I just swallowed ice water. "What do you mean?"

"It's in person. Real-world. Competitors who qualify get invited to a physical location for a live hacking challenge. You show up, prove your identity, and compete against other top players in person."

In person. The words hit me like a punch. Everything we've done (the puzzles, the late nights, the anonymous usernames) has been from the safety of our bedrooms. Behind screens. Protected by layers of encryption and anonymity.

In person means none of that protection. In person means showing your face. Exposing yourself completely.

My pulse quickens. "Melissa, that sounds incredibly dangerous. We don't know who these people are. What if it's a trap? What if KOTR is running the games and they're collecting information on competitors?"

"I know the risks." Her voice has that edge again, the one that says she's already made up her mind. "But Jacob, I've heard rumors. The sponsors of the Shadow Games might actually be there. Not representatives or recruiters, the actual people who created and run this whole operation."

"That's exactly why we should be careful. Maybe do more research first. Figure out who these sponsors actually..."

"Research takes time. Time I don't have." She cuts me off, and I feel a flash of irritation. "My dad's been gone for two and a half years, but it's been eight months since his last phone call. Eight months of total silence. Before that, he at least called on holidays. Now there's nothing. Something changed, and I don't know if he's even still alive."

"I'm not saying do nothing. I'm saying be strategic. Plan ahead. Don't just..."

"Don't just what? Take action? Actually do something instead of theorizing about it?" Her voice gets sharper. "Look, I get that you're a think-it-through-first kind of person. That's great for code puzzles. But sometimes you have to make a move before you have all the information. Sometimes waiting IS the wrong choice."

We're both quiet for a moment. I can hear her breathing on the other end, slightly fast, like she's worked up. Like this hit a nerve.

"Sorry," she says after a beat. "That came out harsher than I meant. I just... I've spent so long being careful. Being patient. Doing exactly what everyone tells me. Focus on school, let the adults handle it, be a good daughter. And nothing changed. Nothing got better. The only progress I've made on finding Dad came from taking risks other people would call stupid."

The frustration in her voice mirrors something inside me. That same trapped feeling. That same desperate need to do something, anything, instead of just waiting and hoping.

I think about that. About my own journey. Breaking into Mom's office, entering the Shadow Games, asking questions that drew anonymous threats. None of that was safe or sensible. And it's the only reason I have any answers at all.

"No, I get it," I admit. "I just... I worry. When you care about someone, the idea of them walking into danger is..."

I stop, suddenly aware of what I just said. When you care about someone. Do I care about her? I've known her for weeks, never seen her face, never been in the same room. But somehow... yeah. I do.

"Terrifying?" she finishes for me.

"Yeah."

She laughs softly. "Welcome to my life. But here's the thing, Jacob. We're already in danger. The moment we started climbing, we became targets. The question isn't whether to take risks. It's which risks are worth taking."

I think about the anonymous text message I received. The warnings about people watching and hunting. The competitors who asked too many questions about KOTR and disappeared. Black-Hat77's frozen profile, their cut-off message still haunting the competitor chat.

"The location could be compromised. They could have surveillance. They could be filtering for people to... I don't know, recruit or eliminate."

"Or they could be recruiting for something good," Melissa counters. "We don't actually know the games are evil. We just know they're mysterious. What if the sponsors are actually fighting KOTR? What if this is the path to finding our fathers?"

I don't have an answer to that.

"Are you going to go?" I ask.

"I'm thinking about it. Seriously thinking. I'm scared. I'd be an idiot not to be scared. But I've been climbing for eight months, Jacob. Eight months of late nights and puzzles and questions without answers. This might be the closest I ever get to the truth about my dad." She pauses. "Would you go? If you qualified?"

The question hangs in the air like the moment before a leap. Would I walk into a room full of unknown hackers, possibly connected to KOTR, possibly responsible for my dad's disappearance?

I think about Dad's face in the White House photo. The pride in his eyes. The secrets he never got to tell me.

I think about Mom's office. The mysteries still unsolved. The feeling that I'm only seeing fragments of a much bigger picture.

I think about BlackHat77's message: "KOTR isn't what you think. They're not the enemy."

"Yeah," I say finally, the word heavy with commitment. Heavy with everything it means. "I would. If it's my best shot at finding answers about my family, I'd take the risk."

A pause. I can hear her breathing on the other end, steadier now, like my answer meant something to her.

"Partners in shadows," Melissa says. "Whatever happens, we face it together. Deal?"

"Deal."

The word feels like a promise. Maybe the first real promise I've made since all of this started.

***

After we hang up, I sit in the dark of my room for a long time. The silence feels different now, less lonely, somehow. The conversation replays in my head. Melissa's voice. Her laugh. Her story. The revelation about an in-person meeting.

We're both looking for missing fathers. We're both stuck in the shadows of secrets our families kept. And we're both willing to risk everything for answers.

It occurs to me that this is what it's like to have an ally. A real one. Not just Ethan, who cares about me but can't fully understand what I'm facing, not without putting him in danger too. Melissa gets it. She's living the same nightmare, just a different version. Two kids with too many questions and not enough answers, stumbling through the dark together.

I pull up my scoreboard ranking. 31st place. 762 points.

How many more points to qualify for The Meeting? How many more challenges between me and the truth? If top 25 is the cutoff, I need to climb at least six more ranks. Maybe more, if other competitors are climbing faster than me.

I open the Phase 2 challenge board. There's one I've been avoiding, a puzzle that requires analyzing an encrypted audio file. The description mentions "spectral analysis," which sounds complicated. Something about converting audio frequencies into visual representations to find hidden patterns. It's worth 300 points. A big chunk. But it looks hard.

I download the audio file and load it into Audacity, a free audio editing program I've used for random projects before. The file sounds like static at first, white noise with no obvious pattern. I zoom in on the waveform, looking for anomalies. Nothing jumps out.

Spectral analysis. I remember reading about this. Some steganography techniques hide images or text in the frequency spectrum of audio files, information that's invisible when you just listen but becomes visible when you convert sound to a visual spectrogram.

I switch to spectral view in Audacity. The white noise transforms into a rainbow of colors representing different frequencies at different times. And there, hidden in the pattern of highs and lows, I see it.

Letters. Actual letters, spelled out in the frequency distribution.

It takes another hour to fully decode. The message was encoded using a technique called SSTV (Slow Scan Television) which amateur radio operators use to transmit images over audio frequencies. Once I figure that out, I download specialized software and convert the audio to an image.

The image is coordinates: 38.8956, -77.0255

I paste them into a map. The pin drops on Washington, D.C., but not just anywhere. It's pointing at a specific building.

The FBI headquarters.

My heart pounds. Is this a hint? A warning? Some kind of misdirection?

I submit the coordinates as my answer for the challenge.

The response comes almost immediately: "Challenge Complete! 'Spectral Secrets' - 300 points awarded. You see what others miss."

My score jumps to 1,062 points. My rank climbs to 28.

Closer. Always closer.

The night stretches on toward dawn. Outside my window, the sky is starting to lighten at the edges, that weird gray-blue color that means morning is coming whether you're ready for it or not. Somewhere across the country, three hours behind me, Melissa is probably doing the same thing, burning the midnight oil, chasing points, chasing truth. Two shadow dwellers, looking for light in the darkness.

I think about her voice. About the way she laughed when she called me weird. About the promise we made.

Partners in shadows.

The Meeting is out there, waiting. And I'm going to make sure I'm there when it happens.

Whatever it takes.

10

The Phone

Mom's phone is on the kitchen counter again.

It's sitting there like it's daring me. Like it knows exactly what I'm thinking.

It's Saturday afternoon, gray and drizzly outside, the kind of day that makes you want to stay inside and do nothing. Rain drips down the windows and makes everything outside look blurry and distorted, like reality itself has gone slightly out of focus. The kind of day where time feels weird, like nothing important is supposed to happen.

My phone buzzes. Ethan: "Gaming sesh at my place? My parents are at some medical conference thing. I have snacks."

I type back: "Can't. Family stuff."

"You've been saying that a lot lately."

He's right. I have been. Every time he asks to hang out, I have an excuse. Shadow Games research, investigating Mom's secrets, trying to piece together the puzzle of my family. I'm lying to my best friend, which feels almost as bad as everything else.

"I know. I'll explain soon. Promise."

"You better. I'm starting to think you've been replaced by a pod person."

I put the phone down without answering. Soon. Once I figure out what's actually going on, I'll tell him everything. Or at least everything I can.

Mom ran out for groceries. A quick trip, she said, back in twenty minutes. That was three minutes ago. I have maybe seventeen minutes to find out what I need to know. Seventeen minutes to cross a line I can never uncross.

Seventeen minutes to betray my mother's trust completely.

The thought sits heavy in my stomach like a stone. I love my mom. Even with everything (the secrets, the locked office, the double life I'm only beginning to understand) I still love her. And what I'm about to do feels like a betrayal of something sacred. Something that can't be taken back.

But I need to know the truth. Even if the price is her trust. Even if it costs me the version of our relationship that exists right now.

I've been planning this moment for days. Every piece of evidence I've gathered (the dark web research, the KOTR connections, the mysterious BetaZone profile, the payment to someone called Alpha) all of it points to answers that might be on that phone. The encrypted messenger I saw her using late one night, hunched over the screen with the intensity of someone receiving orders rather than just texting friends. The conversations she guards so carefully, angling the phone away whenever I walk into the room.

This is my chance. Maybe my only chance.

My hands shake as I pick up the phone. It's warm from sitting in a patch of weak sunlight that managed to fight through the clouds. The screen lights up with her wallpaper, a photo of Dad, Mom, and me at my tenth birthday party. We're standing in front of a cake with blue frosting and too many candles. We all look so happy. So normal. So completely unaware of what was coming.

I stare at Dad's face in that photo for a moment. His smile, wide and genuine. His arm around Mom's waist. His other hand resting on my shoulder, protective and proud. We look like a family. We look happy.

Was he already living a double life then? Was every smile a performance, every family moment a carefully maintained cover?

Was any of it real?

Focus, Jacob. You can have an existential crisis later.

The phone is locked this time. Six-digit PIN required. The screen glows with patient hostility, waiting for me to prove I don't belong here. I've watched her type the code from across the room a few times (over dinner, from the living room couch) but never got a clear look at the actual numbers. Just the general motion of her thumbs, the rhythm of the taps.

I try the obvious ones first: her birthday, 071482. Wrong. The screen flashes red, rejecting my attempt. My birthday, 030909. Wrong again. Dad's birthday, 121576. Wrong.

Three attempts down. My palms are sweating so badly I have to wipe them on my jeans. Most phones lock you out after too many failed attempts, some after five, some after ten. I might have three more tries. Maybe seven. I don't know Mom's security settings, and I really don't want to find out by triggering a lockout that alerts her something happened.

Then I remember the Constitution book cipher from her office. The numbers referenced dates. Specific dates. Important dates. What date would be significant enough for her to use as a password, something she'd never forget, something deeply personal?

The date Dad went missing: February 10th, two years ago. I type 0210 as the first four digits, then pause, my thumb hovering over the keypad. What comes after? What year?

I try random combinations: 021015. Wrong. The phone vibrates with rejection. 021014. Wrong again.

My heart is pounding now, blood rushing in my ears like static. I'm running out of attempts. One more wrong guess and the phone might lock me out entirely, or worse, alert Mom somehow that someone tried to access it. Some security apps send notifications when failed attempts exceed a threshold.

Think, Jacob. Think like Mom. What date would mean something to both of them? Something strong enough to remember but personal enough that no one else would guess?

Their anniversary. When was that? I remember seeing it on a card once. Mom keeps a box of old cards in her closet, tied with a faded ribbon. April something. No, wait. It was February. February something.

Valentine's Day? No, that's too obvious. Mom always said she hated how commercialized Valentine's Day was. They wouldn't choose something so predictable.

I close my eyes and try to remember. There was a photograph in Dad's study, back when he still had a study, before Mom converted it into her secret office. Him and Mom on their wedding day. She wore a simple white dress. He wore a dark suit that didn't quite fit right. The date was printed in gold script at the bottom of the frame. February 10th.

February 10th. The same day Dad disappeared, years later.

Their anniversary became the day he vanished. That can't be a coincidence. That date must have meant everything to them, a day of pure joy that transformed into a day of pure loss. Or maybe not loss. Maybe transformation.

I type: 021004. February 10th, 2004. The year they got married.

The screen unlocks.

For a second, I just stare at it. I'm in. I'm actually in. The weight of what I'm about to do settles on my shoulders like a physical thing.

There's no going back now.

***

I have fourteen minutes left. Maybe less if Mom hit traffic or forgot something and has to come back. Fourteen minutes to find answers to questions I've been asking for weeks. Fourteen minutes to either confirm my theories or shatter them completely.

My fingers fly across the screen, moving with an urgency that feels almost frantic. I go straight to her messaging apps, my thumb hovering over each icon like I'm defusing a bomb. One wrong choice, one wrong move, and everything explodes.

The crypto payment app where I saw the KOTR transaction is gone. Completely uninstalled, no trace in her app drawer or in the recently deleted section. She must have noticed the notification and gotten paranoid. Scrubbed the evidence. Which means she knows something's off, even if she doesn't know exactly what.

But there's another app I don't recognize. An encrypted messenger with a black and gold icon, something that looks like a stylized eye, or maybe an hourglass turned on its side. I've never seen it in any app store. Custom software, maybe. Built specifically for secure communications. The kind of thing that wouldn't show up in a normal search.

I open it. The interface is sleek and minimal, similar to the competitor hub from the Shadow Games. Dark background, neon accents, clean lines that suggest serious purpose rather than casual chat. A list of conversations appears, but instead of names or phone numbers, each contact is identified by a code name.

Overseer_7
Handler_M
Logistics_W
Alpha_Actual

My heart pounds so hard I can hear it in my ears, feel it in my temples, taste it in the back of my throat. Alpha. The name from the KOTR payment. "Thanks for the C2 - $10,000 Paid by Knights of the Republic - Alpha."

Mom was receiving money that was sent to someone called Alpha. But here in her messenger, she's having conversations with someone using that name? Why would she be talking to the same person who received KOTR's money?

Unless Alpha isn't the enemy. Unless Alpha is something else entirely.

I tap the conversation with Alpha_Actual.

***

The messages go back months. Hundreds of exchanges, maybe thousands. I don't have time to read them all. The clock in my head is ticking louder with every second. I scroll to the earliest entries and start scanning, looking for anything that explains what I'm seeing.

Alpha_Actual: "Package delivered. Targets acquired. Awaiting confirmation on timeline."

BetaZone (Mom): "Timeline pushed to quarter 2/April. Resources need reallocation after the near-miss. How secure is the new C2 infrastructure?"

Alpha_Actual: "More secure than the old setup. The modifications you suggested worked perfectly. Running on hardened servers with multiple fallback routes. KOTR suspects nothing."

BetaZone: "Good. Remember. We need evidence, not exposure. If they figure out we're inside before we're ready, everything we've built collapses. Years of work gone."

Alpha_Actual: "I understand. Patience is part of the cover."

BetaZone: "Stay safe out there."

Alpha_Actual: "Always."

I read the exchange three times, my brain struggling to process the implications. Each reading shifts the picture slightly, like adjusting the focus on a camera. "KOTR suspects nothing." "Evidence, not exposure." "If they figure out we're inside..."

Mom isn't working for KOTR.

She's infiltrating them.

The realization hits me like a wave, and I have to grip the counter to keep my balance. Everything I thought I knew about my mother, everything I feared, inverts in an instant. She's not a criminal. She's not the enemy.

She's gathering evidence. Building a case from the inside, just like I suspected Dad might have done. BetaZone isn't a criminal alias. It's an undercover identity. A mask worn to get close to people who would otherwise never trust her.

My mom is a spy. An actual spy. And she's one of the good guys.

Or is she?

But who is Alpha_Actual? The person she's messaging, the person receiving KOTR's money, the person who's "inside" the organization? Someone who knows about C2 infrastructure and hardened servers. Someone who talks to Mom like they're partners in a dangerous game.

***

I scroll faster, looking for more clues. The rain outside intensifies, drumming against the windows like impatient fingers. The messages are mostly operational (coordinates, technical specifications, references to "targets" and "assets") that could mean anything without context. Acronyms I don't recognize. Code phrases that probably have specific meanings I couldn't guess.

Some of it goes completely over my head. References to "cell structures" and "extraction protocols." Mentions of other code names I've never seen. A whole vocabulary of shadow operations that I'm only beginning to understand.

But then I find a message from two weeks ago that stops me cold. My thumb freezes on the screen.

Alpha_Actual: "J is getting too close. The Shadow Games participation wasn't anticipated. Should we intervene?"

BetaZone: "No. Absolutely not. He's doing exactly what we hoped he would, just faster than expected. His instincts are strong. Let him climb."

Alpha_Actual: "And if he makes contact with the wrong people? Some of those competitors are genuine threats."

BetaZone: "Then we adjust. For now, we watch from a distance. He needs to find his own way to the truth. Intervention would raise questions. Make him doubt himself."

Alpha_Actual: "You know him better than I do at this point. I trust your judgment."

BetaZone: "That's all I ask."

J.

That's me. Jacob.

The phone nearly slips from my sweaty fingers. I catch it at the last second, my heart slamming against my ribs. The room tilts slightly, and I have to grab the counter edge to steady myself.

They're talking about me. Discussing my progress in the Shadow Games like I'm some kind of project, an experiment to be observed, a variable to be monitored. "Doing exactly what we hoped he would." "Let him climb."

A hot flush of anger mixes with the shock. All this time, all those late nights thinking I was being so clever, so independent, so brave, I was just a piece on their board. Moving exactly where they expected me to move. Thinking I was finding my own path when really they were watching every step.

Mom knows I'm competing. She's known the whole time, since before I even found her office, maybe. Since before I broke in and started this whole investigation. Every late night I spent thinking I was being so clever, so sneaky, so careful... she was watching. Knowing. Letting it happen.

I don't know whether to feel betrayed or relieved. Both, maybe. Mostly I just feel manipulated.

And there's someone else, Alpha_Actual, who's also watching me. Someone who defers to Mom's judgment about me. Someone who says "you know him better than I do."

Someone who sounds like they once knew me too.

Someone who doesn't anymore.

***

I hear a car's engine outside. The sound cuts through my concentration like a blade through paper.

I nearly drop the phone. My whole body goes rigid, fight-or-flight instincts screaming at me to run, hide, do something.

Headlights sweep across the kitchen window, painting white stripes on the wall and then disappearing. The pattern is familiar. Mom's car, pulling into the driveway. Earlier than expected. Way earlier.

I frantically close the messenger app, my fingers suddenly clumsy with panic. Did I leave any traces? Any indication that I was here? I check the recent apps, make sure nothing's still running in the background, then lock the phone. Place it exactly where I found it on the counter, screen facing up, positioned in that same patch of sunlight that's now fading as clouds roll in.

Then I sprint to my room and dive onto my bed, grabbing the first textbook I see and opening it to a random page.

Biology. Chapter 14. Something about photosynthesis. The words blur in front of my eyes, meaningless symbols that my brain refuses to process. All I can think about is the phone in the kitchen, the messages I read, the questions multiplying in my mind like cells dividing.

My heart is pounding when Mom's keys turn in the lock. I hear her footsteps in the kitchen, the rustle of grocery bags being set down, the soft thud of something being placed on the counter.

Is she picking up the phone? Is she checking it? Did I leave any trace that someone accessed it?

"Jacob?" she calls out, her voice normal. Pleasant. The voice of a mom who just got back from grocery shopping, nothing more. "Can you help with these?"

"Coming!" My voice sounds almost normal. Almost. A slight waver that I hope she attributes to being interrupted mid-study. Or maybe just puberty. Everything sounds weird when you're sixteen.

I walk to the kitchen on shaky legs, my mind still reeling from what I read. Mom smiles at me as she hands over a bag of vegetables. No suspicion in her eyes. No hint that she knows I was just reading her most secret messages. Just warmth and the slightly tired look of someone who spent twenty minutes navigating a grocery store.

"Put these in the fridge? I got that cereal you like. It was on sale."

"Thanks, Mom."

She moves around the kitchen, unpacking groceries, humming something soft under her breath, some old song I half-recognize from car rides when I was younger. Just a normal mother on a normal Saturday afternoon. No trace of BetaZone, high-threat-level malware developer. No sign of the operative coordinating with someone called Alpha about targets and timelines and operations that span years.

But she does know things. She knows about the Shadow Games. She knows I'm "climbing." And she's letting it happen.

Why?

The question burns in my chest as I put away vegetables, as I stack cereal boxes, as I carry in the last of the groceries from the car. Every normal action feels like a performance now. Like I'm the one wearing a mask, pretending everything is fine while my whole understanding of reality shifts beneath me.

Mom chatters about her day (traffic, the produce selection, a funny thing a cashier said) and I nod and respond in all the right places. Playing my part. Being the son who doesn't know anything. Who didn't just break into her phone and read her most dangerous secrets.

But inside, my mind is racing. Processing. Connecting dots.

Alpha_Actual. "You know him better than I do at this point."

Who talks like that about someone's kid? Who would have known me before but doesn't now? Who would care about my progress, my safety, my path to the truth?

The answer hovers at the edge of my thoughts, too big to look at directly. Too impossible to accept. A shape in the darkness that I refuse to let into focus.

Not yet. I'm not ready to think about it yet.

But my heart knows. Somewhere deep down, in the part of me that still remembers what his hand felt like on my shoulder, in the part that's been waiting for two years for a sign that he's still out there...

My heart already knows.

I help Mom finish putting away the groceries, then mumble something about homework and retreat to my room. Close the door. Lean against it and let out a breath I didn't know I was holding.

My hands won't stop shaking.

I slide down until I'm sitting on the floor, back against the door, knees pulled up to my chest like I'm ten years old again, like I'm hiding from monsters under the bed. The ceiling fan spins slowly overhead, casting lazy shadows that circle and circle and circle.

Everything I thought I knew about my family is wrong. Mom isn't just a programmer. The Shadow Games aren't just a competition. And Alpha, whoever Alpha is, has been watching me from somewhere far away.

I think about Dad's face in the birthday photo. His smile. His hand on my shoulder.

"You know him better than I do at this point."

The words echo in my head, over and over, like a code I'm afraid to crack.

The photo in my locker. The one of us at Niagara Falls. Mom, Dad, and me, all smiling like nothing was wrong. I've looked at it a hundred times without really seeing. But now I remember their hands. Dad making an "A" with his fingers, the tips touching to form a triangle. Mom making what I always thought was just a goofy pose, but it could be a "B."

A for Alpha. B for Beta.

Alpha and Beta. Dad and Mom.

What if Dad didn't disappear at all? What if he just became someone else?

What if he's been Alpha this whole time?

What if my father is alive?

The thought hits me like a physical blow. I can't breathe. Can't think. Can't do anything except sit here on the floor of my bedroom while my entire world reshapes itself around an impossible possibility.

Dad. Alive.

11

THE THEORY

D ad. Alive.

The thought is too big to hold all at once. It keeps slipping away, like trying to grab water.

If it's true, if he's really been there this whole time, then every night I cried myself to sleep, every time I stared at his photo wondering where he went, every moment I hated myself for not being able to remember his voice clearly anymore... he was somewhere out there. Alive. Choosing not to come home.

The relief and the rage are so tangled together I can't tell them apart. I don't know whether to laugh or scream or throw something against the wall.

So I just sit there on my bedroom floor, breathing, letting the impossible possibility settle into my bones.

That night, I can't sleep. The questions won't stop bouncing around my head. Every time I think I've figured something out, three more questions show up to take its place. My brain is a hamster wheel that someone forgot to oil.

I stare at the ceiling of my room, the familiar cracks and water stains that I've memorized over years of insomniac nights. There's the one that looks like a rabbit. The one that looks like a crooked tree. The water damage near the corner that Mom keeps saying she'll get fixed but never does.

But tonight the ceiling doesn't hold my attention. Tonight my mind is stuck on two words: Dad. Alive.

Two years. Two years of grief and questions and this gaping hole in our lives where he used to be. Two years of Mom pretending everything was fine. Two years of me wondering if I'd ever know what really happened.

What if he was there the whole time? Just... invisible?

Deep undercover. So deep that even his own family can't know he's alive, because if we knew, if we acted like we knew, it would blow his cover. KOTR would realize their infiltrator is still alive, still feeding information, still building the case against them from the inside.

***

My mind races through the implications, connecting dots I never even saw before.

If Dad is alive, if he's Alpha, then everything I thought I knew is wrong. The White House ceremony wasn't a posthumous honor; it was recognition for ongoing service. His "disappearance" wasn't an accident or an attack; it was planned. Stage-managed. A necessary sacrifice to go deeper undercover than anyone had ever gone.

Mom's secretive work. Her high-threat-level status. Her nights locked in that office with nine monitors and satellite imagery. She's not just continuing Dad's mission. She's coordinating with him. Supporting him from home base while he operates in the field. Two halves of the same operation, separated by distance but connected by encrypted messages and shared purpose.

Operation Teardown.

The code name on Mom's whiteboard. That's what this is all about. A long-term operation to take down KOTR from the inside. Dad started it years ago, got close enough to become trusted, then "died" so he could get even closer. Mom continued the technical work, building infrastructure, maintaining their inside position, keeping the operation running while the rest of the world, including me, thought everything was normal.

And now, somehow, I've become part of it too.

***

I grab my notebook from the nightstand and turn on my desk lamp, ignoring the late hour. I need to write this down. All my theories. All my evidence. The connections I've made.

Dad = Alpha. Secret government mission to infiltrate KOTR.

Mom = BetaZone. Technical support and coordination. Continuing his work after his "disappearance."

Operation Teardown = Multi-year operation to take down KOTR from within? (Best guess).

Shadow Games = Part of the operation? Recruitment tool? Training ground?

Me = "Climbing" on purpose. Being watched by both parents. Allowed to progress toward... something.

But if Mom and Dad (Alpha) are the good guys, if they're working to bring down a dangerous hacker organization, why was KOTR sending money to Alpha? That was the payment notification I saw: "$10,000 Paid by Knights of the Republic - Alpha."

Unless... that was part of the cover.

To stay trusted inside KOTR, Alpha would need to act like a real member. Do real work. Accept real payments. If he suddenly stopped taking money, stopped delivering results, they'd get suspicious. The cover would break. Years of careful work would collapse in an instant.

Accept KOTR's payments to maintain trust. Use their own resources against them. Play both sides perfectly until you have enough evidence to bring the whole thing crashing down.

It's brilliant. And terrifying. And it makes my chest ache with something I can't quite name. Anger? Admiration? Betrayal? All of it, maybe, twisted together into something new.

It means my parents have been living double lives for years, longer than I ever imagined. Every dinner, every movie night, every family vacation... all of it happening alongside shadow operations I never suspected. Every "I love you" at bedtime layered with secrets they couldn't share. Every normal moment balanced against extraordinary danger.

They lied to me. Both of them. For years.

But they lied to keep me safe. To keep the mission safe. To protect something bigger than our family's comfort.

I don't know if that makes it better or worse.

***

One question burns hotter than all the rest: Why didn't they just tell me?

The thought comes with a surge of anger that surprises me. I'm not usually an angry person. But right now, sitting in the dark with my world turned inside out for the hundredth time, I feel it burning in my chest like something physical. My jaw clenches so tight my teeth ache. My hands curl into fists on my desk.

Two years. Two years of thinking I wasn't worth a goodbye. Two years of wondering what I did wrong, what I could have done differently, whether Dad even thought about me wherever he was. Two years of building walls around the part of my heart that used to belong to him, because keeping it open hurt too much.

If Mom knows I'm in the games, why keep up the pretense? Why let me sneak around, break into her office, decode her messages, spend sleepless nights trying to piece together mysteries? Why put me through all this fear and confusion when she could just sit me down and explain? Does she have any idea what these past weeks have been like? The terror? The loneliness? The feeling that I couldn't trust anyone, including her?

I think about Dad's face in the White House photo. The pride in his eyes. The ceremony where the President said, "It's unfortunate they will never know what happened."

Secrecy. Even from family. Because the stakes are too high.

Because knowing could get me killed.

Maybe knowing too much makes you a target. Maybe if I knew the whole truth, I'd act differently, let something slip in conversation, make a facial expression at the wrong moment, somehow reveal that I know things I shouldn't. KOTR has connections everywhere. If they even suspected that Alpha's family was aware of the operation...

Maybe Mom is protecting me by not telling me. Maybe everything I've uncovered on my own is safer than being officially read into the mission. If I'm caught, I can honestly say I was just a curious kid who stumbled onto things. I didn't know. I was never briefed.

Plausible deniability. For my own safety.

Or maybe there's more going on. Maybe the picture is even bigger than I realize. Maybe Mom and Dad don't have all the answers either. Maybe they're pieces on a board being moved by hands I can't see.

I look at my Shadow Games ranking on my phone. 28th place. 1,062 points. The numbers glow in the dark room, a measure of progress I didn't even know I was supposed to be making. Melissa mentioned something about qualifying for "The Meeting," an in-person event where the sponsors might actually appear.

If Mom and Dad are really behind all this, if the Shadow Games are somehow connected to Operation Teardown, maybe The Meeting is where everything comes together. Where the truth finally comes out. Where I get answers directly instead of piecing them together from stolen glimpses of phone conversations.

Or maybe The Meeting is something else entirely. A test. A trap. Another layer of secrets on top of all the others. The only way to know for sure is to keep climbing.

***

I think about texting Ethan. He's my best friend. He should know what's going on. But what would I even say? "Hey, I think my dead dad might actually be alive and secretly working with my mom on some spy stuff"? He'd either think I'd lost my mind or he'd want to help, and I can't drag him into this. Not yet. Not until I know more.

The lie by omission makes my chest hurt. Ethan deserves better. But some secrets are too dangerous to share, even with the people you trust most.

I text Melissa instead: "I need to talk to you. Something major happened."

Her response comes within seconds, like she was waiting for exactly this message: "Same here. I found something too. Video chat tomorrow morning?"

"Yes. 9 AM my time."

"I'll be there. Don't do anything crazy before then."

"Define crazy."

"Ha. Just... be careful, Jacob. I have a feeling things are about to get real."

I put down my phone and stare at my notebook full of theories. Tomorrow, I'll share what I know with Melissa. She'll share whatever she found. Together, maybe we can figure out what comes next. Two shadow dwellers combining their pieces of the puzzle, building a picture neither of us can see alone.

But tonight, I let myself feel something I haven't felt in weeks: hope.

It's a dangerous feeling. Hope can make you careless. Hope can make you see patterns that aren't there, believe things that aren't true, trust people who don't deserve it. I know all of this.

But right now, sitting in the dark with my notebook full of theories and my heart full of questions, I choose to hope anyway. I let myself feel it, really feel it, for the first time in two years. The warmth spreading through my chest. The lightness in my shoulders. The tears that prick at my eyes and don't feel entirely sad.

Dad might be alive. Mom might be a hero working to bring down dangerous criminals. And somehow, I'm part of their mission, not a hindrance to be protected from, but a player being guided toward the truth.

The shadows are starting to give way to light. Or maybe that's just what I want to believe. Maybe hope is just another kind of blindness, seeing what you want to see instead of what's really there.

But you know what? I don't care. For two years, I've lived in the dark. I've wondered and grieved and questioned everything. If there's even a chance that Dad is out there, that he's been watching over me this whole time, waiting for me to find my way to him, then I'm going to hold onto that chance with everything I have.

I close my notebook and turn off my lamp, but I don't sleep for a long time. The questions keep circling, but they feel different now. Less like threats and more like puzzles waiting to be solved. Less like monsters and more like challenges.

When I finally drift off, I dream of oak trees and coded messages and my father's face, smiling at me from somewhere far away. He looks the same as he did in the White House photo. Proud. Determined. Alive.

"Find your own way to the truth," he says in the dream. "I'll be waiting."

And somehow, despite everything, despite all the lies and secrets and years of not knowing, I believe him.

I believe he's out there. And I'm going to find him.

12

Bad Guys Close In

The next morning, right at 9 AM like we agreed, I click the video call link Melissa sent me.

It starts with her face frozen mid-word, mouth open, one hand raised in a gesture that could mean anything. California internet strikes again. The little loading icon spins in the corner of my screen like it's mocking me, and I wait for the connection to stop being garbage.

After a few seconds, she pixelates back to life, the image stuttering through a bunch of incomplete frames before finally smoothing out. For a moment she looks like a ghost, fragments of a person trying to become whole.

"...and that's when I knew something was seriously wrong," she's saying, her voice finally matching up with her lips.

"Wait, start over. I missed the whole beginning. Connection dropped."

She sighs, and I can see the frustration in the way her shoulders tense up. We've been having these calls for weeks now, but this one feels different. Heavier. Even through the crappy pixelated video quality, I can tell something's wrong. She looks pale. Scared. Her eyes keep darting to something off-screen, like she's expecting someone to burst through her door any second.

"I said I got a weird message last night. Not on the competitor hub, on my actual phone. From someone calling themselves 'The Watcher.' They know things about me, Jacob. Things that aren't public anywhere." She pauses, and I see her swallow hard. "My real name. My school. My dad's actual job title. Even my brother's name."

"Can you tell anything from how the message was written?" I ask. "Writing style, word choice..."

"Already analyzed it." Her eyes sharpen despite the fear. This is her thing. Reading people, understanding them even through text. "Formal but trying to sound casual. Like someone educated pretending to be a regular hacker. The vocabulary is too sophisticated, too controlled. Whoever wrote this isn't some random troll. They're trained. Professional. And they're used to intimidating people."

My blood goes cold. Like ice water dumped straight into my veins. "That sounds exactly like what happened to me. The anonymous text telling me I was asking dangerous questions."

"Jacob, they threatened me." Her voice cracks a little. "Said if I didn't drop out of the games immediately, withdraw my competitor status and delete all my research, things would 'get complicated' for my family. Those were their exact words. Get complicated."

I think about Mom's phone. The messages I read. The network probes that keep hitting our router. All the warnings I've ignored because I was too focused on finding the truth.

"It's KOTR," I say. "Has to be. They've figured out people are investigating them through the games."

"That's what I thought too. But Jacob, how did they get my phone number? My home number, not the secure one I use for game stuff. That information isn't connected to my competitor profile anywhere. I've been super careful about that."

I tell her what I found on Mom's phone. The encrypted messenger app. The Alpha_Actual contact. My theory that Dad might be alive and working with Mom on Operation Teardown, infiltrating KOTR from the inside while Mom runs tech support from home.

Melissa listens without interrupting, her face getting more serious with each thing I reveal. When I finally finish, she's quiet for a long moment. I can see her processing, the same way I did when I first figured it out.

"If your parents are running some kind of undercover operation against KOTR," she says slowly, working through it, "and these 'Watcher' messages are coming from KOTR people who've figured out someone's investigating them through the games..."

"Then we're in their crosshairs," I finish. "They don't know exactly who the threat is, but they're sending warnings to anyone who looks suspicious. Trying to scare people off before they find something real."

"Which means they have something real to hide."

"Exactly."

Melissa runs her hands through her hair, and I notice her fingers are shaking. Not just a little. Really shaking, like she's cold even though I can see sunlight streaming through her window.

"Jacob, I'm scared." Her voice drops to almost a whisper. "Not just nervous, actually scared. Someone knows where I live. Where my brother goes to school. Dylan is twelve years old, Jacob. He rides his bike to school. He doesn't know anything about any of this. If they're willing to threaten my family just because I'm climbing in a hacking competition..."

She doesn't finish the sentence. She doesn't have to.

Something cold spreads through my chest. Not just fear for her, though that's there, sharp and urgent, but something darker. The realization that my curiosity, my investigation, my climbing through the ranks might have put her in danger too. If they're tracking me, they're probably tracking everyone I talk to. Everyone I trust.

I might have painted a target on Melissa's back without even knowing it.

"Maybe you should drop out," I hear myself saying, even though part of me screams at the idea. The selfish part that doesn't want to lose the only person who truly understands what I'm going through. "If it's too dangerous..."

"No." Her jaw sets in that stubborn way I've gotten to know. The fear is still there in her eyes, but there's something else now too. Something harder. "I've spent eight months trying to find answers about my dad. I'm not giving up because some anonymous creep sends threatening messages. They want us scared? Fine. I'm scared. But I'm not quitting. I'm getting smarter."

"Partners in shadows," I remind her.

"Partners in shadows," she agrees. Her voice is steadier now. "Whatever happens, we face it together."

***

I go to school the next day in a total daze. The familiar halls of Lincoln High School feel alien now, like I'm walking through a movie set where everyone knows their lines except me. Every face in the hallway feels like a potential threat. Every casual glance could be surveillance. My skin prickles with the constant sensation of being watched.

The guy at the lunch table who looks at me a beat too long. Is he just curious about the kid sitting alone, or is he watching me for someone else?

The substitute teacher in biology who keeps checking her phone. Is she texting a boyfriend, or getting updates about where I am?

Even Jason's usual bullying feels different. He shoulder-checks me in the hallway between classes, calls me a loser loud enough for the whole corridor to hear, but there's something in his eyes that seems sharper. More mean. Like he knows things about me that he shouldn't.

God, I'm losing it. This is what paranoia does to you. It turns everyone into a suspect, every interaction into evidence.

I know I'm being irrational. I know that not everyone is a spy, that most people are just living their lives without any clue about shadow games or undercover operations or hacker groups threatening teenagers. But like Melissa said: just because you're paranoid doesn't mean they're not watching.

And someone is definitely watching.

Ethan corners me at my locker after third period. He looks worried, genuinely worried, not just annoyed that I've been blowing off our gaming sessions.

"Dude, what's going on with you? You look terrible."

"Thanks," I mutter, focusing on spinning my combination. The numbers blur in front of my eyes. I can't remember the sequence. It's the same combination I've used all year, and suddenly it's just... gone. Like someone deleted the file from my brain.

"I'm serious, Jacob." He lowers his voice, stepping closer. "You're falling asleep in class. You've blown off the last two gaming sessions without any explanation. And you keep looking over your shoulder like you're waiting for someone to attack. Is this still about your mom? About the Shadow Games stuff?"

I want to tell him everything. About the phone messages. About Melissa's parallel investigation. About my theory that Dad might be alive, that my whole family has been living a lie for years. About the fact that dangerous people might be tracking us both right now, watching through cameras and monitoring network traffic and building profiles that could get us killed.

But how do you explain any of that to someone who thinks the Shadow Games are just a fun competition? Who sees the world as basically safe and normal, where the biggest threats are pop quizzes and mean kids?

"I'm fine," I lie, finally remembering my combination and yanking the locker open harder than I meant to. "Just stressed about homework."

Ethan doesn't look convinced. His eyes search my face for the truth, and I know he can see something's wrong. We've been friends long enough that lying to him feels physically painful.

But the bell saves me from more questions. The hallway empties around us as students rush to their next classes.

"We'll talk later," Ethan says. It's not a question. "Whatever's going on, you don't have to deal with it alone, okay?"

I nod, not trusting my voice, and escape into the flow of students.

But as I'm walking to fourth period, my phone buzzes. A text from Ethan.

"I know you said you're fine but I don't believe you. So I did something. Remember when you showed me how to search for metadata in documents? I used it. Found some stuff about that KOTR group you mentioned. Sending you what I found after school. Maybe it helps, maybe it doesn't. But you're not doing this alone whether you like it or not."

I stare at the message. Ethan, who can barely remember his own passwords, who once uploaded a Word doc with his home address in the metadata, actually went and did research. For me. Because he was worried.

Something loosens in my chest. It's not much. He probably just found the same public stuff I already know. But the fact that he tried means more than I can say.

"Thanks," I type back. "You're a good friend."

"Obviously. Now go to class before you get detention."

I pocket my phone, feeling slightly less alone. Even if Ethan can't fully understand what I'm going through, at least he's trying. At least someone is.

***

That afternoon, I come home to find Mom sitting at the kitchen table. Not making dinner. Not doing any of the normal mom things I've gotten used to seeing.

Just sitting there. Staring at something on her screen. The light from the laptop casts harsh shadows across her face.

"Jacob." Her voice is weird. Tight. The way it sounds when she's trying really hard to control some strong emotion. "Come here."

I approach slowly, every instinct screaming that something is very wrong. My stomach sinks with each step, like I'm walking toward a cliff I can't see.

On her screen is a ScyberSpace message board. The topic title hits me like a punch to the gut:

"SirBreaksAlot - Who Is This Newbie Climber? INVESTIGATION THREAD"

My username is plastered across discussions analyzing my progress through the Shadow Games. Someone has compiled my solve times, noting the pattern of late-night activity. Cross-referenced my post history on ScyberSpace to build a profile. Made guesses about my real identity based on writing style and geographic clues from the challenges I've solved.

There are theories. Guesses. Someone even found the Reddit post I made two years ago about building a PC, the same post I discovered in my self-analysis for The Analyst challenge.

I profiled myself to be safe. And now someone else has done the exact same thing. Turned my own technique against me.

"Mom, I can explain..."

"You're competing in the Shadow Games." Her voice is flat. Not a question.

I freeze. This is the moment. The confrontation I've been dreading and avoiding and preparing for, all at the same time. The moment where all my secrets collide with all of hers.

But something in her eyes isn't just anger. There's fear there too. Real, raw fear that I've never seen on my mother's face before. The kind of fear that makes my stomach drop, because if she's scared, things are way worse than I realized.

"How did you find out?"

"Someone sent this to me. Anonymously. Along with a message that I'm hoping you can explain." She turns the laptop to show me another window. An email with a single message:

"FROM: The Watcher
SUBJECT: Regarding your son

Your son is good. Maybe too good. His climbing speed in the Shadow Games has attracted attention from people who don't appreciate being investigated. He's asking questions that lead to dangerous places.

Consider this a courtesy warning. We know who you are, BetaZone. We know about Alpha. We know about Operation Teardown. And we know that your son is now a liability, a loose end that could unravel everything you've spent years building.

You have 48 hours to withdraw him from the games and cease all operations. After that, the next message won't be as polite.

-TW"

KOTR. It has to be. They've figured out someone is looking into them through the games, and they've traced it back to me. Worse, they know about Mom. About Dad. About Operation Teardown.

And now they know about my connection to both of them.

***

"Jacob." Mom's voice is shaking now, the controlled calm cracking. "I need you to tell me everything. How long have you been in these games? What have you found? Who have you talked to?"

Looking at her face, really looking, past the BetaZone mask to the terrified mother underneath, I feel something break inside me. Grief, maybe. For the simple relationship we used to have. For the mom who made pancakes and asked "what did you learn?" without any hidden agendas. Was she ever really that person, or was it always a cover? Did she love me as a son or as an asset to be protected?

I hate that I even have to ask those questions. I hate that I can't tell which version of her is real anymore.

I should lie. Protect my sources. Play dumb. That's what you're supposed to do when you're caught. Deny, deflect, minimize. She already knows I've been participating in the Shadow Games and climbing the ranks. Does she already know I've uncovered much more?

But I'm so tired of secrets. Tired of shadows. Tired of the walls between us, the careful performances, the constant exhausting effort of pretending not to know things I know. If this is the end of our double lives, maybe that's not entirely bad. Maybe the truth, painful and dangerous and terrifying, is better than another day of lies. She's already been watching me for a while

"I've been in the games for almost three weeks," I say. "I'm ranked 28th. I've completed most of Phase 2. And I know about Operation Teardown. I know about KOTR. I know that you're BetaZone." I pause, trying to find courage for the rest. The words feel enormous in my mouth, too big to actually say out loud. "And I know that Alpha_Actual is Dad. I know he's alive."

Mom's face goes white. Not just pale, white, like all the blood has drained out of her at once. For a second, I see something shatter behind her eyes, the careful mask she's been wearing for two years cracking under the weight of all the lies. She looks like she might cry. She looks like she might scream. She looks like she's been carrying something impossibly heavy for a very long time, and it just got ten times heavier.

Then her expression hardens into something I've never seen before. Professional. Cold. Calculating. The mask of BetaZone sliding into place over my mother's face.

It's terrifying. And fascinating. Watching the person who made me pancakes transform into someone who could probably kill with her bare hands.

"How did you..." She stops herself. Shakes her head. "It doesn't matter how. You know, and now so do they." She stands up fast, her chair scraping against the floor. "Go to your room. Pack a bag. Enough for a week. Maybe longer."

"What? Why?"

"Because we're leaving. Tonight. And we might not be coming back."

***

I pack in a fog, my hands moving automatically while my brain struggles to catch up. Clothes. Jeans, t-shirts, underwear. My laptop and chargers. A few books I've been meaning to read. My notebook with all my theories and evidence, thick with scribbled notes and coded observations.

I touch the thumb drive hanging from my neck, the one Dad gave me the week before he disappeared. Still password protected. Still a mystery. But maybe, after tonight, I'll finally learn what's on it.

Through my bedroom wall, I can hear Mom on the phone. Her voice is low and urgent, pitched to carry to whoever she's talking to but not to me. I press my ear against the wall, straining to catch pieces:

"...compromised... threat level elevated to critical... extraction protocol Foxtrot-Seven... yes, including him... I know it's ahead of schedule but the timeline is blown... doesn't matter anymore... tell Alpha to go to backup site Charlie... we'll meet there in four hours..."

Extraction. That's a word for pulling undercover agents out of dangerous situations. A word from spy movies and thrillers. A word I never thought would apply to my actual life.

A knock on my door. Mom appears in the doorway, and for a second I don't recognize her. She's wearing clothes I've never seen, all black, tactical-looking fabric with lots of pockets, practical boots instead of her usual flats. Her hair is pulled back tight, and there's something different about how she holds herself. Taller. More alert.

She looks like a different person. A stranger wearing my mother's face.

"We need to talk," she says. "About your father."

My heart stops. Actually stops, the beat suspended in my chest for one long moment.

"Is he alive?"

She takes a deep breath. I see something soften in her eyes, the real Mom peeking through the operative's mask.

"Yes. He's alive. He's been alive this whole time." She steps into my room, closing the door behind her. "And in about two hours, you're going to see him."

***

The car ride is surreal. Mom drives fast, faster than I've ever seen her drive, taking back roads I've never noticed before, routes that avoid main highways and cameras. The headlights cut through darkness that seems thicker than usual, like even the night is helping hide us.

She explains as we go. All of it. The full story, told in pieces between gear shifts and navigation checks.

Dad, Alpha, has been working deep undercover inside KOTR for almost three years. He didn't just discover them; he infiltrated them. Rose through their ranks by proving his skills. Became trusted enough to access their most sensitive operations.

The White House ceremony was real recognition for real service. The "unfortunate that no one will never know" was about him being so deep undercover that even his family had to believe he was gone.

He staged his own disappearance. Planned it months in advance with Mom's help. Walked out of our life one morning and became someone else entirely.

"We couldn't tell you," Mom says, her eyes fixed on the road ahead. The dashboard lights paint her face in shades of green and blue. "If you knew, and someone questioned you (drugs, torture, even just a slip of the tongue) you could have given him away. One wrong word, one hesitation, one flash of hope when someone mentioned his name. KOTR would have known."

"So you let me think he was dead." My voice sounds hollow. Distant. Like someone else is talking from very far away. "Two years of thinking my father was gone. Two years of grief. Two years of wondering what I could have done differently. What I should have said. Whether he knew I loved him."

My throat tightens. I will not cry. Not now. Not in this car, with all these secrets finally spilling out.

"Two years of protecting the mission. Of protecting him. Of protecting you." Her grip tightens on the steering wheel until her knuckles go white. "Do you think that was easy for me? Watching you grieve? Lying to you every single day? Seeing you stare at his photograph and having to pretend I didn't know anything?" Her voice cracks. "It was the hardest thing I've ever done, Jacob. Harder than any mission. Any operation. Any danger I've ever faced. But it was necessary."

I should be angry. Part of me is, this burning coal of rage at the center of my chest, fueled by every tear I cried, every night I stared at his photo, every time I wished I could have said goodbye.

But mostly I just feel hollow. Like someone scooped out my insides and left only the shell. Two years of grief, and it was all based on a lie. Two years of mourning someone who was alive the whole time.

All those nights I lay awake wondering if something I did drove him away. All those moments I replayed our last conversation, searching for clues I might have missed. All that guilt. Did I not tell him I loved him enough? Did he know how much he meant to me?

He knew. He always knew. And he left anyway.

The hollow feeling expands, pressing against my ribs from the inside. I don't know how to process that. I don't know if I ever will.

"The Shadow Games," I say eventually. "Were you really okay with me competing? Or was that part of some plan too?"

Mom's jaw tightens. "I didn't expect you to find my office. I definitely didn't expect you to solve the cipher and enter the games on your own. When I realized what you'd done, I panicked. Wanted to pull you out right away." She glances at me for a second before looking back at the road. "But your father thought it might actually help. You were gathering intel we couldn't get from our existing people. Fresh perspectives. Different angles."

"So I was doing your job for you. Being used."

"You were doing what we spent your whole childhood preparing you for. You just didn't know it." Her voice softens a little. "All those years of teaching you about computers. Encouraging your tinkering. Letting you break things and figure out how they work. We were preparing you for this world, Jacob. Just in case."

"In case of what?"

"In case we ever needed you to carry on the mission. In case something happened to one of us. In case..." She trails off. "In case exactly what's happening right now."

***

We pull into a parking garage I don't recognize. Underground. Concrete walls and harsh fluorescent lights. No windows. The kind of place designed for secrecy, where no one can see who comes and goes, where signals get blocked by tons of reinforced concrete.

Mom parks and kills the engine. The sudden silence feels heavy.

"There's one more thing you need to know before we go in."

I wait, exhausted beyond words but still desperate for answers.

"The Shadow Games aren't just a competition. They're a recruitment and training platform. The people who run them, the real people behind the anonymous 'sponsors,' they're part of the same organization your father and I work for." She turns to face me fully. "An organization that doesn't officially exist. No name on any government budget. No headquarters you can find on a map. But we fight people like KOTR, protect innocent people from the kind of damage cyber criminals can cause."

"So the games are... a good guy thing?"

"It's complicated. Nothing in this world is purely good or bad." She sighs. "But yeah. The games identify people with the skills and mindset to become operatives. People who think differently. Who can solve problems. Who don't give up when things get hard. People like you." She pauses. "People like your friend StarBreaker."

My mind races. Melissa. Is she also being recruited? Has her father been guiding her all along, just like mine? Are our parallel journeys not parallel at all, but orchestrated?

Before I can ask, there's a knock on the car window. Sharp. Urgent.

A man stands outside, mostly in shadow. He's wearing civilian clothes (jeans, a dark jacket) but something about his posture screams military. The way he holds himself. The way his eyes scan the garage even while he waits for us.

Mom opens her door. "Daniel. You made good time."

"Traffic was light once we hit the back routes." The man's voice is calm. Professional. "He's waiting inside. Are we sure about this?"

"We're sure." Mom gets out and waves for me to follow. "Jacob, I'd like you to meet Daniel. He's part of the extraction team."

I step out of the car on legs that feel like they belong to someone else. Daniel nods at me, respectful, sizing me up, then leads us toward a heavy metal door I hadn't noticed before.

Through the door. Down a corridor lit by buzzing fluorescent tubes. Past doors labeled with numbers instead of names. The air tastes like recycled ventilation and decades of secrets.

We stop at a door marked simply "7."

Daniel knocks twice. Pauses. Knocks three more times. Some kind of pattern.

The door opens.

And there he is.

A little older. A little thinner. Lines around his eyes that weren't there before. His hair is different, shorter, grayer at the temples. He's wearing the same boring clothes as Daniel, practical and forgettable. The kind of clothes designed to make you invisible.

But the eyes are the same. The exact same warm brown eyes that stared at me from a thousand memories, that I've seen in photographs every single day for two years, that I've dreamed about so many times I lost count.

"Hi, Jacob," says my father. His voice cracks a little on my name. "We need to talk about your future."

I open my mouth to say something.

Nothing comes out.

After two years of silence, two years of grief and questions and desperate hope, words seem impossibly small. Not enough. What do you say to someone you've mourned? What do you say to someone you buried in your heart, only to find them standing in front of you?

Hi, Dad. I missed you. I hate you. I love you. Where have you been? How could you leave? I'm so glad you're alive. I'm so angry you're alive.

All of it true. None of it enough.

So instead, I just stand there, staring at the ghost who turned out to be my dad. Alive. Real. Close enough to touch if I could only make my arms work.

He takes a step toward me. Hesitant. Uncertain. His hands are shaking. I can see them trembling at his sides. I realize he's scared too, scared of how I'll react, scared that I'll hate him, scared that two years apart has destroyed something that can never be fixed.

And all at once, the anger and confusion and numbness melt away, replaced by something simpler. Something I've been waiting to feel since the day he disappeared. Something that's been locked in my chest for two years, waiting for this exact moment.

I cross the distance between us in three steps and throw my arms around him. He catches me, stumbles a little, then steadies, and his arms close around me in return. He's thinner than I remember. Stronger in different ways. He smells different too, no trace of the familiar cologne he used to wear. But underneath all that, he's still Dad. Still the person who taught me to ride a bike. Still the person who told me bedtime stories about space explorers and made up silly voices for all the characters.

Still mine.

Neither of us says anything.

We don't have to.

For just this moment, in this underground room full of secrets, we're just a father and son, holding on to each other against the darkness. Against the years. Against everything that tried to keep us apart.

Everything else can wait.

13

The Truth

The first thing I do is punch my dad in the chest.

It's not hard, more like a shove, really, but the look on his face is totally worth it. Two years of nothing and now he's just standing here like it's no big deal. Like he can just waltz back into my life and everything will be fine.

The hug that came before, that desperate, shaky embrace where I held onto him like he might disappear again, feels like it happened to someone else. Some other Jacob, in some other timeline where feelings are simple and pure. This Jacob is angry. This Jacob has two years of hurt demanding to be heard.

"Two years." My voice cracks and I hate it. I sound like a little kid, and I hate that too. "Two years I thought you were dead. Or kidnapped somewhere getting tortured while I sat in my room feeling completely useless. I looked at that stupid White House picture every single day trying to figure out what you would've said to me. I made up conversations in my head. Imagined advice you might've given me about school or girls or whatever." I'm shaking now and I can't stop. My whole body is trembling like I'm cold, but I'm not cold. I'm burning up. "And the whole time you were just... alive? Working? You chose not to come home?"

Dad doesn't move. Doesn't try to defend himself or back away. Just stands there with his arms half-open, like he's ready to take whatever I throw at him.

"I know," he says quietly. "And I'm sorry. More sorry than I can ever..."

"Sorry doesn't cover it."

"No. It doesn't."

We just stand there in this concrete room that smells like recycled air and old coffee. The fluorescent lights buzz overhead like they're commentating on my breakdown. Mom watches from a few feet away, her face doing this weird thing where she looks sad and relieved at the same time, like she's been waiting for this explosion and is almost relieved it's finally happening. Behind her, that Daniel guy has disappeared down the corridor to give us space or whatever.

My leg won't stop bouncing. I shove my hands in my pockets so no one can see them shaking. The anger feels safer than the other thing underneath it, the thing that feels like relief, like joy, like wanting to hug him again and never let go. I can't let myself feel that yet. Not until I've said what I need to say.

Finally Dad speaks again. His voice is steady but I can see it's costing him. There's this tension around his eyes that wasn't there before.

"I have explanations. They won't make it better, but you deserve to hear them. All of them." He pauses. "Will you listen?"

Part of me wants to walk away. To tell him to shove his explanations and just leave. To make him feel even a fraction of what I felt all those nights crying into my pillow.

But another part, the part that decoded ciphers and broke into Mom's office and climbed through the Shadow Games just to understand, that part needs to know.

"Fine," I say. "Talk."

***

We end up in a conference room upstairs. Elevator up three floors, through what feels like a million doors that need keycards and retinal scans, into a space that looks exactly like something from a spy movie.

Big table in the middle. Screens on every wall, all dark right now. Weird equipment in the corners that I don't recognize but looks expensive. A whiteboard covered with diagrams and acronyms that make zero sense to me.

The whole place smells like cleaning supplies and secrets. If that's even a smell.

Dad sits across from me. Mom takes a spot by the door, standing guard or maybe just needing the distance. I sit with my hands flat on the table because I don't know what else to do with them.

"So KOTR," Dad begins, and there's something different about his voice now, clipped, professional, the way you'd start a military briefing. "Operation Teardown. Timeline begins approximately four years ago..."

"Wait, what?" I'm already lost. "Can you just... start from the beginning? Like the actual beginning? Not the spy version. The dad version."

He stops. Blinks. Like I just reminded him who he's talking to. "Right. Sorry." He rubs his face with both hands, and for a second he just looks tired. Really, really tired. "I'm used to briefing assets who already know the background. You're not an asset. You're my son. Let me try again."

"KOTR was getting dangerous," he tries again. "Not just stealing data or messing with companies. They started going after hospitals. Power grids. Water treatment places."

"The charities I researched," I say, remembering. "The veterans group. The health organization."

"Exactly." Dad nods. "But it was worse than that. When you take down a hospital's computer network during surgery, people can die. When you mess with emergency services, people who call 911 don't get help. KOTR wasn't just causing problems. They were hurting real people. Killing them, sometimes, even if they never pulled a trigger."

My stomach does this uncomfortable flip thing. I knew KOTR was bad. I didn't know they were that bad.

"So what, you just decided to join them?"

"Infiltrate them." Dad's voice gets this edge to it. "Big difference. I had the skills, the computer stuff, the technical knowledge. I could think like they think. So I created this whole fake identity. Alpha. A mercenary hacker with no morals who only cared about money and chaos."

"And they just... believed you?"

"It took months to set up. Fake history, fake credentials, fake accomplishments. I had to do some actual crimes under that identity, nothing that hurt regular people directly, but enough to get noticed by the wrong crowd."

Mom speaks up from the doorway. "I became BetaZone around the same time. Technical specialist, malware developer. Someone who could provide tools without asking questions."

"Wait," I say, trying to piece together the timeline. "So you both started this when I was like... twelve? And you've been doing it for four years?"

Mom nods. "We met through the organization, actually. Before you were born. Your dad was already doing intelligence work when I was recruited."

"Why were you recruited?" I ask. "I mean, what made you get into this?"

Mom is quiet for a moment, like she's deciding how much to share. "I was a grad student at MIT. Computer science. One of my professors was working on a research project, officially about network security, but really it was about finding vulnerabilities in critical infrastructure. One day, some men in suits showed up at my apartment."

"Government agents?"

"They said they'd been monitoring my work. That I had a particular skill set they were interested in." She almost smiles at the memory. "I was twenty-three and thought I was going to change the world through open-source software. Instead, I ended up changing it through... other means."

"And you just said yes? To becoming a spy?"

"Not a spy, exactly. Technical support. Analysis. The behind-the-scenes stuff that keeps operations running." She looks at Dad. "I didn't do fieldwork until much later. That's how I met your father. He was already deep in the game, and I was his handler. His support system back home."

"That's kinda romantic, in a weird way," I admit.

"It was," Mom says softly. "Is. Even now."

"We got married, had you, and thought we could have a normal life while doing this stuff on the side." She pauses. "It didn't work out that way."

"So my whole life..." I feel dizzy. "Every birthday party, every family vacation, every normal day... you were both secretly spies the whole time?"

"We weren't active for all of it," Dad says carefully. "After you were born, we stepped back. Just monitoring, analysis work, nothing that put us directly in danger. But when KOTR started escalating, when they started hurting people..." He trails off. "We couldn't stay on the sidelines anymore."

I stare at Mom. My mom, who makes me eggs in the morning and worries about my grades and leaves notes in my lunch sometimes, was pretending to be a criminal hacker this whole time. And before that, she was pretending to be a normal person while actually being some kind of spy.

My brain is doing that thing where it can't quite hold onto reality. Like I'm watching a movie of my own life and none of it makes sense.

"So the payment I saw," I say slowly, putting pieces together. "The ten thousand dollars from KOTR to Alpha..."

"Part of my cover," Dad confirms. "To stay trusted, I had to act like a real member. Accept money. Deliver results. If I suddenly stopped, they'd get suspicious."

"Okay but..." I'm picking at my fingernails now, a nervous habit I thought I'd kicked. "The fire. The day you disappeared. Was that all fake too?"

Dad's face does something complicated. Guilt maybe? "The fire was real, an actual electrical fault. Worst timing ever. But we used it. Made it look worse than it was. Let people assume the worst."

"And then you just left." I can hear the bitterness in my own voice and I don't even try to hide it. "You let me think you were gone. For two years. Two freaking years, Dad."

"It was the only way to protect..."

"Don't." I hold up my hand. "Don't say you were protecting me. That's such..."

"...to protect the operation's integrity and ensure..."

"DAD." My voice comes out louder than I mean it to. "You're doing it again. The briefing thing. Stop talking like I'm some agent you're debriefing. I'm your son. Your son who thought you were dead."

The words hang there. Dad's mouth opens, closes. Opens again.

"You're right," he says finally, and his voice is different now, raw, unpracticed, human. "I was protecting the mission. That's different from protecting you. I know that."

Silence. The kind that feels heavy and wrong.

Mom shifts by the door but doesn't say anything.

Dad just looks at me. Really looks, like he's seeing me for the first time in a long time.

"You're right," he says finally. "I told myself it was about protection. And part of it was. KOTR targets families, uses them as leverage. If they knew Alpha had a wife and kid still alive..." He trails off. "But you're right. I was also choosing the mission over being your father. I was scared and I took the coward's way out."

I didn't expect him to admit it. But his honesty doesn't make me feel better. If anything, it makes it worse. He knew what he was doing was wrong. He did it anyway.

"So you admit it." My voice sounds strange even to me. Cold. "You knew you were hurting me, and you just... kept doing it. Every day for two years."

"Jacob..."

"Do you know what it's like?" I'm standing now, though I don't remember getting up. The chair scrapes against the floor behind me, loud in the silence. "To be fourteen years old and think your dad is dead? To cry yourself to sleep and wake up and remember he's gone and have to feel that all over again? Every. Single. Morning?"

Dad doesn't answer. His jaw is tight. Good. Let him hear this.

"I stopped talking to people. Did you know that? After you 'died,' I barely spoke for like three months. Mom had to drag me to a therapist who kept asking about my feelings and I couldn't say anything because..." My voice breaks. I hate it. I hate that I'm crying now, tears streaming down my face when I wanted to be strong. "Because I didn't have words for what I felt. I just had this hole where you used to be. This empty space that hurt every time I looked at it."

I wipe my face angrily with my sleeve. Keep going. Get it all out. If I stop now, I'll never say any of this again.

"I used to wake up on my birthday and forget for just a second. And then I'd remember, Dad's not going to be there. And I'd have to grieve you all over again." My voice is raw now, stripped down to something I didn't even know was there. "I had conversations with your photo, Dad. I asked it for advice. I told it about my day. Because that was all I had left of you."

I'm shaking so hard I have to grip the table to stay upright. Every word is a piece of me I'm handing over, two years of pain finally given a voice.

"And you know what the worst part was? Not knowing. Not knowing if you were alive or dead. Not knowing if you chose to leave or if someone took you. Not knowing if you thought about me wherever you were." A sob catches in my throat, ugly and raw. "At least if you were dead, I could have grieved and moved on eventually. But this, this limbo, it never stopped. Every day, wondering. Every night, hoping. And all along, you were just... alive. Making that choice over and over again to not come back."

The room is so quiet I can hear the fluorescent lights buzzing. Mom is crying silently by the door, tears streaming down her face, but she doesn't move. Doesn't try to comfort me or defend Dad or do anything except stand there and take it.

Good. She should hear this too.

"And now you're back and you want me to just... what? Be happy? Grateful? Oh, Dad's alive, everything's fine now?" I laugh but there's no humor in it. "That's not how it works. You can't just undo two years of grief because you decided the mission was finally over."

"I know," Dad says quietly. "I know, Jacob. And I'm not asking you to forgive me. Not today. Maybe not ever. I made choices that hurt you, and I have to live with that."

"We both do," Mom adds, her voice thick with tears. "We knew we were causing you pain. We did it anyway because we thought it was the only option. But you're right, that was our choice, not yours. You never got a say."

The anger is still there, burning in my chest like something physical. But underneath it, I feel exhausted. So tired of carrying all these feelings by myself.

"Mom knew the whole time?" I ask, even though I already know the answer. The question comes out quieter than before, some of the fire drained out of it. "Like, from the actual beginning? From the day you 'died'?"

"Before that," Dad says heavily. "We planned it together. Three months before the fire, we sat down and mapped out every detail. How to stage my disappearance, what she'd tell you, how she'd maintain the cover story. She was there when I packed the go-bag that I'd take with me. She helped me rehearse my 'last day' so nothing would seem unusual." His voice cracks slightly. "She's the one who held it together at the memorial service, knowing the whole time I was alive and watching from a surveillance feed."

I stare at Mom. She's had this secret for two years, longer if you count the planning, and she never slipped. Never gave me a hint. All those times I cried in front of her, all those times I asked questions about Dad, and she just... played the part of the grieving widow.

"She kept the home base running, maintained my cover, raised you alone while carrying a secret she couldn't share with anyone."

I look at Mom. She's got this expression like she's bracing for me to hate her too.

"I wanted to tell you so many times," she says. "Every time I saw you looking at that picture in the hallway. Every time you cried yourself to sleep (and yes, I heard you through the walls) I wanted to just tell you the truth. But if you knew, and someone questioned you, or you slipped up somehow..."

"KOTR would've figured it out," I finish. "And killed all of us. Yeah, I get the logic."

"Understanding the logic doesn't make it hurt less," Mom says softly. "I know that."

***

"What about the Shadow Games?" I ask after a long pause. My brain is trying to process everything but it's like drinking from a fire hose. "How does that connect to any of this?"

Dad and Mom exchange one of their looks. The silent communication thing that used to annoy me and now makes way more sense.

"The games are run by our organization," Dad says. "Same people who coordinate Operation Teardown and a bunch of other stuff you'll never hear about."

"Wait, so the Shadow Games are like... good guy games?"

"Complicated." Dad stands up and walks to the whiteboard, erasing some of the existing diagrams. "They serve a few purposes."

He writes "TRAINING" and circles it.

"The challenges aren't just random puzzles. Each one teaches specific skills. Cryptography. Network analysis. OSINT, that's open source intelligence gathering. By the time someone reaches Phase 2, they've basically completed a crash course in spy stuff."

I think about all the challenges I've done. The steganography. The frequency analysis. The SSTV decoding. I thought I was just earning points. Turns out I was being trained.

He writes "RECRUITMENT" next.

"The games identify people with the right mindset. Not just tech skills, those can be taught. But the way of thinking. Persistence. Creativity. Pattern recognition." He taps the marker against the board. "Most players never know they're being evaluated. But the best ones get noticed."

Third word: "INTELLIGENCE"

"This is what you stumbled into. Challenges like 'Trace the Knights' aren't just academic exercises. Players think they're earning points for historical research, but really they're helping us build profiles, map connections, identify targets."

Holy crap. My submission for that challenge. The three KOTR operations I documented. I wasn't just solving a puzzle. I was actually helping with a real investigation.

"And the players who disappear?" My voice comes out smaller than I want. "BlackHat77 and the others?"

Dad's expression gets dark. He sets down the marker and turns to face me fully.

"KOTR has their own people in the games. Watchers. Hunters. When they identify someone getting too close, asking wrong questions, making connections that threaten them, they act."

"Sometimes that means threats," Mom adds. "Anonymous messages. Doxxing. Psychological pressure."

"And sometimes worse," Dad finishes. "We've lost players. Not many, but some. People who pushed too hard and attracted attention from the wrong people."

"There was one player," I say slowly, the memory surfacing. "BlackHat77. Their last message said something weird, that KOTR isn't the real enemy, that the games are a recruitment tool for something. They got cut off before they could finish."

Dad and Mom exchange another one of their looks. The kind that says they know exactly what I'm talking about.

"BlackHat77 was getting close to something," Dad says carefully. "But they had it backwards. KOTR plants disinformation in the forums, makes people think we're the bad guys, that they're the ones fighting for freedom against some shadowy government conspiracy. It's effective. Some players buy into it completely."

"So BlackHat77 was... turned? By KOTR?"

"Not turned. Confused. They found real evidence that the games have a purpose beyond competition (which is true) and KOTR fed them a story about what that purpose was." Dad's jaw tightens. "By the time they started spreading that narrative in the competitor chat, KOTR had already identified them as useful. A messenger. And when they'd served that purpose..."

He doesn't finish. He doesn't have to.

KOTR silenced their own asset. Someone who genuinely believed they were exposing the truth, used and discarded the moment they became inconvenient.

That's somehow worse than if BlackHat77 had just been asking dangerous questions. They thought they were helping. They died thinking they were a hero.

"So me and Melissa," I say slowly, "we've been competing in a shadow war without even knowing it. Getting trained for a job we didn't apply for. Being watched by both sides."

"Pretty much."

"Cool. Great. Love that for us." I know I'm being sarcastic but I can't help it. It's either that or completely freak out, and I've already done enough crying for one night. The sarcasm feels like armor, not great armor, but better than nothing.

***

"I never wanted you involved in this," Dad says quietly. He sits back down across from me, closer now. "When you were born, I swore I'd keep this world away from you. Train you to protect yourself, sure, teach you to think critically, understand technology, question things. But never to fight our battles."

A memory surfaces. Dad teaching me to ride a bike in our backyard when I was seven. I kept falling, getting frustrated, wanting to quit. He sat down next to me in the grass and said, "The secret isn't balance. The secret is being okay with falling. You fall, you learn something. You fall again, you learn something else. Eventually you've learned so much that falling isn't the problem anymore."

That was always his thing, turning everything into a lesson without making it feel like a lecture. Making me feel smart instead of stupid. I'd forgotten that about him. Two years of grief has a way of flattening memories, reducing a whole person to a photograph and a feeling of loss.

Now he's sitting across from me, real and alive, with that same patient way of explaining things. The same way of making complicated stuff feel manageable.

"Then why let me into the games at all?" The question's been bugging me since I saw those messages on Mom's phone. "Mom could've stopped me. You could've had someone scare me off. Why let me keep climbing?"

Dad sighs and it's this heavy, tired sound. "By the time we realized you were SirBreaksAlot, you'd already contacted StarBreaker. Already started asking about KOTR. Already solved challenges that showed real talent."

"Pulling you out would've looked suspicious," Mom explains. "A promising climber suddenly withdrawing right after reaching Phase 2? KOTR's watchers would've noticed. They might've investigated. Connected you to us."

"So you watched instead. Let me keep going."

"We monitored. Protected where we could without revealing ourselves." Dad's voice gets heavy with something, regret maybe. "I argued with your mother about it constantly. She wanted to intervene. I thought letting you find your own way was safer long-term."

"'He needs to find his own way to the truth,'" I quote. "That was from your messages. I read them."

Dad's eyebrows go up. "You accessed your mother's phone?"

"I mean, yeah. I'm a shadow gamer. Breaking into stuff is kinda the whole point."

Despite everything, I see the corner of his mouth twitch. Is that... pride? From the man who just admitted to lying to me for two years?

"Melissa," I say suddenly, the thought hitting me. "StarBreaker. Is she part of this too?"

"Her father is one of ours," Mom confirms. "Similar situation, deep cover operator, different target. Melissa entered the games on her own, looking for answers about him. Just like you did."

"So we were both following in our dads' footsteps." My head is spinning. "Without knowing."

"The irony isn't lost on us," Dad says dryly. "You both inherited the same instincts, the same drive to understand. And you both ended up in the same place, asking the same questions."

"Does she know? About her dad being alive?"

"By now, yes. Her father's having a similar conversation with her tonight."

***

"What happens now?" The questions have run out. Now comes the scary part, decisions. "You said we might not be going back. Does that mean..."

"KOTR knows we've been compromised," Dad interrupts. "Not everything, but enough that they're looking harder than ever. The warning they sent Mom was a test. Seeing if we'd react, run, make mistakes."

"So we're in danger. Like, actual danger."

"Yes." Dad doesn't sugarcoat it. "All of us. You, your mother, me, Melissa and her family. Everyone connected to Operation Teardown."

I let that sink in. Not pretend danger. Not the nervous energy of breaking into Mom's office. Real threat-to-our-lives danger.

"Which means we have two choices," Dad continues. "Option one: extraction. We disappear, all of us, start over with new identities somewhere safe. New names, new locations, new everything. The operation continues without us. KOTR wins this round, but we survive."

I wait for option two.

"Option two: we accelerate. Take the risks, burn the covers, and take down KOTR before they can take us down. Use everything we've gathered over three years for one massive coordinated strike. It's faster, more dangerous, way more likely to fail." He pauses. "But if it works, it ends this. For good."

"Which one are you recommending?"

Dad looks at Mom. She gives this tiny nod, like a millimeter of movement.

"That depends on you, Jacob."

"Me?" I actually laugh. It comes out kinda manic. "I'm sixteen. I've been in the games for like three weeks. Why does this depend on me?"

"Because you're a variable we didn't plan for. Your involvement changes everything."

Dad leans forward. His eyes are intense in a way I've never seen before.

"You've proven yourself. Not just in the games, in everything. How you found the office. How you decoded the cipher with zero training. How you've been investigating, gathering intel, making connections, all without giving yourself away to anyone watching."

"I had help. Ethan. Melissa."

"You built a team. Assessed who you could trust and brought them in strategically." Dad's voice has this new weight to it. "That's an operational skill, Jacob. That's what we do."

Mom steps closer to the table. "You have instincts we can't teach. Pattern recognition. Determination. The ability to stay calm under pressure." She pauses. "Skills that took me years to develop, you've shown them naturally."

"So what are you saying?"

Dad takes a breath. I can see this is hard for him, not the conversation, but what he's about to offer.

"I'm saying we can't force you into this life. We won't. If you want to walk away, we'll arrange extraction and you never have to think about any of this again." He pauses. "But if you choose to stay, if you want to help us finish what we started, there's a place for you in Operation Teardown."

***

The question just hangs there. Everything I've wanted for two years (answers, reunion with my dad, a purpose beyond being the kid who breaks stuff) it's all right here.

But at what cost?

"What about school?" I ask. "My friends? Ethan doesn't know any of this. He thinks I've just been stressed about homework."

"If we go with extraction, everything changes," Dad says honestly. "New city. New school. New name, even. You'd have to leave Ethan behind. Leave everything behind."

My stomach drops. Ethan. The guy who just did KOTR research because he was worried about me. The guy who's been my best friend since fourth grade. I'd just... disappear on him? Let him think I moved away, or worse?

"But if we go with the accelerated plan," Mom adds, "and it works, we go back to normal life. Same house, same school, same friends. The threat would be eliminated, and we could actually stop hiding."

"Your cover as a normal student is actually valuable either way," Dad says. "Teenagers get overlooked. Underestimated. You can go places and do things that adult operatives can't."

"You've been using that already," Mom adds. "Nobody suspected a sixteen-year-old was behind some of the best Phase 2 solutions in the games."

So that's the real choice. Run and lose everything, but stay safe. Or fight and maybe get my normal life back, but risk losing everything in a different way.

I think about what I'd be giving up. A normal high school experience. The chance to just be Jacob, not SirBreaksAlot or some junior operative. Lazy weekends with Ethan, arguing about video games without worrying if someone's monitoring our conversations.

Then I think about what I'd be gaining. My dad, actually having him around, working with him instead of just missing him. The truth, not pieced together from stolen glimpses, but the full picture. A chance to stop people who hurt hospitals and charities and emergency services.

"Melissa," I say suddenly. "What about her? If I say yes, does she get the same offer?"

"She's being offered the same choice. Her father is reaching out tonight."

Two kids whose families kept impossible secrets. Two kids who found each other in the shadows and became partners without knowing how deep the connection really went.

Maybe we don't have to do this alone.

"I need to talk to her first," I say. "Before I decide anything. I gotta know what she's thinking, how she feels about all of this. We're in this together, whatever comes next."

Dad nods slowly. Something like approval in his eyes. "That's fair. More than fair, it's smart. You should coordinate with your team before making operational decisions."

He reaches across the table and puts his hand on my shoulder. First real contact since that brief hug, solid, warm, definitely real. After two years of nothing, the weight of his hand feels like an anchor pulling me back to something I'd lost.

"Whatever you choose, Jacob, I want you to know one thing."

I wait.

"I'm proud of you. Not because of what you've accomplished in the games, though that's impressive." His voice catches a little. "I'm proud because you stayed true to yourself through all of this. You didn't give up when things got hard. You didn't stop asking questions when the answers were scary. You kept pushing, kept growing, even when everything seemed impossible."

His eyes get kind of wet. My dad, who I've seen cry maybe twice in my entire life.

"You're everything I hoped you'd become. Everything and more."

I don't trust myself to talk. The emotions are too big, too mixed up, anger and relief and love and confusion all tangled together in a knot I can't even begin to untie. If I open my mouth, I don't know what will come out. Maybe words. Maybe screaming. Maybe just this sound that's been building in my chest for two years.

Part of me wants to say something back. Tell him I'm glad he's alive. That I missed him. That having him here, even like this, is better than the alternative. That the anger is real but so is the love underneath it, and I don't know how to hold both at the same time.

The two feelings are at war inside me, tearing at my chest. Relief so sharp it hurts. Anger so deep it feels bottomless. Love that never went away, even when I thought he was gone. Betrayal that cuts fresh every time I remember he chose to stay hidden.

I love you, I think but don't say. The words feel true even as I think them. But I don't know if I trust you anymore. And I'm not sure if love without trust is enough. Maybe that's the hardest part, loving someone you can't trust. Having your heart reach for them while your brain screams to pull away. How do you hold both at once? How do you love someone who hurt you that deeply and still believe them when they say they'll never do it again?

But another part, the part that spent two years grieving, two years talking to a photograph, two years carrying a hole in my chest where he used to be, that part won't let me say any of it. Not yet. The words feel like they'd be a betrayal of all those nights I cried into my pillow, all those mornings I woke up remembering he was gone.

How do you tell someone you love them and hate them at the same time? How do you say "I'm so glad you're alive" and "I'm so angry you let me think you were dead" in the same breath?

You can't. Not yet. Maybe not ever.

So I just nod. And for now, that's gotta be enough.

Dad seems to understand. He doesn't push for more. Doesn't try to force a moment that isn't ready to happen. Just squeezes my shoulder once, a weight that feels like home and like a stranger at the same time, and lets go.

The truth is out. But that doesn't mean everything's okay.

That's gonna take time. Maybe a lot of time. Maybe more time than we have.

And I'm not sure I'm ready to give it yet. But I'm here. He's here. And for now, that's something.

It has to be enough.

14

THE CHOICE

The secure facility has a small communications room tucked away at the end of a long corridor. Dad takes me there himself, his hand on my shoulder like he's afraid I might disappear if he lets go. The room is tiny, just a desk, a chair, and a video terminal that looks like it could survive a nuclear blast.

"Military-grade encryption," Dad explains as he types in an access code. "Multiple backup servers, rotating IPs, end-to-end protection. Even if someone intercepts the signal, all they'll get is garbage. No one can listen in."

"Not even you?"

He pauses with his hands on the keyboard. "Not even me. This is private, Jacob. You and Melissa need to talk without anyone else in your heads."

I'm surprised by that. After everything I've learned about secret operations and need-to-know and compartmentalized information, I expected them to monitor every conversation. The fact that they're giving us real privacy feels important. Like maybe they actually do want to earn our trust.

Dad finishes setting up the connection and steps back. "Take as long as you need. I'll be in the conference room when you're done."

The door closes behind him with a solid thunk. I'm alone with the terminal, its green cursor blinking in the darkness like a promise.

I type in Melissa's secure handle and wait.

***

When her face appears on the screen, she looks as wrecked as I feel. Dark circles under her eyes that look painted on. Hair pulled back all messy, like she gave up on making it presentable hours ago. The same haunted expression I probably see in my own mirror, the look of someone whose whole world just got turned inside out.

Even exhausted, even scared, even obviously running on coffee and adrenaline and sheer stubbornness... something about her makes it hard to look away. She has brown eyes that somehow look both tired and fierce at the same time. Her hair is dark, falling loose around her shoulders despite her attempt at pulling it back.

I realize I'm staring and force myself to focus.

"Jacob." Her voice is hoarse, like she's been crying or screaming or both. Probably both. "Tell me you're seeing the same crazy stuff I'm seeing."

"My dad's alive." Even saying it out loud still feels surreal. "He's been undercover inside KOTR for three years. My mom's been working with him the whole time, running tech support, maintaining his cover, pretending to be a single parent while actually coordinating secret operations. They want me to join some shadow organization to help take down the bad guys."

Melissa lets out a breathless laugh that sounds more like a sob. "My dad just showed up at our house with two agents in suits. Like, actual government agents with badges and serious faces. He's been 'embedded' with a contractor that tracks international hacker networks. The whole protective custody story was cover. He could have come home anytime, but the mission needed him to stay hidden."

"That's insane."

"It gets worse." She swallows hard. "Apparently my mom knew the whole time. She's been in on it from the beginning."

My jaw actually drops. "Your mom knew? The whole two and a half years?"

"Dad said keeping her in the loop was essential for his mental health. He needed someone on the outside who understood, who could tell him me and Dylan were okay. So she's been lying to us every single day, pretending to be worried about Dad, pretending not to know where he was, while actually getting regular updates."

She shakes her head, anger and hurt fighting across her face. "I'm still processing that one."

My mom had to go through it alone. No one to confide in, no support system, carrying the weight of the secret all by herself. I don't know if that's better or worse than what Melissa's mom did.

We sit in silence for a moment, pixels across screens, both of us trying to deal with the fact that our entire lives have been elaborate lies. That the parents we trusted were playing roles. That everything we thought we knew was a carefully managed illusion.

It's the strangest kind of solidarity, knowing someone else is going through the exact same thing at the exact same time. Like we're two people drowning in identical oceans, reaching for each other across the waves.

Part of me feels guilty for being relieved that I'm not alone. Grateful that someone else understands. But mostly I just feel seen, really seen, for the first time since all of this started. Melissa doesn't have to imagine what I'm going through. She knows. She's living it too.

"They asked me to join," Melissa says quietly, breaking the silence. "To make it official. Use my skills for the good guys. Help finish what our dads started."

"Same here. Dad gave me this whole speech about how I've proven myself, how I have instincts they can't teach. Like I should be flattered that they think I'm good enough for their secret war."

"Are you? Flattered, I mean?"

I think about it honestly. Part of me is, the part that spent years feeling like a disappointment, like a kid who just broke things instead of building them. But another part feels manipulated. Used.

"I don't know," I admit. "I don't know what I feel about anything right now."

"What are you gonna do?" I ask after another long silence.

Melissa is quiet for a while. On screen, I can see her looking at something off-camera, probably her dad, waiting in another room for her answer. Probably wearing that same anxious expression I saw on my parents' faces.

"I've spent eight months climbing the Shadow Games," she says finally, her voice slow and careful. "Eight months of late nights and puzzle-solving and worrying myself sick about what happened to my family. Eight months looking for answers."

"And now you have them."

"Yeah. Dad's alive. He's one of the good guys, at least according to him. Everything makes sense now, all the weird behavior before he disappeared, all the security paranoia, all the times he seemed distracted or worried." She pauses. "It should feel like relief."

"But?"

"But I don't know if I'm ready to be a soldier. Even a shadow one." Her voice wavers, cracking on the words. "I'm sixteen, Jacob. I should be worrying about college applications and AP exams and what dress to wear to prom. Not international hacker networks and undercover operations and people who might want to kill me."

I get exactly what she means. The weight of this decision isn't just about what happens next. It's about who we become. What kind of people we turn into.

"My dad said the same thing," I tell her. "That I shouldn't be involved in this. That he never wanted me in his world. But then he turns around and offers me a spot on the team like it's some kind of honor."

"Contradictory much?"

"Yeah." I lean back in my chair, staring at the ceiling of the secure room. Gray concrete, reinforced steel. The architecture of secrets. "What if we said no? What happens then?"

"I asked that," Melissa says. "Dad said they'd respect our choices. Extract us to new lives somewhere safe. New names, new schools, new everything. The operation continues without us, and we get to be normal kids again."

"Normal." The word tastes weird on my tongue. Like something from a foreign language I used to speak but forgot. "I don't think I know what that means anymore. Did I ever?"

"Me neither." She laughs, but it's hollow. "Three weeks ago, normal meant stressing about homework and avoiding bullies. Now normal feels like a costume I couldn't put back on even if I tried. You can't unknow the things we know now. Can't unsee what we've seen."

The words hit me harder than they should. She's right. Even if we walked away tomorrow, even if we pretended none of this happened, we'd always know the truth. We'd always see the shadows hiding in plain sight, the secrets lurking behind ordinary faces. The world has changed shape, and it's never going back.

***

We talk for over an hour. About our families, the real versions, the ones behind the masks we've been seeing our whole lives. About the games and how strange it feels to know they were never just a competition. About the future we can't quite imagine, the paths branching out in front of us like a maze with no exit in sight.

Melissa tells me about her little brother Dylan, how he's been confused and scared since their dad appeared, how she doesn't know what to tell him. I tell her about Ethan, my best friend who thinks I've just been stressed about homework, who has no idea that I've been living in a spy thriller without knowing it.

"He's gonna freak out," I say. "When I finally tell him. If I can tell him."

"My mom said we'll have to keep some things secret. Even from people we trust. That part never really goes away."

"More lies. Great."

"Necessary lies, supposedly." She doesn't sound convinced.

Eventually, Melissa asks the question that's been hanging between us, the one neither of us has wanted to say out loud.

"Do you trust them? Our parents?"

I think about it carefully. About the messages I read on Mom's phone, the cold way they talked about my progress, like I was a test subject. About the two years of lies, the elaborate cover stories, the nights I cried myself to sleep while Dad was apparently alive and well somewhere. About the fact that they made choices for me without ever asking what I wanted.

"I don't know," I admit honestly. "They kept the biggest possible secret from us. They let us believe our dads were gone, dead or disappeared or worse. That changes things. You can't unhear a lie like that."

"But they did it to protect us." Melissa sounds like she's trying to convince herself as much as me. "To keep us safe from KOTR. To make sure we couldn't accidentally give anything away."

"Maybe. Or maybe they did it because the mission was more important than our feelings. Because protecting their covers mattered more than their kids' mental health."

Melissa winces, the words hitting harder than I meant. "That's harsh, Jacob."

"It's true though. Right?" I lean forward, my reflection ghosting across the terminal screen. "They made a choice. Mission over family. Secret work over honest relationships. And now they're asking us to make the same choice, to put the operation over our own lives, our own safety, our own futures."

"So what do we do?"

I look at the encrypted terminal. At the reinforced walls of this underground facility. At my own face, thin and tired and older than it should be, reflected in the dark glass.

"I think," I say slowly, the idea forming as I talk, "we need to make them prove they've changed. That we're not just pieces to move around a board. That they actually want a relationship with us, not just access to our skills."

"How?"

"Conditions. Terms. If we join, it's on our terms, not theirs. We stay in school, keep our real lives as much as possible. They don't get to rip us out of everything or turn us into full-time operatives. And they tell us the truth from now on, the whole truth, about everything. No more secrets 'for our own protection.'"

Melissa's eyes light up, something sparking behind the exhaustion. "I like that. Force them to treat us like partners, not pawns."

"Exactly. Equal footing. Or as close to it as we can get."

***

We end the call with a plan. Each of us will give our conditions to our parents separately, negotiate as individuals, but as a united front. If they agree to our terms, really agree without trying to weaken them or add loopholes, we're in. If they don't, or if they try to manipulate us into giving up our autonomy, we walk.

It feels good to have some control back. Even if it's an illusion. Even if they could probably force us to do whatever they want. The act of demanding respect changes something basic in how we see ourselves.

We're not helpless kids anymore. We're negotiators. Partners in shadows, about to become partners in something bigger.

"Good luck," Melissa says before we disconnect.

"You too. Message me after?"

"Obviously. We're in this together, remember?"

"Partners."

"Partners."

The screen goes dark. I sit in the communications room for a few more minutes, gathering my thoughts, practicing what I want to say. Then I stand up and walk back to the conference room.

Time to negotiate.

***

When I enter the room, Dad and Mom are waiting. They're sitting closer together than before, like they moved toward each other while I was gone. Their faces are nervous, more nervous than

I've ever seen either of them. Dad's leg bounces under the table. Mom's hands are gripped together so tight her knuckles are white.

For a second, I see him as Alpha, the operative, the undercover legend who infiltrated KOTR and lived a lie for three years. But then he looks up and catches my eye, and I see something else. Hope. Fear. The desperate love of a father who's made terrible choices and knows it. That's not Alpha. That's just Dad, flawed, human, real.

I'm going to spend a long time figuring out which version is which. Maybe they're the same person. Maybe everyone is multiple people, depending on who's looking.

They're scared. Not of me, of losing me. Of having me say no and walk away forever.

That realization gives me strength.

"Well?" Dad asks, his voice trying to sound calm but totally not succeeding.

I take a deep breath. "I'll help. But I have conditions."

Dad's eyebrows go up a little. Mom's expression shifts to something I can't quite read. Surprise? Respect?

"We're listening," she says.

***

I lay it out step by step, the way they taught me to approach problems. Point by point, term by term.

First: school. I stay enrolled. I finish high school, go to college, keep my grades and my friendships and my normal life. The operation doesn't get to eat everything.

Second: transparency. No more lies. No more half-truths. No more "you're not ready for that information." If something affects me or Melissa, we get told about it. Period.

Third: partnership. We're not junior agents or trainees or mascots. We're equals at the table. Our opinions matter. Our safety isn't just something to consider. It's a priority.

Fourth: Melissa. Whatever deal they offer me, they offer her too. Same terms, same respect. We came into this together, and we stay together.

They hear me out without interrupting, which I appreciate. When I finish, there's a long moment of silence. Dad and Mom exchange another one of their wordless conversations, eyebrows raised, heads tilted, a whole dialogue happening in microseconds.

Dad clears his throat. "Some of that's... complicated. The transparency clause especially. There are compartmentalization proto cols..."

"Protocols." I let the word hang there. "You're already doing it again."

"Jacob..."

"You asked what I need to make this work. I told you. If the answer is 'no, operational security matters more than your trust,' then I guess we're done here."

I don't actually know if I mean it. But I hold his gaze like I do.

Another silent conversation between them. Mom puts her hand on Dad's arm, not restraining, just... communicating something. He exhales slowly.

Then Dad nods.

"Those are reasonable terms. More than reasonable. They're things we should have offered from the start. We got so wrapped up in operational security that we forgot you're not just potential assets. You're our son."

"Actions, not words," I push. "No convenient omissions. No 'we'll tell you later.' Full partnership, starting now."

"Full partnership," Dad agrees. "With appropriate safety consid-erations. There are some things that could put you in danger if you knew them, operational details about other undercover agents, for example. But we'll explain why we're holding back, not just shut you out. You'll know there's a secret even if you don't know what it is. That's different from pretending everything's open while lying to your face."

It's a compromise. Not perfect, but workable. Real partnership means understanding that not every piece of info can be shared, as long as the limitations are honest.

"Then I'm in."

Dad stands up slowly. For a second I think he's gonna hug me again, but instead he holds out his hand. Not a hug, something more formal. An agreement between equals. A handshake that means something.

I take it. His grip is firm, his palm rough from work I'm only starting to understand. For a second, I feel like I'm standing outside myself, watching this moment happen, hardly believing it's real. Jacob Mitchell, sixteen years old, shaking hands with his spy dad, agreeing to join a secret operation against international hackers.

What even is my life anymore?

"Welcome to Operation Teardown, Jacob. Let's take down KOTR together."

Mom comes around the table and puts her arms around both of us, a family embrace that feels more real than any we've had in years. Because this time, no one's hiding anything. No one's pretending. The secrets are out, the masks are off, and we're just... us. A family. Damaged and complicated and full of things we haven't said yet. But together.

We're finally all on the same side. For real this time.

***

That night, I lie awake in the small room they've given me at the facility. It's basic, just a bunk, a desk, and a lamp, but clean and secure. The kind of place designed for people who need to sleep somewhere safe, even if it's not home.

Tomorrow, everything changes. Dad will tell me about the current state of Operation Teardown, the intel they've gathered, the targets they've found, the plan to finally bring KOTR down. Mom will fill me in on what I accidentally discovered during my time in the games, connecting dots I didn't know existed.

And somewhere in California, Melissa is probably having the same sleepless night. Staring at the same kind of ceiling, wondering about the same uncertain future.

I pull out the phone they gave me, a new one, with crazy security features and encrypted channels and apps I don't recognize. The interface is sleek, minimal. Designed for people who need to communicate without being overheard.

I open our encrypted messenger and type:

"I'm in. You?"

Her response comes seconds later, fast enough that she must have been waiting: "Same. Guess we're shadow operatives now. Official and everything."

"How does it feel?"

"Weird. Scary. Kinda exciting? Is that messed up?"

"I don't think so. We spent months preparing for this without knowing it. Now we actually get to use what we learned."

"Partners in shadows."

I smile in the darkness, my face lit only by the phone's soft glow. "Partners."

"Terrified?"

"Absolutely. You?"

"Same. But at least we're terrified together."

There's a pause, then another message: "My dad said there's gonna be a briefing in two days. Both families together. Apparently the operation is speeding up."

"Mine said something similar. Guess KOTR forced their hand by threatening us."

"Silver lining: we get to meet in person. Finally."

I hadn't even thought about that. After weeks of text messages and voice calls and video chats, I'm actually gonna meet Melissa. Real handshake. Real face-to-face conversation. Maybe a real hug?

"Looking forward to it," I type.

"Same. Get some sleep, SirBreaksAlot. Tomorrow's a big day."

"Night, StarBreaker."

I put the phone down and stare at the ceiling again. The concrete is gray and boring, but somehow it doesn't feel depressing anymore.

For a long time, I just lie there. Not sleeping. Not really thinking either. Just... existing with the weight of everything that's happened.

The silence in the room is different from the silence at home. No familiar creaks of the house settling. No sound of Mom moving around downstairs. Just the low hum of climate control and the distant echo of footsteps in the corridor, agents changing shifts, maybe, or other operatives going about their mysterious business.

I try to imagine going back to normal life after this. Sitting in English class discussing symbolism in The Great Gatsby. Eating lunch with Ethan and pretending I care about who's dating who. Doing homework like any of it matters compared to what I now know exists in the world.

It feels impossible. Not just hard, literally impossible. Like trying to fit a shape into a hole it no longer matches.

The version of Jacob who did those things, normal Jacob, regular Jacob, the kid who just broke laptops and worried about grades, he feels like someone I read about in a book. A character from a different story. I can remember being him, but I can't quite feel it anymore.

Is this what growing up is? Losing access to the person you used to be, one revelation at a time?

For the first time since I found Mom's office, since I broke into her secret world and started down this path, I don't feel alone. Whatever comes next, the dangers, the challenges, the impossible odds, I'll face it with people who understand.

My dad. My mom. Melissa. Maybe even Ethan, once I figure out how much I can tell him.

The shadows aren't so dark anymore. Not when you have people standing beside you.

Something loosens in my chest, a knot I've been carrying for so long I forgot it was there. The loneliness I'd gotten used to, the constant feeling of being the only one who knew the truth, the exhausting weight of secrets I couldn't share... it's not gone, exactly. But it's lighter. Shared. Split among people who actually understand what it means to carry it.

Three weeks ago, I was just a kid who broke things. Now I'm... what? A junior spy? A shadow operative? A sixteen-year-old who said yes to something he doesn't fully understand and is trying really hard not to freak out about it?

All of the above, probably.

I close my eyes and, eventually, sleep comes. And for the first time in weeks, I don't dream about Dad's empty chair or Mom's locked door or the questions that kept me awake.

I dream about what comes next.

15

The Briefing

The briefing room looks like something straight out of a spy movie. Which I guess makes sense, since we're apparently in an actual spy facility now.

Massive screens cover three walls, each showing different stuff. News headlines scrolling by, weird network traffic patterns with red blotches that probably mean something bad, and this constantly updating map with glowing dots all over the world. I have no idea what any of it means, but it looks super important.

Getting here was insane. We went through like a dozen security checkpoints that made airport screening look like a joke. Retinal scans where I had to stand perfectly still while a blue light mapped my eyeballs. Voice verification where I had to repeat some random phrase three times until the system was satisfied. A full-body scanner that Dad said could probably detect my dental fillings. By the time we reached this room, I felt like the government now had a database entry that knows more about my body than I do.

Creepy? Yes. Cool? Also yes. I hate that I think it's cool.

Dad stands at the front of the room, looking like a totally different person than the father I remember. Professional. Focused. In charge. His casual clothes are gone. Now it's a crisp shirt and tactical pants, posture all military-straight. When he talks, his voice has this weight to it. Like someone who's been doing this forever.

"KOTR has been planning something big," he says, clicking a remote. The main screen changes to show three words in bold red letters: PROJECT NIGHTFALL. "Based on intel we've gathered, they're preparing coordinated attacks on multiple targets across the US."

My stomach drops. The screen changes again to show a list:

- Power Grid (6 states on the East Coast)
- Water Treatment Facilities (12 locations)
- Hospital Networks (NYC, LA, Chicago, Houston, Phoenix)
- Air Traffic Control (several major airports)
- 911 Emergency Services (15 major cities)

I'm staring at the list trying to process what I'm seeing. This isn't just hacking for money or making a statement. This is like... terrorist stuff. Real terrorist stuff. The kind of thing you see on the news and think "that'll never happen here."

Except now it might.

"If they succeed," Dad continues, his voice grim, "it's gonna be catastrophic. Blackouts affecting thirty million people, and that's if we're lucky. Could spread to more connected grids. Maybe half the eastern seaboard goes dark."

He clicks to the next slide. Maps with water systems highlighted.

"Water supplies messed with or shut off completely. The treatment plants they're targeting use these SCADA systems..." He pauses when he sees my confused face. "Sorry. It's like the computer brains that control the water treatment. They're pretty easy to hack if you know what you're doing. One piece of malware and suddenly the chemicals are wrong, or everything just shuts down."

Another click. Hospital stuff now.

"Hospitals can't monitor patients or access records. Imagine someone in the ICU on life support and suddenly all the screens go dark. Imagine a surgeon in the middle of an operation when the power fails."

I feel sick. Actually sick, like I might throw up right here in this fancy briefing room. My palms are sweating and my mouth has gone completely dry. This isn't a game anymore, not that it ever really was. But hearing it spelled out like this, seeing the numbers, imagining the actual human beings who would suffer...

It makes everything we've been doing suddenly, terrifyingly real.

"And this is the worst part." Click. Emergency services. "911 systems go down. Someone has a heart attack, calls for help, and the call goes nowhere. Or it goes to the wrong place. Or it gets through but the ambulance routing is broken."

"When?" I ask. My voice comes out all wrong, thin and scared. Not the voice of someone who just agreed to join a secret operation.

"We think they're about two weeks from launch. Maybe less." Dad pulls up a timeline showing a bunch of intercepted communications and money transfers and movement patterns. Red dots moving across a map of the country, all converging on different cities. "They've been moving people and equipment into position for months. We're watching them test their attack methods right now."

"Can we stop it?" The question that actually matters.

"That's the plan. But we need more info than we have. We know the targets but not exactly how they're gonna attack each one. We know roughly when but not the exact trigger." Dad's voice is steady now, confident. "Every day that passes is another day KOTR gets closer to being ready."

***

The next hour is basically a crash course in how KOTR works. My brain is struggling to keep up, and I'm pretty sure I've missed like half of what Dad's saying.

He walks me through their organizational structure using these diagrams that look like evil corporate org charts.

▾

"They operate through seven cells, each kinda independent." He points to different nodes on the screen. "Cell Alpha does malware development. They created the ransomware that hit those charities. Custom code that's constantly changing to avoid detection."

I nod like I understand, even though I'm only getting about seventy percent of this.

"Cell Beta handles social engineering, that's like, tricking people. Fake emails, pretend phone calls, fake social media profiles. Human hacking, basically."

Okay, that part I get. I've read about that stuff on ScyberSpace.

"Cell Gamma does the physical stuff. Actually breaking into buildings, planting hardware, compromising systems that aren't connected to the internet by getting boots on the ground."

"Wait, so they actually sneak into places? Like Mission Impossible style?"

Dad almost smiles. "More like fake delivery guy style. Walking through the front door with a fake ID and a confident attitude works better than rappelling through skylights."

He goes through the rest. Cell Delta does money laundering with cryptocurrency and shell companies, Cell Epsilon handles recruitment through online forums and the Shadow Games themselves, Cell Zeta runs counter-intelligence to catch infiltrators like Dad, and Cell Eta handles what he calls "direct action."

I'm pretty sure that last one means the people who made BlackHat77 disappear.

"The cells don't know about each other's operations," Dad explains. "If one gets caught, the others stay hidden. Even within cells, everyone only knows what they absolutely need to know."

"But you know about all of them."

"Most of them." There's this weight in his voice. Three years of pretending to be someone he's not. "Every handshake, every encrypted message, every payment I processed, all of it feeding into this picture."

He pulls up a new diagram. An org chart with some photos attached, some question marks.

"This is KOTR's leadership as we know it. Cell leaders here," he points to the middle level, "regional coordinators here, and at the top..."

A single question mark, bigger than all the others. It pulses on the screen like it's mocking us.

"The Architect," Dad says. "That's what the inner circle calls them. The person who founded KOTR, sets the agenda, approves major operations. Nobody knows their real identity, not even the cell leaders. All communication goes through encrypted dead drops and anonymous channels."

"So we don't know who's in charge?"

"Not yet. But we're close. The Shadow Games have helped identify patterns we couldn't see from inside. Melissa's research. Your OSINT work. The combined intelligence from hundreds of competitors, it adds up."

Mom steps forward. "Which brings us to your role, Jacob."

***

"The Meeting," Mom says. "You've heard of it?"

I nod slowly. The invitation-only event that Melissa mentioned. The one where top competitors might meet the mysterious sponsors. The one that sounded too good to be true, and too dangerous.

"It's happening in three days. Here in the DC area." Mom pulls up satellite imagery of a modern-looking conference center. Glass and steel, surrounded by parking lots. Looks like any boring corporate building. "We've confirmed that several KOTR cell leaders will be there, posing as 'game sponsors.'"

"So The Meeting is actually a KOTR thing?"

"Partly." Dad takes over. "Our organization runs the Shadow Games. But KOTR embedded themselves as co-sponsors, a partnership neither side fully trusts. They use the event to scout top performers for recruitment. We use it to identify their agents and gather intel."

"A game within a game," I murmur.

"Exactly. Both sides pretending to cooperate while actually competing. Both watching, waiting for the other to mess up."

I think about BlackHat77 and the other competitors who vanished. About the warnings in the forums. About the feeling I had, even before I knew all this, that the Shadow Games were way more than they appeared.

"The players who disappear," I say slowly. "KOTR either recruits them or..."

"Takes them out. Yeah." Dad pulls up my player profile. Sir-BreaksAlot, rank 24, 1,847 points. "Which is why your participation is valuable."

"You're high enough to get attention from both sides," Mom explains. "Young enough to be underestimated. Talented enough to be interesting. At The Meeting, you'll have access to areas and people that adult operatives can't reach."

"You want me to go undercover." The words sound insane coming out of my mouth. "At The Meeting."

Undercover. At sixteen. In a room full of people who blow up hospitals and make witnesses disappear.

"With full support," Mom adds quickly. She must see the terror on my face. "We'll have operatives everywhere, disguised as competitors, catering staff, security, venue workers. You'll have communication equipment that can't be detected. Extraction plans for every scenario. You won't be alone."

"What am I supposed to do?"

Dad zooms in on the conference center floor plan. Multiple levels, tons of rooms, service corridors winding through like veins. Emergency exits marked in green. Blind spots in the camera coverage highlighted in yellow.

"The Meeting will be a distribution point. Our intel says KOTR will use the event to share final coordinates and timing for Project Nightfall with their cell leaders. Encrypted data, probably on physical drives to avoid network interception."

"You want me to steal the coordinates."

"We want you to identify which attendees are KOTR leadership. Track their movements. Document who they talk to, what rooms they enter, what devices they use. And if you can safely copy any data they share..." He trails off.

"The more we know about Nightfall," Mom adds, "the better our chances of stopping it. Every piece of intel you gather could save lives."

I try to process all this. Undercover at a hacker gathering. Surrounded by people who'd kill me, actually kill me, not just virtually, if they figured out who I really was. Trying to steal information from cyberterrorists while pretending to be just another teenage competitor.

It sounds impossible. Insane. The kind of thing that only works in movies where the hero has plot armor and a guarantee of surviving.

It sounds exactly like what I've been accidentally training for this whole time.

Which is somehow even more terrifying.

***

"One more thing," Dad says, his voice softening a bit. "Melissa's been briefed on the same operation. Her father wants her to participate too."

My heart jumps. "She's gonna be at The Meeting?"

"If she agrees. We're giving you both the same choice, full autonomy. If either of you doesn't feel ready, you don't have to do this. There are other ways to get the intel."

"But none as good as us," I say, getting the unspoken part.

"No. None as good. But that doesn't mean we'll force you into danger. Your safety matters more than any intel. If you say no, we figure out another way."

I think about Melissa. About our promise to face this together. About the months we spent climbing the leaderboard, preparing for something neither of us understood.

"Did you talk to her? About her decision?"

"Her briefing is happening right now. Same time as ours. Her father's walking her through the same stuff."

I pull out my secure phone and text: "Did they tell you about The Meeting?"

Her reply comes almost instantly: "Just finished. My dad looks like he aged ten years explaining it. What do you think?"

"Terrifying."

"Same. Like actually terrifying. Not movie scary. Real world consequences scary."

I glance at my parents. They're giving me space to process, watching with expressions that mix hope and fear.

"Same," I type back. "But also kinda exciting? Is that messed up?"

"I've been thinking about this for 8 months. All those puzzles, all those late nights, all that training we didn't know was training. This is what it was building toward."

"Partners?"

"Partners. I'm in if you're in."

"Then let's do this."

I look up at my parents. Dad's face is carefully neutral but I can see the hope in his eyes. Mom's gripping her own hands so hard her knuckles are white.

"She's in. And so am I."

The relief that washes over their faces tells me more than words ever could. They didn't want to ask this of us. Didn't want their kids in danger. But they also know that sometimes the only way out is through.

"Then we have work to do," Dad says. "Let's get you ready."

***

The rest of the day is intense. Like, way more intense than I expected.

They fit me with a tiny earpiece that sits deep in my ear canal. Totally invisible from outside. Activated by a specific frequency that sounds like background noise to anyone else but carries Dad's voice, Mom's voice, instructions from whoever's watching over me.

A watch that looks completely normal but has a hidden camera inside. The lens is hidden in what looks like a scratch on the glass. Dad shows me how to angle my wrist to record video, how to check storage with a series of button taps, how to wipe the memory if I'm about to get searched.

"Very James Bond," I mutter.

"James Bond wishes he had our tech," Mom says with a rare smile.

Shoes with GPS trackers in the heels. Another tracker sewn into my jacket. "Redundancy," Mom explains. "If one fails, others keep working. We'll always know where you are."

A phone that looks normal but isn't. Encrypted protocols, a panic button disguised as a game app, storage for any data I manage to copy. The lock screen shows a picture of me and Ethan from last summer, normal teenager stuff, but behind it is hardware that cost more than our house.

Then there's a pen that can copy USB drives just by touching them. Hold it against the drive for five seconds and it uploads everything to a secure server.

They drill me on cover stories until I can say them in my sleep. My name stays Jacob, keeping my first name reduces the chance of not responding when someone calls me. I'm a homeschooled kid from Virginia with a single mom in IT. Found the Shadow Games through ScyberSpace about a month ago. Interested in security as a career. Nervous about meeting other competitors but excited to see what the games are really about.

Code phrases for different situations get hammered into my brain. If I say "the coffee here is terrible," it means I'm in trouble and need extraction now, teams move in within thirty seconds. If I tap my right ear twice, I need to talk privately with handlers. If I scratch my left wrist, I've spotted someone from the intelligence briefings. If I say "I'm ready to leave," extraction teams move in within sixty seconds.

"What if I actually just want coffee?" I ask.

"Then you say 'I could use some coffee,'" Dad says patiently. "Or 'is there coffee around here?' Anything except 'the coffee here is terrible.'"

"No pressure," I mutter.

"All the pressure," he corrects. "But pressure creates diamonds. And you're already proving to be diamond-quality."

By the time we're done, my head is spinning with scenarios and signals and backup plans. I know what to do if I'm confronted. What to do if I get separated. What to do if I recognize a KOTR operative. What to do if someone recognizes me.

But underneath all the anxiety is something else. Excitement. Purpose. The feeling that all of this actually matters.

This is what Dad prepared me for, whether he meant to or not. All those years of messing with computers. The tinkering. The curiosity. The pattern recognition. Learning to stay calm when stuff goes wrong.

I'm not just a kid who breaks things anymore.

I'm apparently an operative now. A sixteen-year-old spy with gadgets sewn into his clothes and code words memorized for every disaster scenario. Two weeks ago I was stressing about homework. Now I'm preparing to infiltrate a gathering of cyberterrorists.

Life comes at you fast, I guess.

I have a mission. And for the first time in my life, the things I'm good at, the obsessive puzzle-solving, the pattern recognition, the ability to stay calm when everything goes wrong, might actually matter. Might actually save lives.

No pressure.

***

That night, I video chat with Melissa one more time. Her face appears on screen looking like I feel, exhausted and wired at the same time. Dark circles under her eyes but those eyes are bright with something that could be fear or anticipation. Maybe both.

"Three days," she says. "Three days until we walk into a room full of cyberterrorists."

"When you say it like that, it sounds like a terrible plan."

"It's definitely a terrible plan." She grins, and I find myself smiling back. "But it's our terrible plan. And we're gonna crush it."

"What if we don't though?" The fears I've been pushing down bubble up, breaking through the surface like something I can't control anymore. "What if something goes wrong? What if they figure out who we are? What if we can't get the intel?"

My voice sounds small. Scared. Not the voice of someone who agreed to be a junior operative. Just a sixteen-year-old kid realizing how in over his head he really is.

"Then our parents pull us out. They promised full support, full backup, immediate extraction if needed. We're not alone, Jacob."

"But what if..."

"What if extraction fails? What if they're too late? What if KOTR has better security than we think?" She reads my mind. "I've been through those questions too. Like a hundred times since the briefing. And you know what I realized?"

"What?"

"Every path has risks. Doing nothing is risky. KOTR launches Nightfall, thousands of people get hurt, and we spend the rest of our lives knowing we could've helped but didn't. Doing something is risky. We might get caught, might fail. But at least we're trying."

I want to believe her. And mostly I do. But part of me can't forget that our parents are professional liars. They kept secrets for years, looked us in the face, and said things they knew weren't true. How do I know they're being honest now?

I guess I don't. I just have to trust them.

And maybe that's okay. Trust doesn't mean certainty. Trust means choosing to believe when you can't be sure.

"Get some sleep," Melissa says. "We're gonna need it."

"You too. See you in the shadows."

"See you in the shadows."

The screen goes dark. I lie back and stare at the ceiling, running scenarios through my head.

Somewhere out there, KOTR is planning to hurt thousands of people. Hospitals going dark. Emergency services failing. Power grids crashing.

And somehow, two sixteen-year-olds are part of the plan to stop them.

No pressure at all.

I close my eyes and try to sleep, but my brain won't stop spinning. The faces from KOTR's leadership chart. The floor plan of the conference center. The list of targets that suffer if we fail.

Three days.

In three days, everything changes.

Either we stop them, or we don't. Either we pull this off, or we become another statistic in KOTR's history of making problems disappear.

But lying here in the dark, fear mixing with something else, determination maybe, I realize something. I'd rather face this challenge and fail than never try at all. I'd rather know I did everything I could.

The thought settles something inside me. Not confidence exactly. I'm still terrified. But something more solid than fear. Acceptance, maybe. Of who I am. Of what I'm choosing to do. Of the person I'm becoming.

Three weeks ago, I was a kid who broke things and felt useless about it. Now I'm choosing to be something more. Choosing to try, even when the odds are impossible. Choosing to matter.

The shadows are calling.

And I'm ready to answer.

16

The Meeting

The conference center looks totally normal from the outside. Like, aggressively normal. Generic glass-and-steel building in a boring office park, the kind of place where PowerPoint presentations go to die. The parking lot is full of regular cars. The landscaping is nice but forgettable. Nothing about it screams "secret hacker gathering inside."

Which I guess is the point.

I adjust my tie for like the tenth time. I hate ties. They feel like someone's slowly strangling me, but apparently "young professional" was the cover they picked. Great.

I walk toward the entrance, trying to look casual. Confident. Like I totally belong here and definitely haven't spent the last three days memorizing code phrases and escape routes.

Dad's voice comes through the earpiece, low and steady. "Looking good, Jacob. Posture is relaxed, expression is natural. Remember: observe first, act second. We have eyes on all entrances and exits. You're never alone."

"Copy," I murmur, barely moving my lips. The mic hidden in my collar picks it up.

The lobby is way nicer than I expected. Sleek furniture in grays and blues. Abstract art on the walls that probably costs more than my house. A registration desk where someone in a crisp suit checks my invite.

Something prickles at the back of my neck, that weird feeling you get when you're being watched. I glance around casually, the way Dad taught me during our briefing sessions. Nothing obvious. Just other competitors milling about, checking phones, looking as nervous as I feel. But the feeling doesn't go away. Cameras, probably. Lots of them. Hidden in the ceiling fixtures, behind those abstract paintings, embedded in the walls. This place is a surveillance machine dressed up as a conference center.

I hold up my phone showing the QR code that took our organization two days to fake. According to Dad, there's some constantly-shifting encryption thing that makes it look legit. If anyone scans it too closely... well, let's not think about that.

"SirBreaksAlot, ranked 24th in the Shadow Games competitive division." The guy hands me a lanyard with my screen name in big white letters. "Welcome to The Meeting. Main event is in Ballroom A, starts in about forty minutes. Refreshments in the atrium. Networking on the second floor. Have a good time."

I nod and head for the metal detectors. My heart is pounding so loud I'm sure everyone can hear it. If my equipment gets detected, if alarms go off, if anyone asks questions...

Nothing. No alarms. No weird looks. The regular phone they took at the door is a decoy, loaded with innocent apps and boring search history. All the real stuff (the watch camera, the earpiece, the GPS trackers, the magic pen) passed right through.

I'm in.

Holy crap, I'm actually in. A sixteen-year-old just walked past security at a gathering of cyberterrorists carrying enough spy equipment to outfit a small agency.

My legs feel wobbly. Relief and terror mixing together until I can't tell them apart. Part of me wants to laugh, the absurdity of this whole situation hitting me all at once. Part of me wants to run straight back out the door I just came in.

Either their tech is inferior to ours, or I just used up all my luck for the next ten years.

***

Inside the main venue, I'm hit by a wall of sensory overload.

Hundreds of people everywhere, all wearing lanyards with hacker aliases. NightShade. PhantomByte. CipherQueen. Names I recognize from the competitor chat, now attached to actual faces. Most of them look surprisingly normal, nothing like the hoodie-wearing stereotypes from movies. Business casual clothes. Polished shoes. The kind of people you'd see at any tech conference.

Except everyone here can probably break into systems that regular people don't even know exist.

Giant screens cover the walls showing the Shadow Games leaderboard in real-time (my name, 24th place, glowing in green), live challenge feeds, scrolling chat from the competitor hub. Music thumps from hidden speakers, electronic beats mixed with ambient tones. It's like a nightclub crossed with a security conference.

It's also, potentially, a trap.

Somewhere in this room, hidden among all these competitors and curious newbies, are KOTR cell leaders. The people who planned Project Nightfall. The people who want to crash hospitals and power grids and kill thousands.

I have to find them. Identify them. Document everything without giving myself away.

"Take your time," Dad murmurs in my ear. "You're doing great. Get a feel for the room before you start moving with purpose."

***

The first hour is all about watching. I drift through the crowd, nodding at people whose screen names I recognize from months of online interaction. Most are friendly but guarded. Everyone knows they're surrounded by strangers who might be friends or enemies or something way worse.

I grab sparkling water from the refreshment table, nothing that could mess with my head, and position myself near a group of mid-ranked players talking about Phase 2 challenges.

"The spectral analysis one almost killed me," someone with a CodeMonkey lanyard is saying. "Took me three days to crack the SSTV encoding."

"Three days? Amateur." Another player laughs. "Got it in twelve hours. The trick is recognizing the frequency patterns."

I nod along, contributing just enough to seem engaged. Normal competitor behavior. Nothing suspicious.

Across the room, I spot a familiar lanyard. StarBreaker. Melissa.

She's wearing glasses I've never seen, probably with cameras built in, like my watch. Her expression is carefully neutral, but I can see the tension in her shoulders. She's scared too.

But even scared, she's working. I watch her for just a second, watch her do what she does best. She's not looking at the screens or the tech like I was. She's looking at the people. Reading them. I can almost see her cataloging information: who stands too close together (allies), who avoids eye contact (hiding something), who checks their phones obsessively (waiting for orders). While I analyze systems, she analyzes humans. Different skills, same goal.

Our eyes meet across the crowded room. She gives this tiny nod, barely visible unless you're looking for it.

We agreed not to interact directly. Two players suddenly becoming best friends at The Meeting would look weird to anyone watching. Better to work separately, cover more ground, compare notes later. Partners in shadows, even when we can't acknowledge each other. Me gathering technical intel; her mapping the social landscape.

I look away and keep moving. Work to do.

***

A cluster of people near the bar catches my attention. They're different from the other competitors, older, late twenties or early thirties, and they move with this confidence that suggests they're in charge. While everyone else mingles nervously, these people hold court like they own the place.

One of them has a lanyard that says "Sponsor" in gold letters instead of white.

I drift closer, pretending to check my phone while angling my watch to record video. The camera is invisible, hidden in what looks like a scratch on the glass.

"...timeline is tight, but achievable," one of them is saying. Male, dark hair, expensive suit that doesn't quite fit the tech conference vibe. "Everything converges on Sunday. Final pieces are already in position."

"And the assets are ready?" Another man, older, gray at his temples, eyes constantly scanning the room.

"Waiting for coordinates. Once we distribute tonight, there's no going back. Cells Alpha through Delta get their packages within the hour."

Project Nightfall. They're talking about Project Nightfall. Right here, surrounded by hundreds of witnesses who have no idea what they're hearing.

I keep my face completely blank. Every acting skill I've ever used to lie to Mom about broken computers, I'm using them all right now. My heart is racing so hard I'm surprised it's not visible, but my expression stays mildly bored. Just a young competitor checking his phone.

These are the people we're looking for. Cell leaders. KOTR leadership.

"Phoenix, you're getting too close," Dad warns in my ear. "Circle back. You're in their peripheral vision."

Phoenix. That's my operational code name. I almost forgot.

I start to move away, but not before one of the sponsors looks directly at me. His eyes are sharp, calculating. The kind of eyes that see everything.

"SirBreaksAlot," he says, reading my lanyard. His smile doesn't reach his eyes. "I've been watching your progress. Impressive climb for a newcomer."

Every instinct screams at me to run. Make an excuse and disappear into the crowd. But that would look suspicious. A competitor walking away from a sponsor's attention would raise red flags.

I force a casual smile. "Thanks. Just trying to keep up with everyone else."

"More than keeping up. You've shown real talent, instincts that can't be taught. The way you approached the Analyst challenge was particularly creative." He extends a hand. "They call me Granite. I coordinate... special opportunities for high performers."

I shake his hand, hoping my fear doesn't show. His grip is firm. Confident. The grip of someone used to being in control.

"Special opportunities?"

"Let's just say the Shadow Games are just the beginning. For the right people, people with the right skills and mindset, there are paths beyond the public competition. Greater challenges. Greater rewards. Greater impact."

This is it. The recruitment pitch. The moment we prepared for without knowing it.

"Sounds interesting," I say carefully, trying to keep my voice level despite the adrenaline flooding my system. "What kind of paths?"

***

Granite leads me to a quieter corner of the ballroom, away from the crowd. Every step feels wrong. Breaking away now, making a scene, calling for help, trying to run, would blow my cover completely.

"The games identify talent," Granite explains, his voice low enough that only I can hear. "They filter out the pretenders from the genuine article. But talent without direction is just potential. We offer direction. Purpose. A chance to make a real impact."

"Impact how?"

"Depends on your skills and interests. Some recruits focus on offensive operations, penetration testing, zero-day development, the kinds of challenges that need creativity and precision. Others specialize in intelligence, OSINT, pattern analysis, connecting dots others miss."

"I'm more of a puzzle solver," I say. "I like figuring things out. Understanding how systems work, finding weak points."

"Excellent. Analysts are always in demand." Granite studies me with those unnervingly intelligent eyes. "But I sense you're looking for something specific. Not just skills development. Something personal."

I hesitate. How much does he know? Has KOTR been watching me this whole time? Do they know about Dad, about Mom, about everything?

"I'm looking for the truth," I say finally. The words come out before I can stop them. "About some things that happened to people I care about."

Granite nods slowly. "The truth is valuable. One of the most valuable commodities in our world. But it comes at a cost. Information wants to be free, but freedom is never truly free. Are you prepared to pay that cost?"

Before I can answer, a commotion erupts near the main stage. Someone's talking into a microphone, their amplified voice cutting through the noise. The crowd parts to let them through.

"Excuse me," Granite says, his whole demeanor shifting from recruitment to business. "I'm needed for the main presentation. We'll continue this later, SirBreaksAlot. Don't go anywhere."

He disappears into the crowd. I stand there, pulse pounding, trying to process what just happened.

I was just recruited. By KOTR. By someone who definitely knows more about me than a random sponsor should.

And they're about to hand out the Project Nightfall coordinates.

***

The main stage lights up with dramatic colors. Blue shifting to purple shifting to red. A figure in a completely white mask steps up to the podium. No features at all, just smooth, almost sculptural blankness. The voice that comes out is distorted, processed through speakers until there's no way to identify the original.

"Welcome, champions of the shadows."

The crowd goes quiet. Hundreds of hackers all staring at a masked figure like disciples waiting for a sermon.

Could this be The Architect? The mysterious leader Dad mentioned, the one nobody's ever identified? Or just another layer of performance, another mask hiding another mask? I file the question away. Either way, this person commands the room like they own it.

"Tonight, we celebrate excellence. We recognize achievement. We honor those who have proven themselves worthy of the path we walk." The voice pauses. "And for a select few, we offer something more. We offer... ascension."

The crowd cheers. It's bizarre, all these smart, talented people applauding a mystery figure like fans at a rock concert. But I get the psychology. They've spent months proving themselves. Working toward this. They want to believe it means something.

"The Shadow Games have identified the best among you. The most skilled. The most dedicated. The most aligned with our vision of a world where information is truly free."

Free. I remember that word from the KOTR manifestos I researched. They believe information should be "free" from governments and corporations. Their methods of "freeing" information have destroyed careers, ruined organizations, gotten people killed.

"Tonight, we distribute the next phase," the masked figure continues. "Our highest-ranked competitors will receive encrypted packages containing special assignments. Complete these assignments, and you earn your place in the inner circle. Fail... and your journey ends here."

Encrypted packages. That's gotta be the Nightfall coordinates. The attack vectors. The timing.

"Assignments will be distributed to the top fifty competitors via secure terminal. Access begins in fifteen minutes."

The crowd heads toward a row of computer terminals along one wall, sleek machines with privacy screens so no one can see what the person next to them is doing. I spot Melissa moving that way, head up, posture confident. She's ranked higher than me, so she definitely qualifies.

My earpiece crackles. "Jacob, we need those packages. Can you access a terminal?"

"I'm ranked 24th. I should qualify."

"Then get in line. Copy anything you can to your pen drive. We'll handle decryption on our end."

I start walking toward the terminals, hand in my pocket, fingers wrapped around the pen that looks ordinary but isn't.

But before I get there, a hand clamps down on my shoulder. Firm. Controlling. The kind of grip that says I'm not going anywhere.

Granite. His friendly expression from earlier is gone, replaced by something much more dangerous.

"SirBreaksAlot. We need to talk. Privately."

***

He steers me toward a side room. I realize with growing horror that I have no choice but to follow. Breaking away now, making a scene, calling for help, would blow everything. Everyone in the room would know something was wrong.

The room is small. Empty except for two chairs facing each other. The door closes behind us with a heavy click that sounds very final.

Granite turns to face me. His expression is completely different now.

"You asked about the truth earlier. Let me tell you a truth about yourself." He pulls out a tablet and shows me the screen. A dossier. My dossier.

"SirBreaksAlot. Real name: Jacob. Age: sixteen. Mother: Beth, alias BetaZone, known malware developer and suspected intelligence asset. Father: known as Alpha, KOTR operative. Believed deceased by some, but certain inconsistencies suggest otherwise."

My blood turns to ice. Literally, I can feel the cold spreading through my veins, numbing my fingers, making my legs feel like they're about to give out. They know. They know everything.

The room tilts. My vision narrows to a point. For one terrible second, I think I might pass out, just collapse right here on this generic corporate carpet while a KOTR operative watches. Every nightmare scenario I imagined during those sleepless nights is coming true all at once.

All the training. All the preparation. All the code phrases and escape routes and careful planning. None of it matters now. I walked into a trap thinking I was setting one.

And worse, I brought my parents into it. Whatever happens to me now happens to them too.

"We've been watching your family for years," Granite continues, voice calm like we're discussing weather. "BetaZone was always a curiosity. Too talented to be a simple supporter. Her work on C2 infrastructure was impressive, but her operational patterns never quite fit a true believer."

"I don't know what you're talking about." My voice sounds hollow even to me. Pathetically unconvincing. I wouldn't believe me either.

"Don't insult my intelligence, Jacob." His voice hardens. "Your father is Alpha. He infiltrated KOTR three years ago. We've suspected for months but couldn't confirm until you showed up here tonight. Your registration triggered a deeper background check. The fake credentials were good, but not perfect. Small inconsistencies that led us back to your mother's work, to Alpha's disappearance, to everything." He smiles coldly. "You led us right to him."

I try to think. To find a way out. Some angle I haven't considered.

"What do you want?"

"Cooperation. Simple as that." Granite sits in one of the chairs, gestures for me to take the other. I stay standing. "Your family has valuable intelligence. Information that could help us identify other infiltrators. Names, methods, communication protocols. Everything Alpha learned during his years inside."

"And if I refuse?"

"Work with us, and we might let you live. All of you. Your mother, your father, even you. We have uses for talent." Granite smiles coldly. "Refuse, and... well. Your mother is coordinating from a van outside. Yes, we know about that too. And your father is in the surveillance room upstairs. We spotted him about twenty minutes ago. Did you really think we wouldn't notice Alpha walking back into our territory?"

My stomach drops even further. They've been watching us this whole time. The trap wasn't just for me. It was for all of us.

In my ear, Dad's voice is urgent but controlled: "Jacob, we're tracking your location. We know they've made us. Extraction is already moving. Stall for two minutes. Keep him talking."

Two minutes. I need to keep this guy talking for two minutes while armed agents move through a building full of hackers.

"Why should I believe you won't just kill us anyway?" I ask, letting fear into my voice, not hard since I'm genuinely terrified. "Once you have what you want, we're just liabilities."

"Because you're more valuable alive. Think about it. A young, talented operative with skills we can develop, desperate to protect his family, willing to do anything we ask. You'd make an excellent asset."

One minute thirty seconds. I can almost hear the countdown in my head.

"And if I refuse right now? If I tell you I'd rather die than betray my family?"

"Then this conversation ends badly for everyone. Especially for the girl. Melissa, I think? StarBreaker? She's ranked even higher than you. Her father is another infiltrator, isn't he?"

One minute.

"Let me think about it," I say, playing for time. "This is a lot to process. You're asking me to betray everything I..."

The door bursts open.

Dad stands there, gun drawn, flanked by two agents in tactical gear. His face is cold fury, the expression of a man who spent three years pretending to be a monster and finally gets to drop the act.

"Hands where I can see them," Dad says. His voice is ice. "Don't move. Don't speak. Don't even think about reaching for that tablet."

Granite raises his hands slowly. His expression is oddly calm for someone with guns pointed at his chest.

"Alpha. Finally in the flesh. Your commitment to the role was impressive. Three years of convincing everyone you were one of us."

"Jacob, move. Now."

I don't need to be told twice. I bolt toward the door, past Dad, past the tactical agents, into the hallway where Mom is waiting with more operatives.

"We've got him," she says into her radio. Her voice is tight with relief. "Package is secure. Initiate full sweep. Every KOTR operative in this building, in custody, next ten minutes."

Alarms start blaring throughout the conference center. The party just became a raid.

The last thing I see before they hustle me toward an exit is the main ballroom erupting into chaos, competitors screaming, sponsors running, tactical teams pouring through every door. The giant screens flicker and die. The carefully curated atmosphere of a hacker gathering shatters into something raw and terrifying.

The pen in my pocket never got used. I never made it to the terminals. Never copied the Nightfall coordinates. The whole mission objective, gone because Granite grabbed me thirty seconds too early.

My secure phone buzzes once as we reach the exit. I glance down and see a message from Melissa's encrypted channel, just two words: "Got it."

She made it. She got to a terminal before everything went sideways. Whatever's in that encrypted package, whatever coordinates KOTR was distributing tonight, Melissa has a copy.

The mission might not be a total loss after all.

I have no idea if we just won or lost. I have no idea if the intel Melissa grabbed is enough to stop Nightfall, or if KOTR has backup plans we don't know about. I have no idea what happens next.

But we're alive. My family is alive. That has to count for something.

The adrenaline is crashing now, leaving me shaky and weak. All that fear I'd been holding back during the confrontation, it comes flooding in now, making my hands tremble and my eyes sting. I almost died in there. We all almost died.

All I know is that the shadows just got a whole lot darker.

And we're not done yet.

17

THE RAID

Chaos erupts everywhere. The conference center that felt so controlled a minute ago has transformed into something out of a war zone. Agents pour through every entrance, not just doors but windows too, rappelling down from the ceiling in some areas, popping out of service corridors that guests didn't even know existed.

The noise is insane. Shouted commands in voices trained to carry. The crash of doors getting kicked in. A high-pitched alarm that feels like it's drilling directly into my skull. And underneath all of that, the confused screaming of hundreds of people who just realized their world has flipped upside down.

Competitors scatter in every direction, some trying to bolt toward exits, others ducking under tables and chairs. A woman in a silver dress trips over a fallen lanyard display and crashes into a group of panicked hackers. Someone screams, this raw, terrified sound that cuts through everything. Glass shatters somewhere to my left. The carefully curated vibe of the Shadow Games gathering has shattered into pure animal panic.

I'm frozen for a second, maybe two, my brain trying to catch up with the sensory overload. Flashing lights. Running people. The bitter smell of smoke from somewhere, flashbangs maybe, or actual fire. My legs feel rooted to the floor, like my body has decided "standing very still" is the best survival strategy.

Everything I learned in the briefings about staying calm under pressure has apparently evaporated from my brain. So much for operational training.

A voice in my head that sounds like my own screams at me to move, to run, to do something. But my body isn't listening. This is what they call "freezing," the third F that nobody talks about. Fight, flight, or freeze. And I'm frozen solid, like a deer in headlights, watching the world fall apart around me.

The masked presenter vanishes in a swirl of smoke. Literally, there's some kinda theatrical flash bang on the stage, a burst of light and white smoke that billows outward like a magician's trick. When the air clears enough to see, the podium stands empty. Whoever was behind that mask, whoever might be the Architect themselves, is gone. Just disappeared into the chaos like a ghost.

"Stay with me!" Mom grabs my arm with a grip that's way stronger than I expected, BetaZone's grip, not my mother's. She pulls me through the crowd, moving with practiced efficiency, her eyes constantly scanning for threats. Her free hand hovers near her jacket, where I now know she carries a concealed weapon.

"What about Melissa?" I shout over the noise. The alarms are deafening, mixed with all the shouting and running and the general craziness of hundreds of people realizing they're trapped in what's become a massive law enforcement operation. "I saw her near the terminals..."

"Her father has her. They're getting out through the east wing, different route, same destination." Mom yanks me sideways to avoid a cluster of people rushing past, their faces twisted with terror. "Keep moving. Don't stop for anyone. Don't look back."

Behind us, I hear sounds of struggle. Agents tackling suspects who tried to run. The distinctive zip of plastic restraints getting tightened. Shouted orders: "On the ground! Hands where I can see them! Don't move!" It sounds like something from a movie, dramatic, cinematic, unreal. But the fear running through my veins is very, very real. This isn't a movie. This isn't a game. This is actually happening.

We push through a service door into a kitchen area. The shift from chaos to relative quiet is jarring, like stepping out of a hurricane into the calm eye. Stainless steel counters gleam under fluorescent lights. Industrial ovens line one wall. The smell of catered food (stuffed mushrooms, chicken skewers, the finger food from the reception) mixes with the acrid taste of fear coating the back of my throat.

Two agents in tactical gear flank us immediately, weapons up, sweeping the room with professional efficiency. Their movements are precise, coordinated, the kind of discipline that comes from years of training and countless operations.

"Clear," one of them reports into his radio. His voice is calm, almost bored, like this is just another Tuesday for him. "Package moving to secondary extraction point."

"Copy," Mom responds. She's in full operative mode now, completely transformed from the mother who made me eggs and worried about my homework. This is BetaZone, high-threat-level asset, running an extraction with military precision. "Jacob, through here. Stay low, move fast."

We wind through the kitchen, past stunned catering staff pressed against the walls with their hands visible, terrified civilians caught in the middle of something they don't understand. A young guy in chef's whites stares at us with huge eyes, his hands shaking so badly the ladle he's holding clatters against his leg. One woman is crying quietly, mascara running down her face in dark streaks.

I want to stop, to tell them this isn't about them, that they're not in danger, that everything will be okay. But Mom's grip doesn't allow for hesitation. Every second we spend here is a second something could go wrong.

Out a loading dock door. The night air hits my face like a slap, cold and sharp, carrying the distant sound of sirens getting closer. A black SUV idles on the concrete, engine running, no license plates visible. The back door is already open, interior lights off, just a dark rectangle waiting to swallow me.

I'm shoved into the back seat before I can process what's happening. The leather is cold against my palms. Mom slides in beside me. The door slams with a heavy thunk, and we're accelerating before I can even reach for a seatbelt. The driver doesn't look back, doesn't speak. He just drives with the focused intensity of someone who's done this a thousand times.

Through the tinted back window, I watch the conference center shrink away. Blue and red lights are converging on it from every direction. Police cars. What might be FBI vehicles. An ambulance, maybe more. The whole emergency response machine descending on a building that, an hour ago, looked like nothing more than a boring corporate event.

***

"Status report," Mom says into her radio, her voice clipped and professional. The SUV swerves through traffic, running red lights, taking turns at speeds that press me against the door. Normal rules don't seem to apply. We're cutting through the city like a knife through water, and nobody's stopping us.

Voices crackle back with updates. Fragments of operational chaos, each report painting a piece of a bigger picture.

"Sixteen arrests confirmed so far. Granite in custody. He was still in the room where you found him. Didn't even try to run."

The image of Granite's face flashes through my mind. Those cold, calculating eyes. The way he smiled when he told me he knew exactly who I was. Part of me is relieved he's been caught. Another part wonders if prison can even hold someone like that.

"The masked presenter escaped. We're still trying to track the exit route. Heat signature disappeared somewhere in the basement level. Possible secret exit we didn't have mapped."

The Architect. It has to be. The one person at the top of KOTR's food chain, the one who might have founded the whole organization. And they slipped away while everyone else was getting arrested.

"Multiple suspects attempting to flee through the north parking structure. Teams intercepting now. Three in custody, two still running."

"What about the packages?" I ask, the question bursting out before I can stop myself. My voice sounds wrong, too high, too young, too scared. "The encrypted files with the Nightfall coordinates? Did anyone get them?"

Mom looks at me with something like pride, or maybe relief. Maybe both, all mixed together.

"Melissa got them. She downloaded five packages from the terminals before the raid started. Saw her window when the masked figure was giving their speech and most of the sponsors were distracted." A small smile crosses Mom's face, the first crack in her professional armor since this whole thing started. "But that's not all she did."

"What do you mean?"

"When we breached, one of the KOTR techs was trying to trigger a switch, something that would have wiped all their servers remotely. Destroyed everything we needed. Melissa saw it happening from across the room." Mom shakes her head, something like wonder in her voice. "She social-engineered her way past two guards by pretending to be a panicked civilian, got to the tech's station, and pulled the network cable right out of the wall. She physically severed the connection before the wipe signal could transmit."

I stare at her. "She what?"

"Saved the entire operation, basically. All that intel our techs are working on right now? The target coordinates, the cell assignments, the attack timeline? Gone if she hadn't acted. She had maybe three seconds to make that call, and she made it." Mom's smile widens slightly. "Her father's team is rushing the drives to decryption right now. She did more than we trained either of you for. She improvised under fire and saved everything."

Relief floods through me so hard I feel dizzy. My vision blurs for a second, and I have to blink hard to clear it. We didn't fail. We got something. All of this (the terror, the running, the feeling of Granite's eyes boring into me) wasn't for nothing.

"Is it enough?"

"We'll know soon. The packages should have target coordinates, attack timing, and cell assignments. If we can decode them fast enough, we can stop every attack before it happens." Mom's radio crackles again, and she holds up a hand for silence. "Copy. We're five minutes out."

The SUV turns onto a highway, blending into normal traffic as best it can. Just another black vehicle among thousands, nothing to see here, nothing unusual about the way it's moving a little too fast, changing lanes a little too aggressively.

Through the tinted windows, I see the conference center shrinking in the distance, surrounded by a constellation of flashing lights (police cars, ambulances, fire trucks, the whole emergency response machine that gets called when something this big goes down). Helicopters circle overhead, their searchlights cutting through the darkness like accusing fingers.

"What happens to the regular competitors?" I ask. "The ones who were just there for the games? Who didn't know about KOTR or Nightfall or any of it?"

I'm thinking about the people I saw tonight. The kid my age who was so excited about finally meeting other hackers in person. The woman who talked about using her winnings to pay for college. The countless faces I passed in the crowd, people who came here because they loved puzzles and challenges and competition, not because they wanted to hurt anyone.

"They'll be questioned and released," Mom says. "Most of them are just talented kids who got caught up in something bigger than they knew. Background checks will clear them quick. Anyone without KOTR connections will be home by morning. The ones who are clean will go home with a scary story and probably a lifetime suspicion of any future 'exclusive gaming events.'"

"And the ones who aren't clean?"

"They'll be held for more questioning. Asset interviews. Some will be charged. Some will be offered deals in exchange for information. The intel we gather tonight will keep giving for months, maybe years." She trails off, and I understand: some of those competitors were KOTR. Some of them knew exactly what they were part of.

"And the games? The Shadow Games themselves?"

"That's above my pay grade. But I imagine there'll be some restructuring. The games were always a recruitment tool, but now they're compromised. KOTR knows we were using them for intel, and we know KOTR was using them for recruitment. The whole dynamic has to change." She puts her hand on my shoulder, and for a second she's just Mom again, not BetaZone, not an operative, just the woman who used to tuck me in at night. "You did good, Jacob. Really good."

"I got caught. Granite knew who I was."

"And you stalled long enough for extraction. You didn't panic, not visibly, anyway. You didn't break cover until we reached you. You kept him talking, kept him focused on you instead of checking his security feeds or warning other KOTR people." She squeezes gently. "That's not failure. That's adaptation. That's exactly what good operatives do when plans go sideways."

"Melissa would've done better," I say, and I'm surprised to realize I mean it. "If she'd been in that room with Granite, she would've read him. Known what he was going to do before he did it. People are like puzzles to her. She sees patterns in behavior the way I see patterns in code."

Mom nods. "Different skills. Both valuable. You analyze systems; she analyzes humans. That's why you work well together. You cover each other's blind spots."

I don't feel like a good operative. I feel like a scared kid who got lucky. But I don't say that. Maybe because I don't want to disappoint her, or maybe because some part of me wants to believe what she's saying is true.

The highway gives way to suburban streets, then a quiet neighborhood that looks like a thousand other quiet neighborhoods around DC. Split-level homes. Trimmed hedges. Cars parked in driveways. The kind of place where people mow their lawns on Saturday mornings and wave to their neighbors.

Our destination looks completely boring from the outside.

***

The safe house is this unassuming colonial home in a cul-de-sac, the kind of place where normal families have normal lives. White siding. Blue shutters. A manicured lawn that suggests someone actually cares about curb appeal. A basketball hoop in the driveway, slightly rusted from weather. Nothing about it screams "intelligence operations center." Nothing hints at the secrets behind its walls.

Inside, it's anything but ordinary.

Walls of screens showing news feeds, satellite imagery, and scrolling data streams. Banks of computers humming with processing power, their fans creating a constant white noise. Agents moving with purpose, headsets on, hands flying across keyboards, voices murmuring into microphones. The living room has been converted into a command center, couches shoved against walls to make room for folding tables covered in equipment. The dining room holds communication gear (radios, encrypted phones, devices I don't recognize). What was probably once a family room is now packed with tactical gear and weapons.

The contrast with the exterior is jarring. Step through the front door and you leave suburban normalcy behind, entering a world of encrypted communications and real-time intelligence and the infrastructure of shadow operations.

Dad is already there when we arrive. He looks exhausted but wired, adrenaline still flowing from the raid. There's dust on his tactical vest, probably from the breach. A scratch on his cheek that's already stopped bleeding. His eyes light up when he sees me, relief mixing with something deeper, something that might be pride or love or both.

"Jacob." He crosses the room in three strides and pulls me into a hug, not a quick one, but a real one. The first genuine father-son hug since we got back together. I can feel his heart pounding against mine, his breath shaky with emotion he's not quite controlling.

Something breaks open in my chest. All the fear I've been holding (from Granite's cold eyes, from knowing they could have killed me, from wondering if I'd ever see my parents again) comes pouring out in a single shuddering breath. I grab fistfuls of his tactical vest and hold on tight, like I'm seven years old again and afraid of the dark.

For a moment, all the complexity falls away. He's not an undercover operative. I'm not a junior asset. We're just a father and son, grateful to be together, grateful to be alive. And that's enough. That's everything.

"I'm sorry you had to go through that," he says into my hair. "The plan didn't account for Granite making you so fast. We should have had better surveillance. Should have pulled you out the second he showed interest."

"How did he know?" I ask when he finally lets go. The question has been burning in my head since that moment in the private room when Granite pulled out my file. "I was careful. I followed all the protocols."

"We're still figuring that out." Dad guides me to a couch in a corner that's relatively quiet, away from all the operational chaos. Someone has left a water bottle and a protein bar on the cushion, small comforts in the middle of madness. "There may be a leak somewhere in the organization, someone feeding KOTR info about our people. Or their intel network was better than we thought. They've been watching us while we were watching them."

"Granite said they'd been suspicious of Mom for years."

"Your mother is too talented to fly under the radar. We always knew her BetaZone cover was thin. Her work was too good, her skills too advanced for someone who was supposedly just a mid-level malware developer. But the cover was necessary for the mission." Dad sits down beside me. "For now, rest. You've earned it. The hard part is over, at least for you."

But I can't rest. My mind is still racing with everything that happened (the conference center, Granite's cold eyes, the door bursting open, the chaos of the extraction). Every moment replays on a loop. The sound of glass breaking. The feel of Mom's grip on my arm. The smell of smoke and fear.

"Can I talk to Melissa?"

"She's on her way here. Her extraction went smooth. She and her father made it out through the east wing without any problems. The route was clear the whole way." Dad checks his watch. "Should be here any minute."

***

Twenty minutes later, Melissa walks through the door. She looks as wired as I feel, eyes wide with leftover adrenaline, hands trembling a little, the same disconnection from reality that comes from experiencing something too big to process in real time. Her clothes are messed up, her hair escaping from its careful styling, but she's whole. She's here. She's safe.

"Jacob!" She crosses the room in seconds and pulls me into a fierce hug. I can feel her shaking against me, tremors running through her body like aftershocks. "They told me Granite had you in that room. I was terrified. I couldn't do anything. My dad wouldn't let me go back..."

Her voice breaks. She's crying now, really crying, tears soaking into my shoulder. I hold on tighter because I don't know what else to do. Because I was scared too. Because we almost lost everything tonight.

"Hey. Hey." I pull back a little so I can see her face. There are tear tracks on her cheeks, her eyes red and swollen. "I'm okay. And I heard what you did, with the network cable, the switch. You saved everything."

She shakes her head, dismissing it. "I just saw what was happening and... I don't know, I didn't think. I just moved."

"That's exactly the point." I hold her by the shoulders so she has to look at me. "You didn't freeze. You improvised. You saved the entire operation."

"You would have done the same thing."

"Maybe. But you're the one who actually did it. That's what matters."

She sniffs, wipes her face with her sleeve. "We're partners, remember? Partners don't leave partners behind."

"Partners in shadows."

"Partners in shadows." She takes a shaky breath, visibly pulling herself together. "Did we do it? Did we get what we needed?"

Before I can answer, a frustrated voice cuts through the room. One of the tech analysts, a guy with wire-rim glasses and about three days worth of stubble, slams his palm against his desk.

"We've got a problem."

Everyone gravitates toward the main screen. Dad pushes through the crowd, his expression shifting from relief to operational focus in an instant. "What is it?"

"The packages Melissa grabbed, they're layered." The analyst pulls up a display showing what looks like digital gibberish, blocks of random characters scrolling across the screen. "We cracked the outer encryption in about twenty minutes. Standard AES-256, nothing fancy. But underneath that there's a second layer. Custom cipher. Nothing in our databases matches it."

"Can you brute force it?" Dad asks.

"Not in time. We're talking weeks of processing, maybe months. Whatever algorithm they used, it's not standard. It's bespoke. Built from scratch."

The room goes quiet. The kind of quiet that means everyone understands how bad this is. We have the data. We're holding it in our hands. But we can't read it. And somewhere out there, seventeen targets are counting down to disaster.

I stare at the screen, watching the garbled text scroll by. Something about it tugs at my brain. The pattern of the characters. The way certain symbols cluster together, then spread apart in these irregular waves. The spacing between blocks.

I've seen this before.

The realization hits me like a punch to the chest. My heart starts racing again, but this time it's not fear. It's recognition.

"Wait." The word comes out before I can think about whether I should say it. Every head in the room turns toward me, this sixteen-year-old kid surrounded by professional intelligence analysts. "Can you scroll back? To the beginning of the second layer?"

The analyst gives me a skeptical look, but Dad nods. "Do it."

The screen rewinds. I lean closer, my eyes tracing the patterns. There. Right there. The way the character frequency shifts every forty-eight symbols. The specific ratio of alphanumeric to special characters. The subtle repetition in the spacing.

"That's not random," I say, my voice coming out steadier than I expected. "It's a modified book cipher. I've seen this exact structure before."

"Where?" Dad's voice is sharp now, intense.

"Phase 2 of the Shadow Games. Challenge 7, called 'Gutenberg's Ghost.'" The memories flood back. Three brutal days of staring at my screen, cross-referencing patterns, testing theory after theory until my eyes burned. Most competitors gave up on that one. I was too stubborn. "The solution required identifying a specific public domain text as the key. Without the right text, the output looks exactly like this. Random garbage."

"You're saying KOTR based their encryption on a Shadow Games challenge?" The analyst sounds skeptical. Also maybe a little insulted that a teenager is telling him how to do his job.

"Think about it," I say, the pieces clicking together in my head as I talk. "The Shadow Games are recruitment and training for KOTR. The challenges teach skills they actually use. Why wouldn't they use the same methods for their real operations? Anyone who completed Phase 2 would already know how to decrypt their communications."

Dad and Mom exchange a look. That silent parent communication thing they do.

"It makes sense," Mom says slowly. "Compartmentalized knowledge. Only people who've proven themselves through the games would have the skills to access sensitive data. It's elegant, actually."

"So what's the key text?" the analyst asks, leaning forward now, skepticism replaced by something like hope. "For this Gutenberg challenge?"

I close my eyes, trying to remember. The original challenge used a public domain book, something obscure enough that random guessing wouldn't work. The pattern in the encrypted text had pointed toward political philosophy. Manifestos. Declarations of information freedom.

"The Crypto Anarchist Manifesto," I say, opening my eyes. "Timothy C. May, 1988. That was the key for Gutenberg's Ghost. KOTR's whole ideology is built on the same principles, information wants to be free, encryption for the masses, all that stuff. If they based their cipher on the same challenge..."

The analyst is already typing. His fingers fly across the keyboard, pulling up the text, feeding it into the decryption algorithm. The room holds its breath. I can hear my own heartbeat pounding in my ears.

The screen flickers.

And then the gibberish starts transforming into words.

"Holy..." The analyst trails off, staring at the screen like it just performed a miracle. "It's working. It's actually working."

Readable text floods the display. Target names. Coordinates. Timestamps. Cell assignments. Everything KOTR was planning, laid out in clean, organized lists.

"We're in," Dad breathes.

For a second, nobody moves. Then the room erupts into controlled chaos. Agents grabbing headsets, pulling up secondary screens, coordinating with teams across the country. But Dad turns to me first, and there's something in his eyes I've never seen before. Not just pride. Something deeper. Like he's seeing me properly for the first time.

"Jacob. How did you...?"

"I like puzzles," I say, and my voice sounds weird even to me. Shaky. Overwhelmed. "I just... I remember patterns. It's what I do."

He puts his hand on my shoulder and squeezes. No words. He doesn't need them.

***

Melissa appears beside me as the analysts work through the decrypted data. Her eyes are wide, taking in the organized chaos unfolding around us.

"Did you just crack their encryption?"

"Kinda." I still can't quite believe it myself. "The Shadow Games taught me how. Turns out all those late nights weren't just for points."

She stares at me for a long moment, then breaks into this huge grin. "Partners in shadows."

"Partners in shadows."

We stand together, watching the screens fill with information. Target coordinates for seventeen different facilities across the country. Power substations in six states. Water treatment plants in four major cities. Hospital networks in New York, LA, Chicago. Air traffic control systems at three major airports.

"Attack windows scheduled within 72 hours," one of the analysts reads aloud. "They were gonna hit everything at once. Coordinated across all time zones. Maximum chaos, minimum response time."

"Cell assignments matching everything we suspected about KOTR's structure," another adds, pulling up supporting data on a second screen. "This confirms the seven-cell model. We have names, roles, operational details. Handler identities. Communication protocols. This is everything."

I'm scanning the data alongside the professionals now, my brain doing that thing it does where patterns jump out at me. And something about the hospital targets is bothering me. Something that doesn't fit.

"Wait," I say, pointing at the screen. "The timing on the hospital attacks. Look."

Dad leans in. "What about it?"

"Every other target has attack windows at round numbers. Power grid hits at 2:00 AM, water treatment at 2:30 AM, air traffic at 3:00 AM. Nice clean times. But the hospitals are all scheduled for seventeen minutes past the hour. 2:17, 3:17, 4:17. That's weirdly specific."

The room goes quiet again. The analysts exchange glances.

"You're right," one of them says slowly. "That's not random. Seventeen minutes..."

"It could indicate a dependency," I continue, the theory forming as I speak. "Like the hospital attacks need something else to happen first. A staged trigger. Maybe the power grid going down is supposed to create the vulnerability they exploit at the hospitals. The seventeen-minute delay gives time for backup systems to fail."

Dad's already on his radio. "All teams, priority update. Hospital targets may have precursor dependencies. Check infrastructure linkages within a seventeen-minute window of scheduled attack times. Power grid failures may be required triggers. Adjust protection protocols accordingly."

Mom appears at my other side. "How did you see that?"

"I don't know." And I really don't. It just... jumped out at me. The way patterns always do. "It looked wrong. Everything else was so organized, so clean. The seventeen-minute thing broke the pattern."

She looks at me like she's never seen me before. Maybe she hasn't. Maybe none of us have really seen each other until now. All those years of secrets and lies, and it took a crisis to strip everything away and show what's actually underneath.

"Can we stop it?" someone asks. The question that matters most. The question everything has been building toward.

"We're already moving." Dad's voice is steady, confident, the voice of someone who's been waiting three years for this moment. "Alerts going out to FBI, DHS, NSA, and partner agencies. Every target is getting protection teams deployed right now. Every cell is getting raided simultaneously within the next two hours."

He looks back at me and Melissa.

"This is it. This is everything we've been working toward. Because of what you two did tonight, the intel you gathered, the risks you took, the patterns you recognized, we have a chance to stop Project Nightfall completely."

Melissa grabs my hand. I squeeze back. Her fingers are cold but her grip is strong.

All those months of Shadow Games challenges. All those hours I thought I was just killing time, solving puzzles that didn't matter. They led here. They led to this moment. The skills I built without understanding why, they actually meant something. They actually saved something.

I'm not just watching anymore. I'm not just a bystander in someone else's operation. I actually helped crack this thing open.

Three weeks ago, I was just a kid who accidentally fried his laptop, who spent his days worrying about homework and bullies and whether his mother was hiding something in her locked office. Now I'm standing in an intelligence command center, holding hands with another teenage operative, watching the takedown of an international cyberterrorist network happen in real time.

The world is a much stranger place than I ever imagined. And somehow, impossibly, I helped change it.

That thought hits me like a physical thing, making my knees wobble. Me. Jacob Mitchell. SirBreaksAlot. Kid who breaks stuff.

I actually did something that mattered.

My eyes sting suddenly, tears threatening to spill over, catching me off guard. Not sad tears. Something else. Relief, maybe. Or pride. Or the overwhelming weight of realizing you've been part of something bigger than yourself, something that will save lives you'll never know about, prevent tragedies you'll never see avoided.

I blink hard, not wanting anyone to see. But Melissa's grip on my hand tightens. She knows. She feels it too.

***

The next few hours are a blur of activity I can barely follow. Agents coordinate with partner agencies through secure channels, speaking in code words and abbreviations I don't understand. Alerts spread across the country through networks I don't even know exist. Radio chatter fills the room, status updates and urgent instructions, the voices of people putting their lives on the line to stop something terrible.

One by one, reports start coming in. Success stories, mostly.

"Cell Alpha neutralized. Six arrests, no casualties. Seized equipment includes malware development workstations and what looks like a command-and-control server."

"Cell Gamma hit. They were already at the target location. They caught them with equipment in hand. Physical infiltration gear, fake IDs, building layouts. They were hours from going live."

"Cell Delta's financial infrastructure seized. Cryptocurrency wallets frozen. Bank accounts flagged. They're not going anywhere."

Each report brings a small cheer from the gathered agents. Each green marker that appears on the map represents a victory, a disaster prevented, a piece of KOTR removed from the board.

By 4 AM, the main screen shows a map of the United States covered with green markers, each one representing a successful operation, a KOTR cell taken down, an attack prevented.

"Fifteen of seventeen targets secured," Dad announces, his voice hoarse from hours of coordination but still strong. There's a weariness in his posture now, the adrenaline finally fading, but his eyes are bright with satisfaction. "Two cells went dark before we could move on them (probably got tipped off somehow), but their attack windows have been blocked. Infrastructure at those targets is locked down. Extra security deployed. Nightfall is officially a failure."

Cheers erupt in the room. People hug, high-five, shake hands. Three years of undercover work. Months of Shadow Games intelligence gathering. One terrifying night at The Meeting. All of it building to a single, coordinated action that stopped something catastrophic.

And I was part of it. Melissa was part of it. Two sixteen-year-olds who found their way into the shadows and helped bring light.

Mom finds me in the corner of the room, too tired to celebrate properly. My legs feel like they're made of lead. My eyes burn from exhaustion and leftover adrenaline. The couch I'm sitting on feels like the most comfortable surface in the world. I could sink into it and sleep for a week.

"How are you holding up?"

"I don't know." It's the honest answer. "This is a lot to process. Like, a lot a lot."

"I know it is." She sits down beside me, and for a moment we're just a mother and son, the way we used to be before secret offices and coded messages and international spy operations. "When this is over, when things calm down, we're gonna have real conversations. About what happened. About what you went through. About what comes next."

"What does come next?" It's the question I've been avoiding, the one lurking at the back of my mind through all the chaos.

"That's up to you." Mom's voice is gentle, no pressure, no expectations. "You could step back, return to normal life as much as possible. Go to school, hang out with Ethan, be a regular teenager. We've earned that option. We could relocate, start fresh, put all of this behind us."

She pauses.

"Or you could keep training. Become part of this world officially. Not full-time (you're still young, and school matters), but as a junior operative. Part-time stuff during summers and breaks. The organization has programs for people like you and Melissa."

I think about it. The fear I felt when Granite confronted me, his cold eyes seeing through every lie I tried to tell. The excitement when the decryption worked, when I realized I'd actually contributed something nobody else could. The exhaustion hitting me now, bone-deep and absolute.

"I don't have to decide right now, right?"

"No." Mom smiles softly. "You don't. This isn't a choice that has to be made tonight, or tomorrow, or even next week. Take your time. Figure out what you want."

"Okay." I lean back against the couch. "Then that's what I'll do."

She stands up, kisses the top of my head the way she used to when I was little, and goes back to the operational chaos still unfolding across the room.

I close my eyes. For the first time in weeks, I don't feel the pressure of unsolved mysteries. KOTR is broken, not destroyed completely, maybe, but hurt enough that they can't hurt anyone for a long time. Dad is home. The secrets are out. The lies that defined my family for years have finally given way to something like truth.

Somewhere across the room, I hear Melissa's quiet voice talking to her father. Around us, agents continue their work, coordinating the aftermath of the largest anti-hacking operation in recent history.

The shadows are receding. And maybe, finally, I can rest.

I lean against the arm of the couch and let exhaustion take me. Just before I drift off, I feel someone drape a blanket over me, Mom probably, or maybe Dad.

For the first time since I found Mom's office, since I broke into her secret world and started down this impossible path, I feel safe.

The shadows will be there in the morning. But for now, I sleep.

18

LOOSE ENDS

I wake up to the smell of coffee and quiet voices. Real coffee, not the gross instant stuff Mom keeps for emergencies. The good kind, all fresh and aromatic, cutting through the stale recycled air of the safe house. Sunlight streams through the safe house windows, warming my face. Dust motes float in the golden beams like tiny stars.

The sound of a radio crackling somewhere in the distance. The soft hum of electronic equipment that never quite turns off in a place like this. Outside, birds are singing, a normal, ordinary sound that feels almost surreal after everything.

Somehow it's already afternoon. I slept for like nine hours straight without dreaming, without waking up, without any of the restless tossing that's been haunting me for weeks. My body is stiff from sleeping on a couch, but my head feels clearer than it has since this whole thing started.

Melissa is curled up on the other end of the couch, still out cold. Her face looks soft and peaceful, way different from the tense, alert expression she usually has. Someone (Mom or Dad or maybe one of the agents) put blankets over both of us at some point. Tucked us in like little kids. Which, I guess, is what we still are. Despite everything.

I sit up carefully, trying not to wake her, and see Dad at a nearby table with a laptop. He's changed clothes since the raid, casual now, jeans and a sweater, looking more like the dad I remember than the operative who burst through that door with a gun.

For a second, my brain can't reconcile the two versions. Last night's Alpha, cold-eyed, tactical, a stranger in Dad-shaped clothing who talked about "threat matrices" and "extraction protocols." And now this: just Dad, in jeans and a sweater, drinking coffee and working on something, the familiar way he tilts his head when he's concentrating.

Which one is real? Both, maybe. Neither. I don't know yet.

"Morning, sleepyhead." He closes the laptop and pushes a mug toward me. Steam curls up from the surface. "Well, afternoon technically. You've been out for a while."

For a second, I just stare at him. My dad. Sitting there like it's the most normal thing in the world. Like he hasn't been gone for two years while I thought he was dead. Like we're just a regular father and son having a regular morning.

Except nothing about us is regular anymore. Maybe nothing ever was.

The anger flickers in my chest, that same hot coal that's been burning since I found out the truth. It's smaller now, dampened by exhaustion and relief and the bone-deep gratitude that he's here at all, but it's still there. Still smoldering. I don't know if it'll ever go away completely. Maybe it shouldn't.

I push it down. Not because I'm over it (I'm definitely not over it), but because there's too much else happening to deal with it right now. There'll be time for anger later. Right now, I just want coffee.

But as I reach for the mug, I realize something. The anger isn't all I feel anymore. There's something else underneath it, something warmer, more complicated. Relief that he's here. Gratitude that I get a second chance. The strange, disorienting hope that maybe things can be okay. Not perfect. Not like before. But okay in some new way I haven't figured out yet.

"What'd I miss?" I wrap my hands around the mug, feeling the warmth seep into my fingers.

"Oh, just a few things." His voice is light, almost teasing. "Collapse of an international criminal network. Arrests on four continents. Your mother being debriefed by like seventeen different agencies who all want to know how we pulled this off. Minor stuff."

"Oh, is that all?"

Dad grins, a real grin, the kind that crinkles the corners of his eyes the way I remember from when I was little. It's weird seeing him this relaxed. Three years of living a double life, carrying secrets that could get us all killed. And now... it's over?

"How do you feel?" he asks. The question sounds genuine, not just checking off a box.

"Like I slept on a couch." I stretch, feeling joints pop. "But also... lighter? Like something that was pressing on my chest for weeks finally went away."

"That's the adrenaline dump," Dad says. "Your body's been in survival mode way longer than you realized. Now that the immediate threat is gone, everything catches up."

***

The next few hours fill in details I missed while passed out. The safe house feels different now, less like a command center, more like a recovery station. Fewer tactical screens, more coffee cups and paper plates scattered around.

Granite (real name Anthony Morrison, forty-two years old) turns out to be a former tech executive who went off the deep end after his company crashed during some financial crisis. He blamed "corrupt systems" for his failure, and KOTR gave him a story that made sense of his anger. Within two years, he was running their entire North American operations.

"He'll be tried in federal court," Dad explains, pulling up a file on his laptop. "Conspiracy to commit terrorism, computer fraud, money laundering, a bunch of other stuff. The charges stack up to several hundred years. He's not seeing daylight again."

"What about the others? The cell leaders?"

"Arrests are still happening. We got most of them during the raids, but some ran before we could grab them. A few went completely dark, probably heading for countries that won't send them back."

"What about the two cells that got away? The ones that were tipped off before we could move?"

Dad's expression darkens. "We're looking into that. Someone warned them. That's the only explanation. Until we find out who, we have to assume there's still a leak somewhere in the network."

A mole. Someone on our side, feeding information to KOTR. The thought makes my stomach turn.

"And the Architect?"

Dad's face does something complicated. "That's our biggest loose end. Whoever they are (whoever founded KOTR, whoever was behind that mask at The Meeting), they escaped. We've got theories, leads, but nothing solid. That's an ongoing investigation."

I file that away. The Architect. The mystery figure at the top of everything. Still out there. Still a puzzle.

Another problem for another day.

"What about the Shadow Games?" I ask. "What happens to them now?"

Dad's expression turns thoughtful. "The games will keep going. Our organization is restructuring them to be what they were always supposed to be: training and recruitment for people who want to fight on the right side. No more KOTR influence."

"Melissa's dad is taking point on that," he adds. "Given his background and his daughter's involvement, he's the obvious choice to rebuild the games into something clean."

That means Melissa would have inside access to everything. We could keep training together, keep climbing, even after she goes back to California. Unless...

"So I could keep competing? If I wanted?"

"If you want. You've earned it, more than earned it. Your ranking is real, your skills are real." He pauses, meeting my eyes. "But there's no pressure. After everything you've been through, nobody would blame you for walking away. Putting this whole world behind you and just being a normal kid."

I think about it. The Shadow Games started as my path to answers, a way to figure out what Mom was hiding, what happened to Dad. But they became something more. A world of challenges that pushed me to grow. Connections with people like Melissa who understood what it meant to live in shadows.

"I'll think about it," I say finally. "Give me some time."

"All the time you need."

***

Melissa wakes up around 3 PM, totally out of it and starving. She blinks at the sunlight, looks around the safe house with a confused expression, then seems to remember where she is.

"Please tell me there's food," she groans, shoving herself upright. "I could eat like an entire restaurant."

We raid the safe house kitchen together, throwing together sandwiches from whatever we can find. Bread that's a little stale. Peanut butter from a giant jar. Jelly that's probably been here since forever. Not exactly gourmet, but it's food.

"This is so weird," she says between bites, sitting on the counter because all the chairs have equipment piled on them. "Yesterday we were undercover at a cyberterrorist recruitment thing. Today we're eating PB&J like normal kids."

"We're not normal kids," I point out, hoisting myself up to sit next to her. "We kinda stopped being normal when we entered the Shadow Games. Maybe even before that."

"True." She takes another bite, chewing thoughtfully. "So what now? Back to school? Pretend none of this happened? Tell everyone we were just out sick?"

"Part of me wants that," I admit. "Just be Jacob again. Hang out with Ethan (who's probably sent me like a million texts by now), worry about homework and tests and normal teenage stuff."

My regular phone is still somewhere in this safe house, probably full of Ethan's worried messages. That conversation is coming, and it's going to be hard. But that's tomorrow's problem.

"And the other part?"

"Wants to keep going. Learn more. Get better at the skills I've been developing." I pause, trying to put it into words. "I found something when I was competing. Not just answers about my family, something bigger. A feeling like I could actually make a difference. That breaking things could be about more than just breaking things."

Melissa nods slowly. "I've been thinking the same thing. It's like... now that I know this world exists, I can't unsee it. Can't pretend the shadows aren't there. Every time I see a news story about a data breach, I'll know there's more going on. People like KOTR, threats that most people never see."

"So what do we do?"

She's quiet for a moment, then smiles, the first real smile I've seen from her since before The Meeting.

"Maybe we do both? Be normal kids most of the time. Go to school, have friends, do regular teenager stuff. But keep training. Keep our skills sharp. And when the shadows need us, when there's a threat only people like us can handle..."

"We answer the call," I finish.

"Partners in the shadows?"

"Partners in the shadows."

We bump fists. Whatever comes next (another investigation or just getting through finals), we'll face it together.

***

That evening, Dad pulls me aside for a private talk. The safe house has quieted down, most of the operational staff moved to other locations. It's almost peaceful now, just a big suburban house with a lot of empty rooms and leftover equipment.

We sit on the back porch, watching the sun set over the anonymous neighborhood. Orange and purple streaking across the sky.

"There's something I need to tell you," Dad says. His voice is quiet. "Something I should've said two years ago. Before I disappeared."

I wait. A neighbor's kid is riding a bike in lazy circles at the end of the cul-de-sac. Normal life happening just yards away.

"When I disappeared, it wasn't just about the mission." Dad stares at his hands, not meeting my eyes. "Part of me was running away. From the fear that I'd put you and your mom in danger just by being connected to this work."

"Dad..."

"Let me finish." He takes a deep breath. "I told myself it was for your protection. And it was, partly. KOTR would've targeted you if they knew. But it was also cowardice. It was easier to disappear completely than to figure out how to balance being an operative with being a father."

He finally looks at me. His eyes are wet.

"I missed two years of your life, Jacob. Two years of watching you grow up. I missed your fifteenth birthday. Missed you getting your learner's permit. Missed all the moments, big and small, that make up a childhood."

"I can never get that back," he continues, his voice cracking a little. "I can never undo the grief you went through. All I can do is promise to be here now. To be present. To be honest with you, even when it's hard."

I don't know what to say. The anger is still there, quieter than before, but real. I think about the nights I cried myself to sleep missing him. The times I saw other kids with their dads and felt this hollow ache in my chest. The way I'd look at that White House picture and wonder what he would've told me about my problems, my fears, my stupid crush on a girl in math class.

All those moments he missed. All those moments I needed him and he wasn't there.

"I'm still mad at you," I say, and the words come out rougher than I expected. Then rougher still. "Actually, no. I'm not just mad. I'm furious. I'm so angry I can barely look at you sometimes."

The dam breaks. All the measured, mature conversation from before? Gone. Replaced by something raw and ugly that's been building for two years.

"You want to know what it was like? Every morning I'd wake up and forget for just a second that you were gone. And then I'd remember, and it was like losing you all over again. Every. Single. Day." My voice is rising, cracking, and I don't care. "I used to lie in bed and imagine conversations with you. Ask your photo for advice about school, about girls, about all the stupid stuff dads are supposed to help with. I talked to a PICTURE, Dad. Because that was all I had."

I'm on my feet now, pacing, my hands shaking. The neighbor kid on the bike looks over, startled by my voice.

"And you know what the worst part was? The hope. Every time the doorbell rang, part of me thought maybe it's him, maybe he's back, maybe it was all a mistake. And then it wasn't you, and I'd have to kill that hope again. Over and over. For TWO YEARS."

"Jacob..."

"NO." I spin to face him. "You don't get to explain anymore. You've explained. I understand the mission and the danger and all the logical reasons. But you know what? Logic doesn't help when you're fourteen and crying yourself to sleep because your dad is dead. Logic doesn't fix the hole in your chest when you see other kids with their fathers and you want to SCREAM because it's not fair."

Tears are running down my face now. I wipe them away angrily.

"I had to grow up without you. I had to figure out everything on my own. And the whole time, the WHOLE TIME, you were out there. Alive. Choosing every single day not to come home."

Dad doesn't move. Doesn't defend himself. His own eyes are wet, but he doesn't interrupt.

"So yeah," I say, my voice dropping to something raw and exhausted. "I'm glad you're back. I'm so glad you're alive that it physically hurts. But I'm also so angry I don't know what to do with it. Both things are true at the same time, and I don't know how to hold them both."

I sink back down onto the porch step, suddenly drained. My whole body is shaking.

My chest feels tight. Saying this out loud, actually letting myself feel it instead of swallowing it down, is harder than any challenge I faced in the Shadow Games.

Dad nods slowly. He doesn't try to defend himself or explain again. Just sits with me in the wreckage of everything I've been holding back.

"Maybe someday it won't be so hard," I say finally, my voice hoarse. "Maybe eventually I'll think about those two years and it won't feel like a knife in my chest. But that day isn't today."

"I understand," Dad says quietly. "And I don't expect you to forgive me quickly. Or at all. You get to feel however you feel for as long as you need to feel it."

Something loosens in my chest. Not the anger (that's still there, probably will be for a long time), but the pressure of pretending everything's fine. Of acting like reunion erases betrayal. Of smiling when I feel like screaming.

I can be angry and relieved at the same time. I can love him and be furious at him. I'm learning that feelings don't have to make sense. They just have to be real.

"Okay," I say finally. "But no more disappearing. No more cover stories where I don't know the truth. If you have to go somewhere for a mission, you tell me. Even if it's just 'I've got a classified thing, be back in a week.' I need to know you're coming home."

"I promise."

"And Mom too. No more secrets between us. Not about anything important."

"Agreed."

Dad extends his hand. Not for a hug, but for a handshake. An agreement between two people who respect each other.

"Partners?"

I shake it. "Partners. But also..." I hesitate, feeling the weight of what I'm about to say. "Also dad and son. Because that part matters more than any of the other stuff."

His eyes get misty. He pulls me into a hug, holding on like he's making up for two years of absence. I let myself lean into it this time, not holding back, not armoring myself against disappointment. Just... being his kid. Letting myself need him the way I've needed him for two years.

"Yeah," he says into my hair, his voice thick. "That too. That most of all."

We stay like that for a long time. The streetlights flicker on one by one. The sunset bleeds from orange to purple to deep blue. And somewhere in that moment, something shifts between us. Not forgiveness (that's still a long way off). But the beginning of something. A foundation we can build on.

It's not much. But it's a start.

***

Mom joins us for dinner, Chinese takeout from a place nearby. Containers spread across the kitchen table: orange chicken, beef and broccoli, fried rice, egg rolls. The smell fills the whole room.

It's the first real family meal we've had in over two years. Just the three of us, no operational staff, no urgent communications, no encrypted messages demanding attention.

"So what happens with the house?" I ask between bites. "Our actual house. The office with all the monitors?"

"We're keeping it for now. The organization wants a presence in the area, and it's already set up with secure stuff." Mom uses chopsticks like a pro. "But I'll move the more... sensitive equipment... elsewhere. You shouldn't have to live in an intelligence station."

"And you'll both be home? Like, actually home?"

"As much as we can be," Dad says. "Some travel will still happen. The organization doesn't stop just because KOTR is disrupted. But nothing like before. The worst of it is over. We're in cleanup mode now."

"Cleanup mode," I repeat. "Sounds glamorous."

"It really isn't," Mom laughs. "Lots of paperwork. Lots of debriefings. Lots of explaining to partner agencies how we took down an international network without anyone noticing we existed."

I look around the table. My parents. Together. Alive. No more secrets between us (at least, none that matter). We'll never be a normal family. Mom's job will never just be "programming" and Dad's job will never be boring and safe. But we can be a family that tells each other the truth. That supports each other. That faces the shadows together instead of hiding from them separately.

"One more question," I say, setting down my chopsticks. "What was in the little box? At the White House. The thing you gave back to the President."

Dad and Mom exchange one of their looks, silent communication in a single glance.

"It was a medal," Dad says finally. "Intelligence Star. Awarded for acts of valor in covert operations. Highest recognition the intelligence community gives for classified work."

"You earned a medal?" I'm not sure why this surprises me after everything, but it does.

"I earned a medal," Dad confirms. "For the work I did infiltrating KOTR, the intelligence I gathered, the operations that saved lives. But I gave it back because..."

He trails off. Mom finishes for him.

"Because accepting it would've created a record. A paper trail that could be traced to his real identity if someone dug deep enough. He had to refuse the formal recognition so the mission could continue."

"That's why the President said 'it's unfortunate they'll never know,'" I realize. "Because Dad couldn't keep proof of what he did. The sacrifice had to stay invisible."

"Exactly." Dad's voice is soft. "Sacrifices in the shadows. No glory, no recognition, no medal to display. Just the knowledge that you did the right thing, and the people you protected will never know you protected them."

I think about that. About what it means to give up credit and a normal life, all for a mission you believe in. To be a hero nobody can acknowledge.

It's different from the movies. Quieter. Harder, maybe, because there's no applause at the end.

"I get it now," I say slowly. "Why you did what you did. I still wish you'd told me. I still wish I hadn't spent two years thinking you were gone. But I get the why. The sacrifice."

Dad reaches across the table and squeezes my hand. His grip is warm, solid, real.

"That's all I can ask."

We finish dinner in comfortable silence. Chopsticks clicking, occasional requests to pass containers. Outside, night falls over the suburban neighborhood.

Normal life, happening all around us.

And in the middle of it, a family rebuilt from secrets and sacrifice, finding their way back to each other one truth at a time.

19

Coming Home

Two days after the raid, I'm back in my own bedroom. It feels smaller than I remember. Maybe because I've grown. Maybe because the world feels so much bigger now. Or maybe because my brain is still calibrated to bunkers and safe houses and rooms designed to survive attacks.

My desk is exactly how I left it, scattered with electronics parts, half-finished projects, the keyboard I've been meaning to fix for months. The hacker movie poster still hangs crooked on the wall. The window still looks out over the same suburban street, the same neighbors' houses, the same oak tree that's been there since before I was born.

Everything is the same. And nothing is.

I stand in the doorway for a long moment, trying to make sense of it. Trying to figure out how to fit back into a space that used to be mine but now feels like a costume that doesn't quite fit. The kid who lived here three weeks ago didn't know his father was alive. Didn't know his mother was a shadow operative. Didn't know that the Shadow Games were anything more than an interesting distraction from homework.

That Jacob feels like a stranger now. A different person wearing my face, living my life, blissfully unaware of everything lurking in the shadows.

Something tightens in my chest. Not quite grief, more like nostalgia for a version of myself I can never get back. I used to be innocent. Ordinary. Now I know too much, seen too much, been through things that most people will never experience. Part of me misses the before-time, when mystery was just something in books and danger was just a word.

But a bigger part knows I can never go back. Even if I wanted to.

My first order of business: calling Ethan.

I sit on my bed (my actual bed, not a safe house cot or a government facility bunk) and pull out my phone. Not the secure one from the operation, but my regular phone. The one with Ethan's number saved under "Best Bro" because he programmed it that way freshman year.

He picks up on the second ring.

"Oh. You're alive." His voice is flat. Cold. Nothing like the Ethan I know, the one who talks a hundred words a minute, who can't help making jokes, who fills every silence with nervous energy.

"Ethan..."

"I was wondering when you'd call. Or text. Or literally acknowledge my existence in any way." There's real anger underneath the flatness. "I've been texting you for three days, Jacob. Three days. Nothing. Your mom called and gave some vague 'family emergency' excuse, and I've been sitting here freaking out imagining the worst, and you couldn't even send a single emoji to let me know you were okay?"

The words hit me like punches. I knew this was coming, knew I'd hurt him, but hearing it is different from knowing it.

"I'm sorry. I couldn't..."

"Couldn't what? Pick up a phone? I know you had access to one because I could see you reading my messages. The little 'read' receipts showed up, Jacob. You saw them. And you still didn't respond."

I don't have an excuse. The secure phones blocked most outside communication, but he's right. I could have found a way. I just... didn't. I was too wrapped up in the operation, too focused on everything happening with my family, too deep in my own drama to think about how it would feel from his end.

"You're right," I say. "That was wrong. I should have..."

"Should have what? Remembered I exist? Remembered that I'm your best friend and I spent three days having actual panic attacks about whether you were dead or hurt or kidnapped?" His voice cracks. "Do you have any idea what that was like? Jason cornered me at school asking where you were, and I couldn't even tell him to shove it because I was too busy trying not to cry in the hallway."

"Ethan..."

"And this isn't even the first time! You've been pulling away for weeks. Blowing off game nights. Being 'too busy' every time I wanted to hang out. I keep making excuses for you ('he's stressed, he's going through something'), but you never tell me what. You just keep me at arm's length while apparently living some secret double life with mysterious online friends."

The anger in his voice breaks into something rawer. Hurt.

"I thought we were best friends, Jacob. Best friends tell each other stuff. Even hard stuff. Even secret stuff. But you've been treating me like an outsider for months, and I just..."

He trails off. I can hear him breathing on the other end, unsteady, like he's trying not to fall apart.

"You're my only real friend," he says quietly. "Do you get that? My siblings are annoying. The people at school are whatever. You're the one person I can actually be myself with. And finding out that you've been hiding this whole massive thing from me, that there's this entire side of your life I didn't even know about..."

"I wanted to tell you." My voice comes out small. Guilty. "So many times, I almost did. But it was dangerous, Ethan. These weren't normal secrets. People were threatening my family. If KOTR found out you knew things..."

"So instead you just made me feel like I was crazy for thinking something was wrong? Made me feel like a clingy friend who couldn't take a hint?" The anger flares back. "That's not protecting me, Jacob. That's lying to me. There's a difference."

He's right. The justifications that seemed so solid in my head (need-to-know, operational security, protecting him from danger) don't sound as good when he lays out what it actually felt like on his end. I was so focused on the mission that I forgot he was a person too. A person who cared about me. A person I was hurting.

"I'm sorry," I say, and this time I mean it fully. "You're right. About all of it. I was scared and overwhelmed and I made bad choices about who to trust with what. And you deserved better. You've always deserved better."

Silence stretches. I can almost see him on the other end, probably pacing his room, the way he does when he's upset, running one hand through his hair.

"What actually happened?" he asks finally. Still angry, but willing to listen.

I take a deep breath. This is the hard part. Dad and I talked about this, a modified truth, close enough to reality to be honest, vague enough to protect the mission.

"My dad is alive."

The silence that follows is different from before. Shocked instead of hurt.

"Say that again?"

"My dad. He didn't die or get kidnapped. He was working undercover. Deep undercover, for the government. And he came home."

"Jacob, if this is some weird deflection joke..."

"It's not. I swear it's not. The Shadow Games were involved. And KOTR, that hacker group I was researching. My dad was infiltrating them. Has been for three years." I pause, letting him absorb it. "I found out by accident. The coded messages in Mom's office, the mysterious phone calls, all of it, it was part of an operation he was running. And I stumbled into the middle of it without knowing."

"That's..." He trails off. I can hear him processing, trying to fit this information into any normal category. "That's completely insane."

"I know."

"Your dad is alive? He's been alive this whole time?"

"Yes."

Another long pause. When he speaks again, his voice is different, still hurt, but something else creeping in. Wonder, maybe. Or just the sheer absurdity of it all.

"And you've been, what, working with him? On spy stuff?"

"Not exactly. More like... I kept investigating things I shouldn't have, and it led me into an actual operation, and then things got dangerous fast." I tell him about The Meeting. About Granite. About the raid. Not everything (there are still things I legally can't share), but enough. The real stuff. The scary parts.

He's quiet for a long time after I finish.

"That's why you couldn't tell me," he says slowly. "Not just 'didn't want to,' actually couldn't."

"Some of it, yeah. But Ethan, you were right about the other stuff too. I could have tried harder to include you. Could have at least let you know I was okay. I got so wrapped up in this whole shadow world that I forgot about the people who matter in the real one."

"I just wish you'd trusted me." His voice is quieter now. "Even if you couldn't tell me details, you could have told me something. 'I'm dealing with serious family stuff and I can't explain yet, but I'm okay.' That's all. Just so I knew I wasn't losing you."

"You're not losing me." The words come out fierce. "You're my best friend, Ethan. That hasn't changed. That's not going to change."

"Promise?"

"Promise."

He exhales, a long, shaky breath that carries weeks of tension. "Okay. I'm still mad at you. Like, actually mad, not pretend-mad. But... okay. We can work with okay."

"That's fair. You can be mad as long as you need to be."

"Good. Because I plan to milk this for at least a month of you buying my lunch."

Something loosens in my chest. That's the Ethan I know, already turning hurt into leverage, processing heavy emotions through jokes. We're not okay yet, not completely. But we will be.

"Deal."

"And if you ever disappear like that again without warning me, I will personally hunt you down and lecture you until your ears fall off. I've been practicing with my siblings."

Despite everything, I laugh. "Noted."

"Good." There's a pause, and when he speaks again, his voice is softer. The joke-Ethan mask slipping to show the real one underneath. "I'm glad you're okay, Jacob. Like, actually glad. I was terrified."

"I know. I'm sorry."

"Yeah. I know you are." Another breath. "So. Your dad's a spy. That's going to take a minute to process."

"Hey," he says after a moment. "Are you glad? That you know the truth now?"

The question catches me off guard. Like it's simple. Like there's an obvious answer.

Part of me misses the kid I was three weeks ago. The one who thought his mom was just a programmer and his dad was dead. That kid was ignorant. Blissfully, painfully ignorant. But he also slept through the night. He didn't flinch at shadows or scan crowds for threats or wonder if the person behind him in the grocery store was running surveillance.

"I don't know," I admit. "Knowing the truth is better than believing lies. But knowing also means I can never go back to not knowing. You can't unsee what you've seen. And sometimes..." I trail off, not sure how to finish.

"Sometimes ignorance was easier?"

"Yeah. Exactly."

There's a long pause. Then Ethan says, quietly: "That's actually really wise, dude. Deep. You should write fortune cookies."

I laugh, and it feels like releasing pressure from a valve. "And there's the Ethan I know."

"I have depths. They're just very shallow depths." He pauses. "Anyway. When do I get to meet your not-dead dad?"

"Soon. He's doing some transition stuff first. Apparently coming back from the dead involves a lot of paperwork." I pause, realizing how much I want this. "But I want you guys to meet. He's... he's actually pretty cool. When he's not, you know, pretending to be a terrorist to infiltrate criminal organizations."

"Casual. Very casual." Ethan snorts. "I'll prepare my best 'glad you're not dead' speech. I'm thinking handshake, eye contact, maybe a comment about the weather. Keep it professional."

"Sounds perfect."

"Does this mean you're done with the Shadow Games? Or is that still a thing?"

I think about the question. I got a message from SystemAdmin offering a new account, a fresh start. About the leaderboard still running, the challenges still waiting.

"I don't know yet. I'm figuring that out."

"Well, figure faster. Because if you're still competing, I want in. I've been practicing my metadata removal."

I smile. "I'll keep you posted."

***

School is weird after everything. Kids worrying about home-work and drama and cafeteria food, completely unaware that cy-berterrorism was stopped three days ago. They don't know. They can't know. And maybe that's the point.

At lunch, Ethan gives me a knowing look. "You look different. Like, same face, but something behind it changed."

"I feel different. Like I know things now that I can't unknow."

He nods slowly. "That's very deep for a Wednesday."

"Sorry. I'll try to be more shallow tomorrow."

He laughs, and for a moment everything feels normal again. Then his voice drops. "By the way, there's a rumor. Someone's older sister works at a coffee shop near the federal building and saw your mom going in. Now everyone thinks your family knows the FBI."

Great. So much for operational security.

"'Jacob's family knows the FBI' is way better for your reputation than 'Jacob's family is boring and normal,'" Ethan points out.

He has a point. A terrible, gossip-fueled point, but a point.

***

That evening, I log into the Shadow Games for the first time since The Meeting.

The login screen is familiar, the glowing green terminal font, the prompt for my alias and password. But something about it feels different now. Like looking at a childhood bedroom after you've grown up and moved away. Same objects, different eyes.

I type my credentials. SirBreaksAlot. The name Ethan gave me as a joke. The identity that climbed from nothing to the top 25.

The competitor hub has changed. A banner at the top announces "NEW LEADERSHIP - SAME CHALLENGE" in bold letters that cycle through shades of green. Several familiar names are grayed out on the leaderboard, arrested players, I'm guessing.

People who were actually part of KOTR, not just competitors caught up in something bigger.

The leaderboard itself has been reset. Everyone starting fresh. Level playing field. New beginnings.

I scroll through the changes. New challenge categories. New point values. Something called "Verified Competitor Status" that supposedly tells real players from potential threats.

A direct message waits in my inbox. The notification pulses gently, demanding attention.

From: SystemAdmin
Subject: Recognition

I click it open.

"SirBreaksAlot,

Your contributions to recent events have been noted at the highest levels. While public recognition is not possible (for reasons you now understand), please know that your actions helped save thousands of lives.

The power grids remain operational. The water systems remain clean. The hospitals remain connected. These outcomes are not guaranteed in a world full of threats, but because of what you did, they were guaranteed this week.

The Shadow Games continue. The competition remains valuable for identifying talent and developing skills. Should you wish to resume your participation, your previous rank has been preserved as historical record. However, your current alias is compromised. A new account awaits you with a clean slate.

Choose your next alias carefully. It may define your journey for years to come.

Welcome back to the shadows.

- The Committee"

A new alias. A fresh start.

I sit back in my chair, staring at the message. SirBreaksAlot was who I was when this started. A kid who broke things accidentally and felt bad about it. A joke name that became something more.

But that's not who I am anymore.

I type a reply: "I'll think about it."

But already, ideas are forming in the back of my mind. SirBreaksAlot was who I was when this started. Maybe it's time to become who I'm going to be.

Then I close the laptop and look out my window. The sun is setting over the neighborhood, painting everything in shades of gold and orange. The oak tree casts a long shadow across the lawn, its branches bare now as winter approaches.

Somewhere out there, the world keeps spinning. Hackers keep hacking. Threats keep emerging. The shadows never fully disappear.

But for now, for this moment, I'm just Jacob. A kid in his bedroom, watching the sunset, thinking about what comes next.

And that's enough.

***

Mom knocks on my door an hour later. Three soft taps, the way she's always done it, a small piece of normalcy that survived all the revelations.

The sound makes something loosen in my chest. BetaZone wouldn't knock like that, soft, patient, giving me time to respond. BetaZone would use a coded pattern or just walk in. But Mom (real Mom, the one who's been here all along underneath the operative mask) knocks three times and waits.

Maybe that's the answer I've been looking for. Maybe she was always both people at once, and the mom who asked "what did you learn?" wasn't a cover at all. Just one half of a whole person, doing impossible things to keep her family safe.

"Someone here to see you."

I follow her downstairs, curious. The house smells like the takeout Chinese we had for dinner, lingering aromas of orange chicken and fried rice. Normal domestic scents that feel almost surreal after the institutional cafeterias of the safe house.

Dad is in the living room, standing near the fireplace that we never actually use. But he's not alone. A girl about my age stands beside him, looking awkward but determined, her hands shoved in her jacket pockets.

"Melissa?"

"Hi." She waves shyly, a small gesture that seems weird coming from the confident operative I worked with during the raid. "Surprise?"

For a second, neither of us knows what to do. Do we shake hands? Hug? High-five like teammates after a winning game? We've been through so much together. The strangeness of it makes me want to laugh and hide at the same time.

She apparently has the same problem, because she just stands there with her hands half-raised, like she started a gesture and forgot how to finish it.

I look at Dad, then at Melissa, then back at Dad. "What's going on?"

"Melissa's family is relocating to the area." Dad's voice is casual, like this is totally normal. "Her father will be helping run the restructured Shadow Games (apparently dismantling a terrorist organization from within earns you a promotion), and they wanted to be closer to our organization's hub."

"Which means," Melissa adds, a smile breaking through her nervous expression, "we'll be at the same school. Starting Monday. Same grade, even. Though I might be in different classes depending on how the schedule works out."

Partners in the shadows. And now, apparently, classmates.

The news takes a moment to sink in. The idea of seeing her every day, in the mundane context of school...

"That's... actually really cool."

"I thought so too." Her grin widens. "Also, Ethan sounds hilarious from everything you've told me. I can't wait to meet him."

"He's gonna freak out. In a good way, probably. He already thinks my life is a spy movie."

"Isn't it, though?"

"Apparently so."

***

We spend the evening catching up properly, not through encrypted messages or surveillance-safe video calls, but face to face. Real conversation. Real laughter. Real moments that don't need to be analyzed for hidden meanings or operational implications.

Melissa tells me about the drive from California. Her little brother Dylan, who spent the whole trip playing car games and asking if they were there yet. Her mom, still processing everything, bouncing between relief that the secret-keeping is over and anxiety about the new life they're building.

I tell her about school. About Ethan and his million questions. About the weird moment when Jason showed unexpected humanity. About the rumor mill already spinning theories about my family.

Mom and Dad drift in and out, occasionally joining our conversation. It feels almost like a normal family gathering, if normal families included teenage hackers and undercover operatives.

At one point, Dad's expression shifts. He pulls out his phone and shows us something, his face grim despite the relaxed atmosphere.

"The Architect," he says. "We still don't know who they are. But we intercepted a message during the raid cleanup. Hidden in the data packets of a regular-looking communication."

He shows us the text: "This round goes to you. But the game isn't over. See you in the shadows."

A shiver runs down my spine. The Architect is still out there. Still planning. Still a threat. The mysterious figure at the top of KOTR's hierarchy, the one who escaped during the raid, the one nobody has ever identified.

"So KOTR isn't completely done," Melissa says, voicing what we're all thinking.

"Not completely. The organization is crippled. Most of their cells are taken down, their funding is frozen, their infrastructure is messed up. But someone is already rebuilding. The Architect doesn't give up easy." Dad puts away the phone. "That's a problem for another day. For now, we heal. We train. We prepare."

"And when they come back?"

Dad looks at me. At Melissa. At Mom, who's standing in the doorway with an expression that mixes worry and pride.

"We'll be ready."

It's a promise. A declaration. And hearing it from my father, from the man who spent three years in the shadows to protect his family, it feels like something solid. Something real.

***

Later that night, after Melissa leaves and my parents have gone to bed, I sit at my desk and pull the air vent cover off my closet wall, the hiding spot I've used since this all started.

The notebook is still there. The one where I wrote down everything I was learning about Mom's secret life. It feels like an artifact from another era. From the time before I knew the truth.

I flip through the pages. My handwriting, documenting clues. Sketches of the network diagrams I found. Questions I was trying to answer, mysteries I was trying to solve.

Most of those questions have answers now. Not all of them (the Architect remains a mystery), but enough. Enough to understand my family. Enough to know who we really are.

I flip to a blank page and write:

"Chapter 1: Behind the Closed Door

I gasp for air as a thick cloud of white smoke hits me in the face. I just broke my laptop and can't believe it..."

Maybe someday I'll tell this story properly. Let people know what happened in the shadows. Help other teenagers who might be facing their own mysteries, their own secrets, their own families hiding things they don't understand.

But for now, it's just for me. A record of who I was, who I became, and who I'm still becoming.

I close the notebook and look at Dad's picture on my desk. I finally moved it here from the hallway. The one from the White House. He's standing there, shaking hands with the President, accepting a medal he couldn't keep.

"We did it, Dad," I whisper. "We actually did it."

The words feel small in the darkness. Inadequate for everything we've been through. But also true. Against all odds, against every threat, against the weight of secrets that nearly crushed us... we made it.

My eyes sting. Happy tears, maybe. Or exhausted ones. Or just the release of pressure that's been building for weeks, finally finding a way out.

And somewhere in the shadows of the house, I imagine I hear his voice respond:

"We're just getting started."

The laptop screen glows in the darkness. The Shadow Games portal waits. And tomorrow, Melissa starts at my school.

New chapter. New challenges. New shadows to navigate.

I close my eyes and, for the first time in weeks, fall asleep without fear.

20
New Beginnings

Monday morning. First day with everything changed.

I wake up to the sound of Dad making breakfast. Actual Dad. In our actual kitchen. Like it's the most normal thing in the world.

Except it's not normal. Not at all. And that's what makes it so incredible.

The smell of pancakes drifts up the stairs, mixed with the bitter aroma of fresh coffee, the good kind, not the instant stuff Mom keeps for emergencies.

For a moment I just lie there, listening. The sizzle of butter in the pan. The clink of plates being set out. The muffled sound of Dad humming something I don't recognize, some tune that's probably been stuck in his head for years, through all the missions and covers and hiding. These are sounds I forgot existed. Sounds from the before-time, when I was young enough to believe my family was ordinary.

I didn't realize how much I missed them until now.

Something warm spreads through my chest. Not the sharp relief of crisis averted, but something softer. Steadier. The quiet recognition that this, this moment, this ordinary morning, is exactly what I've been fighting for. Not exciting. Not dramatic. Just... home.

"Pancakes?" he calls when I appear in the doorway, still rubbing sleep from my eyes.

"Sure."

He slides a stack onto my plate, perfectly golden with crispy edges just the way I like them. Steam rises from the surface. "Your mom left early, meeting with her handler about the transition. But she'll be back for dinner."

"Transition?"

"Paperwork. Debriefs. Legal stuff. You'd be amazed how much bureaucracy is involved in intelligence work." He pours himself coffee and sits across from me. "Turns out faking your death for three years creates a lot of complications when you un-fake it. Social security records. Tax documentation. Insurance claims that need to be quietly reversed."

"I bet."

"There was apparently a life insurance payout that your mother never cashed. Which is now causing some confusion at the insurance company, because they have records of a death but no beneficiary claim. Someone has to untangle all of that."

I try to imagine the bureaucratic nightmare of coming back from the dead. Forms to fill out. Explanations to give. Systems that don't have a checkbox for "actually was deep undercover, not deceased."

We eat in comfortable silence. It's strange how quickly this has become routine, or how much I wanted it to become routine. Dad being here. Mom being home more. The secrets finally out in the open. It's only been a few days, but already this feels more real than the years that came before.

"Ready for school?" Dad asks.

"As ready as I'll ever be. Melissa starts today."

"I know. Her father texted this morning. He's nervous, more nervous than she is, probably. First day at a new school is always hard."

"She'll be fine. She infiltrated a cyberterrorist gathering. I think she can handle junior year."

Dad laughs. "Fair point."

***

Ethan is waiting at our usual spot by the bike racks, practically vibrating with excitement. "I prepared talking points," he announces.

"...You prepared talking points?"

"For meeting a girl who helped take down an international hacker network? Yes. I have conversation starters and a list of topics to avoid. 'Have you ever killed anyone' seemed like a bad opener."

I laugh. Even when everything else has turned upside down, Ethan remains exactly who he's always been.

***

Melissa is already by the flagpole, chatting with a girl from the soccer team like they've known each other for years. Social engineering isn't just a skill for her. It's her default mode.

When she spots us, she heads our way with confident strides. "Jacob! Hi."

Ethan steps forward with exaggerated formality. "It's an honor to meet you, StarBreaker. I myself am skilled at forgetting to remove metadata from documents, which I understand is a form of very bad hacking."

Melissa bursts out laughing. "You're exactly like he described."

"Is that good or bad?"

"Definitely good."

***

Lunch brings the three of us together. Ethan shakes his head in disbelief as Melissa recaps the raid.

"And now you're both just... going to school? Like normal people?"

"Mostly normal," I say. "Training, occasional missions, security briefings. But school comes first."

"My biggest accomplishment this month was beating a video game on hard mode," Ethan sighs.

"Which game?" Melissa asks. "Cyber Siege?"

"The firewall puzzle in level seven is brutal!"

They launch into video game strategies, and I sit back, watching them connect. Melissa fitting into my normal life. The two worlds merging. Maybe we can have both.

***

After school, Dad picks me up. The car is the same boring sedan he drove before, recovered from some government impound lot, apparently, where they'd been storing his "estate" while he was legally dead.

"How was it?" he asks as I climb into the passenger seat.

"Weird. Good weird though."

"Melissa settling in?"

"Yeah. She's already made Ethan's talking points obsolete. They spent lunch debating video game strategies."

Dad laughs. "Sounds about right. Her father mentioned she's been using gaming as stress relief. Something about shooting virtual enemies being therapeutic."

"Any update on the leak?" I ask, the question coming out before I can stop it. "The cells that got tipped off before the raids?"

Dad's jaw tightens. "Still investigating. These things take time. But we'll find them."

The way he says it, flat and determined, tells me it's more complicated than he's letting on. Another shadow to deal with later.

We drive in comfortable silence for a while. The neighborhood slides past. Familiar streets, familiar houses, everything looking exactly the way it always has. Like the world didn't almost end two weeks ago.

Then Dad clears his throat. The preparatory throat-clear that means he's about to say something important.

"There's something I wanted to discuss. About the future."

I tense slightly. "Okay."

"The organization has a training program. For young operatives, people your age who show promise in the work we do. It's optional, completely voluntary. But given your talents, they've offered you a spot. Starting next summer."

"Summer training? Like... spy camp?"

"Something like that. Cybersecurity focus, given your skills. They'd teach you advanced techniques: penetration testing, social engineering, network defense. Things beyond what the Shadow Games could offer."

I think about it. A summer of learning from actual professionals. Building skills beyond what YouTube tutorials and late-night experiments could teach. Preparing for... whatever comes next.

"Melissa's been offered the same," Dad adds. "Her father was going to tell her tonight. And they're thinking about adding a research track, for people who want to help from the analysis side. Your friend Ethan's name came up."

"Ethan?" I stare at him. "Seriously?"

"He found patterns in KOTR data that trained analysts missed. That's not nothing, Jacob. The organization notices talent, wherever it comes from."

I think about Ethan. MetaDataKing, the guy who accidentally exposed himself through a homework file and then spent weeks researching cybercriminals just because he was worried about me. He'd probably love this. Or be terrified. Or both.

"So we could all train together?"

"If you all choose to participate. Like I said, it's voluntary. No pressure. You've earned the right to make your own decisions about your involvement."

"Can I think about it?"

"Of course. No rush. We've got months to decide."

***

That night, I video chat with Melissa. Boxes still stacked in corners behind her. The in-between state of a life in transit.

"They asked you about the summer program too?"

"Yep. What are you thinking?"

"Part of me wants normal," she admits. "Make lanyards. Swim in a lake. The other part wants to be ready for whatever comes next." She sighs. "The Architect is still out there."

"Partners in complexity?"

"Partners in complexity."

Whatever decisions we make, we'll make them together.

***

Before bed, I check the Shadow Games one last time. A message notification blinks.

"Have you chosen your new alias?"

SirBreaksAlot was the old me, the kid who broke things accidentally and felt bad about it. I'm not that kid anymore.

I type: "ShadowDweller."

"Welcome back, ShadowDweller. The shadows await."

New name. New challenges. New chapter.

***

The next few weeks settle into a rhythm. School by day, training exercises by afternoon. Melissa and I compare notes each evening. She's better at social engineering, I'm better at technical challenges. Together, we're pretty formidable.

Ethan joins us for gaming sessions on weekends. He's gotten surprisingly good at the Shadow Games, competing under the alias "MetaDataKing," a callback to his infamous metadata mistakes.

"You taught me that small mistakes have big consequences," he told me. "I want to be someone you can count on."

He'll never be a field operative. He doesn't want to be. But he's part of our team now. The one who keeps us grounded.

Our trio against whatever comes.

The shadows await. But so does the light.

And for the first time in a long time, I'm looking forward to both.

21

The Shadows Await

One month later.

I'm sitting in the park under the oak tree, the same one where Ethan and I decoded Mom's cipher all those weeks ago, back when I thought the biggest mystery in my life was figuring out why she locked her office door. Back when I was still SirBreaksAlot. Back when I had no idea what the shadows really contained.

The bark is rough against my back. The leaves have mostly fallen now, carpeting the ground in shades of brown and gold. Winter is coming. You can feel it in the air, that sharp edge that wasn't there last month, the cold that seeps through your jacket if you sit still too long.

But I don't mind the cold anymore. I've learned that some things are worth being uncomfortable for.

Ethan is beside me, laptop open, working on a coding project for his computer science class. He's hunched over the keyboard, muttering about syntax errors and missing semicolons. The eternal struggle of anyone learning to code.

Melissa sits on my other side, scrolling through something on her phone. The sunlight catches her hair as she shifts position. She's been at Lincoln High for three weeks now, and already she's made more friends than I have in three years. That's her gift. She can read people, connect with them, make them feel seen in a way that comes as naturally to her as breathing.

We've become a trio now. The three of us against the world.

"You guys ready for the full training program?" Melissa asks, not looking up from her phone.

Ethan groans. "I still can't believe they actually wanted me for this. Research track or not, I'm going to spy camp. A whole summer of that instead of video games and sleeping until noon."

"You didn't have to say yes," I remind him.

"Yeah, I did. You two would've gotten into trouble without me there to point out the obvious dangers." He grins. "Besides, someone needs to handle the research while you two are busy being action heroes."

He's joking, but there's truth in it. Over the past few weeks, we've fallen into natural roles. Melissa handles the social engineering (reading people, building connections, extracting information through conversation). I tackle the technical challenges (code, encryption, system analysis). And Ethan does the deep-dive research, finding connections and patterns that neither of us would spot on our own.

We complement each other. Three different skill sets that combine into something stronger than any of us alone.

"I'm ready," Melissa says. "My dad's been running me through training exercises for weeks. I think I can pick a lock faster than I can unlock my phone now."

"Show-off."

"Just stating facts."

I look at both of them, my best friend since freshman year, and the girl who started as a competitor and became something more. Partner. Ally. Someone who understands the shadows the same way I do.

"We're really doing this, aren't we?" I say. "Actually becoming operatives. Fighting threats that most people don't even know exist."

"Having second thoughts?" Melissa asks.

"No. Just... making sure it's real. That I'm not going to wake up tomorrow and find out this was all some elaborate dream triggered by inhaling laptop smoke."

Ethan laughs. "If this is a dream, it's the weirdest one I've ever had. And I once dreamed I was a sentient toaster fighting crime."

"A sentient toaster?"

"Don't ask."

The three of us sit in comfortable silence for a moment. The wind rustles the skeletal branches above us. Somewhere nearby, a dog barks.

Normal life, happening all around us. People walking their dogs, kids playing in the distance, cars passing on the street. None of them know what we know. What we've seen. What we're preparing to face.

And maybe that's the point. We do this so they don't have to. So they can keep walking their dogs and playing with their kids without ever knowing how close everything came to falling apart.

"You guys ever look up my new alias on the leaderboard?" I ask suddenly.

Both of them look at me.

"ShadowDweller," Melissa says. "I saw it when you changed it. It fits."

"Better than SirBreaksAlot?" Ethan asks.

"Different. SirBreaksAlot was the old me. He grew up." I look at my hands, the same hands that used to accidentally destroy every piece of electronics they touched. "SirBreaksAlot was about the things I broke by accident. ShadowDweller is about the places I choose to go on purpose. The darkness I navigate because someone has to."

"That's very philosophical," Ethan says. "I'm sticking with MetaDataKing because it's funny and also because I genuinely could not think of anything better."

"It's perfect for you," Melissa says, and she's not even teasing. "You find the hidden data. The stuff other people miss. That's your superpower."

Ethan looks genuinely touched. "Thanks. That's... actually really nice."

"Don't get used to it."

"Too late."

***

That night, I log into the Shadow Games for the first time with my new alias.

ShadowDweller.

The name feels right. Like putting on a jacket that fits perfectly after years of wearing one that was always a little too big or a little too small. This is who I am now. Not the kid who breaks things by accident. The person who navigates the shadows on purpose.

The competitor hub welcomes me back. Messages from players I've connected with over the past months. Challenges waiting to be solved. A whole digital world that most people don't even know exists.

But there's something new on the board. A challenge I haven't seen before, highlighted in red, the color reserved for elite-level puzzles.

"The Architect's Riddle."

The description reads: "For those brave enough to seek the mastermind. Three phases await. Winner receives... the truth."

My blood goes cold.

The Architect. Still out there. Still watching. Still planning.

I stare at the challenge for a long moment. Part of me wants to dive in immediately, solve whatever puzzles they've laid out, prove that I can match wits with whoever is pulling strings from the shadows. That's who I am now. Someone who doesn't back down from challenges.

But another part remembers what Dad said about careful, methodical approaches. About not rushing into things just because you're impatient.

I screenshot the challenge and send it to Melissa and Ethan in our secure group chat.

"Looks like the Architect wants to play," I type.

Melissa responds within seconds: "I saw it too. What do you think?"

"I think we take our time. Analyze it properly. Loop in Dad and the organization before we do anything stupid."

"Look at you, being responsible."

"I'll show Dad in the morning. Do this the right way."

Ethan chimes in: "This is terrifying and also kind of exciting? Is that a normal reaction?"

"For us? Yeah. Pretty much."

"I learned from my mistakes," I add. "Most of them."

I close the laptop and lean back in my chair. Outside my window, the neighborhood is quiet. Normal life, continuing as always. Lights in windows. Cars in driveways. Families going about their evenings without any idea what lurks in the digital shadows.

The Architect is still out there. Still a threat. Still planning something that we can't see yet.

But so are we. Three teens who stumbled into a world of secrets and chose to stay. Who found out that the skills they thought made them weird were actually preparing them for something important.

The shadows await.

And we'll be ready.

***

THE END

...of Book One.

Epilogue

The oak tree image on the Shadow Games scoreboard flickers.

For just a moment (so brief that most would miss it) the image changes. The branches twist into new shapes. The negative space between leaves forms letters, words, a message hidden in plain sight:

"THE NEXT PHASE BEGINS"

Then it's gone. Back to normal. Just an oak tree, just a decorative element on a gaming website that millions of people never look at closely.

But somewhere, someone is watching.

The Architect smiles.

Jacob and his friends have proven themselves. They stopped Project Nightfall. They reunited their families. They chose to embrace the shadows instead of running from them.

Good.

Now the real game begins.

▼

A message goes out through hidden channels: "Activate Protocol Omega. Target: ShadowDweller. Objective: recruitment or elimination."

In the shadows, nothing is ever truly over.

It just transforms into something new.